KANE

Also by Michael Prescott

Shiver
Shudder
Shatter
Deadly Pursuit
Blind Pursuit
Mortal Pursuit
Comes the Dark
Stealing Faces
The Shadow Hunter
Last Breath
Next Victim
In Dark Places
Dangerous Games
Mortal Faults
Final Sins
Riptide
Grave of Angels
Cold Around the Heart
Steel Trap & Other Stories
Chasing Omega
Blood in the Water

KANE

MICHAEL PRESCOTT

writing as Douglas Borton

Kane
By Michael Prescott
Originally published as *Kane* by Douglas Borton

ISBN-13: 978-1502448903
ISBN-10: 1502448904

For Jeanine Basinger and John Frazer

A teacher affects eternity; he can never tell where his influence stops.

—Henry Brooks Adams

1

Where the desert met the sky, there was a man.

A tall man dressed in black, a distant figure shimmering like a mirage behind a tremulous curtain of heat. He was out there alone, and he was walking slowly, deliberately, crossing the bleak stretches of gray shale and alkaline sand, coming toward the town.

At first, he'd been no more than a smudge on the landscape, a wavering shadow amid the ghost flowers and the skeletonweed, like the shadow of a hawk cast by the westering sun; but there had been no hawk. There had been only the shadow, creeping over the pinkish, blistered desert soil that looked so much like sunburnt, peeling skin, moving closer, ever closer, until at last it resolved itself into a human form, tall and dark, smoky with distance, but unmistakable now.

At the corner of his service station, Bill Needham leaned against the Coke machine and watched.

Bill Needham had inherited two things from his father—a long, angular, oddly pinched face and the service station. Of the two, only the latter had proved to be of any real value; and as the years had slipped by and the town had emptied out, there had been fewer tanks to be filled, less work to do, until finally things had reached the point where, on a good day, Bill was lucky to see three cars in his place.

Still, he showed up for work every morning at nine sharp and hung around till eight at night—seven thirty in the summertime—just like in the old days. The old days.

God, he hated to think of it that way. A man shouldn't be nostalgic at thirty-two; it wasn't natural. Shouldn't be idle, either, but he couldn't help that part of it. He would sit in his office all day, listening to the whir of the air conditioner in the window, riffling through the pages of a magazine or a paperback book while the daytime programs flickered on his black-and-white portable. Whenever a car did pull in, he attended to it with anxious concern, checking under the hood, squeegeeing the windshield, wiping the tires with a damp cloth, and making conversation to pass the time.

What little money he made was mostly in repair jobs, which he did from time to time when his services were needed, everything from tune-ups to body work. His customers were all local people, the folks he'd known for years, the handful of diehards who hadn't drifted away like tumbleweeds over the horizon.

He got no other business. No passersby, no travelers, no truckers. No outsiders ever passed through this town, not anymore. Nobody ever came here.

But it looked like somebody was coming now.

Bill Needham squinted, shading his eyes against the sun that had set the western sky aflame. He'd first caught sight of the man about twenty minutes ago, at seven o'clock, when he came out to get a soda from the Coke machine. The machine was the old-fashioned kind that coughed up bottles, not cans. Bill liked that; he appreciated the coldness of a bottle's frosted glass against his hand. He stood there sipping his Coke and looking at nothing, and that was when he saw what he had thought was a shadow, but was not. He'd been watching ever since, studying the man's progress. Once, when he'd finished the soda, he turned away briefly to deposit the bottle in a garbage pail full of empties; when he turned back, he half-expected to find that the man had vanished like the mirage he was; but he was still there.

And getting closer, closer by the minute. But not hurrying. No, just sort of ambling along, nice and easy, taking his sweet time about it. Strolling, you might say. Strolling through the southern Mojave, where the mercury on this mid-July day brushed a hundred fifteen, where the air was so dry it cut your skin like a fine spray of glass and your body would cry out in an agony of thirst after a half hour or so. The man didn't seem to mind. Didn't even seem to notice.

Things were quiet in the service station, as they nearly always were nowadays. There was no sound save a low, rhythmic slapping, the sound of Johnny playing paddleball. Johnny was Todd Hanson's boy, grown to sixteen years, tall, gangly, and slack-jawed, all knees and elbows; with school out for the summer, he'd taken to hanging around at the gas station, for no reason Bill could guess. That paddleball game was his sole diversion. Bill had his back to the boy at the moment, but he could picture Johnny flicking his wrist, staring with hypnotized fascination at the small rubber ball as it struck the paddle again and again. Thwack. Thwack. Thwack.

He blinked a bead of sweat out of his eye and felt it run down his cheek, dancing briefly like a drop of water on a hot griddle, evaporating in the next instant, a victim of the heat and the dryness that sucked the moisture right out of your skin.

The man was perhaps a mile from town. He was tall and lean, long-boned and thin-shouldered, a skeleton man. He wore a hat of some kind, wide-brimmed, battered, and dark, throwing his face into shadow. A rectangular hump loomed on his shoulders; it looked like a backpack. A long black coat fell from his shoulders to well below the knees, enfolding him like bat wings. Black boots tramped the sand in a slow, steady march.

"Johnny," Bill said, his voice low. The boy, intent on the game, didn't hear. "Hey, Johnny." He raised his voice a fraction. "Come over here, will you."

He heard Johnny give the ball one more bounce. Then there was a low crunching of footfalls, which stopped at his side. Bill kept his eyes on the man.

"See that?" he asked quietly.

There was no answer, but he knew that the boy had seen what he saw, that he was staring at it and was held by it, just as he himself was.

The Coke machine rattled briefly, then fell silent.

After a long moment Johnny cleared his throat. "Car broke down," he said matter-of-factly.

Bill had already considered that possibility. He shook his head. "No road out there." He jerked his thumb toward the other end of town. "Highway's that direction."

He heard the rubber ball bounce at the end of its elastic band. Thwack. Thwack.

"Got lost," Johnny said.

"Don't look lost. Don't even look tired."

"He's prospecting something. Digging up Indian bones."

"Not exactly dressed for it."

"Well, then ... what?"

"I don't know."

Silence.

Bill kept watching the man. He was almost afraid to look away. Afraid that if he did, even for a split second, the man might vanish like a mirage.

The man walked on, moving inexorably closer. Now he was perhaps three-quarters of a mile away. Heat rippled over him like waves of distortion in a sheet of glass.

"So," Johnny said, "you think we ought to go pick him up?"

Bill took a moment to think it over. And as he did, he felt something, something that started as a coldness in his gut, then moved through him, shivering up his spine, shimmying down his legs, and set his skin tingling with gooseflesh. For the first time since he'd thrown out the Coke bottle, he let his eyes wander from the vision in the desert. Suddenly he didn't mind if that man vanished like smoke.

His gaze dropped to his hands, hanging at his sides. They were shaking.

He drew a long, deep breath, feeling the brittle air scrape his throat. Slowly he raised his eyes again. He looked toward the horizon.

The man was still there. He hadn't winked out like a dream. He was just walking along, same as before, in that same slow, regular, oddly stiff-legged gait. Nearer now. Closing in.

So he was real, then. No apparition, no fancy born of heat waves and dust devils. Only a man. Well, there was no reason to be afraid of a man.

But all of a sudden, Bill knew he *was* afraid. Because when he looked at that man out there alone in the desert, that man all dressed in black, he saw something more than a man. He saw death.

"No," Bill Needham said softly. "No, I don't think we should pick him up."

- — -

Tuskett, California, was a little town dying by the side of an untraveled road. It sprawled under a mesh of high-tension wires, a checkerboard of closed shops and homes with shuttered windows, of mesquite bushes crawling over trailers streaked with rust-colored dust, of peeling paint and skin, of the mingled smells of sweat and kerosene. A small, forgotten, ugly town. Sixty miles to the west lay San Bernardino; twenty miles to the east was the Arizona border. Where Tuskett was, there was nothing.

The road, a weary strip of cracked macadam sprouting weeds in the double yellow, hadn't always been empty of traffic. Once it had carried smiling young families in Ford station wagons, setting out to see America with their backseats full of squealing laughter and Mickey Mouse ears; and truckers tooling along in their big diesel rigs with Ernest Tubb and Hank Williams singing songs of the workingman on the AM radio; and restless men with cigarettes in their mouths and the unfamiliar feel of civilian clothes against their skin, moving west to find jobs in Southern California, where everything was possible. Each day some of them stopped off in Tuskett for a bite to eat or a road map or a cup of java. A few stayed forever. Most moved on. They kept the town alive, even thriving, in those days when it seemed that the line of cars stretching to the horizon would never end.

But all that was long ago, ancient history, lost to memory ever since the interstates. Now traffic flowed along concrete arteries called Route 10 and Route 40 and Route 15, soulless things, and the back roads were forgotten, and the little town of Tuskett was left to bake in the broiling sun, clinging to its patch of dirt like a hardy desert plant, withering slowly.

Viewed from a height, Tuskett was a perfect square, divided from north to south by a single thoroughfare,

Joshua Street, named after the row of Joshua trees that lined its western side. The surviving business establishments were strung between the corpses of dead stores with boarded-up windows and untended lawns gone to seed. Here you could find Charlie Grain's coffee shop and Dick Lewis' barbershop and the police department, where Lew Hannah worked part-time as police chief, when he wasn't minding his grocery store.

Four side streets, unimaginatively numbered First, Second, Third, and Fourth, crisscrossed Joshua Street at regular intervals. Houses lined the streets, mainly prefab, single-story units with flat roofs and aluminum-siding walls and one-and-a-half baths, the kind of things that had gone up in such great numbers after the war, during Tuskett's brief, heady boom. Most stood empty now, their front walks split into webworks of jagged cracks like dry riverbeds, their yards overgrown with shepherd's purse and dogbane. Faded For Sale signs poked their heads out of thickets of weeds with stupid, stubborn optimism.

Tuskett's southern border was defined by the road that had been its lifeline. The road had had a name once, but it was long forgotten; the Old Road, folks simply called it now. Billboards stood along the roadside, their messages peeling off in ragged tatters. NEEDHAM'S SERVICE STATION, one sign warned, LAST FUEL FOR THIRTY MILES; a huge yellow arrow pointed toward Joshua Street like the finger of God. WELCOME TO TUSKETT, CALIFORNIA—another billboard greeted the empty blacktop—YOUR OASIS IN THE DESERT.

Just east of town, not far from the billboards, lay the dump, a pile of rusted automobiles and tin cans and yellowed newspapers smoking in the heat, where down through the years Tuskett's children had been warned not to play.

At the town's four corners, there were four landmarks, each with its own story to tell. To the southeast, at the tip of Joshua Street, lay a trailer park, which had once been crowded with homes and life; most of the trailers had been hitched up and driven off long ago, but a few stayed, as if rooted in place. To the southwest, opposite the trailer park, stood the Tuskett Inn, a motel that had done a fine business in the old days; it had been shut down ten years ago, and for a few years after that, kids had gone there on restless summer nights to throw stones through the windows and scrawl messages on the walls, but now all the windows were busted and nearly all the kids were gone. To the northeast lay the town's only church, open to all denominations and all faiths, its little congregation shepherded by the Reverend Chester Ewes, who had a framed certificate of graduation from the Sacred Heart Divinity School on the wall of his office and a golden statuette of the crucified Christ on his desk. And to the northwest was Bill Needham's service station, his father's legacy.

But the town's greatest landmark was located in its exact center, like a bull's-eye. It was a water tower, six stories high, which loomed over Joshua Street like one of the three-legged Martian war machines in that Orson Welles Halloween show. In years past, kids had been known to climb up there, though naturally it was forbidden; from the roof you got a fine view of the town, the road, and the desert stretching to the matte-blue outline of the Sheep Hole Mountains fifteen miles to the southwest.

There was little to do in Tuskett except watch the time pass, and there was precious little reason to stay; but there were those—fewer each year—who did stay, though they couldn't have said why. On this Tuesday evening in mid-July, the town's population numbered twenty-three. Twenty-three people who still called Tuskett their home. People who'd lived most of their lives here, and who, in most cases, expected to die here as well.

They had stayed, and they got by, living their quiet lives, adjusting the tempo of their days to the slow crawl of the shadows across the desert floor, marking time by the beat of ceiling fans; they rose with the sun, they talked with friends, they sweated out the heat of the afternoon, and they retired to their beds, another day gone; and on summer nights, in the heat and stillness, the older folk among them would lie awake and listen for the hum of traffic on the Old Road, the traffic that would never come again.

It was nearly eight o'clock, and Johnny had gone home for supper about twenty minutes ago, but Bill Needham, who lived alone and had no supper waiting, had stuck around, held by curiosity.

The man was still coming. He hadn't changed direction or altered his course in the slightest. It seemed almost as if he were headed straight for the spot where Bill stood, still leaning against the Coke machine, his position unchanged from half an hour before. As if he'd come out of the desert, out of all those trackless miles of waste, out of nowhere and nothingness, simply to get to this one place and this one time. Bill thought of that, and for a crazy moment he was sure that it really was death he was seeing, the Reaper, old Mr. Bones himself, striding out of the dusk-mottled sky to carry him away.

He shook his head.

The man was nothing to be scared of. He was just some outdoors type, maybe not quite right in the head, who got his kicks hiking through the desert. Bill had read somewhere about a guy who'd walked across the continent and back again, just for the fun of it. Maybe that was the story here too. Maybe.

Except he knew it wasn't.

He waited.

The man reached the edge of town, where Joshua Street began. He walked down the middle of the street, still moving slowly, cautiously, as if testing the ground with each step. He paid no attention to the service station or to Bill Needham. He just kept walking, his eyes fixed straight ahead, his boots crunching on the blistered pavement. It seemed that he wasn't aiming to take Bill with him to the beyond, after all; he was just walking on by.

Bill almost let him go. He had no real desire to talk with this man, to trade pleasantries and shake hands. But, hang it all, he was curious. He wanted to know just what this fellow was up to, what had brought him here, and from where. And besides, it just plain wasn't natural for a man to stroll out of a hundred miles of desert and pass by the first human being he'd seen in hours or days, with not so much as a sidewise glance.

Bill took a breath, then called out, "Hello."

The man stopped. He turned, swinging his whole body around in one slow, sure pivot. He stood motionless, staring at Bill Needham from ten feet away, and Bill stared back, and a long moment passed that way, while a gust of wind sent pebbles pinging noisily against the gas pumps on the service island.

For the first time, Bill could see the man clearly. On his head he wore a cowboy hat, blotchy with dust and sweat, strapped loosely to his chin by a cowhide lanyard. The packsack's straps were looped over his shoulders and under his armpits; the sack itself bulged in odd places and sagged ponderously in a way that suggested weight. His black coat draped him nearly from head to toe, its hem all but brushing the ground; the coat was soiled, its pockets tattered, its original shape lost to time and wear; it hung on his gaunt frame like a bed sheet on a hat rack.

The coat was unbuttoned, exposing a black denim shirt in the western-yoke style, open at the neck but loosely laced across the chest by a leather thong strung through ragged eyelets. His belt was faded rawhide, bowing a little under the weight of a large brass buckle, green with age. His pants were black corduroy, patched at the knees. His boots, it appeared, were snakeskin. Rattlesnake, from the look of them, though it was hard to tell plainly, since they'd been dyed jet black.

Bill lifted his gaze and gave the man's face a good hard stare. He was beardless and pale. His eyes were sunken, lost in the black recesses of their sockets. His nose was a blade-sharp wedge. His mouth was a thin bloodless line. Tri-cornered shadows lived in the hollows under jutting cheekbones. His hair was close-cropped, largely concealed under the hat, with only a few stray yellowish wisps plastered across his high unlined forehead like bits of straw. He looked to be about thirty, though it was hard to say; he showed no visible signs of age, yet there was no youthfulness in him, no faintest echo of childhood.

He made no reply.

"Hot one today," Bill said.

The man turned to look at the town before him. Bill watched his profile, the hawk nose and narrow, angular jaw in semi-silhouette against the purple sky.

"What is this place?" the man asked in a low voice, a gravelly whisper that made Bill think, absurdly, of the first spadeful of dirt on a casket.

"Tuskett." He kept his own voice even, although suddenly his heart was racing and his mouth was dry and that awful coldness in his gut was back. "Ever hear of it?"

The man shook his head. He stared off into the distance, where the handful of homes and shops lay scattered under a sprinkling of stars.

"How many people?" he asked.

"Twenty-three."

The man made a sound like a chuckle.

"May not look like much," Bill added, feeling a sudden need to defend his town against this man, this outsider. "But we like it. Quiet, you know. No crime here. No hassles. You don't even need to lock your door at night. There's none of this crazy stuff you hear about in New York and LA. There's nobody running guns, or shooting heroin, or doing dope, although not long ago Rile Cady did catch Johnny Hanson, Todd's boy, out in the desert with a jug of Night Train apple wine and his dad's pistol, shooting at the sky ..."

His voice trailed off as he realized he was talking too much. Nervousness, maybe. Or maybe not. There was something disquieting about this man, something that made you want to talk, need to talk, to tell all you knew.

He took another breath, long and slow, drawing in a lungful of the parched Mojave air. "So what brings you here?"

The man looked at him. "Nothing."

"Planning to stay?"

"No."

"Just passing through?"

"Yes." A smile flicked at a corner of his mouth, quick as a lizard's tongue. "Passing through."

"I notice," Bill said, while his heart thudded louder in his ears, "you're wearing a pack. Hiking across country, maybe? Seeing the sights?"

The man lifted his head a fraction, catching the last rays of the sun; and for the first time Bill looked into his eyes. They were ice-blue, with half-closed lids and spiderwork patterns of wrinkles at the edges, and they were cold, so cold, arctic cold. They seemed to look inside you and see the fear twisting your gut like acid. They seemed to see too much.

"You ask a lot of questions," the man said. "Guess you'd like to know just who I am and what I'm doing here."

Bill tightened his grip on the Coke machine, feeling the cool, hard steel. He held on to it as his knees trembled and slow currents of fear rippled through his body. He licked his lips. "Yes, sir. I believe I would."

"Then I'll tell you," the man said. That half-smile flicked again, a twitch playing at the edge of his mouth. "I'm paying a visit. A visit to Tuskett, California, population twenty-three, where there's no crime, no hassles, where you don't even need to lock your door at night. You see, I've been looking for this town. Been looking a long time."

"Thought you said you'd never heard of it."

"Haven't." A real smile this time. Chipped teeth, pale gums. "Been looking, just the same."

Bill took a step back. He was cold all over now. There was something in that smile, something he didn't want to see.

"What's your name?" Bill asked, his voice suddenly hoarse.

"Kane."

The word was clipped, toneless, a single tick of the clock.

Bill swallowed. His head moved a little in time with the hard snap of his Adam's apple.

"I don't think you're welcome here, Mr. Kane."

Kane laughed, a soft, dark sound like the trickle of molasses or of blood. "No," he said. "I don't suppose I am."

He turned and walked on, down the street, into the

gathering night. Bill Needham watched him go.

Jenny Kirk splashed half a jar of Ragu into the saucepan, then chopped up three tomatoes, two green peppers, and an onion, and stirred them into the sauce. That, at least, was one advantage of working at Lew Hannah's grocery store; she got to take home fresh produce every day, and because Lew was a sweetheart, it was always on the house.

The big disadvantage, on the other hand, was that the store stayed open till six thirty on summer evenings, and then she had to help with the sweeping-up, which wasn't part of the job, but she couldn't let poor old Lew do it all by himself. So she rarely made it home before seven fifteen, rarely got dinner on the table before quarter of eight. Not that she minded for herself, but it wasn't healthy for a growing boy—and growing so darn fast—to eat so late. She remembered how, a year ago. Tommy had come down with stomach cramps and gas pains from waiting too long between meals; ever since, she had been sure to leave him a snack in the fridge, maybe half a sandwich or a chicken leg. Not the ideal solution, but the best she could manage. She had learned long ago that compromise was the key to survival in circumstances like hers. And she was a survivor. She and Tommy both.

The sauce bubbled and simmered on the stove. She tasted it and rated it passable. Well, she made no claims to being a master chef, but Tommy didn't seem to mind, and he was the one she was cooking for. If it had been just for her alone, she probably would have lived off TV dinners.

She stirred a colander's worth of spaghetti into the sauce, then ladled the mixture onto two plates, heavy china plates with columbine and ivy embroidered in bluish patterns around the edges. The plates had been a wedding present from Lew and Ellyn Hannah, the only wedding present she and Mike had received. She had been using them ever since. Sometimes, when she looked into their enameled shine, she saw her own face, not as she was now, but as she had been then, a young woman—a girl, really—with all of life's possibilities open and reaching out to her like an outstretched hand. There had been six plates to the set; now there were five; a few years ago, she had dropped one and watched it shatter on the kitchen floor, and there was something about that sunburst of china shards that had made her cry.

She blinked, wondering why she should choose tonight to be remembering that. She had been in a funny kind of mood all day, feeling sad and vaguely apprehensive. She shrugged. Maybe her period was coming early.

"Tommy," she said, not raising her voice too much, because it was a small house, and in small houses there was no need to shout. "Supper."

A clatter of racing footfalls answered her. Tommy Kirk, eight years old, bedraggled, perpetually flushed with excitement and out of breath, stood in the kitchen doorway.

"Mom, after supper, can I go out and play?"

"We'll see how late it gets."

"Just for a little while."

"We'll see."

He heaved a huge sigh, a sigh that was almost too big for him to handle. Without needing to be told, he went to the refrigerator, filled two glasses with milk from a plastic jug, and carried them to the kitchen table,

"Have you washed your hands yet?" Jenny inquired as she sprinkled the spaghetti with Parmesan cheese.

"Huh-uh."

"Do it, pal."

"Both sides?"

"Palms 'n' knuckles. Make 'em shine,"

He turned on the tap water and thrust his hands briefly under a soapy stream, then dried them on a dish towel.

"Hey, Mom," he said, "what did Count Dracula's mother say to him at dinnertime?"

"You got me. Take your plate. Careful, it's hot."

"She said, 'Go on, son. Eat your soup before it clots.'" He laughed. "Get it?"

"Ugh. I get it." She sat down at the kitchen table opposite him. "Where'd you hear that one?"

"Rile."

"That figures."

They ate in silence for a few minutes. The spaghetti was steaming hot, too hot for a summer night; Jenny felt beads of sweat blossom on her face with each bite. She looked down at the vinyl tablecloth, which had once sported a pleasing blue-green checkerboard pattern, but which had faded over the years to a pale, sickly yellow. She thought about how things faded with time. Memories, and youth, and hope. She shook her head, dispelling the thought, and wound another mouthful of spaghetti around her fork. Damn, was she ever in a weird mood tonight.

Tommy was talking again. "Rile says he was here before there even was a town. Before it had a name, anyhow. Think so?"

He chugged down half his glass of milk, leaving a film of white on his upper lip.

"It's possible, I suppose," Jenny said. "Old Mr. Tuskett put up the water tower in 1921, so I've been told. I guess Rile's old enough to have witnessed that. He would've been your age then, or younger. On the other hand, he might just be funning you. He's been known to do that, on occasion."

"He don't mean no harm."

"Doesn't," she corrected. "Doesn't mean any harm."

"Uh-huh. Like I said."

Jenny pursed her lips. Her son, she often felt, was doomed to grow up illiterate. And there was precious little she could do about it. The nearest school was in Jacob, twenty miles away, and it was a crummy hole of a place, staffed by incompetent teachers nearly as ignorant as their pupils. Still, it was the only school around.

"Mom."

"Umm."

"What's a rubber?"

She looked at him. "A what?"

"A rubber."

"Where'd you hear that word?"

"Johnny Hanson said it. Said you got to wear one when you kiss a girl, or else you catch germs and die."

She almost smiled, but stopped herself, seeing the serious look on his face. "When you kiss a girl, huh?"

"When you make love. That's kissing, ain't it?"

She did not correct his grammar this time. She spoke carefully. She had made a vow never to lie to him, not even about things like this. Especially about things like this.

"No, it's not kissing. Making love is ... You remember what I told you about sex?"

"Intercourse?" He still called it that.

"Yeah. Well, that's making love. And a rubber is ... Well, that's a nasty word for it. What it's really called is a condom, and it's made of rubber, and you put it on your ... on your penis."

"So you don't catch germs there?"

"That's right. And so the ... the girl doesn't catch any of your germs, and also so you don't make a baby."

"Huh." He seemed to have lost interest in the subject.

"How'd you happen to get on this subject with Johnny Hanson, anyway?"

Tommy shrugged. "Just talking. Can I go out and play now?"

She looked at his plate, picked clean. She sighed. "Okay, but only for an hour or so. I want you back in this house by nine o'clock sharp. You got that?"

"Got it."

He was gone in a flurry of motion. The screen door banged shut. Jenny sat alone at the kitchen table, finishing her supper and thinking.

So her boy had been talking with Johnny Hanson about making love and wearing rubbers. Well, he'd be doing more than just talking before long. Another few years and he would need advice on that subject, advice she wouldn't know how to give, advice only a father could supply.

She pushed back her chair, too abruptly, scraping the tile floor. She carried her plate and Tommy's to the sink. She washed the dishes by hand under a stream of cold water. She kept on running the water and scrubbing the dishes long after they were clean, till her hands were numb from the cold. She thought about that shattered dish, that faded tablecloth. She thought about losing things she loved. She did not know why she was afraid.

Kane walked down Joshua Street in the twilight darkness, then turned down Third. He passed rows of houses abandoned to the weeds and the desert dust. In one untended yard, a rusted-out tricycle lay on its side amid a bed of dogbane. The leaves of a desert willow shivered in the breeze, swaying like long tresses of hair. A raven hopped amid a forest of toadstools, cawing grouchily.

Halfway down the street, there was a rare sight, a house that was still a home. A flowerbed lay on the verge of a well-watered lawn, neatly trimmed and weeded, brown in spots but holding out the hope of becoming a carpet of green in the winter months, when the rains fell and the air lost its harsh sandpapery feel.

A mobile of wind chimes hung on the front porch, tinkling unmelodically in gusts of wind. Near the chimes was a sign, gray with age, its hand-printed letters barely legible now. ROOM FOR RENT, it said, INQUIRE WITHIN.

Kane stopped. He stood looking at the sign. He looked at it for a long time. A smile played like a tic at the corner of his mouth. His narrowed eyes glinted, cobalt blue.

He crossed the lawn in long swift strides. He walked through the flowerbed, casually trampling a patch of angel's trumpets just spreading their petals to take in the night air. He climbed the steps to the porch, his boots sinking briefly into the spongy softness of each wooden plank. He stopped at the front door, where a screen of wire mesh framed a view of the living room.

It was an old person's room. It had the look and feel, even the musty smell, of age. Antique chairs and coffee tables were arranged at the borders of a frayed Persian rug on a hardwood floor. A lamp with a stained-glass shade cast a rainbow of pastels over a rolltop writing desk scattered with snapshots in silver frames. The snapshots looked like pictures of family members and friends; many were faded, the corners curling up; somebody's memories of years past.

Kane rapped on the screen. It shook, rattling in the doorframe. Nobody answered. He rapped again, louder.

"Coming," whistled a high, flutish voice.

A woman, blue-haired and parchment-creased, appeared out of the dim recesses of a hallway. She wore a blue dress printed with flowers and darkened by half-moons of sweat at the armpits. Gold-rimmed glasses sat on the bridge of her nose. Her eyes, cloudy with cataracts, peered over the tops of the lenses. She stopped at the screen door, looking up at Kane, who stood two heads taller.

"Yes?" Her voice quavered, dovelike.

"I'm here about the room."

She blinked, uncomprehending. Kane waited. He said nothing more. After a long moment a cloud lifted.

"The room for rent?" she said, the words trilling up the scale in childlike astonishment.

Kane nodded.

"Well, if that doesn't beat all." A pale pink tongue clucked at white dentures. "Do you know how long it's been since I've taken in a boarder? If you do, I hope you'll tell me, 'cause I surely don't." She laughed, amused at the witticism. "It's been a time, let me tell you. But look at me, standing here jawing while all you want to do is rest yourself."

She fumbled with the screen door and pushed it open. It creaked.

"You come right on in, Mr. ...? I'm sorry, I didn't catch your name."

"Kane."

"Mr. Kane. I'm Mrs. Walston, Ethel to her friends. And I've got nothing but friends. You got a lot of friends, Mr. Kane?"

"No."

"Well, I'm surprised to hear that. A nice-looking young man like yourself."

She led him through the living room. An electric fan sat on a low end table, whirring; another fan hummed in a window. In one corner of the room loomed a television set, blank and silent; it was a big old-fashioned boxlike thing sprouting a pair of rabbit ears joined by an arc of tinfoil to improve the reception. Next to it was a bookcase, its shelves lined with books in large type for easy reading; a pair of bookends made out of seashells bracketed one row. The shells looked incongruous in this place, so far from an ocean breeze. Outside, the wind chimes tinkled softly, like fairy dust.

"The room's in back," Ethel Walston said as they went down the narrow hall. "It used to be my son Bobby's room. Now Bobby is in Orlando. That's Orlando, Florida." She put a faint stress on the last word, as if to emphasize the exotic distantness of the place. "Have you ever been there?"

"I've been lots of places."

They passed a bedroom. A small dog, a mixed-breed spaniel crotchety with age, trotted out of the room into the hall and cocked his head, staring up at Kane.

"Oh." Ethel Walston smiled. "I nearly forgot. This here is Scooter. That was Harry's name for him, anyhow. I'm afraid he doesn't do a whole lot of scooting nowadays." Worry flashed on her face. "You don't mind dogs?"

"No."

She relaxed. "That's good. I always say you can trust a man who likes animals."

Scooter stared at Kane a moment longer, then approached him, lowered his head, and began to lick the toe of Kane's snakeskin boot industriously, as if in friendship or in supplication.

Kane stood unmoving. He watched the spaniel at his feet as the small pink shape of its tongue worked the boot. The hint of a smile passed over his face like a glimpse of sun on a cloudy day.

"Well, what do you know," Ethel said happily. "Old Scooter seems to have taken a shine to you."

Scooter finished cleaning the boot, lifted his head, and stared intently up at Kane for another moment. Then he turned and padded back into the bedroom.

"Now that you've become acquainted," Ethel said, "I'll show you to your room."

At the end of the hall there was a door. It swung open on a small guest room, four bare walls enclosing a bed with a cotton spread. There were no fans here to move the air; heat lay over the room, thick and heavy as a blanket.

"This is it. Ten dollars a night." She looked at him. "Or we have a weekly rate. Fifty dollars."

Wordlessly Kane pulled a wrinkled ten-dollar bill from his pants pocket and handed it to her.

"You won't be staying long, then?"

"Just the night."

"Mind if I inquire what your business is in Tuskett?"

"None." He smiled briefly. "Just happened to see your town. I liked it."

Ethel shook her head sadly. "Very kind of you to say so. But I'm afraid Tuskett's not what it was. All the young people are moving out." Her lips formed a smile around her dentures. "If you wanted to settle here, you'd be welcome. We could surely use some fresh blood."

Kane smiled again. "Well, you never know," he said quietly. "You just might get some."

Johnny Hanson's father was a large graying bear of a man who'd developed a paunch and a tendency to suck at his teeth, but who was otherwise not substantially different from the young man fresh from action in Korea who'd won Debbie Bascomb's heart. Johnny had seen pictures of his mother as she'd been at nineteen; she looked like a high school cheerleader—fresh-faced, clear-skinned, bright-eyed, with a cute little upturned nose that brought the word "perky" to mind. Todd Hanson had been passing through Tuskett, the way lots of men just out of uniform used to do on their way to Los Angeles, when he'd met Debbie, a local girl, and decided to stay awhile. It had turned into a long stay, thirty-eight years. In that time they'd raised four children, three of them grown and moved away, and Johnny, who'd been, as folks liked to say, a bit of a surprise.

Johnny could never quite shake off the suspicion that the surprise hadn't been entirely welcome. His folks treated him okay, he guessed—they kept him fed and clothed and sheltered, and they didn't mess with his record collection or look for his stash of *Penthouse* magazines—but they ignored him most of the time. He had the feeling they were just itching to pack him off to college in another two years and have the house to themselves.

Which was okay with him, because if there was anything he was looking forward to, it was the day when he could wave good-bye to this piss-ant one-stoplight town. Hell, not even one stoplight. There wasn't a single traffic signal anywhere along Joshua Street, which was the closest thing Tuskett had to a main drag.

Johnny figured he was probably the only kid in high school who didn't like summer vacation. Hated it, in fact. Because for the three stiflingly hot months of summer he was stuck in Tuskett, with nothing but that stupid paddleball game to keep him occupied, and nobody to talk to except a bunch of old farts and Tommy Kirk, a runt of a kid who didn't even know what a rubber was.

Today, at least, something had happened. And he was just about breaking out in hives to spill the news. He'd waited anxiously all through dinner, afraid to say anything because the rule at the table, strictly enforced, was that his dad held court and Johnny was permitted to speak only when spoken to; and tonight, as was the case on most nights, he hadn't been spoken to, not once. But now, finally, dinner was over; his mom was doing the dishes and his dad had settled down in front of the tube.

"Hey, Dad. You won't believe this."

"Hmm," his dad said, exhibiting a marked lack of curiosity. He was slumped in a careworn easy chair, a can of Bud in one fist, his gut overspilling his belt. The Dodgers were facing off against San Francisco. Gibson was at the plate, swinging his stick; the picture rolled. His dad, Johnny knew, had little interest in baseball, probably wasn't even paying attention, probably would nod off to sleep pretty soon with that beer still in his hand—but right now his bleary gaze was focused, more or less, on the action, and he seemed hardly aware of Johnny's presence.

Johnny plunged ahead anyhow.

"There was this guy. Mr. Needham saw him first." His dad insisted that Johnny call all adult men "mister," even though Bill Needham himself had no beef with Johnny using his first name. "He was out on the desert—this guy, I mean—walking toward town. *Walking*. Would you believe it? I would've stuck around, except I figured I'd be late for dinner if I did." That was another thing about his dad; he had strict rules on the subject of punctuality. Being late for dinner was a mortal sin in the Hanson household. "The guy was sort of creepy-looking. I mean—"

"What do you mean, safe?" Todd Hanson snarled in the direction of the TV set. "He was out by a car length, for cripes' sakes."

Johnny sighed. It was no use.

He gave up on his dad and went into the kitchen, where his mom was cleaning up after dinner. He never had to help out with stuff like that, because his dad was of the opinion that it wasn't right for a man to work in the kitchen. That was a woman's place.

"Great dinner, Mom," Johnny said because he knew it was expected of him. In truth, the chicken had been stringy and dry.

Debbie Hanson smiled, acknowledging the compliment. She was still a pretty woman; rigorous dieting reminiscent of the asceticism of medieval monks had kept her dress size unchanged in thirty-eight years.

"You know, there's a new guy in town," Johnny said, affecting a casual tone.

"Is there?"

She, at least, was listening.

"Yeah," Johnny said, dropping any pretence of indifference and fairly machine-gunning the words, "we saw him—Mr. Needham and me—over at the gas station, and he was walking the Mojave like it was a golf course, I mean, just sort of taking a stroll, and he's really dressed weird too—"

"Isn't that nice," Debbie Hanson said, still smiling, always smiling, the Stepford mom.

Johnny realized with a sinking heart that she wasn't listening, after all.

"Yeah," he said, his voice tinged with bitterness; he knew she wouldn't hear that either. "Yeah, it's nice."

He went to his room, shut the door, put on headphones, and cranked up the music. The metal band Rush roared in his ears. He flopped down on his bed, cocooned in noise, and thought about going off to college or getting a job or doing anything, anything at all, just as long as it was far away from here.

In his sixty-odd years in Tuskett, his whole life, Charlie Grain had never seen a man look quite like Bill Needham did now.

"Hey, Billy boy," he said, forcing a smile. "I guess you must've just seen a ghost."

"I don't know," Bill said in a beaten voice. "I don't know what I saw."

He parked himself on a stool at the counter, next to

Lew Hannah, who was sipping black coffee as usual. Lew was the closest thing Tuskett had to a police department; he was the only man to wear a badge in this town, pinned to his plaid short-sleeved shirt—though the last time he'd needed to use it was sometime back in the sixties, when some hippie characters had floated into town in a psychedelic van and made trouble.

At the far end of the counter, Meg Sanchez glanced up from this week's edition of the Tuskett *Clarion* to assess Bill's condition for herself. She made no effort to hide her curiosity; she was a born snoop and everybody knew it; she even looked like one, what with those bird-bright eyes and pencil-fine nose. Blue smoke curled from the tip of the unfiltered Camel in her mouth, rising sluggishly through waves of heat to the spinning blades of the ceiling fan.

The three of them were the only customers in Charlie Grain's coffee shop at the moment, which made it, in Charlie's mind, a full house. At the back of the room PattiSue Baker was scrubbing off the tables with Formula 409.

Bill rested his elbows on the counter and cupped his head in his hands. His skin, always deeply tanned from long days in the open air, looked strangely sallow tonight.

Charlie studied him. "Hey, what is it, Billy? I'm serious. I've seen cowflop that looked livelier than you."

Bill did not raise his head. "Just fry up a cheeseburger for me, will you. And pile on the onions, the way I like it."

"Sure," Charlie said, baffled. "Sure, Billy boy. Coming right up."

He busied himself with the job, molding a beef patty with his brown, age-spotted hands, then slapping it down on the griddle, where it hissed and shivered in a puddle of fat. Nobody said anything. Lew sipped his coffee and made low slurping sounds which sounded oddly like snoring. Meg stared at Bill a moment longer, then managed an elaborate shrug and went back to her newspaper. She turned the page; it crinkled irritably.

Charlie glanced at Bill and saw him staring out the window into the night. He asked no questions. He figured old Billy boy would get around to talking about it eventually. That was why he'd come in, after all. Not to grab a cheeseburger with extra onions, but to talk. Charlie Grain might not have been Albert Einstein, but he could puzzle out that part of the equation.

He flipped the burger onto a bun, sprinkled it with onions and doused it with ketchup, and slid the plate across the counter. Bill stared down at it blankly, as if it were an artifact dredged up from the ocean floor.

"Want a cola or something?" Charlie asked.

Bill raised his head, and Charlie saw, for the first time, that his eyes were wide and haunted and unblinking.

"There's a stranger in town," Bill said simply. "Walked in off the desert. I talked to him."

Everyone was listening now. Lew had put down his coffee. Meg peered over the top of her newspaper.

"Walked in?" Charlie asked. "I don't get it."

"Neither do I."

"Who was he?"

"Said his name was Kane."

"What's he doing here?"

"He wouldn't say, exactly. But I think I know."

Charlie let a moment pass. "Well, what?"

Bill looked around, as if suddenly aware that he was in a room with other human beings and they were watching him. "Oh, hell. Never mind."

Lew Hannah tapped his spoon on the Formica countertop, a low, rhythmic sound.

"Whoa there, Bill," he said in the deep, slow, friendly voice that could have gotten him elected mayor, had he ever chosen to run. "Just hold on, now. You can't come in here telling a tale like this and then say never mind. What is it about this fellow, anyhow? He one of these punk kids with purple hair and a needle in his arm?"

Bill shook his head. "No. He's nothing like that. He's just ..." He seemed to grope for words. "He's ... dark."

Meg snorted. "Bill Needham, I'm ashamed of you. I just hope Rile Cady doesn't hear you talk like that."

Bill flushed. "I didn't mean it *that* way. This man, he's fish-belly white on the outside. But ... but something in him's dark." His voice was hushed, his eyes downcast. "He's evil. That's what I mean."

"Horse puckey," Meg said. She fairly spat the words. "You've been breathing in too much goddamn auto exhaust, is all. It's burned out what little sense you had."

Bill said nothing.

"Charlie." The voice made them all jump, but it was only PattiSue, standing at the far end of the counter with a half-empty spray bottle in one hand and a roll of paper towels in the other. "Tables are all scrubbed clean. Can I take off now?"

"Sure, honey. You have yourself a nice night."

She nodded gratefully, stowed the cleaning supplies in the closet, and undid her apron, all in a dizzy whirl of motion. She was halfway to the front door when it swung open from the outside. She jumped back, her mouth forming a perfect round O of surprise.

A man stood in the doorway.

It was Kane, of course. Had to be. The odds of two strangers in Tuskett at the same time were too low to calculate.

He was tall and bony, his clothes hanging off his gaunt frame like hand-me-downs. He stood in a funny sort of way, his feet planted wide apart, hands hanging limply at his sides, looking relaxed and wary at the same time. His face was strange, all sharp edges and hard angles, a face like cut glass.

PattiSue stood frozen, watching him, her urgency forgotten. Meg looked over at him sharply. Lew swung around on his stool in a languid, unhurried fashion. Bill didn't even turn his head. He sat rigid, gripping the edge of the counter with one white-knuckled hand.

Charlie Grain fancied himself a fair judge of character. In years gone by, when Tuskett had been a town and not a graveyard, a steady stream of people had flowed through that door. He'd seen all kinds. He'd learned to look at a face and read the story written on it. So he studied this man Kane, trying to see what he could see.

He saw nothing. No bitterness or optimism, no friendliness or anger, no fear or fearlessness. The man's face was a blank. Charlie thought of a starless sky, an empty box, an open grave.

A shiver coursed through him and made the muscles of his stomach knot up. Suddenly he wondered if Bill Needham had been right, if maybe there was something wrong about this man. No, ridiculous. His imagination was running away with him.

Kane moved forward. He brushed past PattiSue. She stared after him, her eyes wide and glassy and unblinking, doll's eyes. He crossed the room. His boots clunked like peg legs on the linoleum floor. He took a stool at the far end of the counter, across from Meg. His long, bony fingers drummed the countertop.

"Coffee," he said. "Black."

Charlie poured a cup, too quickly. His hand shook and he spilled some. He set down the cup and saucer in front of the man. Steam rose like a white ghost. Kane didn't touch it.

Nobody said a word. There was something in the air—Charlie sensed it, and he knew the others did too—something that set your teeth on edge, a kind of electricity, like the dry tingle smelling of ozone that is the forewarning of a storm.

Then Meg folded her newspaper noisily and gave the man called Kane a hard, no-nonsense look.

"So, mister. Just who the hell are you?"

Kane raised the coffee cup to his lips and sipped.

Somewhere a clock ticked. There was no other sound.

Meg's words, so bright and mocking and fearless, hung unanswered in the air, going stale, like the odor of hamburger grease from the grill.

Meg took a long drag off her cigarette, then tried again. Suddenly her voice was harsher, throatier than usual.

"We don't get visitors in these parts too often. What brings you here?"

Kane took another sip of coffee. Charlie watched him, feeling certain he wasn't going to speak at all, and then Kane set the cup down on its saucer with a soft thud and looked at Meg Sanchez.

"Nothing," he said, his voice neutral, his face still as empty as before.

"People don't just go wandering around in the desert like Moses."

"I do."

"You from these parts originally? California, I mean?"

"No."

"Where, then?"

"Nowhere."

"Oh, so you're the mystery man." The cigarette in Meg's hand was trembling, and her voice was breaking up like a weak radio signal. "You come from nowhere and you're looking for nothing. That about the size of it?"

"About."

"Well, you've been in Tuskett a little while now. So tell me, mystery man. What do you think of us here? What do you think of our town?"

"I think," Kane said, "it's a good place to die."

"You fixing to die?"

Kane looked at her, into her, through her. "No."

She kept staring at him, and all the breath seemed to go out of her in time with the cloud of cigarette smoke from her nostrils, and then she drew back slowly, her thin body appearing to fold into itself like a Swiss army knife. She looked down at the newspaper in her lap. She did not raise her eyes to him again.

Kane took another sip of coffee.

Lew Hannah tapped the counter with his spoon. He gazed down into the black depths of his coffee, lost in thought. Then he looked up, and on his face there blossomed a broad, friendly, man's-man sort of smile.

"Don't mind Miss Sanchez, mister," he said, his voice purring in lazy reassurance like a forty-five record slowed down to thirty-three. "She's our resident journalist, you see. She's got a right to stick her nose in. That's her job, if you get what I mean."

"Stuff it, Lew," Meg said sourly, but the retort was just reflex.

"Tuskett is really a most neighborly town," Lew said, still wearing that good-old-boy smile, like a party mask he had neglected to take off. "Hope you didn't get the wrong impression. But as you may have noticed from the star on my lapel, I'm chief of police, and sometimes it's my duty to be a bit less than neighborly." The smiling mask slipped, exposing the hardness beneath. "That remark you made about dying—it doesn't sit too well with me. I'd like to hear you explain it. I'd like to know what you're doing here. I'd like to know it right now."

Kane tipped the coffee cup to his mouth and drained the last drops, then set it down. He looked at Lew, and Lew held his gaze, because everyone knew that a man couldn't flinch in a situation like this.

Charlie Grain watched them both. And then he saw a remarkable thing. Slowly, almost imperceptibly, Lew Hannah seemed to soften up, his shoulders sagging, the line of his jaw going slack. It was a change so slight as to be almost nonexistent, and Charlie wasn't completely sure he'd seen it at all.

My imagination again, he told himself. Running hog-wild tonight.

Kane and Lew watched each other a moment longer, and then Kane spoke.

"You meaning to arrest me?" he asked.

Lew hesitated. Slowly he shook his head.

"Can't arrest a man without good reason," he said, his voice low and tired.

Kane nodded. He pushed back his stool and got up. He dug in his pants pocket and pulled out a fistful of coins. They clattered on the countertop. Charlie watched them roll lazily, like marbles, then come to rest. He didn't pick them up.

Kane moved away from the counter to the door, where PattiSue stood frozen, watching him. He paused, looking at her, and she made a swallowing sound. Then the door creaked open and slammed shut, and Kane was gone.

The blades of the ceiling fan rotated slowly, making whispery sounds in the sudden stillness.

"Well," PattiSue said finally, "I ... I guess I'd better be getting along. I'll see you, Charlie. 'Night."

"Wait a minute." That was Lew. He was blinking too much. "I'll walk with you, if you don't mind. I could use the air."

"Police escort," PattiSue said lightly. "Fine by me."

It was funny, Charlie thought, how everybody was acting all of a sudden—everybody but Bill. It was as if they all smelled smoke but none of them wanted to be the first to holler "Fire!" As if the smoke wouldn't be real unless someone acknowledged it. He noticed that Bill was looking at them, turning his head slowly from one to the other, and nobody was looking back.

Lew got off his stool. He glanced at Charlie. "Put the coffee on my tab," he said calmly, easily. It was a very natural thing to say. Except Charlie always put Lew's coffee on his tab. He did the same for everybody. He knew folks would pay him when the bills came due.

He could have pointed that out. Instead he said, "Okay, Lew." He heard the same bright pretense of normalcy in his own voice.

Lew held the door for PattiSue. Beyond the brightness of the coffee shop the night rustled and shivered fitfully. A warm breeze, dry as bone, gusted through the doorway and started the napkins on the tables flapping like sheets on a clothesline.

PattiSue stepped outside, and Lew followed, and the two of them were gone together, into the night. Charlie and Bill stared after them. Meg kept her eyes on the newspaper in her hand. Nobody said anything, until finally Charlie felt he had to break the silence.

"I'll admit he's a strange one," he heard himself say in that same casual tone. "But I've seen some that were even stranger."

"Sure," Meg said, playing along. "He's the antisocial type, is all. Nothing to get all bothered about."

"The way I figure," Charlie said, "he's seeing the country the shoe-leather way. Sleeps out under the stars in the wide-open spaces. Travels here and there. Hardly surprising a man like that would lose the habit of speech." He found the words comforting; they served to dispel the lingering aura of strangeness Kane had left behind. "A free spirit, you could say. Got to admit I envy him a little. If I were a younger man, I might do the same."

"Well, I don't know," Meg said. "I wouldn't want to glamorize him. He might be a trifle, er, touched. That coat of his—an odd thing, isn't it, to be wearing this time of year?" She took another puff and blew a smoke ring at the ceiling. "Tell you what I think. I think he's one of those poor souls they've got so many of in LA. Those that sleep in the gutter and eat out of trashcans. They wear all kinds of gear even in the hottest weather, and some of them are even more taciturn than this one."

"Could be," Charlie agreed. "Only, what do you suppose he's doing here?"

Meg shrugged. "Got to be somewhere."

Bill stood abruptly. "I'll be seeing you folks." He half-turned away, then glanced back at his hamburger, untouched on his plate. "Hey, Charlie, Maybe you could put that burger on my tab too."

Charlie could feel Bill Needham's eyes on him. He looked down at the counter. "Sure thing," he said in that lying coward's voice, the voice that insisted everything was fine, just fine, because Kane was an outdoor type or a homeless bum or anything at all except a dark man with a dark soul.

He didn't look up again until the door to the coffee shop had opened and closed and Bill Needham was gone.

Lew Hannah and PattiSue Baker walked together down Joshua Street. Neither of them said much of anything. She was heading for the trailer park, Lew figured. Eddie would be waiting for her, as usual.

But at the intersection of Joshua and Fourth, PattiSue hesitated. "I'd like to stop in at my folks' place for a second," she said, not looking at him. "If it's all right with you."

"Sure," Lew said easily. "I'm in no hurry."

He did his best to act natural about it, but the truth was, she'd caught him by surprise. It was common knowledge around here that PattiSue and her folks were not on speaking terms, and hadn't been ever since PattiSue started shacking up with Eddie Cox. Not that George and Marge Baker had anything against Eddie, mind you. Everybody figured him to be a fine young man, good-looking and pleasant-tempered, the kind of fellow who'd make any girl a first-rate husband. Only, right there was the rub. Eddie wasn't PattiSue's husband, not even her fiancé. The two of them were living together without benefit of matrimony.

Now, Lew himself was a tolerant sort, and privately he didn't give much of a hang about a piece of paper called a marriage license or a loop of gold-plated tin called a wedding band; true love was what counted. But George and Marge didn't see things that way.

The whole business had come to a boil about two months ago, when PattiSue stopped merely seeing Eddie and decided to move in with him full-time. Harsh words had been exchanged, and PattiSue, it was said, had stormed out of the house after yelling at her folks to go to hell. They'd rarely spoken since. But now she was stopping off at home.

Lew and PattiSue strolled down Fourth Avenue. The Baker house, the only two-story home in Tuskett that was still occupied, rose up on the right-hand side of the street. They climbed the front steps, and Lew waited while she rang the doorbell. From inside came the sound of footsteps, rising over the mosquito whine of a power drill.

A moment later the door opened. Marge Baker stood

there. She was a matronly woman, what you might call full-figured, with a round, flat, but kindly face. She stared at PattiSue as if at a stranger.

"Hi, Mom," PattiSue said without enthusiasm.

"Why ... hello, darling." Marge almost smiled, then thought better of it. "I must say, this comes as something of a surprise—you being here." Her eyes tracked over to Lew; she noticed him for the first time. "Oh. Evening, Lew."

"Evening, Marge."

Marge forced a smile for his benefit. "My daughter's not under arrest, is she?"

Lew smiled. "Nothing like that. We were just taking a stroll together. It's a nice night."

"Uh-huh. A trifle warm."

"But clear."

PattiSue had been shifting her weight restlessly throughout this exchange. Finally she spoke up.

"I'm here to pick up something of mine," she said curtly.

Marge frowned. "You've already cleaned out your clothes closet and your record albums and—"

"There's something I forgot."

A beat of time passed in silence, and Lew wondered if Marge was going to refuse to let her own daughter into the house where she'd been raised from infancy. Then Marge sighed and stepped back, out of the doorway.

"Well, come on in, then."

They went into the living room. Lew waited downstairs with Marge while PattiSue ran up to her bedroom on the second floor.

"Nice night," Lew said again, foolishly.

"Sure is." An awkward pause. "Catch any criminals lately?"

"Not a one."

They both smiled at that. Tuskett had experienced no crime worthy of mention for over a decade. Of course, even in the town's heyday, law enforcement had never been better than a part-time job; Lew's real business had always been the grocery store. He ran it by himself, with only Jenny Kirk to help out, and everybody knew he'd taken her on only out of kindness. Jenny had been in a bad way, what with little Tommy to take care of; somebody'd had to help them, and Lew had taken it on himself to be the one.

Folks around here liked him for doing things like that; he had a good reputation in town, and he knew it. Part of the reason, no doubt, was the good appearance he made. He was a big man, large-shouldered and square-jawed, friendly to a fault most of the time, but tough when toughness was called for. His meaty hands could grip yours in a firm shake or bloody your nose with equal ease.

He was aware of all that; he was human enough to desire the respect of his neighbors and enjoy their good opinion. He kept himself fit and reasonably trim, so as not to disappoint local expectations; and despite the threads of gray at his temples and the spare tire inflated around his waist, folks seemed to feel he was doing okay for a fellow approaching retirement age.

So yes, he felt good about himself. Except ... except for the way he'd handled that man Kane. Or failed to handle him, as the case might be. He wasn't sure what had come over him tonight, but he'd been the one to blink first in the small contest of stares and wills they'd played out in Charlie's coffee shop. The memory disturbed him.

Then George Baker came tramping into view, his overalls stained with machine oil, and Lew let the bad thoughts slide.

"Hey, George," he said with a smile.

"Lew. Good to see you. Didn't hear you come in, with all the noise that drill press of mine makes." He sighed. "Darn thing's acting up again. Don't know if I can fix it this time."

George had hung up his postman's hat two years ago, and now lived off Social Security and his personal savings, like most of the folks in town. He spent most of his time in his workshop at the back of the house, where he had a mess of power tools, lovingly collected over the years. He rarely built anything; mostly he just fussed with his equipment like a nervous old woman fussing over her cats.

"What's the matter with it?" Lew asked politely.

"Aw, I don't know. The motor's giving out, I think, and the drill heads are worn down to pencil stubs, and—"

"George," Marge interrupted, her voice low. "PattiSue's here."

George looked at her. "PattiSue?" he repeated, as if he'd never heard the name. His face brightened. "She ... she moving back?" There was an unmistakable note of optimism in his voice.

Marge shook her head. "She's picking up something of hers. That's all."

"Oh." George looked down at his grease-stained pants. "Lew, I just don't know what's the matter with that girl. Guess we didn't raise her right. I've half a mind—"

But nobody learned what he had half a mind to do, because at that moment PattiSue reappeared, bounding down the stairs with a large stuffed panda in her arms.

"Hi, PattiSue," George said quietly.

"Evening, Daddy." Her voice was polite but empty of feeling.

Marge was staring at the panda. "That's what you wanted?" she asked incredulously. "Trevor?"

"Uh-huh." PattiSue stroked the bear's slightly ratty fur. "Good old Trevor. I missed him." She set her mouth in a pout, keeping her head down. "He was always there when I needed him. I could talk to him, and he wouldn't talk back. Never tried bossing me around. Never stuck his nose into situations he didn't understand."

George took a step toward her. "You watch how you talk to your mother and me," he said, his words stretched taut with tension.

PattiSue blinked in innocent surprise. "I was only talking about my teddy bear." She looked at Lew, "Want to go now?"

"If you're ready."

"Oh, yes."

Lew winced, hearing the way she said it—as if she were fairly burning up with the need to escape this house, and she wanted her parents to be informed of that fact. He guessed there would be no reconciliation tonight.

Nodding at the Bakers, he led PattiSue to the front door. "Nice to see you, Marge. George, good luck with fixing that drill."

"Oh, it'll come around," George said, his eyes on PattiSue. "It's just ... just stubborn, you know. Got a mind of its own, that drill."

Lew and PattiSue left the house together and walked swiftly away. PattiSue clutched the stuffed bear close to her chest and said nothing; but Lew noticed she was sniffling a little, and her eyes were glittery with tears.

The Reverend Chester Ewes dined alone, as was his custom, in his living quarters at the rear of the church. He had a stove and a compact refrigerator and a small cache of canned goods; being of modest means and humble tastes, this was enough for him. He ate while reading, another custom of long standing. He liked to cut up his food in advance so that he could eat with only a fork, leaving his left hand free to turn the pages.

He never read the Bible at the table, or any of his many books on the history and varieties of religion. He preferred lighter reading at the dinner hour. Tonight's selection was a crime novel set in Chicago in the twenties. Quite a good little thriller, filled with violent death and sexual frenzy, the very things some ministers had such a difficult time with. Chester Ewes was inclined to think such fainthearted souls had never read the Bible all the way through; had they done so, they would surely have noticed that it was chock-full of murder and sex, adultery and incest and assorted perversions, and that no small part of these goings-on was the work of those holy figures whom God was said to have taken under His wing. Take David and Bathsheba, for instance. Now, there was a sordid story, the equal of anything penned by Raymond Chandler.

He shrugged and went on reading. He rarely troubled himself with other people's opinions, prejudices, and conceits. He was a man of quietly firm convictions, convictions born of a calamity ten years ago that had tested his intellect and his will as had nothing before or since.

Ten years ago, Chester Ewes had experienced a crisis of faith. He'd been aware that it was coming, in the same unspoken, mysterious way that dogs were said to sense the prelude to an earthquake; but he'd put off acknowledging it as long as possible. He'd gone on delivering sermons and reading the Bible and pretending to himself that he had no doubts or questions, until finally, one chill February night, he awoke in a cold sweat and a fever of fear, knowing that he could keep the truth from himself no longer.

He stayed up the rest of that night, staring out the window at the bleak desert and gazing into the bleaker landscape of his soul. There was no denying it anymore. He'd lost his faith. He no longer believed the words he spoke in Sunday sermons, no longer felt touched by a higher power when he prayed. He felt nothing. His belief, which had once been so strong, was now only reflex and habit, lip service and empty ritual. And he was afraid.

Part of his fear was simple enough. He was forty years old. If he gave up the ministry, what would he have in its place? What would he do? Where would he go? He had no skills. At what trade could he earn a living?

But there was a deeper, more elemental, less soberly practical dimension to his fear. He'd devoted his whole life to his faith. And if his faith were a lie, a delusion, then his years of pious service had been wasted. He'd thrown away half his life, denied himself everything, subsisted on a meager income in a dying desert town—and for what? A daydream, a mirage on the horizon.

The night passed. His doubts did not. He said nothing to his friends. He went about his business. He delivered his sermons. He kept up appearances. Only, every other week or so, he would get in his car and drive out of town, all the way to Phoenix, for the purpose of visiting some bookstores there; and each time when he returned to Tuskett, his trunk was loaded down with books on psychology, philosophy, religion, and myth. He spent many nights reading long into the wee hours, nursing cold coffee or hot tea.

After a time, he arrived at some conclusions. To be honest, he could never be quite sure whether he'd lighted on an objective truth or merely rationalized an answer for himself. But it didn't matter. He'd found an answer that satisfied him.

Religion, he decided, was a tissue of falsehoods, just as he'd feared. But those falsehoods served a useful purpose. They gave meaning to the mundanities of daily life.

People needed more to their existence than washing the dishes and taking out the trash. They needed to feel they were part of a grand drama, an epic clash of good and evil. Religion gave them that drama, illustrated by symbols, dramatized in stories, and acted out in rituals. His job was merely to keep the show going. Belief was irrelevant.

He'd kept the show going, without any further twinges of conscience, ever since.

Past eight o'clock, marked with reasonable precision by the tolling of the bell in the church belfry, Chester Ewes finished his dinner and retired to the spare room to begin work on this Sunday's sermon. Tomorrow he would post the sermon's title on the bulletin board out front, and it would help to know what the subject was.

He reclined in his easy chair, kicked his shoes off, and put his stockinged feet on the footrest. He flipped through his dog-eared King James, looking for an appropriate passage. It wasn't necessary to be too particular; he'd found that almost any Bible verse could serve as the basis for a sermon. The only real requirement was that the thought expressed must be obscure enough to allow for tediously elaborate exegesis. That was why he liked the King James version; even when the original meaning had been clear, the archaic language usually served to muddle it.

He was narrowing down his choice to something from Leviticus, for no reason except that he hadn't used that one in a while, when he heard footsteps in the church.

He frowned. Unusual for anybody to come here on a Tuesday night. And at—he checked his watch—eight thirty. That was late for this sleepy little burg.

The footsteps stopped. Chester waited to hear them resume, or to hear a familiar voice call hello. Nothing happened. That, too, was strange. Nobody he knew would be shy about coming back to his room for a social call.

He put down the King James and left the room. He went through his kitchen, down the short hallway to the worship hall. The hallway opened on the rear of the pulpit. The altar was there, under a large wooden figure of Christ crucified. And standing before the altar, at the chancel rail, gazing up at the icon, was a man.

Chester Ewes stopped short, looking at him. The man was a stranger. A stranger in Tuskett. Well, what did you know. It seemed miracles were possible after all.

The stranger was tall and lean, and he wore a black coat that draped him like a shroud, and a blotchy cowboy hat he'd neglected to take off. He stood with his feet planted wide apart, hands hanging at his sides, head lifted. No flicker of expression showed on his face, no whisper of breath stirred his body. He seemed no more alive than the statue he gazed upon.

Chester studied him for a long moment, saying nothing.

"Sacrifice," the stranger said in a whispery voice that echoed off the far corners of the room.

Chester hitched in a breath. He hadn't thought the man was aware of his presence. "Beg your pardon?" he asked, approaching the altar.

The man didn't look at him. He kept his eyes on the figure mounted over the stage.

"Sacrifice," he said again. "That's what it means, doesn't it? The Lamb of God. The innocent, spilling its blood to purify the guilty."

Chester blinked. It wasn't the kind of notion he'd ever encountered outside his books.

"Why, yes," he said softly. "So it does."

"Blood washes clean," the man whispered, his eyes fixed on the Savior's image. "It's the universal solvent, blood. Leastways, that's how the rituals see it."

"Some do."

The man turned his head a fraction, and his eyes, blue as a postcard sky, met Chester's own.

"A man who spills blood," he breathed, "who makes sacrifices—you'd think he was doing good work, wouldn't you? The Lord's work?"

Chester couldn't tell if he was serious or not. There seemed to be a hint of a smile riding the man's mouth. But those eyes weren't smiling.

"I'd have some trouble with that interpretation," he answered.

"Yes." The man chuckled, a dry-cough sound. "You would. It's a fact, though. Without a devil, there'd be no God. Ever think of that?"

"Hardly an original concept." Chester shrugged. "The Manichaeans, the Zoroastrians—all the dualistic faiths would be with you on that one."

"There's no day," the man went on as if he hadn't heard, "without night to border it. No light without dark."

"No good without evil."

"No life"—the man smiled—"without death."

"You talk like you've given these matters some thought."

The man turned to the statue again. "Some."

"Rare to find a person with an interest in such things. What brings you here?"

"Passing through."

"Staying till Sunday?"

"No."

"Shame. You could've heard my sermon."

"What's it on?"

"Don't know yet. I was just sitting in back, hunting up a Bible verse." Chester had a thought. "You got any ideas?"

The man shook his head. "You'll find something."

Abruptly he turned, just like that, and began to walk away, down the wide nave between the rows of pews. As he reached the door to the narthex, Chester called to him.

"Hey. What's your name?"

The man looked back, and even from this distance Chester could see the brilliant blue of his eyes.

"Kane."

He disappeared through the narthex door, and a moment later the big double doors at the front of the church boomed shut, and he was gone.

Chester stood at the altar for a long time, trying to figure out just what had happened here.

A strange bird, he told himself at last. Sure. Nothing more than that.

He left the worship hall and returned to his sitting room. He settled down in his chair once more, doing his best to persuade himself that he'd simply shared some thoughts of a philosophical nature with a man who was passing through. But he couldn't shake that vague sense of disquiet, the feeling that he'd just awakened from a bad dream, a dream too unpleasant to remember but too vivid to forget.

He shrugged and picked up his King James. It was his intention to turn to Leviticus again, but oddly his hand seemed to have acquired a will of its own; it flipped instead to the beginning of the book, where his finger marked a passage in the fourth chapter of Genesis.

He read the words: "And now art thou cursed from the earth, which hath opened her mouth to receive thy brother's blood from thy hand; when thou tillest the ground, it shall not henceforth yield unto thee her strength, a fugitive and a vagabond shalt thou be in the earth."

Chester sat very still. He stared at the verse. He knew

it well. The words were spoken by the Lord, and addressed to a son of Adam. A dark and savage son, Abel's murderer, mankind's evil brother.

Good and evil, he thought. Light and dark. Abel ... and Cain.

Cain ...

He closed the book with a hard snap and held it in his lap, not looking at it; but the words still hung before his eyes, as if printed on air.

Cursed from the earth. A fugitive and a vagabond.

Passing through, the man had said.

The man named Kane.

Chester Ewes knew it was irrational, yes, foolish to the point of absurdity—but for the first time in ten years, he felt it again, that old fear, the fear that chilled him to the marrow of his bones.

Ethel Walston had been widowed four years ago, when Harry collapsed in the kitchen with a dish of vanilla ice cream in his hand. She still remembered the hollow clatter of the spoon on the tile floor and the look on Harry's face, the empty bewilderment in his eyes. It was heart failure, Dr. Evans had said. "Myocardial infraction," Ethel explained to her friends, inadvertently making it sound as if Harry had been guilty of some criminal offense for which God or nature had taken his life.

Ever since, she had been alone except for old Scooter, and the aging spaniel made poor company nowadays. She lived a quiet life, content to let the days go by; and didn't they go quickly as you got older. She received a meager monthly stipend from Social Security, but it was more than enough with the house paid for and no expenses except the electricity, the groceries, and her arthritis medicine, which didn't do much good but which Jack Evans insisted she take anyway.

The appearance of a boarder at her house, even if only for an overnight stay, was the most exciting thing that had happened to her in years.

Any guest would have been a welcome relief from her routine; and this man was more welcome still. Because he was interesting, mysterious, in a way that was strangely romantic. There was something about his eyes, some brilliant light shining there, that made her wish she were a younger woman.

Occasionally Ethel Walston read romance novels—"my diversions," she called them, or "my guilty pleasures"—and it had occurred to her that Mr. Kane could've stepped right out of one of those books, the tall dark stranger from a faraway place who arrives at the heroine's boardinghouse, his eyes giving no hint of his secret past.

She remembered asking him if he'd been to Orlando.

"I've been lots of places," he'd said.

The answer, with its overtones of mystery, thrilled her. It was the kind of thing one of those romance-novel men would've said.

The first thing he'd done in the guest room, after handing over his ten dollars, was to take off the packsack he was wearing on his shoulders. He'd removed it with elaborate care, first unhooking the straps, then gingerly lifting the pack over his head, holding it all the while in both hands as if it were a Ming Dynasty vase. Very gently he set it down on the bed.

She looked at the pack, bent out of shape by its contents—most delicate contents, to judge by the way he'd handled it. She wondered what exactly was in there. She didn't dare ask.

She hoped he'd want to talk, but after a few futile efforts to ensnare him in conversation, she gave up. Reluctantly she retreated to the living room, where she puttered about with her framed snapshots and potted plants, wondering who he was and what he wanted in town. Maybe he was a writer, doing research on small-town life. Or maybe he really was looking for a place to settle down, as she'd hoped; and Tuskett, for whatever unimaginable reason, had struck his fancy.

She resisted the urge to call her friends and spread the news, for fear that he might overhear her end of the dialogue. Then, shortly past eight o'clock, he emerged from the guest room, still shorn of his backpack but otherwise unchanged. He was walking differently now, she noticed; without the weight of that pack bearing down on him, he moved with athletic gracefulness, his long legs covering ground with the supple, boneless fluidity of a panther on the prowl.

He crossed the living room, brushing past her, saying nothing, forbearing even the small courtesy of a smile; it was behavior she would have found rude in anybody else, but in this case it merely added to the strangeness that was part of his charm.

She saw that he was headed for the door.

"Going out for a spell?" she asked.

Kane turned to look back at her, and for the first time she got a good look at his eyes. They were steel-blue and diamond-hard. Dangerous eyes that hinted at hidden mysteries, at sunken treasures nestled in their unsounded depths. She did not know why her heart was suddenly fluttering against her ribs like a caged bird.

"That's right," he said.

"It's a nice night for a walk." She raised her voice, needing to hear it over the thudding pulse in her ears. "Nice and warm and quiet. Of course, it's always quiet around here."

"Yes." He smiled, and his blue eyes flashed. "Quiet as the grave."

He left. She watched his back shrink into the darkness until he became one with it. When his footfalls had died away and her heart was back to nearly normal again, she ran to her telephone and spun the rotary dial, calling Ellyn Hannah, Lew's wife.

"Lynnie? Ethel ... I know I'm out of breath, and you would be too if you were here. Guess what? We've got a visitor in town. I'm putting him up ... Yes, in Bobby's old room. Can you believe I still had that sign out front? I forgot to take it down ... First off, between you and me, he's a handsome devil. Well, maybe not *handsome*, exactly, but he looks like a man who's been around. You should see his eyes. They glow like blue coals ... No, I'm not meaning to ask him out! He's thirty years my junior, about Bobby's age, I expect, though it's hard to say. He looks old and young at the same time, if that makes any sense ... Nope, no suitcase, only a packsack ... How should I know what's in it? Whatever it is, he takes good care of it. He's like a man holding a newborn baby in his arms ... Okay, Lynnie, I'll let you go. Just wanted you to hear the news. Bye now."

She hung up the phone but kept her hand on the receiver, wondering who next to call. She settled on Gretchen Lewis, Dick's wife, but the line was busy. She sighed, and decided on Judy Perkins instead. Judy listened as Ethel ran through the story again, this time embellishing it slightly with the detail that Mr. Kane had smiled at her in the most disarming way.

Next on her list was Millicent Evans, but her line was busy too, so she tried Gretchen Lewis again and this time she got through, only to learn that Gretchen had heard the whole story already, in slightly garbled form, from Ellyn Hannah. That was why Gretchen's line had been busy before. Ethel shook her head; it seemed Lynnie had gotten all the fun of breaking the story to Gretchen and hearing her coo like a turtledove at every tidbit. Still, Gretchen pressed for details from the original source; and Ethel, happy to clear up a few particulars and still more happy to be the bearer of news again, was somewhat mollified.

Around town, phones rang and were answered, and whispered conversations commenced, and the same bare facts were endlessly repeated, first over the phone and then in living rooms and bedrooms. Judy Perkins called Millicent Evans, and Millie told her husband Jack, and Jack called Todd Hanson, and Todd told his wife Debbie, and Debbie called Lynnie Hannah, who already knew, and meanwhile Stan Perkins got the phone away from his wife long enough to call Charlie Grain, who knew about it, since Kane had left his coffee shop not ten minutes earlier, and who was able to add new details that spiced up the story considerably.

Nobody called Jenny Kirk. She was not disliked, merely forgotten in the rush of breathless excitement. And so Jenny had no cause to worry too much when nine o'clock came and went, and Tommy was not yet home.

"Just because I express some concern about what exactly this fellow wants with us," Stan Perkins said testily, "you're calling me paranoid."

"Darn tootin' I am," Judy answered from across the kitchen, where she was brewing up a pot of coffee, her principal source of nourishment. "A man comes into town—"

"*Walks* in." Stan leaned against the refrigerator, his hands in his pockets, settling in for the fight. "I'd call that peculiar."

"All right, then, *walks* into town. Takes a room at Ethel's. Pays for it, so we know he's not a cheat. And just because folks find him standoffish, you're ready to call out the National Guard."

She was looking right at him, giving him a good hard stare, her green eyes burning in vivid contrast to the bright red of her hair. An artificial red, Stan knew. His wife was two years past fifty, and lately she'd taken to dyeing her hair on the sly to keep the gray out; he'd found the evidence in a trashcan. It was knowledge he held in reserve, not out of kindness, but because information was power, and this particular piece of information might come in handy someday.

"Stan," Judy said with that special tone of contempt she'd honed to a knife edge over three decades of nightly spats, "you're more distrustful of people than any man I've ever known." She looked away from him, affecting a tone of impersonal speculation. "'Course, seeing as how the people around here keep electing you to high office, I suppose there's good reason not to trust them, or their judgment anyhow."

"Folks in Tuskett know a good mayor when they see one."

"Running unopposed the last three times didn't hurt either."

"Nobody would dare take me on."

"Nobody else wants the job."

She had him there, and they both knew it. She was putting him on the defensive, and that was bad. He switched tactics.

"You're changing the subject again," he said. "As usual."

She wasn't rattled. "The subject is you, and your paranoia. 'Cause that's what it is, Stan. Paranoia, plain and simple."

"Oh, she's a psychiatrist now," he said, addressing the room in general. "I suppose she got herself a degree from one of those mail-order outfits."

"I know a nutcase when I see one."

"Just because I'm skeptical of this man Crane—"

"Kane, you nitwit."

"Well, whatever he's called. Just because I'm skeptical of his intentions hardly qualifies me as a nutcase." He smiled, sensing an opening. "Of course, putting up with a Gila monster like you for thirty years is a candy cane of a different stripe. I sure must've been crazy to do that."

That one got her. She was thrown off-balance for a moment, but the woman was quick, he had to give her that much. "Now who's changing the subject?" she asked, waggling an index finger at him like a schoolmarm. "You are a classic case, textbook-perfect, of a paranoid schizophrenic with delusions of grandeur and a persecution complex to boot. And it's not just this Kane fellow. It's this bug up your butt you've got about the Russians. This A-bomb nonsense."

Oh, she was pulling out the big guns now. She was hitting him where he lived.

"Nonsense, my rear end," he retorted. "If you had the sense to read the books I keep recommending to you—"

"Pamphlets, is more like it. Mimeographed pamphlets put out by nutcases and nitwits like you. Nutcases who are scared out of what little sense they've got. Scared silly about the Russians."

"You'd be scared too," he said lamely, "if you weren't so damned ignorant."

Stan Perkins had this theory about the Russians. He was convinced they were getting ready to launch a sneak attack, Pearl Harbor-style, and take out a hefty chunk of America's deterrent force before the lard-asses in DC had the wits to scramble the bombers and fire the land-based missiles. Every time a news bulletin came on the tube, cutting into one of Judy's soaps, Stan predicted that this time it was the big one for sure. One of the best things about living in Tuskett, he often thought, was that it was way out in the middle of nowhere, far from any likely target of nuclear attack.

In his hardware store he stocked survivalist paraphernalia—freeze-dried foods, first-aid kits, even a battery-operated TV that was really something. Nobody ever bought any of it, but, hell, it wasn't his fault if other folks wanted to stick their heads in the sand. Folks like his know-nothing wife, for instance.

"I'd be scared," Judy said sharply, "only if I was a witless coward like some folks I could mention. Scared of my own shadow. Scared of any man who comes to town to stay the night. Yes, sir, it would take one scaredy-cat of a man to feel that way, or maybe just your classic paranoid schizoid type with all those delusions and complexes I was referring to a moment ago. You know, Stan. *That* type."

Stan frowned, unsure how to respond. The witch had backed him into a corner. Then blessedly the phone rang.

"Wonder who that could be," he said, trying not to show his relief.

He retreated into the living room to pick up the phone. George Baker, PattiSue's dad, was on the line with more gossip and rumor about Crane, or Kane, or whatever his name was. Stan chatted with George, and the two of them speculated on what the man might want here, and after a good deal of back-and-forth and give-and-take on the matter, they reached the conclusion that nobody in town, themselves included, had the faintest idea.

PattiSue Baker lay sprawled on the floor of the trailer, naked, moaning softly and praying to God that Eddie wouldn't hit her again.

"Bitch," Eddie Cox said quietly in a way that made her blood run cold.

"No," she whispered, "don't." But it was too late; already she felt the meaty smack of his knuckles against the small of her back. She tried to crawl away, but he followed, kicking her in the ribs, in the butt, in the shins, till finally she reached a corner and there was nowhere left to crawl, so she curled up in a fetal ball and whimpered like a beaten dog.

"Don't," she muttered, knowing it was hopeless. "Don't, Eddie, please don't, don't, don't, don't. ..."

After a while he stopped. She felt his heavy footsteps vibrating through the floor as he went into the kitchen area to pour himself some milk or maybe some orangeade. He said it helped to settle his stomach, and he nearly always got an upset stomach after he beat her. He was getting upset stomachs a lot these days.

Eddie Cox didn't drink, but it might have been better if he had. PattiSue had often thought that a drink or two, now and then, might have served to release some of the volcanic tension always boiling below his surface. But no, his father had been a lush, and Eddie had seen him come home with his breath stinking of Jack Daniel's one too many times for him to even pick up a beer. He drank only milk and orangeade and decaf coffee with NutraSweet. He was, to all appearances, a man of few vices. Even her mom and dad thought so. They liked Eddie, though they'd nearly disowned their daughter for carrying on with him; their objection was to sleeping together without benefit of clergy, nothing more. In the old days, when she and her folks were still on more or less civil terms, they'd actually urged her to get Eddie to "pop the question," as her dad put it; and they would have been thrilled if he had.

She thought about that, and an image flashed in her mind, a perfect photo-album snapshot of herself and Eddie standing at the altar, taking their vows from the Reverend Ewes, while her mom and dad looked on, beaming with pride. She shuddered.

To marry Eddie—God, no—then there would be no escape, no hope, only an endless series of beatings to look forward to, forever and ever, amen. She'd rather be dead.

PattiSue closed her eyes. There was so much her folks didn't understand. But it wasn't their fault. It was hers. She should have let them know what went on in this trailer. Should have told them about nights like tonight—nights when that awful anger of his came up like a blast of pumice and black smoke and left her body battered by its fury.

But she hadn't told them, or anyone. She couldn't. If she ever did tell, there would be hell to pay, worse hell even than nights like this.

Because Eddie would find her. In a town this size, it wouldn't be hard.

And he would mess up her face.

PattiSue Baker had a beautiful face. It was the only thing about her that had ever inspired pride. She was quick-witted enough, but no good with books or figures or mechanical things; she moved gracelessly, her body lumpy and ill-proportioned, her breasts too small and her hips too big. But her face was lovely. It was composed of pink skin soft with down, of wide lips and pearl teeth, of finely traced eyebrows over sky-blue eyes, all framed by a torrent of ash-blond hair. It was a face as nearly devoid of imperfection as a girl could desire—a face which, so she had been told, belonged in *People* magazine.

Eddie had hurt her, sure; he'd punched her in the ribs, kicked her, left blue-black welts on her skin that were sore for days afterward; but never had he gone for her face. Maybe it was because a mark there could not be concealed by clothing the next day, or maybe it was because he knew she'd leave him if he ever went that far; but she suspected she knew the real reason. Her face was a kind of hostage in the blackmail game he was playing. He knew where she was vulnerable. And she knew that he knew it; and she was afraid.

So she'd kept on seeing him in the trailer he'd bought dirt cheap from Joe Willoughby when Joe went east to resettle in Maine for some reason nobody could guess, except that he'd kept talking about the Atlantic Ocean as if it were some Mecca to which he'd been bidden to make a pilgrimage. She let Eddie kiss her all over, and sometimes he was gentle, but other times—more and more often in the past two months—he was crazed, brutal, and there was nothing she could do but lie in bed in a sobbing heap while his fists hammered her and the mattress springs creaked.

At first, it hadn't been like that. For a few precious weeks at the start of their courtship—if that was what this was—Eddie had been kind. Their first episodes of lovemaking had been quick, not entirely satisfying for her, but tender enough. She still remembered with a pleasant glow of nostalgia the way he would take her in his arms and unbutton her blouse slowly, then the sudden warmth that flooded her body and set her skin tingling as his naked body straddled hers, and the size of his manhood, so hard and thickly veined and knotted with wire-tough hairs, and the feel of it as he drove it between her legs and set the mattress vibrating crazily like one of those Magic Fingers beds, the kind she'd seen in movies on late-night TV. He always came too fast, sometimes even before penetration, and the sticky rush of semen squirted over her legs and dampened the rumpled sheets. He seemed not to care and, really, she didn't either, not so long as he kissed her breasts and called her beautiful, beautiful, in his husky voice.

Then things changed. His anger, long dormant, hidden from public view—hidden, perhaps, even from himself—began to emerge like a shaggy, grunting beast crawling out of its cave.

It started on a night last March, when he demanded that she eat him.

"No," she said, shaking her head, not realizing the request wasn't open to refusal. "No, I don't want to do that, Eddie. I don't like that."

"Eat it," he said again, and there was something wild and dangerous in his eyes.

"Please," she said, "I don't want to." She could not tell him that the thought of that huge, hairy, veined thing in her perfect mouth disgusted her. "I really just don't," she said, hoping that would be the end of it.

"Fuck you," Eddie said in a stranger's voice. "Whore. Goddamn cockteasing *whore*!"

And his hand was a fist pounding her ribs, blindly, savagely, and she was crying in shock and bewilderment, unable to fight back.

Maybe—she'd sometimes thought in the months since—maybe if I *had* fought back, right then and there, I could've put a stop to it.

But she hadn't. She couldn't fight him. She was too scared and felt too helpless—too worthless, even, to make standing up for herself seem worthwhile. And so she had not put a stop to it, then or since.

The same encounter had been repeated two dozen times in the past four months, each time with very nearly the same exchange of dialogue, until PattiSue had begun to feel that she and Eddie were two actors caught in an endless rehearsal for a play nobody was allowed to see. Or maybe it was only a nightmare, the kind that kept coming back. Sometimes he wanted her to eat him, though she never had or would, and sometimes another thing would set him off—something she said, or an item in the news, or anything at all.

She hadn't expected any trouble tonight. She had the event in Charlie Grain's place to report, and she thought the story would be interesting enough to hold him at bay. She was partly right; for a while he was quiet and attentive. He sat across from her at a folding table in a corner of the trailer and listened, saying nothing, as she told him about the man named Kane.

"What's this bastard look like?" Eddie asked when she finished her story. Beads of perspiration dotted his forehead like measles. The light from a naked bulb threw his shadow on the window shade.

"Tall," she said. "Dresses funny. Wears a long coat, in this heat—can you imagine? And a hat. Like a cowboy hat, I guess. I don't know."

"Good-looking?"

"Huh-uh." She said it too quickly; he had a streak of jealousy in him that was nearly as wide as the mean streak she knew so well.

"You don't seem so sure." His eyes were narrowed, watchful.

"No, honest"—a mistake: he always knew she was lying when she used that word—"he's a strange one. Spooky, kind of. I didn't like him."

That much, at least, was true. But the deeper truth was that she had found the man ... well ... *interesting*. There was an air of intrigue about him that had made her heart speed up.

"Okay," Eddie said, seeming mollified. He took a sip of ice water from a plastic cup. "So. You notice anything else about him?"

"Not really. Except that when Lew Hannah tried to chew him out, this man Kane just stared him down. And Lew gave in, too. Backed down like a scared dog."

"Hard to imagine. I've never seen Lew back down."

"Neither have I, till now. But I can't blame him. That

man, there's something about him ..." She realized Eddie might take this as a compliment to Kane, which in a way it was. "Something I didn't like one bit," she added hastily.

"He say anything to you?"

"Huh-uh." She hesitated. She couldn't resist telling a little more. "He did look at me awful funny, though."

"Like how?"

"Like a rattler. I mean, he's got rattlesnake eyes. Cold. Almost hypnotizing. When he looks at you, it's like he's seeing right inside you."

She shivered, thinking of how she had stood at the doorway, less than a foot away from him, while he stared at her as if spying on her very soul, learning her dearest secrets and most private thoughts. It had scared her, yes; but it had thrilled her too—at least, a little. She could imagine losing herself in those eyes if she wasn't careful.

"What are you smiling at?"

She jerked her head up. She hadn't realized she was smiling, but she must have been, because Eddie was studying her with the dark light in his eyes that said he was displeased.

"Nothing," she said, fighting to keep the quaver out of her voice.

"You liked him, didn't you?" His voice had lowered to a whisper. "You liked the way he looked at you. Nothing funny about it."

"No, Eddie. I didn't like it. I already told you."

"You lied. You're a lying bitch, girl." The words came out slurred, as if with drink. "You've always been a lying bitch. And you know what a lying little girl needs to get from her daddy." He licked his lips. "Needs a spanking. A good spanking."

She didn't argue, didn't plead; she knew it was no use. Instead she got up and stripped, knowing that if she didn't, he would tear the clothes off her body with his bare hands; he had done it before. Then she was naked and huddled on the floor, and he was smacking her around, working her over, and she was whimpering and crying out.

When it was done, she had about half a dozen black-and-blues on her midsection and legs; but he'd been careful; there was nothing that might show.

The heavy tread of his footsteps, returning, cut off her thoughts. She raised her head and stared past a web of sweat-matted hair at Eddie Cox, framed in the doorway.

Eddie was—she couldn't escape it—a handsome man. He was tall and big-shouldered, with a barrel chest and a neck seemingly as thick as a tree trunk. His head was blocky, bright with close-cropped sandy hair; his eyebrows made two brief horizontal slashes over the dark brown slits of his eyes. He was twenty-nine years old but could have passed for forty.

"Get into bed," he said.

She rose to her feet. She was just beginning to feel the pain in her back, her sides, her legs—the pain that would dull to an ache and then hang on like an uninvited guest for days. She looked down at the bed.

"You going to wallop me some more," she said in a voice too lifeless to express the thought as a question.

"Want me to?"

She shook her head.

"Okay, then. I'd say you got enough for one night."

She climbed into bed, feeling grateful to him and hating herself for it. She lay on her stomach and pressed her cheek to the pillow and tried not to think about the pain in her back. The bedside light snapped off, and a moment later the bed rocked once as Eddie lowered himself to the mattress beside her, and then she felt one big clumsy arm reach out to hold her in a way that was almost tender.

"Love you," Eddie Cox whispered in the darkness.

She took a breath. She had to say it. Or he would be mad again.

"Love you too," she breathed into the pillow, and she felt the sting of tears at the corners of her eyes, and a hot stab of shame.

Eddie sighed, a contented man. His grip on her arm tightened; his fingers drove like spikes into her flesh. He didn't know he was hurting her. Maybe—she thought—maybe, in some crazy way, he never knew.

She knew what was coming next. He would make it up to her. He would be her lover. And he would be gentle. Oh, yes. At times like these, he always was.

He lifted himself on top of her, slow and easy. The bed rocked under them, swaying to the rhythm of his body against hers. PattiSue felt his hardness inside her, probing deep. She pressed her cheek against the mattress and listened to the sighing of the springs. She shut her eyes. And in the darkness behind her closed eyelids, a face took shape, a hard face blazing with blue eyes, rattler's eyes. For just one instant she permitted herself to imagine that those eyes were watching her now, and that the body entwined with hers belonged to the man in the coffee shop—that Kane, not Eddie Cox, was her lover tonight. The thought—the forbidden, deliciously dangerous thought—sent a spasm of pleasure shivering through her, racking her body.

For the first time in months, she was the one who came first.

After leaving Charlie Grain's place, Bill Needham took a stroll in the night air. He did it with a secret purpose, one he was reluctant to admit even to himself: he was looking for Kane. He didn't know what might happen if he found the man, and somehow it didn't matter; all that mattered was that there was a stranger in Tuskett, an outsider, a dark man with eyes of ice, a man who liked the thought of a town with unlocked doors.

Why the hell did I ever tell him that? Bill asked himself, feeling like a fool. Why couldn't I tell him we're all gun-crazy and paranoid and we shoot on sight?

But there was something in that man's eyes that had made him tell. The same mysterious something that had made Lew back down in the coffee shop, that had mesmerized Meg and Charlie and PattiSue and made them act as if nothing was wrong. Some hypnotic quality of his stare that drowned all your doubts and canceled out your better judgment. Bill didn't know how such a thing could be possible, but there it was.

He shook his head, pushing the thoughts away. He headed south down Joshua Street, glancing idly at the rows of boarded-up storefronts passing him by.

There was Claude Lapham's bookstore, and what a fine store it had been, with a stock of hardbound classics by Dickens, Twain, and Kipling; a store that had always smelled of the big Cuban cigars Claude got from God-knew-where. Claude was gone ten years now—not dead, just moved away; but then, what was the difference? In either case, he would never be back.

Next door was Louise and Marty Gallagher's gift shop. They had sold paperweights made from bits of sandstone Marty collected in the Mojave, along with sketches of the local scenery done by Lou, who had an artistic touch. The Gallaghers were in Oregon now; Bill had gotten a postcard from them last Christmas, privately printed from one of Lou's drawings, a sketch of the Pacific hurling itself against the rocky shore. He guessed they were happy there.

Other stores passed by. Jim Heinz's toy shop, where a model train used to run all day long through a wonderland of miniature trees; Estelle Farraday's dry-cleaning place, which once guaranteed same-day service if you brought in your stuff by noon; Raymond Valdez's pharmacy; Rupert Glascon's shoe store; Wally Chin's pet shop; others, so many others, each as poignant to Bill's eyes as a marker in a cemetery.

He reached the south end of Joshua Street and kept going, onto the Old Road. It was empty of traffic, as always. A line of utility poles marched along the roadside at five-hundred-foot intervals, their topmost masts strung with glittering streamers that were high-tension lines, the lower branches bearing the darker, hose-like strands of telephone cable. The power lines hummed and crackled, the sound of electric current leaking into the air. Bill liked that sound. He liked the thought of all that power, three hundred thirty kilovolts, channeled along miles of aluminum wire just to reach this town and feed it and keep it alive. There were precious few other travelers that still bothered to pass this way.

He craned his neck, gazing up at the nearest pole. A dozen wire leads and three black ribbons of phone line traced a graceful curve in the sky, linking the roadside pole to one of Tuskett's own. He turned, following the cables' path with his gaze. They receded down Joshua Street, carried by a ragged line of smaller utility poles that supplied electric current and phone service to the few surviving business establishments; other wires branched off from the main line at each side street to feed rare homes. Rooftops shone in the pale light of a three-quarter moon and a brilliant scatter of stars. The row of Joshua trees that had given the town's central thoroughfare its name shivered in the dry breeze.

It all looked so peaceful that for a moment Bill wondered if he'd been wrong to be afraid. Then he shook his head. He wasn't wrong. That man Kane had mischief in mind. And Bill intended to keep looking till he learned exactly what it was.

But he surely wouldn't find him here. There was nothing down the road except the town dump, and nobody ever went there.

So he doubled back, heading up Joshua Street again. Rising up on his left was the empty hulk of a closed-down motel, the Tuskett Inn. On the other side of the street lay what had been the trailer park, a handful of homes scattered in a flyblown field. Nearly all the trailers had been abandoned, too dilapidated to sell even for scrap metal. Only two were still occupied. Rile Cady lived in one; Eddie Cox in another.

Tonight Rile's beat-up Chevy van was gone and the windows of his place were dark; it looked like he was out of town, maybe cruising the Old Road in that rattletrap of his. Eddie was home. His window shades were drawn, but slivers of yellow light played at the edges, winking in and out as the shades shifted under the breeze.

From inside the trailer came a sudden sharp cry. Bill's breath froze in his throat, and he was sure that his worst fears had been confirmed, that Kane was in there and up to no good. Then he realized it was only PattiSue carrying on, as usual. Damn girl had the noisiest orgasms in the state.

He walked on. Up ahead was the intersection with Fourth Avenue, the first of the four side streets. He turned right, covering the eastern end of the street first. He kept his eyes open as he strolled past empty houses and a few that still supported human life. One of those was the Baker place; George and Marge were visible as moving shadows on a yellow window shade.

Cars were parked at the curb here and there. In Tuskett there was no such thing as a garage-kept car; in the name of economy, all the houses had been built without such luxuries as garages or even carports. Nobody minded. The weather was kind—no snow and ice to contend with, and little rain—and even in the town's heyday there had never been a shortage of parking spaces on the street.

Now, with only twenty-three people living here and most of them getting on in years, there was a grand total of eight vehicles left. Eight. Was it any wonder his service station was quiet all the time?

He saw nothing out of the ordinary on the eastern end of Fourth, so he returned the way he'd come, then crossed Joshua Street and continued west. He passed Stan and Judy Perkins' house. Stan was the mayor of Tuskett, and had been for twenty-two years, but his real job was running the hardware store, which had been a going proposition once but which was now, like Bill's gas station, merely an old habit, hard to break.

From the house came the sound of voices raised in anger—hardly surprising, seeing as how this was Stan and Judy. Rile Cady called them Punch and Judy, and they were the fightingest couple Bill had ever seen, forever scratching and clawing like alley cats.

"... and if I didn't have a bloodsucking pasty-faced harpy for a wife, I might just *be* a happy man!"

"Give it a rest. You wouldn't be happy if you married Priscilla Presley and won the Lotto to boot. You're a born complainer, Stan!"

"That's 'cause when I was born, they told me someday I'd wind up hitched to you!"

No, nothing unusual here.

He doubled back to the main street and went north. At the western corner of Joshua and Third was Charlie Grain's coffee shop, where Bill had started his walk thirty minutes ago; the shop was dark now, closed for the night.

There were no homes still occupied on the eastern side of Third, so he turned left, passing the coffee shop. Almost instantly the Lewis place came into view, marked by the huge gray Oldsmobile Delta 88 sitting at the curb. Dick and Gretchen had held on to that car for years; Bill sometimes thought they might be buried in it.

He passed by the house. Dick Lewis, the town barber for going-on-forty years, was out on his front porch having a smoke. Bill stopped at the edge of the yard and waved to him.

"Dick," he said by way of hello.

Dick leaned forward in his chair and squinted hard—he was nearly seventy now, and his night vision was poor—then made him out. "Hey, Bill. Come on up."

Bill mounted the steps and took a seat on a porch swing with rusty chains. It creaked under his weight; he leaned back and dangled his legs, making the swing sway slowly. Dick Lewis sat across from him in his favorite chair, which wasn't a rocker because Dick insisted that only old folks liked rocking chairs. He puffed contentedly on his pipe.

"Out for a stroll?" Dick Lewis asked at length.

"You bet."

"Fine night for it."

"That it is."

The screen door creaked open, and Gretchen Lewis stepped out onto the porch. She was a small, slender woman with a penchant for wearing too much makeup, perhaps in an effort to recapture the delicate loveliness of her youth. Bill had seen photos of Gretchen as a young woman, and she had been a beauty, all right. Still, she was not old—not by Tuskett's standards, anyhow. At fifty-nine, she was ten years younger than her husband.

"Time for my constitutional," she said brightly, and pecked her husband's cheek.

"Don't I get a kiss too?" Bill joshed.

"Don't tempt me, Bill. You know I'm a married woman." She turned to Dick again. "I'll be back in a little while.

There's peanut butter in the cabinet over the fridge if you want a snack."

"Okay."

Bill watched Gretchen go. He knew that lately it was her custom to take a stroll every night at about this time. Tonight it occurred to him to wonder if it was safe for her to walk the streets alone. A peculiar thought to have in Tuskett, but one that was hard to shake off. Maybe he ought to have said something, tried to warn her about the stranger in town. But then he remembered how Lew and Meg and Charlie had reacted to that notion in the coffee shop.

"You hear the news?" Dick asked, cutting into his thoughts.

Bill started. "What news might that be?"

"New man in town. Staying overnight. Passing through, it seems."

"I met him," Bill said, keeping his voice even.

"Did you, now? What's he like?"

"Different. Hard to put words to it. How'd you come to hear about him?"

"Oh, Lynnie Hannah called Gretchen to pass the word. It seems Ethel's putting him up for the night."

Bill swallowed. He hadn't known about that, and he wasn't pleased to find it out. He'd been half-hoping Kane would stroll out of town and disappear over the horizon.

"You don't say," he answered flatly.

"Yeah. You know, she's got that extra room. Bobby's old room."

"Is the fellow there now?"

"Couldn't say. Why?"

"No particular reason." Bill hesitated. "You haven't seen him around, by any chance?"

"You appear to be very interested in his whereabouts."

Bill shrugged. "Curiosity."

"Well, I've not laid eyes on him." Dick studied his pipe. "Wish I had. Maybe he could use a haircut."

"Maybe."

"Did his hair look long to you? In need of a trim, you think?"

"Hard to say. He wears a hat."

"A hat, now?" Dick chuckled. "Covering up a bald patch, I bet you. Old trick."

"Could be," Bill said. "Covering up something, that's for sure."

Dick looked up. "What was that? Didn't catch that last part."

"Nothing. Just talking to myself."

"Means you're going crazy."

"I don't doubt it."

"Crazy from loneliness. Need a woman by your side. Like my Gretchen. She's been my salvation, let me tell you." Dick smiled slyly. "That Jenny Kirk would make somebody a good wife."

"A shame she doesn't think so," Bill answered. He got up, setting the swing rocking again. "I'll be on my way."

"Got things to do, I suppose?"

"Right."

Dick Lewis considered the pipe in his hand again. "You're looking for that man," he said, "aren't you?"

Bill didn't know what to say. He figured the truth was best.

"Uh-huh."

"Why?"

"I'd rather not say."

Dick nodded, then brushed away an insect that wasn't there with a gentle sweep of his hand, as if to let Bill know he was hereby dropping the matter. That, Bill thought, was the good thing about a barber. He knew when you wanted to talk, and when you didn't.

"Well," Dick Lewis said, taking another slow puff on his pipe, "if you do see him, let him know this town's got a barbershop. Tell him I'll give him my best haircut at a special discount. It'd be worth it, just to have him tell me a story I haven't heard before."

"I'll do that. Evening, Dick."

"Evening."

Bill left the porch and moved on. He passed Jack and Millie Evans' place, a few doors down from the Lewises'. Jack had been the local doctor for as long as Dick had been cutting hair. A good doctor, skilled with the tools of his trade and adept at the human side of his business as well. The Lewises' living-room window flickered in a wan blue light; canned laughter reached Bill's ear.

He kept walking. He saw nobody else on Third Avenue. He returned to Joshua and went north again, turning right onto Second. From down the street he heard a woman's voice calling out. It was Jenny Kirk, standing in the doorway of her house.

"Tommy! Tommy, you come here this instant! *Tommy* ... !"

Bill smiled, because he'd been a boy himself once, and he could still remember the pain of hearing the call that would summon him home for the night. And then he felt something cold in his gut, something like a block of ice deposited whole in his belly, as he remembered the reason for his evening stroll; and he wondered just how late Tommy might be, and how long his mother had been worrying after him.

He walked closer, trying not to hurry his pace.

"Tommy!" Jenny Kirk cried again, an odd, piping note of urgency in her voice. She saw Bill and smiled nervously, brushing a stray hair off her forehead. "Hi, Bill."

"Evening, Jenny."

"I don't suppose you've seen that boy of mine?"

"Sorry." He wanted to ask how long Tommy had been missing. He didn't dare. "I'm sure he's around somewhere," he said pointlessly.

"Yes. Somewhere. He's not usually this late, though." She forced another smile. "He'll turn up."

"They always do," Bill said with a forced smile of his own.

There was an awkward moment when neither said anything. The two of them had passed many such moments together. Folks around town—folks like, say, Dick Lewis with his sly smile—were always pointing out that it would be only natural if Bill and Jenny were to hook up, them being the only two eligible young people in Tuskett, both of them certainly good-looking enough, and Bill so good around kids. And the funny thing was that Bill was inclined to agree with the conventional wisdom on the matter.

But Jenny had always been distant with him. Not rude, just aloof, as if she were sending him a silent signal to keep his distance. It was nothing you could put your finger on, but it was there, and Bill knew it, so he'd never pressed the point. But sometimes he sat up late and thought about Jenny Kirk, and how her hair lay around her shoulders in chestnut waves, how her eyes flashed with a smoky gray light.

"If you see him," Jenny said, "send him on home, will you?"

"Sure will."

He considered saying something about the new man in town. But he couldn't see what good it would do. Anyway, with Ethel and Lynnie and all the other gals talking up a storm, Jenny must've heard the news by now.

"You take care now," he said, and walked on.

Behind him, Jenny Kirk's voice rose once more in a

high, plaintive cry, the cry a hawk would make as it dipped and bobbed over the desert floor.

He covered the other side of Second, then all of First, seeing nothing of interest. He wound up at the northernmost tip of Joshua Street. On the eastern side of the street, almost directly across from his service station, was the church. Light filtered through a stained-glass window depicting the Blessed Virgin and her child, both of them haloed in magenta. Reverend Ewes would be inside, tucked away in his sleeping quarters at the back of the church; perhaps he would be settling down to read after supper.

Bill thought of stopping in to see him, unloading some of his troubles. He decided against it. He wasn't a religious man; he was perhaps the only person in town who didn't attend the Sunday services; and it felt hypocritical for him to seek help from the minister.

He walked over to his gas station. The place looked small and unprotected, strangely vulnerable to the darkness on all sides. He shivered a little and turned back.

His own house was halfway down First Avenue's east end. He mounted the three steps to the front door—unlocked, of course—and entered.

The living room was dark; he never left a light on when he wasn't home; in Tuskett there was no need. But tonight the dark scared him. His fingers fumbled at the wall, groping for the switch. He flicked it down and the floor lamp in the corner snapped on, casting a cone of light over a framed oil painting of a desert sunrise which Louise Gallagher had made as a Christmas present for him, years back.

He looked around, checking to make sure nothing in the room had been disturbed. His eyes passed over the sofa filling one wall, a piece of history that had been here when this house was his father's, and his grandfather's—

the shelves lined with potted cacti, which he watered too often, just out of the need for something to do, some living thing other than himself to care for—his TV set and stereo, their electronic voices so good at creating the illusion of company and life.

He looked everywhere. Part of him was certain Kane had come here and was lying in wait.

No one was here. The house was empty, as it always was. Empty and heavy with silence.

He was used to silence, emptiness. He'd lived alone for ten years. Even before that, the house had always seemed empty. His mother had died when Bill was ten years old, and his dad, shattered by the loss, had never been himself again. His old man had spent most of his time at the service station, even as the town's slow death robbed him of customers and work. He must have found some sort of peace at the service station, and that was good; but it meant Bill had grown up alone.

It was to escape loneliness that Bill had gone off to college with the ambition of earning a physics degree; he'd always been intrigued by how things worked—electricity, magnetism, gravity—and he wanted to get to the bottom of it all, study the forces that moved the universe.

He lasted in college only a semester and a half. He dropped out after his dad suffered a heart attack that left him too badly incapacitated to run the service station by himself; if the business was to stay afloat, Bill would have to help out. It was only temporary, of course. Everything was only temporary. His dad would get better and Bill would finish school and move away for good. But three years later, a second heart attack had finished his father, and the only thing Bill still had in the world was the service station. He'd been here ever since.

The service station, like the house, had been paid off

in his father's time, and Bill's income and savings were still sufficient to pay for the groceries and utilities. He didn't live well, but he lived. Like everyone else in Tuskett, he got by.

He could have moved on, of course. But he had good reasons for staying. Loyalty to the family business, for one. His dad had sweated his life away to build that service station out of nothing, and it would have been wrong to abandon it like so much scrap. Loyalty to the town, for another. Folks depended on him; Tuskett was isolated, and the few cars left had to be kept in working order in case of emergency.

Sure, he had reasons, sound, even noble reasons, the kind of reasons Jimmy Stewart was always finding in *It's a Wonderful Life* to keep him safely nestled in mediocrity while other people lived the life he secretly wanted. People admired Jimmy Stewart in that movie, and maybe they admired Bill Needham too.

But it was all a crock. Bill knew what really kept him anchored to this patch of desert, letting his life slip away. Not loyalty, not conscience, not anything noble or heroic. It was fear. An ugly, shameful, childish fear of the unknown and the untried.

His father's heart attack had been only an excuse to cast aside his big dreams and return to the comfort of the safely familiar. If there had been no heart attack, he would have found some other pretext to give up. One way or another, he would have wound up precisely where he was now, living out his days in the house of his childhood, with family heirlooms for furniture, with no children in his life or woman in his bed, with no future but to pump gas till Tuskett died or he did, whichever came first. He wondered what kind of movie Frank Capra could make out of that.

Christ, was he ever in a foul mood tonight. It was

Kane, he thought. The man had got him all worked up, jumping at shadows, dwelling on old memories and fears, things best left undisturbed.

He went into the kitchen and poured himself a glass of water, not from the tap, but from a bottle chilled in the refrigerator; it always tasted better that way. He drank it down in three long swallows.

"I wonder if Tommy Kirk is home yet," he said suddenly. He hardly even noticed that he was speaking aloud. He was used to that, too. "Oh, hell. Of course he is."

But deep down, Bill knew he wasn't.

2

Gretchen Lewis rested her head on the pillow and sighed.

"I'd better be going," she whispered in the darkness. "Dick will be getting worried."

Beside her, Charlie Grain frowned. "Or suspicious, maybe."

Gretchen rose without answering and began pulling on her clothes. She was tired of allaying Charlie's fears. Dick would not be suspicious. Her husband was too dull-witted to see the truth even if it knocked him flat on his can. If Dick were to wander into Charlie's bedroom right now and see the two of them here, Charlie in his undershirt and nothing else, Gretchen herself half-dressed, her skin glistening with jewels of sweat—if he saw all that, he'd merely blink, say hello to Charlie, and ask Gretchen if she could remind him where she'd left that jar of peanut butter she told him about.

It wasn't that Dick was a bad man, but he'd sure gotten old in a hurry—too damn old for her. At sixty-nine, he was ten years her senior, and seemed a good ten years older than that. His hands were starting to shake, and pretty soon he wouldn't be able to hold a pair of barber shears for the life of him; his eyesight was failing; and his interest in lovemaking, never strong, was now as much a part of history as the Battle of Bull Run. All he did at night was sit on the front porch and smoke that pipe of his. It was enough to drive a woman to drink—or to other vices.

And so, every night for the past two and a half months, Gretchen had gone out for a walk; and always her path led her to Charlie Grain's house on Second Avenue for a half hour of hurried, frightened intimacy.

She really couldn't say just how she and Charlie had gotten started like this. Part of it was simple availability on both their parts. She was desperate for a man who'd make her feel like a woman again, and not just a piece of furniture; and as for Charlie, well, he was a bachelor at the age of sixty-three, a regular hell-raiser in his youth who'd seen the good times go by, a man with nothing in his life now except his Merle Haggard records and his coffee shop; the records were getting scratchy and hard to play, and the coffee shop was nearly always empty these days.

She didn't think she loved Charlie, not really, and she was sure he didn't love her; still, they were good company for each other, and that was something. But their time together was so brief, only a few minutes each night; and then she would have to return to a husband who was barely more alive than a corpse at a viewing. There were moments when she was sure she couldn't stand it another day.

She finished dressing and began straightening her hair. Behind her, the bedside light snapped on.

"Gretchen."

She turned. Charlie was watching her from the bed, a funny look on his face.

"I've been thinking about something," he said slowly. "I'd like to know your opinion of it."

"Fixing to redecorate?" she asked lightly.

"No. Nothing like that. This business I want to bring up with you—well, it's serious."

"Okay, Charlie," Gretchen said, with no trace of humor this time. "I'm listening."

Charlie had dropped his gaze. "Well, here it is, then. This town's through. Everybody here knows it. Not much point in fighting it anymore. I'm only sixty-three; I ought to have some good years left, and I don't want to spend them wasting away in a place that's hardly better than a graveyard. So I've been thinking ..." He took a breath, then said it. "I'm going to close up shop and move on. To Arizona, maybe, or New Mexico. Someplace where there are golf courses—I've always meant to take up that game—golf courses and maybe a fishing hole. And people. Lots of people."

"You ... you're leaving, Charlie?" she whispered, and in that moment she knew he meant much more to her than she'd believed.

"Yes, I believe I am."

"When?"

"Next month."

"Oh, God ..."

Suddenly her knees were weak. She sat on the edge of the bed. She felt his hand touch hers.

"But, Gretchen," he whispered, "there's something else I wanted to say."

She kept her head down, ashamed to let him see the tears blurring her vision. "You mean there's more?"

"A little more."

"Well ... what, then?"

"Will you come with me?"

She heard the words. At first they had no meaning; they were only a string of empty sounds. *Will you come with me? Will you leave Tuskett, this place of weeds and boarded-up windows and old people killing time till the Reaper comes? Will you leave your husband, a man sliding into senescence as surely as a dinosaur into a tar pit? Will you leave all that behind, and come with me to start a new life in some green, laughing place of golf courses and fishing holes?*

"Charlie," she breathed, "are you serious?"

He squeezed her hand.

"Will you?" he asked again.

"Yes."

"You mean it? Really?"

"Yes, Charlie, yes, oh, Lord, *yes*!"

Then they were crying and hugging each other and rocking back and forth on the bed while the rusty springs creaked. A long time passed that way, and while it did, Gretchen knew the purest joy she'd known in years.

Finally they separated.

"What will we live on?" Gretchen asked as she collected herself.

"I've got money saved up. A lot. The coffee shop used to do land-office business, you know. Years ago. I've got plenty squirreled away. And there's my Social Security too. We'll do fine."

"Yes," she said happily. "Of course we will. Oh, God, this is wonderful. We're getting out. We're leaving Tuskett. We're not going to have to grow old and die here, like I figured we would."

"Huh-uh. Let all the rest of 'em stay here and rot. We'll live it up." Charlie was smiling, but the smile left his face as he added, "It's going to be hard on Dick, though."

"I know it."

"But we have to do what's best for us. Right?"

She nodded firmly. "Right."

"Anyway, he's got plenty of friends here."

"Sure, he does."

"He'll make it all right."

"I'm sure he will."

It was a lie. They both knew that. This would kill Dick. She pictured him waking up to find his wife gone, along with her clothes and all her other belongings. He would wander the house in his pj's, calling her name and blinking back tears. And when he found out Charlie was missing too—when he found out that his wife of forty years had left him for another man, and not just any man, but a friend, a fellow who'd come to Dick's place regularly for a shave and a trim—when he learned all that, he would curl up like a sick old dog and die.

The thought pained her. But if she stayed in Tuskett, she would be the one to die. And she wanted to live. She was still young enough, still had her strength and her health. She had a right to do whatever it took to save her life. Of course she did.

"Of course," she said out loud.

Charlie glanced at her. "What?"

"Nothing." Her eyes flicked to her wristwatch. "Look at the time. I've really got to get home. I'm late as it is, and Dick will be fretting now, for sure."

Charlie kissed her, briefly and awkwardly, on the cheek.

"I figure a month from now," he said, "or six weeks at the most, and I'll be ready. And we'll say adios to this town."

"If Tuskett lasts that long," she answered cheerfully, and they both laughed, and Charlie kissed her again, a real kiss this time, and it was good being kissed that way.

By nine thirty Jenny Kirk was getting seriously scared.

Tommy still hadn't come back, and he never, absolutely never, stayed out this late.

She paced the living room, ignoring the drone of the TV set from the parlor. Her teeth tugged at her lower lip, a nervous habit. She wondered what could have happened to her son. Most of her was afraid, just plain scared, the way an animal might be, with no mitigating complications about it; but one small part of her, a part she didn't care to acknowledge, was angry too—angry at Tommy for scaring her like this, and angry at the world for making it her problem and hers alone. She had known that anger before. She'd known it for nine years—ever since she stopped off in Tuskett for a bite to eat, on her way to a better life in LA, or any kind of a life at all.

Back then, the Tuskett Inn had still been alive, if not exactly thriving, in those days when the town was only beginning to die its lingering death. She still remembered the meal she'd ordered there, an open-face roast-beef sandwich with a gravy boat of mashed potatoes on the side. The food was good, amazingly good under the circumstances, and she made the mistake—if it was a mistake—of telling the waiter to give her compliments to the chef. She'd lain awake on many nights in the years since, wondering how things might have turned out for her if that roast beef had been a tad less tender or the mashed potatoes just a touch undercooked.

The waiter, she later learned, had passed along her compliment with a lascivious grin; it was the grin that persuaded the chef, a young man named Mike Kirk, to pay a visit to the lady's table. She was startled when she saw him; he looked like a lifeguard with his wavy blond hair and sky-blue eyes; he was, she thought, Malibu incarnate—the mystical paradise for which she'd begun her cross-country odyssey, embodied in the person of a man. They hit it off right away, and she found an excuse to stay over, and that very night she slept with him. Yes, it was that fast. Love at first sight, or so it seemed at the time; months passed before she realized that what they'd had between them was not love and never had been; and by then it was too late, because they were married and she was pregnant and he was gone.

Just gone. He'd never been the type to think things through, she guessed. The marriage, like his courtship, had been merely an act of impulse, and when the consequences began to dawn in his brain, when he saw her belly swelling, he'd panicked and run. She had no idea where he'd gone. Frankly, my dear, she didn't give a fuck.

There had been no men since. Tuskett was not known for an overabundance of eligible bachelors—for an overabundance of anything, in fact. Of course, there was Bill Needham, a sweet man, decent and thoughtful, serious and reserved, a man who no doubt would make a caring husband and father. And he was interested in her; she'd seen the look in his eyes when they made small talk to pass the time. But she'd never shown him any interest in return. She told herself she had no time to get involved with a man; she had her hands full raising Tommy while holding down a full-time job. This was true, but it wasn't the whole truth. The whole truth was that she was scared to go through it again. She'd gotten used to sleeping alone, snuggling up to a pillow rather than a man, and it did have its advantages; a pillow couldn't hurt you the way a man could; it couldn't take off one day and leave you alone and crying.

So she kept her distance; and good old Bill, who seemed to sense what she wanted, kept his.

And, truthfully, life wasn't so bad. She had a son she loved, a job she tolerated, friends and neighbors who cared for her and didn't look at her with that awful, pitying, good-Christian expression too often. She had her health. And, modesty be damned, she still had her looks.

She was thirty-one but could have passed for twenty-five, especially when she unclipped her hair and let it cascade around her shoulders in waves of chestnut silk. Yes, things were fine.

Only now things weren't fine. Now it was nine thirty on a Tuesday night in July, a cop show was blaring in the parlor, pots and pans were soaking in the sink, and Tommy wasn't home.

Jenny completed another circuit of the living room, then stopped. She stood stock-still, thinking.

She knew her son well enough to be sure he wouldn't stay out without a damn good reason. And the only good reason she could think of was that he'd gotten hurt. Maybe he'd twisted his ankle in a vacant lot or tumbled out of a tree and knocked himself cold. Or maybe—God forbid—he'd gone over to the old motel and fallen through the rotted floor or ... or the dump ...

That decided it. She had to find her boy, and find him now. She couldn't do it alone. She needed help.

With sudden determination she marched into the kitchen, where a rotary-dial phone hung on the wall near a bulletin board. Pinned to the board, nearly lost among the shopping lists, recipes, and clippings from the *Clarion*'s comics page, was a slip of paper marked EMERGENCY with two phone numbers written underneath. One was the number of the police department; the other was Lew Hannah's home phone. It was a number she must have dialed a thousand times, a number she knew as well as her own name; but just now—funny thing—it seemed to have slipped her mind.

She picked up the phone with a shaking hand and dialed, while thinking in dull wonder that in the entire time she'd lived in Tuskett, this was the first emergency she could remember.

- — -

At ten minutes to nine Tommy Kirk had been thinking quite seriously of heading back. He wore his very own digital wristwatch, a birthday present from Mr. and Mrs. Hannah two years ago this October; its display glowed greenly in the gloom, and he knew that it would take him five minutes, at least, to get to his house from the dump.

He'd been warned not to play in the dump. His mom had told him that there were germs and rats and other creepy-crawlies there, and that it was no place for a boy of eight to be fooling around. She'd said he'd darn well better mind her or there would be the devil to pay.

Tommy had listened respectfully and promised—crossed his heart and hoped to die—that he wouldn't go. He'd meant it too; but the town was so small, and there was hardly anything for a kid to do on a restless evening. The dump might be dangerous, but it was fun, and the fact that it was forbidden only made it better.

So Tommy went to the dump. He went often, but only in the evenings, when darkness concealed his entry and exit. In a small town, there were eyes everywhere, eyes that never seemed to shut or even blink. The twilight was Tommy's ally; it screened him from any possible observer as he ran down Joshua Street to the Old Road, then east a quarter mile to the dump's rusty gate, and slipped inside. Once in the dump, he no longer feared being caught; no grown-ups would come here; there was nothing for them to find.

Plenty for him, though. He liked to prowl among the rusted car frames and the broken glass, looking for treasure. So far he'd collected three dollars and sixteen cents in change, a can opener, and a copy of *Playboy* magazine bloated with rain. He'd looked through it, intrigued by the naked women who were—he was sure of it—performing intercourse.

His discovery tonight had been of less moment. Toward the rear of the dump, lying in a corner on its side, was a dead refrigerator. He'd crawled inside, wondering idly what he could make out of the thing. He supposed he could flip it on its back, put wheels on it, and run it like a racing car. That might be pretty neat.

But now it was time to hurry back through the darkened streets, climb into his pj's, run a toothbrush over his teeth, and crawl into bed with Duncan the Dragon, who lay resting on the pillow with his cheery gap-toothed grin. His brief hour of freedom was up, the hour when he could pretend to be a man, all grown-up and on his own with a world to explore and remake to his own design; now he would have to resume the dreary routine of childhood.

He sighed and climbed out of the fridge. He got to his feet, brushing the dirt from his cut-off jeans and bare knees. He looked around, A hundred feet away, a huge tangled heap of scrap metal poked its snout at the sky, a volcanic cone streaked with lava flows of rust, encircled by islands of junk and archipelagos of abandoned automobiles. The moon, three-quarters full, was rising; the summit of the scrap heap glowed chalk-white. No moonbeams reached the lower portions or the surrounding detritus; they remained lost in a well of purple shadow.

Tommy stared at the scene, struck by its strange beauty. And if there could be beauty even here, in a town dump in the middle of the desert, then what must the rest of the world be like—those places he saw on TV, Los Angeles and New York, Paris and Tahiti? He experienced a sudden fever of impatience about growing up, the kind of fever that came on at odd times and made him itch with the need to escape this town and see the world, all of it, every inch; and then the fever broke and he was left feeling sad and a little afraid.

He couldn't say why. There was nothing to be afraid of here.

He shook his head and started walking. He made his way through a maze of irregular walls looming up out of the ground cover of garbage. Each mound had its own distinctive silhouette, sharp against the sky. His eye picked out animal shapes—giraffe, bear, gorilla—a topiary of trash.

He was halfway through the dump when he heard a sound.

He stopped, listening. It was a low rasping sound, the sound that skeletal fingers might make as they clawed their way out of an unmarked grave. For the first time, Tommy wondered if there were bodies buried in the dump. The thought made a kind of twisted sense; this was a place for dead things.

He screwed up his face, disgusted with himself. Of course there were no dead bodies here, and even if there were—even if somebody like, say, old man Tuskett had been buried here in secret, years ago—even then, it wouldn't matter because the dead stayed dead, they stayed in the ground with the earthworms and maggots where they belonged, no matter what went on in those scary movies his mother did her best not to let him watch.

But something sure as heck was making that sound.

He stood rigid, head cocked, eyes half-shut, doing his best to pinpoint the location of the noise. As best he could tell, it was coming from the other side of that huge central scrap heap, less than fifty feet away. Close by. He could take a look. Would only cost him a minute or so.

He hesitated, torn between curiosity and fear. Part of him wanted to find out what the thing was; another part was flashing a warning at him, like the digital readout on his watch.

Then he shrugged. What was the worst it could be? A stray dog or coyote, maybe, rooting with its snout in the trash, sniffing out rotted food. Or a raccoon, pawing at the garbage heap and licking up grubs. Or a rat, just like his mom had warned him about. He knew there were rats here—he'd seen them—though he'd never heard one make this kind of noise.

Well, there was one way to find out.

Slowly he approached the junk heap. He moved silently, treading on the balls of his feet, so as not to scare away whatever was on the other side. The mound towered over him, blotting out the night sky. Wind gusted up, spraying a fine scatter of dirt.

He reached the scrap heap and began to circle around it, taking each step with slow caution, watching the ground at his feet. He avoided the broken bottles that would crunch under his sneakers, the tin cans that, if kicked, would bounce and jangle in that hollow way tin cans had, the loop of barbed wire that could have snagged his leg and made him cry out. He was careful. He made no sound. And meanwhile the noise on the other side of the mound was growing louder, closer. He thought he could detect breathing, low and regular, but it might have been only the sighing of the wind.

After some endless length of time—half a minute, at least—he was nearly within sight of the source of the noise. Slowly he peered around the edge of the pile.

It was not a coyote, or a raccoon, or a rat.

It was a man.

He was crouching with his back to Tommy, rummaging through the trash, and the low rasping was the sound of his hands—long-fingered hands with smooth, hairless backsides and bone-white knuckles—digging. Searching for something.

The man was a stranger in town. Tommy knew that much, right off, even though he couldn't see the man's face. Nobody in town wore a long black coat or a dirt-blotted cowboy hat, or had hands like that. And nobody in town made Tommy shudder, a brief involuntary spasm, the way he'd shuddered just now.

Part of him—an old, wise, instinctive knowledge at the base of his brain—told him to run now, run away, run and don't look back. Tommy didn't run. He stood unmoving and watched the man as he continued to root in the garbage like some immense black insect with its legs folded under it and its pale, grasping forelegs poking at a dunghill.

The man found something. A length of pipe, rusty and cracked, ten inches long. He turned it over and over in his hands, studying it, and nodded—Tommy saw the hat bob briefly—and then the black coat opened up like the wings of an insect unfolding, and the man tucked the pipe inside, and it was gone.

He went on searching. He unearthed an empty plastic milk carton and tossed it aside; it made a dull thud in the darkness. He found an old shoe, the neck of a whiskey bottle, a tattered telephone book, a phonograph record. He kept none of those things. Then his questing hands, crawling like pale whitish scorpions over the mound, closed over another length of pipe, this one slightly shorter than the last. A sound like a mirthless chuckle, a dark death-rattle sound, greeted the discovery. This pipe, too, disappeared inside the coat, swallowed up by its black folds.

Tommy stared, his gaze riveted on the stranger. He didn't know why he had to keep watching, what it was about this man that made him unable to turn away. Somehow it seemed terribly important to know what he was doing, to see him dig up still more of those cracked and rusted pipes he seemed to prize.

Then the man stiffened, his shoulders hunching. Slowly his hat turned on its axis and his face swiveled into view and his eyes, ice-blue and ice-cold, met Tommy's own.

Tommy stared into those eyes, into their depths, drowning in them as he might have drowned in an arctic sea. The night was warm, but a freezing wind seemed to have kicked up in the confines of the dump, or maybe it was simply blowing like a gale through his own body as he stood trembling with his knees threatening to buckle.

As Tommy watched, unable to tear his eyes away, the man rose to his feet in one swift, effortless motion and stood staring down at him from that dizzying height all grown-ups enjoyed. He was smiling.

"All alone," the man breathed in a voice like dust, "little boy."

It was not a question.

Tommy's heart was doing dance steps in his chest. His breathing was quick and shallow; he was sucking in the dry night air and getting no oxygen. He tasted something nasty, like puke, at the back of his mouth. His brain buzzed.

"Stay away," he whispered bravely.

The man laughed, and the worst thing about that laugh was that it was perfectly ordinary, not a movie villain's chortle, merely a brief bark of amusement. Tommy remembered a cartoon he'd seen on TV about Mickey Mouse and an evil giant, and how little Mickey had faced off against the giant, his tiny mouse body swallowed by a looming, monstrous shadow, and how he'd tried to act brave.

"What brings you here?" the man asked in a voice neither cruel nor kind, but faintly ominous, like a distant rumble of thunder.

"Playing," Tommy said, fighting the dryness in his throat.

The man nodded. "Me too," he said somberly. "What's your name?"

Tommy knew he shouldn't tell him, knew he shouldn't talk to strangers at all—that was another thing his mother had warned him about—but he couldn't help it. Those eyes drew him in and made him tell.

"Tommy Kirk."

"How old are you?"

"Eight."

"Are you afraid of me, Tommy?"

Say no, his mind ordered. Say no. Say no.

"Yes," he said, then added uselessly, "a little."

The long-fingered hands made two fists, then unclenched, then clenched again, slowly, rhythmically, as if keeping time with a melody only their owner could hear.

"Well," the stranger said softly, "you should be."

Tommy knew he had to run. Had to get away. Because this man was the devil his mother had warned him he would pay if he broke his word and played in the dump. This was his punishment, this man of ice and dust. This was the bogeyman.

That thought broke his paralysis at last. Tommy took a step back, and another, and one more, and the stranger followed, and they matched each other stride for stride, the boy retreating and the man advancing, and all the while the night shivered and stirred around them like the folds of the man's great black coat, rustling fitfully.

Then with a burst of energy Tommy turned and broke into a run, and behind him footfalls hammered in pursuit, and he knew with sudden clarity that he was running for his life.

Twisted shapes rushed past him. A clawed hand, which was a loose coil on the spring of a mattress, snagged his shirt. He tore free, the shirt ripping loose with a zipper sound. He ran on. He glanced back and saw the man following swiftly, swallowing great gulps of ground in long strides. The coat flapped like bat wings.

His hat bobbed on its chin strap, crazily askew, exposing a bird's nest of hair sticking out at all angles. His lips were parted in a pale crescent that was a smile.

Oh, God—Tommy heard himself praying—please don't let him get me. I promise I won't play in the dump anymore.

He sucked air in shallow gasps. His sneakers pounded the ground, racing in a mad blur. One of his shoelaces came undone and flapped at his ankle, threatening to trip him up. He felt a sudden spurt of warmth and moisture in his underpants and realized with a stab of shame that he'd wet himself. It seemed like such a stupid, babyish thing to do. He hoped his mom wouldn't see the stain.

He glanced back over his shoulder and saw that the man was gaining on him.

The stranger wasn't running, not quite. He seemed disdainful of the need to run. But he was striding at a fast clip, closing the gap between himself and his prey. And he was still smiling. That was the worst thing of all, his awful, sickly smile—that, and his eyes, gleaming like the blazing night-vision orbs of a coyote or a timber wolf.

Tommy ran faster, ignoring the ice-pick stabs of pain in his lungs, the racing crescendo of his heart. But when he looked back, the man was less than ten feet away, and closing in.

Up ahead, two heaps of trash formed a narrow alley bordered by a sofa bed on one side and a rusted-out Buick on the other. The alley tapered to a slot just barely big enough for him to squeeze through, too small for his pursuer. He arrowed toward it, knowing the man would have to go around, and meanwhile he would be out the front gate, home-free.

It was a good plan, except that halfway down the alley Tommy realized it narrowed more than he'd thought. It was too narrow for him to get all the way through. He was trapped.

When he looked back, the man had reached the entrance.

"I'm coming, Tommy," he said in a voice as soft as velvet, and then the velvet became sandpaper. "Coming to get you."

Tommy felt tendrils of fear creep over him. He stood frozen as the man moved forward, his shoulders brushing the heaps of glittering rubbish on either side. He walked calmly and casually now, in a way that was hardly threatening at all; he might have merely been out for a stroll, enjoying a breath of the night air. But those eyes still glinted, shading from blue to green to yellow, and he still smiled, an unholy smile laced with some hidden purpose, a purpose Tommy didn't want to know.

Tommy backed up as far as he could, until his shoulders made a pincushion for random scraps of metal poking out of the pile. Another few steps and the man would be right there. Tommy thought about shouting for help. No use. Nobody would hear.

Well, then, he would just have to escape.

He grabbed hold of the first thing within reach, which was the handle of the Buick's door, and hoisted himself onto the roof of the car, and then a hand caught his sneaker from below, trying to drag him down, and with a final effort he kicked at the hand and knocked it free.

He clambered over the car. Its roof was level with the summit of a low, shapeless hill of junk. He stepped onto the pile. Tin cans and broken bottles shifted under his feet. He took a step forward and brought his foot down on the reassuring solidity of a toilet seat, but the seat scooted out from under him like a skateboard and he came down on hands and knees. He landed on someone's baby doll. It giggled mechanically and kept on giggling as he struggled to get up with his heart thumping at his eardrums and his breath coming in gasps.

He shut his eyes, listening.

Something else was moving on the junk heap.

He looked back—God, let it be a rat, only a rat—but it wasn't a rat. It was him. It was the bogeyman. He had climbed over the car, just as Tommy had, and was now setting foot on the top of the pile.

Tommy grabbed the doll and hurled it at him. The man didn't even move. The doll whirled dizzily into space, missing him by a yard or more. It hit the ground somewhere below, still unspooling its idiot laugh.

Tommy threw himself upright and staggered forward, sliding drunkenly on the mound, fighting its quicksand softness and the sucking holes that appeared out of nowhere, tugging at his feet, trying to pull him down. He fell again. His arm scraped a scrap of wood studded with nails, gouging deep grooves in his flesh. He barely noticed. He looked back at the man, who was following slowly, one cautious step at a time, moving with the graceful hesitance of a high-wire artist. He was less than a yard away.

Tommy gave up on walking. He crawled over the garbage pile, scrambling madly, cutting his hands and legs. He kept his head down, eyes glued to the crap passing by, inches below his face—buttons shining like coins, pencils worn down to stubs, mismatched socks with holes in the toes, a Richie Rich comic book, a spiral notebook littered with somebody's scribblings, a can of Alpo Liver and Gravy Dinner encrusted with flies like raisins, more stuff, an endless river of it, and God, did it ever stink. The stench of rotten food, of maggots and rodent droppings, stung his nostrils and made his gut heave.

A voice was droning on his mind, the voice of a very scared little boy who didn't want to die. Make him go away, the voice was pleading, make him leave me alone, and don't let him hurt me, please don't, please please please—

A hand grabbed him by the loop of his belt.

Tommy twisted onto his back. The man loomed over him, black as night, even his eyes lost in shadow now. With one hand he held on to Tommy; with the other he reached into his coat. Tommy caught a glint of metal there, a cold steel spark that wasn't one of the rusty pipes but something else.

He screwed up his face against a flood of tears, and with the last of his energy he pistoned out both legs and delivered a vicious kick to the man's midsection, and the man let go, doubling over, hissing like a deflating balloon.

Tommy dived into the trash, heedless of injury, and propelled himself forward like a swimmer doing a breast stroke, flinging his arms over his head in quick, rhythmic jerks while his legs kicked wildly. With each thrust he sucked in a great gasping lungful of air. White spots danced in his field of vision. He reached the edge of the pile. With a final thrust he plunged over the edge, down the side, rolling over and over, while sharp things bit and clung and tore and the night spiraled around him in a dizzy glittering whirl.

He thudded headfirst on the ground. A red spray jetted from his nose. Scraps of tin and shards of glass clung to him like porcupine needles. He didn't care. He'd gotten away.

Thank you, God, he thought. I'll never play in the dump again, I swear, I swear.

"I swear," he grunted aloud, not aware he was saying it, as he struggled to his feet, trying to find the strength to run. And then he stopped, in time with another warning from that wordless instinct he'd never known was his.

Very slowly, he turned and raised his head to look up at the pile of junk; and there, at the very edge, was the man. He stood looming against the sky, a great black bat with its wings folded around it; and as Tommy watched, he spread his arms like the wings of a bat unfolding and leapt from the mound. He sailed into the air, executing a perfect leap, almost beautiful in its grace and athleticism. He landed catlike on both feet, a yard away. He stared at Tommy, his eyes cold, his face composed. He didn't seem even to be out of breath.

"You shouldn't have tried to get away," the man said. "You're going to be very sorry for that, young man."

Absurdly, hurtfully, the words reminded Tommy of his mother and the way she always called him "young man" before she sent him to his room without supper, and it was that thought, no less than the certainty of what was to come next, that brought bitter tears to his eyes.

"Don't hurt me, mister," he whispered, knowing that all words were useless now.

The man only smiled. He raised his left hand, and again Tommy saw that silver glitter, which was a knife.

The blade, so long and sharp, caught the starlight prettily, trembling like a drop of dew on a leaf. Tommy made a low whimpering sound and took a stumbling step backward, and his feet tangled up on him, and he fell on his butt. He lay helpless, staring up as the man approached, his boots crunching with a dry-leaf sound.

The man stopped a foot away. He clasped the knife in both hands and turned it slowly, arrowing the knife point at Tommy's chest. The blade shone like a sliver of moon against the sky. Tommy imagined that awful sharpness whistling down to puncture his heart like a paper bag. He was crying.

Slowly the man raised the knife, lifting it high over his head. The wind tugged at the loose straw of his hair. His eyes blazed with a cold, psychotic fire. Clad in his flowing black coat, he might have been a priest standing at the altar of a human sacrifice.

There was no place to run this time.

Tommy scrabbled at the ground, and his fingers closed over a scrap of plywood.

"Good night, Tommy," the man said in a voice as quiet and as dry as the night wind. "Sweet dreams."

The knife swept down in a shining arc. And in the same instant Tommy flung up the plywood plank to cover his chest, a makeshift shield. Steel met wood. The knife punched through up to the hilt, then stopped, held in check, inches from Tommy's heart.

The man laughed, a dark sound, like the gurgling of black waters.

"It's no use. Tommy. You're no match for me."

He tugged at the knife, working it loose. Tommy let go of the scrap of plywood and tried to get to his feet and run, but his body wouldn't obey him, and he could only backpedal frantically on the ground, grunting like an animal, kicking up a spray of dirt and pebbles. He felt a sting of pain as his hand skidded into a broken bottle neck. He seized it, thinking it might make a weapon, and then the man wrenched the knife free.

He tossed the plywood plank aside and moved forward with the knife in his hand. Tommy twisted around to a crouching position, clutching the bottle neck. The knife flashed. Tommy dodged the blow and thrust the bottle at him, sinking its jagged glass teeth into his knife hand. Drops of blood pattered on the ground in a fine red rain.

He bleeds, Tommy thought with a rush of hope. I can *hurt* him. The realization made him giddy, lightheaded.

The man lashed out again. Tommy leapt to his feet, avoiding the knife by inches, then flung the bottle at the man, aiming for his face. A spray of glass shot up in time with a howl of animal rage. The man hissed like steam. His left cheek was scored with a webwork of crimson lines. He drew back, pressing a hand to his face, and for the moment—just one moment—Tommy knew he had been forgotten.

He ran. He cut a zigzagging course through scattered mounds of trash, heading for the rear of the dump, where he could climb the fence and get away. But it was no use. Already the man was following, and he was quick, so quick; Tommy knew he couldn't outrace him.

Directly ahead, a familiar shape came into view. The refrigerator. The one he'd been playing in only a few minutes ago. He could hide in there. Like an animal holing up in its cave. If he could get inside and wedge the door shut, he might be safe, at least for a while, and maybe help would come before the man found a way in.

A faint hope, but better than no hope at all.

Tommy reached the refrigerator, snatched a tire iron from the litter at his feet, and pitched himself inside. He twisted around to grab the door. Through the rectangle of the open doorway, the man was visible, bearing down on him, his face a blood-smeared mask.

Tommy yanked the door shut. Darkness closed over him. His fingers groped for the built-in shelf on the inside of the door. He found it. Running along the shelf was a metal bar. He wedged one end of the tire iron behind the bar, then braced the other end against the side of the refrigerator, jamming the door shut.

In the next instant, bestial grunting sounded just outside, and hands scratched at the door, seeking to pry it open.

"Come on out, little boy," the man muttered, his voice muffled. "You can't hide in there for long. Not enough air for your little lungs. You want to suffocate? You want to die that way?"

Better than your way, Tommy thought, his face set and grim.

The door rattled. A fist or a boot pounded it savagely. It did not yield.

Tommy licked his lips and tried not to think about the closeness of the walls, the mustiness of the air in here, the awful feeling of being trapped. The refrigerator was like a coffin, and being locked in it was like being buried alive. He'd heard about a kid who'd crawled into a fridge in a junkyard in Jacob and had gotten locked in; that kid had croaked when the oxygen ran out, just like the man had said. Tommy figured the same thing would happen to him before long. But he guessed it didn't make much difference anymore.

The refrigerator gave a hard sideways lurch. It teetered, then crashed on its side. Tommy banged his head. Involuntarily he cried out. The tire iron shuddered but held, still wedging the door shut.

He hugged himself, shivering, in a corner of the lightless box. From above, he heard noises. Scrabbling sounds, then echoing hammer blows. He understood. The man had hurled the refrigerator onto its side, hoping to crack it open. He'd failed. In a frenzy of frustration, he'd climbed on top of the thing and was pounding it with some blunt object—one of those rusty pipes he'd salvaged, probably. Tommy reached up and ran his hand over the smooth plastic above his head. He could feel it dimpling with each blow. The metal casing underneath had been dented, but it hadn't cracked. Not yet.

"Game's over, Tommy," the voice rasped with a lunatic chuckle. "Olly olly oxen free ..."

The man would break through soon. And he would be angry. Tommy had hurt him, humiliated him. He would do things. Awful things. Things Tommy didn't even want to think about.

The wall caved in a little more, in time with another sledgehammer strike. Tommy shut his eyes against the burn of tears, and waited.

- — -

The Ford Tempo glided down silent streets, its headlights cutting the darkness. Lew Hannah peered through the windshield, looking for any sign of the Kirk boy.

Jenny had called him ten minutes ago, her voice threatening tears the way a dimming sky might threaten rain. Lew knew Jenny as well as anyone did; he and Lynnie thought of her almost as a daughter, the child they'd never been able to have. God knew, they were old enough to be her parents; but then, Lew Hannah didn't like to think about encroaching old age—the stiffness in his knees on damp mornings, the ringing in his ears that kept him up nights. Watching over Jenny—even if she didn't quite realize he was watching over her—was one of the things that kept him feeling young.

So, yes, he knew her, all right, and he'd thought he knew her every mood, every nuance of her personality; but he'd never heard that particular choked tone of voice from her before.

"Tommy's missing," she said.

Lew hadn't answered right away, just pulled in a breath. He felt Lynnie's eyes on him, the movie on Channel 11 forgotten. His wife had been the one to answer the phone, before handing it over to him, so she knew it was Jenny, and from his face she knew with equal certainty that something was wrong.

"Okay, Jen," Lew said softly. "Don't panic on me. Just tell me what's going on."

Briefly, her voice trembling only a little, Jenny summarized the situation. "He should be home by now," she finished. "He's never late. He wears a watch. The one you gave him."

"All right. Do you have any idea where he might have gone? Is there someplace he likes to play? The motel, maybe?"

"I told him not to go there."

"How about the dump? I remember you telling me he wandered in there once."

"He's not supposed to go there anymore. He knows that."

"But do you think he might've?"

"Dammit, Lew, I don't know!"

"Okay, hon. Take it easy. We'll find your boy."

He was sure of it too. This was Tuskett, after all. How much trouble could a boy find in a town with a population of just twenty-three? Then he recalled the incident at the coffee shop an hour ago. Twenty-four, he realized. There were twenty-four souls in Tuskett tonight.

For the first time he felt a faint stirring of fear. He brushed it impatiently aside.

"We'll find him," he told Jenny again, keeping his voice calm and confident. "You sit tight."

He hung up and turned to Lynnie. She was watching him intently, her gray eyes narrowed, lips pursed. It was the same look she wore when she was reading one of her mysteries or doing the crossword. He liked to watch her when she looked like that. The prettiest thing about her, he'd been known to say, was the intelligence that was so often visible on her face.

"Tommy missing?" Ellyn Hannah asked after a long moment.

Lew nodded.

"You think it's got anything to do with that man Kane?"

"I doubt it."

"Pretty tall coincidence, don't you think?"

"The boy's probably just lost track of time. Let's not go making a federal case out of it."

"This Kane, he might be a child molester or something."

Lew winced. "Dammit, Lynnie, don't say that."

"These things happen."

"Not here."

She said nothing.

"Look," Lew said, "I'll find him. Okay? Meantime, if Jenny calls again to say that he's come home on his own, buzz me on the police band and give me the good word."

"Roger wilco," Lynnie said, and smiled. But Lew noticed a hint of dampness sparkling in her eyes.

In the ten minutes since leaving the house. Lew had made two complete circuits of the town, stopping now and then to shout Tommy Kirk's name. He'd gotten out at the trailer park to look around, but had seen nothing. Now he was at the south end of town for the second time, looking out on the Old Road, which lay empty and silent under the three-quarter moon and the star-flecked sky.

He thought about the motel ... and the dump. His gut told him a little boy would be more than likely to hang out in such places; certainly enough of them had, in the years when there were lots of kids in Tuskett. He remembered how Rick Duarte, all of nine years old, had taken a tumble down a flight of rotted stairs in the Tuskett Inn and broken his leg. Rick had worn a cast for weeks; in the summer heat it must have itched like the very devil.

Tommy might be there, or at the dump. Lew hesitated, weighing the two possibilities. The dump seemed the more likely of the two, though he couldn't have said why. Maybe simply because it was the kind of place he would have gone if he were a boy of eight with a summer evening to spend.

He guided the Tempo to the front gate of the dump. The gate was half-open, but that in itself meant nothing; the lock had rusted through long ago and had never been replaced. In a dying town, such small deaths went unnoticed; they happened every day. He cut the engine and almost got out, then hesitated, held in place by a sudden thought.

Pretty tall coincidence—Lynnie had said—don't you think?

He didn't believe it, of course. Didn't believe there was a man in town who'd kidnap a child ... or do something worse. Or was it merely that he didn't want to believe it? He remembered sitting at the counter and staring into Kane's eyes and feeling chilled to his very soul. He hadn't wanted to admit, even to himself, how much those eyes had scared him. They were eyes that seemed to speak to him, and what they spoke of was death.

A dark man, Bill Needham had said. An evil man.

That was crazy. No logic to it, none at all. Still ...

Lew Hannah unlocked the glove compartment and took out the gun he kept hidden there. It was a snub-nosed Colt .38. The Detective Special, it was called. The kind of thing real cops—you know, the ones on all the TV shows—had been known to use.

He checked the cylinder. The gun was fully loaded, six rounds. He wedged the gun in his belt on his right side, where he could reach it in a hurry. If it came to that.

It wouldn't, of course. Kane was probably soaking his feet in Ethel Walston's tub by now, washing off the desert dust. And Tommy Kirk was just bending his mother's rules a little, the way kids would. Sure. He knew that.

But there was no harm in being careful.

He picked up the flashlight from the passenger seat, where he'd left it after his search of the trailer park. He switched it on and got out of the car. The wind plastered his shirt sleeves against his bare arms. It was a dry wind, dusty and warm, but he shivered anyway, and told himself it was from the cold.

His shoes crunched on the bone-dry ground. He

walked up to the gate and pushed it open, hating the sound it made, the screeching whine of fingernails on a blackboard. Then the gate was behind him and he was inside the dump, its chicken-wire fence boxing him in, cutting him off from quick escape. Now, why would he think of it like that? Escape—from what?

He shook his head, disgusted with himself, and tried to launch a gob of spit at the darkness. But, funny thing, his mouth was dry. He didn't have any spit, none at all.

He swung the flashlight slowly, its beam spotlighting heaps of refuse that glittered like gemstones. He recognized the remains of old Dominic Torres' Bonneville, a boat-size monster that ate gas like a kid eats candy. Dominic had put two hundred thousand miles on that baby and would have put on two hundred thousand more if he hadn't gone out onto the interstate, dead-drunk and lead-footed, and smashed head-on into a semi truck. Back in '82, that was. Then Dominic wound up in a cemetery in Carlyle, twenty miles away, and the car wound up here, in this other graveyard. Lew found the incident oddly appropriate. The interstate had killed everything else in Tuskett; why not its people too?

Something rustled behind him, and he turned too quickly, his hand going reflexively for his gun. Then he relaxed, feeling foolish, as he saw that it was only a yellowed scrap of newspaper drifting like a tumbleweed on a current of wind.

See? he told himself. That's what you get for acting like a skittish old woman.

He faced the scene before him, sweeping the flashlight over the dump in a searchlight arc.

"Tommy?" he said. His mouth was still unaccountably dry, and the word came out hoarse, rasping. He cleared his throat. "Tommy?" he said again, louder. "This is Mr. Hannah. Police Chief Hannah," he added pointlessly, but somehow it didn't seem pointless to stress that particular fact, just in case someone other than Tommy Kirk might be listening. "If you're here, I want you to come out now. No fooling around. Your mom's worried sick."

Nothing.

Lew Hannah could have turned back then, knowing he'd checked out the dump. But somehow he knew, just knew, that Tommy Kirk was here.

He crept forward, beaming the flashlight into the darkness on all sides. The circle of light bobbed over the ground, illuminating scraps of garbage that littered the dirt like flecks of scum on a stagnant pond. He saw a tattered handbag, a smashed pair of eyeglasses, an empty shampoo bottle. And ...

Blood.

Fresh blood, not yet dried, lying in a shapeless puddle at his feet. He stared down at it while the darkness shifted around him and the night wind clawed at his shirt and spread goose pimples over his arms.

Well, so what? he thought. So it's blood. There are rats galore in this place. Cat or coyote might've gotten hold of one. It happens.

Lynnie's voice wafted through his mind: Pretty tall coincidence, don't you think?

Yes. He did think so. Most likely the blood was Tommy's. But that still proved nothing, except that the boy had come in here and cut himself on some scrap of metal or shard of glass. Maybe he was hiding out for fear of going home and letting his mother see the damage.

Raising his flashlight, Lew made out a second puddle, a few feet farther on. And beyond that, shrinking with distance, a third and a fourth. A trail of blood snaking through the dump into the dark.

"Tommy," he said again. "Tommy. You there?"

Nothing.

Slowly, deliberately, Lew Hannah pulled out the Colt and drew back the hammer. He was past the stage of pretending to himself that everything was normal. He was scared. Scared for Tommy, and for himself. His mouth was terribly dry, and his forehead was hot, fever-hot. He wanted very much to turn back. But he couldn't do that. He had a job to do. He'd promised Jenny he was going to find her boy.

The trail of blood led him deep into the recesses of the dump, far from the gate and the car headlights shining like twin beacons at his back.

"Tommy," he called again, no longer expecting a response.

A low sound, half-whimper, half-sob, answered him.

Lew caught his breath. Tommy was here.

He moved forward with the flashlight in one hand and the gun in the other.

"It's me," he called out. "Lew. Lew Hannah."

A high, thin voice, ragged with fear, rose to his ears.

"Help me. *Please!*"

Then Lew was running, oblivious of danger, the gun cocked and ready, the flashlight bobbing wildly in his hand and making long luminous streaks in the darkness like shooting stars.

It had taken a long time for the man to break into the refrigerator, and there was nothing Tommy could do but wait, curled in a knot of fear, wincing at each new hammer blow that shook the darkness like thunder. Then suddenly he heard a new sound, a harsh crackle like the splintering of dry wood. He raised his head reluctantly, almost afraid to see what was happening, and watched in dumb horror as a hole opened in the side of the refrigerator.

The man had ruptured the metal casing at last, and

now with his bare hands he was tugging at the edges of the crack he'd made, pulling it apart, widening the gap.

Tommy drew back into the far corner of the refrigerator, his breath trapped in his throat.

Slowly an arm snaked through the opening like an eel gliding out of its cave. The five fingers, long and bony, flexed. They groped in the dark, seeking prey.

Tommy knew he had only one hope now. He reached out to the door of the refrigerator and found the tire iron, still wedged in place. He wrenched it loose. Now the door could be opened from the outside. But the man might not know that.

The hand loomed closer, brushing his head. Tommy lifted the tire iron. When the fingers spread wide, preparing to close over his throat, he lashed out. He felt a rush of air whistle past his face, then heard the crunch of impact as the tire iron slammed down on the man's knuckles.

The man hissed. Instantly the hand was withdrawn. Tommy waited, gripping the iron bar in both fists. He heard soft scrabbling noises from outside, as if the man were searching the ground for something. So far, at least, he hadn't tried to open the door. He must think it was still sealed.

Then the hand burst through the opening again, and this time something sharp and deadly as an icicle gleamed in its fingers—the knife. Tommy jerked his head to one side. The blade flashed past. He swung out blindly with the tire iron, beating at the hand, trying to smash it like some loathsome insect that had crawled in here to sting him. The hand withdrew once more, defeated. For the moment.

Tommy lay in the corner, his heart thudding at his eardrums, his breath coarse and ragged in his throat. A slimy trickle ran down the tire iron onto his hands. Blood.

He'd drawn blood again. Good.

Then the hand, shorn of its knife, came at him once more, bloody and battered but refusing to give up. Tommy lashed out again, but this time the hand did not flinch or back off; instead those red fingers closed over the tire iron and gave a good hard tug, nearly yanking it free.

Tommy moaned. The hand pulled harder, refusing to surrender its grip on the thing, dragging it slowly, inexorably toward the hole. Tommy clung to the iron bar with all his strength, but the metal was slick with the man's blood and his own sweat, and he could feel the weapon slipping away, inch by inch, shuddering free in fits and starts, and there was nothing he could do about it. Finally the tire iron popped loose and slithered away out the hole, and he was defenseless and trapped and doomed.

A small sound, a scared-little-boy sound, escaped his lips. He sniffed back a sob. He waited.

"I'm going to kill you now, Tommy," the man said from some great distance. "And I'll do it slowly."

He reached through the hole again, and Tommy lashed out in desperation at that awful looming hand. He kicked and scratched and bit. It was no use. The hand just kept coming, inexorable as death. Tommy arched his back and pressed his shoulders against the rear of the refrigerator, rigid with terror, as those bone-white, blood-dripping fingers inched toward his throat.

And he heard a voice—Lew Hannah's voice—calling his name.

"Tommy!"

The hand paused, as if listening.

Tommy tried to scream an answer, but only a strangled sob came out. Lew called for him again, and this time Tommy found his voice.

"Help me ..." The words were a warbled cry. "*Please*!"

Abruptly the hand vanished through the hole.

"Tommy," a different voice, a frighteningly familiar voice, whispered. "Look at me."

Against his will, Tommy Kirk lifted his head. Framed in the narrow opening was the man's face. He was gazing down, blue eyes glowing with moonlight or perhaps with something more. Tommy peered into those eyes and felt that cold wind gusting through him again, as it had the last time he looked.

"You will say nothing," the man whispered. "You will keep silent. Do you understand, boy?"

Tommy wanted to say no. Wanted to leap up and thrust his hands through that hole and claw those evil eyes right out of their sockets. But he only stared.

From the distance came the clatter of footsteps.

"Understand?" the man said again, with greater urgency.

Tommy jerked his head once in a nod of assent.

Then the man was gone. His boots crunched on the dry soil, receding into the distance.

Tommy blinked, fighting the swirls of fog in his brain. Slowly he crawled to the refrigerator door and pushed it open and collapsed in a shaking heap.

Lew rounded a trash heap and stopped, staring down at Tommy Kirk, who lay halfway inside an upended refrigerator. One side of the fridge had been battered open; the edges of the hole were smeared with sticky snail-trails of blood. A red-glazed tire iron lay nearby. Lew didn't know what had happened here, but it hadn't been pretty, that was for damn sure.

He crouched by the boy and touched his head. "Tommy. It's me, Lew."

Tommy looked up, his eyes wide with shock and fever-bright with fear. Lew scanned his body, taking in the numerous cuts and bruises covering his bare legs and arms. There was no sign of any major injury.

"What happened, Tommy?" Lew asked. "Tell me."

Tommy stared down at the ground. He said nothing.

Lew hesitated. "Was it a man? A stranger? A stranger in a black coat?"

Tommy started to tremble. Still he didn't speak. But he almost didn't have to. The fear that was racking his body, as nakedly visible as an animal's terror, was enough.

"Okay, now. It's okay."

But it wasn't, of course. It wasn't okay at all. Lew figured they both knew that.

He forced himself to think clearly. As he saw it, he could do one of two things at this point. He could lead Tommy out of the dump, drive him over to Jenny's, and call the state police. That would be the easy way out. He could even justify it to himself. Tommy might be on the verge of going into shock; he needed medical attention. Nobody would blame Lew for thinking of the boy first.

But there was another option. One he didn't like to think about, but there was no way around it. Kane had been here just moments ago. He was bleeding, leaving a trail that was easy enough to follow. Lew beamed his flashlight at the ground and saw fresh droplets of blood receding into the darkness. Somewhere in that darkness, Kane was hiding. If Lew left the dump now, the man would have a chance to slip away, leave town, escape into the vastness of the desert from which he'd come. He might never be found.

Lew tightened his grip on the Colt .38. He felt a stab of anger at himself—anger for being afraid, and for having been so slow to recognize the danger Kane posed. If he'd been quicker on the uptake, if he hadn't let that man saunter out of the coffee shop to go about his business, none of this would have happened.

The anger decided things. He wasn't backing off. It was possible Kane had already climbed the fence or slipped through the gate. But if he was still here, Lew would find him. And if the son of a bitch put up any resistance, Lew Hannah would put a bullet in his chest.

He helped Tommy to his feet and checked him over. He was pretty sure the boy could make it to Jenny's house. It wasn't that far, and his cuts and contusions were only superficial.

Lew looked him straight in the eye. "Okay, Tommy, I want you to do exactly what I say. You've got to run. Run for the gate. It's not a long way, and I'll keep an eye on you the whole time. And once you're out of here, keep on running till you get to your mom's place. Tell her what happened. Have you got that?"

Tommy still didn't react. He looked like a boy in a coma. He just stared and stared, his eyes big and round. Lew thought of those tacky paintings of overly cute children with saucer eyes. Tommy looked like that. Only there was nothing cute about it.

"All right," Lew said. "Get going." To punctuate the thought, he swatted Tommy lightly on the butt.

Tommy broke into a run. He raced away, streaking through the darkness. Lew kept his flashlight on him till the boy was too far away for the beam to reach; then he squinted, following his progress. Tommy slipped through the gate and was momentarily caught in the Tempo's headlights; he blurred past them and was gone down the street, out of sight.

Safe.

Lew released a breath. Then slowly he turned to face the tangled shadowland that might conceal, somewhere in its midst, a dark man named Kane, a man who had come to Tuskett out of nowhere, and who liked to hurt little boys.

He gripped the Colt tight. He started forward, following a trail of pinpoint drops of red. He was unnaturally aware of each step he took, each breath he drew, every beat of his heart. Above all, he was aware of the darkness. The awful, blind, empty darkness on all sides, darkness which seemed to be folding in on him like the petals of a jungle plant closing over its prey. There were shadows everywhere, and the man he was seeking was a shadow, and who knew which shadow might hide him, might *be* him ...

A rat, squeaking shrilly and twitching its whiskered nose, scurried out of his path. Lew felt the short hairs at the back of his neck stand up. He made his way through the piles of garbage moldering like compost heaps, exploring the shadows that loomed on all sides. His flashlight swept the ground, making the fresh blood sparkle like drops of spilled wine.

He felt funny. He supposed that was the word for it: funny. His stomach hurt. Gas pains, he told himself. But he knew it wasn't gas. It was fear twisting his gut like a knife. The same fear that made his head seem suddenly weightless, like a balloon floating free of his body, carrying him away.

He turned down an alley of trash, and his flashlight stopped on a pale oval that might have been a man's face, half-hidden among a jumble of tin cans and old newspapers. Then he realized it was only somebody's dinner plate, broken nearly in two. He shook his head and walked on.

Ten minutes or a lifetime later, he followed the winding trail to the back of the dump, where the chicken-wire fence was rusted through in spots. It was possible Kane had gotten out through one of the holes. Lew shone the flashlight on the fence, looking for drops of blood on the ragged wire mesh. He saw none.

A hand closed over his shoulder.

He whirled, raising the gun, then relaxed. It was not a hand. It was only a tattered rag, blown by the wind to wrap his arm. He tugged it free, and it ghosted away into the dark.

"God damn," he whispered. His teeth chattered. He ground his jaws together to stop their castanet clicking.

The blood trail was harder to follow now. The telltale droplets were petering out. He did his best, picking out rare splashes of color with his flashlight. He climbed over the ruins of a bicycle, somebody's kitchen table, the dead hulk of an air conditioner. An empty plastic bag, the kind that had once held corn chips or popcorn, fluttered past him.

Finally the trail ran out. Kane had stopped bleeding, apparently.

Lew felt a mixture of frustration and relief. Frustration because he hadn't found the man. Relief because now he was free to leave in good conscience, knowing he'd done his duty.

He hurried back to the gate. The Tempo sat where he'd left it. The headlights remained on, a pair of glassine eyes staring blindly into the night. He approached the car, then stopped a yard away from the driver's-side door, thinking of something.

A man could hide in there. Could climb into the backseat, like killers were always doing in horror movies, and wait for Lew to return. With a weapon in his hand, a scrap of steel or glass.

Lew hesitated, then cautiously shone his flashlight into the car. He played the beam over the front and back seats. He saw nothing.

Still ...

The man might be huddled on the floor of the backseat, out of the flashlight's reach. It was possible.

Lew got right up against the car, the open window on the driver's side inches away. He expected at any moment to see Kane pop up out of that window like a demented jack-in-the-box. The Colt trembled in his hand.

He aimed the flashlight at the floor of the backseat.

The car was empty.

It had been foolish to get so worked up. Kane must be a mile away by now, scared witless at the prospect of being caught.

He was smiling at this thought when something seized him by the legs and yanked him off-balance, throwing him to the ground, and before he could do more than raise his head, Kane was snaking out from underneath the car, where he'd been hiding on his belly, lying in wait.

Lew tried to point the gun and shoot. Too late. Kane was already on top of him, holding him spread-eagled on his back. His right hand clamped on Lew's wrist, pinning his gun uselessly to the ground. In his left hand he held a knife. Lew felt its razor-sharp tip testing the tender skin of his throat. He knew with utter certainty that if he put up the least resistance, if he so much as looked at Kane cross-eyed, the knife would open him up like a filleted fish.

So he lay still, gazing up into Kane's face, the face that filled his field of vision like a giant close-up on a movie screen. Lew was close enough to see the pores in Kane's skin, the shadows bruising his eyes, the fine black lashes there. He could smell the man's breath, hot and foul with a carrion stink.

On Kane's left cheek was a meshwork of bloody cuts. The wounds were crusting over, starting to dry, but still oozing pinpricks of blood. Tommy had done that, Lew realized. Had slashed Kane's face.

"You're going to tell me some things," Kane breathed,

his voice a low, tenebrous rasp, like the scraping of bare branches in an October wind. "You're going to tell me everything I need to know."

Lew swallowed, thinking of that knife and what it would do to him. With all the courage he had left, he shook his head.

"Fuck you," he whispered.

Kane tightened his grip. The steel-hard fingers dug into Lew's wrist. Shock waves of pain shot through his arm.

After a moment, the killing pressure lessened. Lew lay flat on his back, breathing hard, with Kane on top of him.

"Who has a gun in this town?" Kane asked.

"Everybody," Lew said between gasps. "Every fucking person. So you might as well be on your way, no easy pickings here—"

"Shut up."

Lew waited for another burst of agony, or maybe the deadly thrust of the knife.

"Look into my eyes," Kane said.

Lew jerked his head away. Somehow the prospect of meeting Kane's stare frightened him more than pain, more than death.

"No," he whispered.

"Come on, now. Don't be afraid." The voice had softened, becoming gentle and almost kind, but an inhuman cruelty lay just below the surface of that kindness, hidden there like a razor blade in a polished apple. "I'm only asking you to look. Just looking can't do any harm, can it?"

Yes, Lew thought. Yes, it can.

He had looked into Kane's eyes once before, in Charlie Grain's coffee shop; and what he'd seen had haunted him. He didn't know how to put words to it, but there was something terrible in those eyes, the hint of some evil power Kane possessed. Hypnotism, mind-reading, or maybe the same insane spark that had gleamed in Hitler's eyes and Charles Manson's, too. Those men had mesmerized their followers just as surely as a python holds its prey fascinated with its stare. Through the centuries a few in each generation could weave a spell to cloud men's thoughts. Maybe Kane was one of them.

"Please," Kane whispered. "Look at me. Look, and tell me what you see."

Lew tried not to listen. But that voice, so sweetly seductive, was doing something to him; it was weakening his resolve the way a caress might melt the heart of a woman, the way a snatch of melody might move a man to tears.

Slowly, Lew Hannah turned his head and looked up into Kane's face, into his eyes. He stared into their icy waters, their swirling depths. He saw something there, he couldn't say quite what. But whatever it was, it was beautiful. It held him, just as it had before. He couldn't turn away.

"Do you see?" Kane asked.

Lew's mouth was dry. His tongue was paste. "I see."

"Who has a gun in this town?"

He didn't want to answer; but, funny thing, he had no choice. All his willpower was gone.

"I ... I've got most of them," he whispered.

"Where do you keep them?"

"A few in the police station. The rest, at home."

"Where, at home?"

"Locked up. In the hall closet."

"Where is your home?"

Don't tell him that. Lew ordered himself. Lynnie's there.

"Second Avenue," he said, the words coming out slow and thick, like dollops of molasses. "West of Joshua, third house down. Number wouldn't mean anything to you; it's all worn off anyway ..."

"Who else has a gun?"

To answer was to sign a death warrant for every name he gave. Lew knew that. But those eyes—how they stared—they saw right through you. It was no use keeping secrets from them. They already knew everything you were about to tell.

So he told. He told about George Baker, PattiSue's dad, who had a hunting rifle in his bedroom closet, and Rile Cady, who kept a shotgun in his trailer, and Todd Hanson, who had a pistol he'd gotten by mail order, an exact replica of the one he'd used in Korea.

Kane listened patiently. When at last he spoke again, his voice had a queerly sated sound, as if he had fed well.

"Now," he said, "who has a radio? A shortwave?"

"I do. In the police car. And ... a portable one at home."

"Who else?"

"Nobody."

"Good. Very good."

"Why do you"—Lew's voice cracked with the strain of forcing out the question—"want to know? What are you meaning to do?"

Kane seemed to almost smile, but his mouth didn't move; it was his eyes that were smiling, smiling at some very fine joke Lew couldn't see.

"There are twenty-three people," Kane said softly, "in this town of Tuskett, California. A nice, quiet little town, no crime, no hassles, where you don't even need to lock your door at night. Just twenty-three people. That's all."

Then he did smile, but Lew wished he hadn't. It was the hard, brittle smile of an executioner.

"Soon," he whispered, "there will be twenty-two."

Lew swallowed. He said nothing. There was nothing to say.

After a long moment Kane spoke again, his voice lower now, hushed as if with reverence.

"And then there will be twenty-one. Then twenty. Then nineteen. One by one, hour by hour, they will fall to me. Like flies to the spider. Until there is no one left."

Kane gazed down at Lew Hannah, his blue eyes shining with what had to be madness.

"I'm going to kill you all, you see. Every last one of you. Every man, every woman, every child. By morning, there will be nothing left alive in this town of Tuskett, California. Nothing but weeds."

"You won't get away with it," Lew Hannah said. "You ... you can't."

A chuckle answered him, dark and mirthless. Nothing more.

3

In the driver's seat of his Chevy van, speeding down the Old Road at eighty miles an hour, Rile Cady was putting on a show.

That was how he thought of it, every time he started singing as he drove, admiring the rich basso-profundo tones of his voice as they echoed off the dashboard and the windshield. He was far from being a trained singer, and he had no illusions about the quality of the performance he turned out; he was, at best, a talented amateur, and at age seventy-seven he didn't expect to advance beyond that stage. Still and all, the singing pleased him. There was nothing he liked better than to take the van out for a spin, east to Jacob or south to Carlyle, streaking down the empty road killed by the interstates, with the windows rolled down and the dusty night air sweeping through, and open his pipes.

Of course, a little gin didn't hurt. Certainly it hadn't hurt tonight. He'd gone to Jacob earlier for the express purpose of getting snockered, and he'd succeeded admirably.

Rile never drank in Tuskett. For one thing, there were no bars in town; the last one had closed three years ago, when Wally Taylor went to San Diego to live with his sister in a retirement home by the sea. But even when Wally and the other barkeeps had been around, Rile had avoided drinking in town. He liked a good snort, but he wasn't eager to have his gossipy neighbors see him prancing like a stumblebum, especially when one of his several odd jobs required him to drive kids to and from the Jacob public school five days a week.

But when he was far from the town and its many eyes, he let her rip. He liked to pull up a barstool and knock back a few and tell the folks his favorite stories about how things used to be, long ago, when this part of the Mojave had been even less developed and less densely populated than it was now, assuming such a thing was possible. And if anybody, drunk or sober, was in a position to tell those stories, he was. He'd spent his whole life in Tuskett, though in the early days it had carried another and perhaps more fitting name: Desolation.

Rile Cady was born in Desolation on June 28 of the year 1913, precisely one year to the day before an archduke by the name of Ferdinand got himself shot. He remembered his childhood as a blessed time; and if, half a world away, men were gasping out their lungs in clouds of poison gas as tanks rolled over corpse-lined trenches, he was thankfully unaware of it.

Where he was, there was no war; there was only the great hot sweep of the desert, the biggest playground any boy ever had, filled with rare and beautiful treasures—the shimmering thickets of paintbrush and beardtongue blooming in the spring; the merry dance of the butterflies, viceroys and admirals, ladies and blues; the song of the white-throated swift and the flight of a golden eagle. Some people thought the desert was dead, but only because they had never lived on it, had never seen its abundance of marvels.

There were few people in Desolation, and they lived

with nature always close at hand. It was a hard life—harder, no doubt, than he was willing to remember—but a rewarding one. His father, Justin, ran a general store, an outfit not too different from the grocery store Lew Hannah looked after now. Rile had reached his sixteenth year before he realized that Justin Cady was something special, that in the larger world outside Desolation's borders, a colored man didn't own a business in a town where nearly everyone else was white. But this was the desert, and it hadn't been too long ago that settlers had banded together in these parts to fight off raiding parties of Yumas and Mojaves; even in the dawning decades of a new century, enough of the frontier spirit remained to ensure that a man was judged on performance and nothing else. Justin Cady was good at what he did; his store was the best in town. People respected him for it. They tipped their hats to him.

There were a few other stores in Desolation, and a filling station to service the Model T Fords and similar contraptions that came chugging down the Old Road. Even then, the road had been the town's lifeblood—even before there was a town worthy of the name.

The town proper began in 1920, when Kirby Tuskett settled in Desolation. The old man Tuskett, as he was called. Unlike everyone else Rile had ever met, the old man Tuskett had money, scads of it. What he was doing in the hinterlands was a question nobody raised with him. There were rumors, however, rumors of business deals back east that had gone bad, the sort of business deals that flourished beyond the law. It was whispered that Kirby Tuskett had planted himself in this forsaken patch of desert to save himself from being planted, in a more permanent fashion, in concrete.

But nobody really cared about that, any more than they cared that Justin Cady was a black man. In Desolation, as in dusty desert towns the world over, there were many men without a past.

Kirby Tuskett owned a fine car, a GM roadster with the loudest horn Rile Cady had ever heard, before or since, and a chauffeur to drive it for him. He paid to have a house put up, the nicest house in town for thirty years thereafter, until it was lost in a fire in 1950. He even hired a butler, a thing unheard-of in Desolation. Kirby Tuskett, it appeared, believed in making the best of a bad situation. If he had to live in the trackless isolation of the Mojave, at least he was going to do it in style. And so, when he had settled in at his new house, he set about improving the town itself.

Out of his own pocket he put up the money for the water tower that, ever since, had loomed over Joshua Street. He had the streets paved and a sewer system installed. By some means never discovered, most likely a threat or a bribe, he arranged to have power and phone lines strung all the way from Jacob to Desolation, across fifteen miles of desert; Rile Cady was eight years old when electricity and telephone service came to his town.

Folks had tolerated Kirby Tuskett from the start; but by the time he was done making his improvements, they loved him. He could have been elected mayor on a unanimous vote, had he ever chosen to run. He didn't. He had no interest in politics, in local affairs, or even in getting to know his neighbors on more than a passing basis. He kept to himself mostly. He avoided conversation. He wasn't gruff, not exactly, but he was distant, and on his face he wore a look somewhere between sadness and resignation. Sometimes, in the evening hours, folks would see him standing at the edge of town by the side of the Old Road, under the humming power lines his influence had bought, gazing eastward, like a man expecting company.

On a hot summer night in 1926, a night very much like this one, his company arrived. All over town, folks heard the sound of gunshots, six in all, from Kirby Tuskett's house. Some claimed to have heard the squeal of tires on the Old Road as an unknown car sped away into the night; but others swore there had been no car, only those gunshots, then silence.

The party of men that went inside the house, Justin Cady among them, found two corpses on the ground floor—the butler, garroted, and the chauffeur, his throat cut. Both men must have died silently, because it was clear that Kirby Tuskett never suspected anything amiss. He was found in his bathtub, the bathwater stained red, a half dozen bullet holes scoring his chest. In death his features had smoothed out into an expression that might have signified peace.

In the days that followed Kirby Tuskett's burial, the people of Desolation debated how to best remember him. He had been, after all, their greatest benefactor. And it was remarked by more than one person that after all the good works the old man Tuskett had done, the name of Desolation scarcely suited the town anymore.

Now, nobody in these parts ever doubted for a minute that the man they'd known as Kirby Tuskett had been living under an assumed name. But nobody knew his real name either; and for that matter, nobody much cared. The name on his grave marker was Tuskett; and it would be only fitting, they concluded, if the name of the town he'd helped to build was the same.

And so Desolation was no more. From then on, the town was Tuskett, California. It had been Tuskett ever since.

Rile Cady smiled, thinking of that story. He enjoyed telling it, even embellishing it some when the fancy took him. It was, perhaps, the only genuinely romantic incident in the town's history.

A billboard, half eaten away by time and wind and the rare but punishing desert rains, swept past. TUSKETT, TWO MILES, it said, STOP AND STAY AWHILE. A man peered over the steaming rim of a coffee cup, flashing a frozen smile at the dead road.

Rile eased his foot down on the brake pedal and slowed the van to forty. He kept on singing. The song was a drunken sailor's ditty he'd learned from an ex-Navy man who'd passed through town decades ago on his way to LA. It was salted with vulgarisms and laced with obscenities; not the sort of thing he'd care to have Jenny Kirk or Debbie Hanson hear out of his mouth—they being the only two moms who still had children of schooling age in Tuskett. He shook his head sadly, thinking of that. The only two. Once, his van had been loaded full up on morning and afternoon runs; now his cargo consisted entirely of Tommy Kirk and Johnny Hanson, and Johnny would be out of school in two years, probably to vanish over the horizon on the trail of the same Pied Piper that had carried off all the other kids.

The outline of the Tuskett Inn swam into view, looming like a haunted house against the sky. He stopped singing, as he always did when he got within sight of home territory. It just didn't feel dignified to be carrying on like that in your own backyard.

He slowed to a crawl and eased off the main road onto Joshua Street, a maneuver he'd performed so many times he could have done it by feel, his headlights off or eyes shut. He turned into the weed-littered field where his trailer was parked, killed the van's engine, and got out.

The night was clear and warm and still. He stood by the van, listening to the slow tick of the engine as it cooled, hoping to catch a cry of girlish pleasure from Eddie's place. He heard nothing. The lovebirds must be pooped out already, fast asleep or sharing a cigarette, if that Cox boy ever took a smoke—which, considering his absence of vices, seemed unlikely.

Rile started walking toward the door of his trailer, feeling his joints pop the way they always did after a long drive. Halfway to the trailer, he stopped, looking at the front steps, where a small shadowy figure was huddled in a fetal pose.

Rile blinked. "Tommy? That you?"

Tommy Kirk lifted his head into the pale moonlight. His face was an expressionless mask. His eyes glinted, wide and unblinking. His mouth was set tight, as if to dam up a flood of screams. His lower lip trembled like a plucked rubber band.

"Tommy. Jesus jumped-up Christ in a chariot-driven sidecar. What are you doing here?"

The boy stared at him, just stared, his eyes brimming with tears and with some terrible secret he would not share.

Rile let a moment pass while he took a deep breath, hoping to clear his head of the alcohol swimming in his brain. Then he walked over to the boy and crouched on the steps, his bones creaking with the effort. He stroked Tommy's hair.

"How long have you been sitting here, son?"

There was no answer. Tommy stared into space. His T-shirt rose and fell with slow, steady breathing.

"Come on, now," Rile pressed. "You can tell me. What happened? You get into a dogfight with your mom? You know, she's bound to be worried sick over you."

Still nothing. Tommy sat and stared. Rile thought of a cat mesmerized by a dangling string.

He searched the boy's face for any flicker of life. Slowly a realization came to him. The child was in shock.

Something had happened to him, something that had left him stunned and speechless.

Slowly Rile got to his feet, feeling a momentary rush of tipsiness and wishing to Christ that he hadn't chosen tonight to tie one on.

"Okay," he said quietly, collecting himself. "What I say is, we go inside and pour ourselves some milk. And make a phone call."

He took Tommy by the hand, such a small hand, pale and delicate, like a fragile desert flower. He helped the boy up the stairs to the door of the trailer, pushed the door open, and led him inside, out of the night.

Tommy hadn't meant to go to Rile Cady's place. He'd intended to run straight home, just like Chief Hannah had told him. But when he got a few dozen steps from the dump, he found himself outside the pale circle drawn by the headlights of the police chief's car; and the sudden sense of being alone in the dark hit him like a blow. He staggered and nearly fell. He looked back over his shoulder, thinking of going back to hide in the car, but it was too close to the dump and to the shadows where the man—the bogeyman—must still be hiding.

So he started running blindly, zigzagging up the Old Road till he reached Joshua Street, and finally stumbling into the trailer park. He ran past Eddie Cox's trailer, dark and silent. Briefly he considered banging on the door to wake up Eddie. Something stopped him. He'd never liked Eddie Cox, though he couldn't say why. The man was big and husky and friendly—too friendly—and he had a smile that wasn't quite right, like a jack-o'-lantern's lopsided grin. Thinking of that smile, Tommy remembered the sickly crescent that had bloomed on the stranger's face as he strode out of the night.

He ran faster. He had to get away from that trailer,

from anything that reminded him of the man with ice-blue eyes and bony, bloodied hands.

He raced across the field, trampling bunchgrass and locoweed. Rile Cady's trailer shot up in his path. When he realized what it was and who lived there, he took the steps two at a time and hammered the door and wished he could call Rile's name, but his voice still seemed to be stuck at the back of his mouth.

Nobody came to the door.

For the first time, Tommy noticed that Rile's beat-up old Chevy van was gone. He must be away somewhere, out for a drive. Out of town. And Tommy was still alone. Alone, in a night crowded with shadows and death.

All his energy left him, like water spiraling down a drain. He had no strength even to go inside the trailer, though he was sure the door was unlocked. His legs folded, and he sank onto the steps and lay in a boneless heap, shivering and crying and wishing he wasn't so afraid, and the night wind hissed in its chortling, secretive whisper behind his back.

Some unknown length of time passed that way, before Rile Cady returned.

Tommy had lifted his head to gaze up into the old man's face. It was a face he knew as well as his own. Rile was his best friend, except for his mom, and moms didn't count. With Rile, you could do things you'd never do at home, like swear and spit and laugh at dirty jokes. Tommy had passed many happy hours in Rile's company, sitting in his trailer and hearing him spin stories of the way things used to be around these parts when he was a younger man, or taking rides with him in that rust-bucket van to explore the desert and learn the names and ways of the wild, secret things that lived there.

So if there was anyone in Tuskett he could talk to, it was Rile. But when Tommy tried to talk, he couldn't, just couldn't. It was exactly like when Chief Hannah asked him those questions in the dump; he'd wanted to answer, but nothing had come out. He seemed to have lost the power of speech, or even the power to nod or point, to communicate in any way. It was as if a barrier had been put up between him and the world, an invisible wall, and embedded in that wall was a pair of disembodied eyes commanding him to keep silent.

He wanted desperately to disobey that order. He heard his own voice, loud in his mind, pleading with Rile to hear him. But of course Rile couldn't hear. Nobody could hear. Tommy thought of those nightmares where you know you're dreaming and you want to wake up, but you can't. This was like that. Only worse, because he wasn't dreaming.

And worst of all, he knew that the nightmare had only begun.

In the darkness of their bedroom, Todd and Debbie Hanson lay peacefully asleep on opposite sides of their double bed. Moonlight, filtering through the curtains, rippled over their faces. Debbie Hanson was on her back, motionless save for the slow rise and fall of her chest. Next to her, Todd Hanson rested on his side with his cheek pressed to his pillow, his gray head tinted silvery-blue.

As they slept, a shadow crept over them, an elongated, almost skeletal shadow, a shadow in the shape of a man.

The shadow hesitated, as if selecting its prey. Then it moved forward, silent as a breeze. Darkness swallowed Debbie Hanson. She slept on.

Out of the dark came a knife, a carving knife with a serrated blade. It was a knife from the kitchen drawer, a knife Debbie had used earlier this evening to cut up the frying chicken she'd bought at Lew Hannah's grocery store. After dinner, she'd washed the knife, dried it with a dish towel, and put it neatly in its place, and there it lay till the drawer opened under the pull of a pale hand with long fingers and bony joints. That hand held the knife now, guiding it toward Debbie Hanson's throat.

In her sleep, Debbie made a tiny, scared noise, a kind of whimper, and her eyelids twitched as if with dreams.

Another hand, a twin of the first, reached down out of the dark and closed over her mouth, choking off further sound. The sudden pressure shocked her awake. In the instant when her eyes opened, the knife plunged into the soft flesh underneath her jaw and drove upward at an angle, bursting through the roof of her mouth and into her brain.

Debbie moaned. Her eyes bulged. She tried to struggle, but some vital connection had been broken, some circuit linking brain and body; her muscles twitched as feebly as the limbs of a dissected frog touched by an electrode.

Beside her, Todd Hanson mumbled under his breath but did not wake.

The knife was forced in deeper, an inch at a time, sinking into her flesh in fits and starts, trembling like a dowser's rod. Debbie moaned again, a low, piteous sound, barely audible; she shuddered all over and lay still.

The hand released its grip on her mouth. Her jaw hung down. Her tongue lolled.

With infinite care, the knife was withdrawn from her neck. It came away slick with blood, dripping on the sheets.

The shadow glided around the bed, circling like the shadow of a hawk on the desert floor, a hawk spiraling toward its prey. It reached Todd Hanson. Slowly it extended, draping him in black, a funeral shroud.

This time it was quick. The knife vanished up to the hilt, buried in Todd's neck. His head jerked up. His eyes were open wide, their irises rolled up in his skull, only the whites showing. He tried to scream, but emitted only a brief hiss of breath through gritted teeth. Then his features smoothed out and he dropped his head back onto the pillow, gently, with no fuss, like a man nodding off to sleep.

The knife was pulled free. The shadow receded like a black tide, leaving behind two corpses. Their wounds leaked slow trickles of blood, flowing like molasses, thick and glittery. It made a low gurgling sound.

The shadow stole away, silent as an angel of death.

Johnny Hanson lay rigid in his bed, staring into the dark, listening.

He'd been sound asleep until a minute ago. All of a sudden he'd sat upright, heart racing. Bad dream, he figured.

He didn't get bad dreams too often. Most of the time he had no trouble sleeping. Getting up was the problem, rising to face another summer day in this dead Dogpatch town, a town with more geriatrics per square inch than the average nursing home, where the only way for a guy of sixteen to pass the time was to hang out at Bill Needham's gas station and play paddleball and watch the bugs die of heat prostration.

He tried to remember what kind of nightmare he'd had. He drew a blank. But something sure as shit had made him wake up with his heart beating like a rock drummer.

Well, whatever it was, it didn't matter. His heart was already slowing down to the legal speed limit. Waves of sleepiness washed over him. By morning, he wouldn't even remember that he'd awakened during the night.

He had just eased his eyelids shut when he heard a muffled moan from his parents' bedroom.

That was when he started listening. He couldn't be sure, but it had sounded like his mother's voice. Maybe she was having a bad dream too. Or maybe ...

A slow grin blossomed on Johnny Hanson's face.

Were they making it? His mom and dad?

The thought was funny, but at the same time it kind of gave him the creeps. It just didn't seem natural for your parents to fuck. That was something other people did. It occurred to him that never before had he heard any noise from their bedroom that might be the least bit indicative of passion.

The moan came again, softer this time, fading out.

Yeah, he thought. They're doing it, all right. Dad's getting some tonight.

He felt a stab of pride for the old man. He guessed there was some life in him yet.

He wondered what had gotten them hot. His dad had fallen asleep watching the Dodgers game; shortly after, his mom had switched the channel to an old Burt Reynolds movie while her husband snored beside her in his easy chair. Around nine o'clock Johnny had walked through the living room on his way to the kitchen to get a soda; he'd glanced at his mom and dad, one comatose with sleep, the other blank-faced and waxy-pale, and he'd flashed on an image of corpses laid out in an embalming room.

And now, from what he could hear, they were going at it like newlyweds. He shook his head. It just didn't figure.

He heard a new sound, different from before. A low, prolonged hiss, like steam escaping from an overheated radiator. Then silence.

He didn't know what the hell that was. Orgasm, maybe. His dad might have sucked in breath to keep from crying out. Christ knew, the two of them were secretive enough about doing it. He guessed small-town folks were just uptight by nature.

Drawn by curiosity, he pressed his ear to the wall.

At first he couldn't tell just what it was he heard. The sound was faint and indistinct. Not conversation, that was for sure. And not rustling sheets or laughter or any other noise you might expect. This was more like ... running water. Or like his dad gargling with Listerine.

The sound went on, reminding him of a babbling brook on the relaxation tape his mom sometimes played. A low, gurgling sound.

Johnny Hanson drew back from the wall. For the first time he wondered if something was maybe not quite right in his parents' bedroom. If maybe the noises he'd heard were not what he'd assumed.

He was still thinking about it when the door to the master bedroom creaked on its hinges, swinging open.

In the hall, a footstep. A quiet footstep, muffled by the carpet and by stealth, but unmistakable.

Slowly he turned his head to face his bedroom door. The door was almost, but not quite, shut. A hairline crack let in faint orange light from the bathroom down the hall, where a night-light glowed.

Another footstep. Closer.

Well, so what? asked a small, rational, but oddly unpersuasive part of Johnny's mind. Your mom's just gotten up for a drink of water, that's all. And she's checking on you first. To make sure you're sleeping okay. Moms always do shit like that. It justifies their existence.

Except he knew it wasn't his mom. He knew the sound of his mom's footsteps, and his dad's too. The person outside his door was neither of them.

He heard another step, very close. His door began to inch open, making no sound.

He stared at it as if hypnotized. At first he thought it was his imagination—the door wasn't really opening—but then he saw that the crack of light was almost imperceptibly widening.

The door eased open the rest of the way, revealing a tall figure in silhouette against the orange glow, the figure of a man in a battered cowboy hat and a shapeless coat that fell below the knees. A man Johnny had seen once already, walking toward the town out of the sunset sky.

There was a knife in his hand. It dripped.

Johnny felt his Adam's apple jerk once, like his paddleball on its rubber string.

The man stepped into the room. His coat rustled around him. The floorboards creaked under his slow approach. He made no other sound, not even breath.

Johnny stared up at him. He knew he had to get away. Had to get out of bed and climb through the window. Had to do something, anything, except lie here with his heart hammering in his ears. But he couldn't move. His body was as rigid as a block of ice.

The man reached his bedside and leaned over, masking the light from the hall, leaving nothing but darkness. Johnny caught a glimmer of light directly above him, which was the knife, and an answering flash of silver, which was a canine grin.

"No," Johnny said. "Don't."

The words came out as a throaty rasp. They sounded dull and hollow and useless, which of course they were.

He waited, knowing what would come next.

He didn't have to wait long.

Jenny Kirk nearly screamed when the telephone rang.

She'd turned off the TV long ago, not to hear its maddening chatter, then paced the living room till her legs threatened to give out. She didn't know what to do. She wanted to leave the house and search for Tommy on foot, but she was afraid to miss Lew's call.

For the thousandth time she checked her watch. Ten thirty. An hour and a half had gone by since Tommy should have been home. There was no way he could have lost track of that much time. Which meant he was in trouble, some kind of trouble. Hurt or sick or ... She didn't know. She ran a shaky hand through her hair and felt her gorge rise dangerously, and that was when the telephone in the kitchen went off like an alarm.

She spun to face the kitchen doorway, then ran for the phone, nearly tripping herself in her haste to grab the receiver. "Hello?"

"Jenny? Rile."

She wondered why he sounded so funny. No, not funny. Upset. Scared, maybe. The way people sounded when they had bad news to report. She experienced the sudden terrifying certainty that Tommy was dead and Rile had been chosen to let her know. But no, that couldn't be. Because Rile wouldn't do it over the phone. He would come in person. He and a dozen other people with grim expressions and downcast eyes. That was how it was always done around here. She herself had been a member of a group like that, six years ago, when Betty Andersen's girl Laura fell off the water tower and broke her neck.

All of that went through her mind in the instant it took for her to reply, "Yes, Rile? What is it?"

"I've got your boy here."

Relief washed over her and started her trembling worse than before. She felt sick at her stomach all over again. She lowered her head against a rush of faintness and groped for something to hold on to, finding the kitchen wall. She pressed her palm to it and watched her fingertips whiten as the blood was squeezed out.

Rile was still speaking, rather slowly, his words oddly slurred. Part of her wondered if he'd been drinking. It seemed unlikely. She'd never known him to take a drink.

"... so I took him in," Rile finished. "Poured him some milk. He's here now."

Jenny took a breath. "He's not hurt?"

A pause. "No. Not so far as I can tell. But I'm afraid he is acting a bit peculiar."

"What do you mean?"

"Well"—he chuckled, a weak, forced sound, like a cough—"he's not talking, is what. Giving me the old silent treatment." He said it lightly, but tension lay under the words like a body under a sheet.

"You mean he's not saying anything? Anything at all?"

"Not a word."

The fear that lived in her gut was back, twisting her insides like strands of spaghetti around a fork. Her son was a talker. He loved questions and noise and showing off, all the things that were as healthy for a growing boy as air and sunshine. For him to just sit there, dumb as a ventriloquist's dummy in a carrying case ... She didn't know how a thing like that could happen or what it might mean. But it scared her.

In that moment Jenny Kirk understood a little something about herself. She'd never really been tested by life. She'd allowed herself to take this detour on her way to Malibu, and she'd stayed in this shitty, dying town with the excuse of a steady job and a dirt-cheap house to hold her here, and she'd shunned romance and even close friendship the way a diabetic shuns sweets. She'd cocooned herself in a dull job and a safe routine, unthreatened by outside forces.

Now, for the first time since she'd awakened to find

Mike gone nine years ago, she was faced with a crisis. And she couldn't handle it.

Panic clawed at her. She forced herself to stay in control. If not for her sake, then for Tommy's.

"Okay, Rile." She kept her voice inflectionless. "Thanks. I'll be over."

"I can bring him to you, if you like."

"Oh, yes. Please. If it's no bother."

"None at all." He hesitated. "It'll be all right, Jenny."

He clicked off. She stood holding the phone to her ear. The dial tone hummed its idiot tune.

She had to figure out what to do. But it was so hard to think straight. She set down the receiver and leaned against the wall, eyes closed, trying to bring order to the chaos of her thoughts. The first thing was a doctor. Yes. Take Tommy to the doctor. That meant Jack Evans, naturally. Jack would be asleep by now. He and Millie turned in early. Well, she'd have to wake them up, that's all. Of course. Everything was so simple when you just stayed calm.

She pressed her hand to her mouth and chewed at her knuckles, unaware that she was doing it. Fragments of what Rile had told her broke into her thoughts like shards of glass punching through cloth.

He's not talking ... Giving me the old silent treatment ... Not a word ...

The room spun. She found a chair at the kitchen table and sank into it and willed herself to be strong.

After a long moment she raised her head, remembering something. Lew. He must still be out looking for Tommy, probably just as worried as she herself had been. Not to mention Ellyn, waiting in her house for some word. Getting more nervous and worked up by the minute, most likely, and not knowing which to worry over more—Jenny's boy or her own husband.

Jenny drew in a deep breath, then got to her feet. She picked up the phone to call Ellyn Hannah and let her know that Tommy had been found and Lew could come home.

"Lew. Come in, Lew. This is Ellyn. Answer, if you can. I've got some good news for you. Lew, do you read me? ... Lew ...!"

Ellyn Hannah sat at a table by the bedroom window, hunched over her husband's police-band radio, the microphone in her hand. She'd been trying to reach Lew for ten minutes, and so far she'd had no luck. And that was strange.

Of course, there were plenty of reasons why he might not have answered. Most likely, he'd simply left the car to explore some spot where a small boy might be—the old motel, maybe. That made sense, perfect sense. Ellyn really wasn't worried at all, and what she couldn't understand was why the short hairs at the nape of her neck insisted on standing up, the way they always did when she was afraid.

"Lew," she said again, expecting no response, receiving none. Static crackled over the radio like a hard, steady rain.

She put down the microphone and gazed out the window, which framed a view of the darkness outside. Normally the Ford Tempo would be parked at the curb. She didn't like seeing the street empty. A flash of motion at the corner of the window made her shift her focus. She watched a tiger moth beat its yellow wings against the window screen. The screen, she noted, was getting ragged; there were two or three small holes in the wire mesh that would allow an enterprising insect to get through.

She looked at the radio, still hissing like a fuse. It was

a small, squat, ugly metal box, a virtual antique. It always sat on this low table by the window, ready for use in case of emergency. There were few emergencies in Tuskett, though. The last one had been three summers ago, when Toby Wilks had gone off wandering in a dead drunk. Lew had been sent to look for him, and not until he'd circled the town fifty times had Nora Wilks realized her husband was curled up asleep behind their house, with fat August horseflies buzzing on his rugose nose. Nora had been so embarrassed, she and Toby had picked up and moved to Arizona the next month.

Ellyn Hannah shook her head. Even that hadn't been the same. She'd felt none of this slow, creeping worry then. The worry had been brought on by the fact of an outsider in Tuskett—a pale man, with something unsettling about his eyes. And, yes, she'd noticed the unsteadiness in Lew's voice and the nervous flicking of his tongue when he recounted the incident in the coffee shop. That man Kane had put a scare in him, though he'd refused to admit it; and anybody who could rattle her husband was a man she wanted very much not to meet.

She tried the radio again.

"Lew ... Come in, Lew. Damn it all, answer me!"

Abruptly the radio sputtered to life.

"Hello, Mrs. Hannah."

She drew back in her chair, staring at the radio as if it were a living thing.

It had been a man's voice. But not Lew's.

Remembering the microphone, she pressed it to her lips. "Who's that? Who's on the other end?"

"You don't know me."

"How'd you get on this frequency?"

"I'm using the radio in your husband's car. But you already knew that, didn't you?"

"What's going on here? Who the hell are you?"

"My name," the voice said, "is Kane."

Suddenly she was cold all over. The room was far away. She looked down at the microphone in her hand. But it was not her hand. It belonged to somebody else, somebody who was living through this, somebody who would surely know what to do.

Her lips worked, forcing out speech like paste through a tube.

"Where's Lew? What's happened?"

The radio barked with a brief burst of laughter.

"What have you done to him?"

There was no answer, only the mindless static hiss.

She dropped the microphone and stood. The room tilted, spun, then steadied. She took a step away from the table. The radio gazed up at her with its grillwork of insect eyes.

She had to call somebody. Call the police. But Lew was the police. The only policeman in town. And he was ...

She couldn't think about it.

The police band sizzled with a new transmission.

"I have a surprise for you, Mrs. Hannah." A beat. "Look out the window."

She didn't move.

"Go on," the voice said. "Look."

Reluctantly she raised her head toward the window. And there it was. Their Ford. It was parked at the curb where it belonged, not ten feet away. The headlights were dark, the motor off. It must have coasted down the street, silent as a barracuda, while she was preoccupied with the radio.

A man was at the wheel. She could see him clearly. He wore a hat on his head and a dark coat, just as Lew had described him to her. He was turned sideways, looking at her. Even from a distance she caught the feral glint of his eyes.

Then he shifted in his seat and raised his right hand. Something was clutched in it, clutched tight in bony fingers that reminded her of a falcon's claws.

Two thoughts hit her simultaneously.

He can see me just as sure as I can see him.

He's got a gun.

There was a crack of sound, and a new hole was punched in the wire mesh of the window screen.

Ellyn staggered backward. Suddenly her chest was shot through with dizzying pain, pain so intense it was almost unreal. She'd never felt such a terrible hurt in all her life. She looked down and saw something dark and sticky flowing from a round hole in her blouse. It took her a moment to realize that the hole was a bullet hole and the tacky wetness was blood.

"Oh, God," she whispered.

She put her hands to her chest and pressed tight, trying to plug the wound, but the blood kept running, pouring down her blouse in crisscrossing rivulets, like rainwater or tears. Then there was another distant bang, and she thought for a terrified moment that he'd shot her again; but when she raised her head to look out the window, she saw that he'd merely slammed the car door after getting out.

He paused at the side of the car, a scarecrow figure with a gun in its hand. Then he started walking. Walking toward the house. Coming for her. Coming to finish the job.

She made a sound that was more than a whimper, not yet a moan. She backed away from the window, moving in soundless slow-motion, unable to take her eyes from the man centered in its frame. He walked casually, in no hurry, taking his sweet time. Distantly, past the high, thin cicada buzz in her ears, she heard the crunch of his boots on the dead lawn.

What she had to do was simple enough. She had to run. Get out of the house. Get away. Now.

She turned and stumbled into the bed and fell sprawling across the rumpled bedspread. She tried to get up but, oddly, she seemed to have lost control of her body. Her fingers were all tingly with that pins-and-needles feeling you got when your hand went to sleep on you, and her eyes were dazzled by white spots whirling like the plastic flakes in a snow globe.

She swayed with a rush of faintness. The world lost its colors, going gray. She looked down at the bed and saw spilled blood everywhere. The bedspread was soaked, dripping.

That's me, she thought. That's me all over.

She tried to laugh, and coughed up a ribbon of red spittle.

Behind her, the window screen rattled in its frame.

She turned her head, drawn by the sound. He was prying at the edges of the screen, the gun tucked under his belt. He was smiling.

She made a last effort to get off the bed and run, but it was like moving underwater; her limbs were heavy, her reactions slowed to one-quarter time, and she couldn't get her legs to work. She slid off the bed onto the floor and rolled over on her back and lay there, helpless as an upturned tortoise, staring at him as he tugged the screen loose and tossed it aside.

He hoisted himself through the window. His boots thudded on the floor. He took a step toward the radio and shut it off, silencing its hiss. Calmly he removed the gun from his belt.

It was Lew's gun. His Colt .38, the one he carried in the glove compartment. She moaned, seeing it.

Kane heard her. Slowly the corners of his mouth curved up in a smile. His teeth were stained red. Stained ... with blood.

Still smiling, he crouched on the floor by her side and leaned in close. His breath was hot on her cheek. His face filled her world. She thought of her dentist in Jacob, Dr. Whitter, and how he would smile as he loomed over her with a syringe full of Novocain. It was a comforting thought. She never minded trips to the dentist, even when there was drilling to be done. And she would much rather imagine she was reclining in that cushioned chair in Dr. Whitter's office than ... than what? She didn't know. Of course she was in the dentist's chair. Where else could she be? She'd gotten a bit lightheaded there for a minute, but that was okay; Dr. Whitter was an understanding man; he wouldn't mind.

The doctor reached out with his free hand and tugged at her chin to open her mouth. She let her jaw drop loosely, unresisting, while part of her heard him say in his calm voice, "Don't you worry, my dear. This won't hurt a bit."

I know it won't, Doctor, she wanted to say. But since she could say nothing with her mouth hanging open, she only smiled.

The needle slid into her mouth. She tasted it with her tongue; it was smooth and cold, and had an oddly metallic flavor. And it was so large. This must be an awfully big dose of painkiller that Dr. Whitter was giving her.

"Good-bye, my dear," Dr. Whitter said softly, and she just had time to wonder what he meant—such a peculiar thing for a dentist to say—in the moment before he pulled the trigger.

Ten minutes earlier, at a quarter to eleven, Wendell Stoddard's police-band radio had come unexpectedly to life.

He was cruising down a stretch of the Old Road between Jacob and Tuskett, watching the shine of his high beams on the cracked macadam and drumming his fingers on the steering wheel. His thoughts were far away. In his mind he was replaying a memory of the great event that had taken place three days ago, that priceless, forever-to-be-treasured moment when Melody Stoddard, eighteen months old and cute as a button, had struggled to her feet and, with tremulous concentration, taken her first steps. Her tiny feet had carried her nearly a whole yard before she lost her balance and plopped down on her rear. Then, naturally, she started crying, and Jill comforted her and told her what a good baby she was, while Wendell himself just stared, his jaw slack and eyes wide, struck dumb by the miracle he'd witnessed.

His daughter ... had ... walked.

He'd been unable to get the memory out of his mind. It kept coming back to him, mixed in with other images, images that weren't even real. Melody walking to school ... Melody walking out the door on her first date ... Melody walking down the aisle in a bridal gown ...

Come on, Wendell, a reproachful voice—his own—whispered in his ear. She's only eighteen months old.

Then the radio started crackling like old newspaper, cutting into his thoughts.

"Lew," a faint female voice was saying. "Come in, Lew. This is Ellyn. Answer, if you can ..."

The woman, Ellyn, kept talking, but the rest of her words were lost in a blizzard of static. Still, Wendell had heard enough to have a fair idea of what was going on. The Lew in question must be Lew Hannah, Tuskett's chief of police; most likely he was out on patrol, and his wife, Ellyn, was signaling him.

Wendell knew all the local cops, Lew Hannah included. Not that Lew was a cop. Well, okay, technically he was. But there were so few people left in Tuskett, so little law and order to worry about, that Lew's badge was largely a formality. By Wendell's way of thinking, a real cop didn't run a grocery store to keep up the payments on his Ford Tempo. A real cop didn't carry his gun in his glove compartment instead of on his hip.

Wendell, on the other hand, was indisputably a real cop. State trooper. Highway patrol. Riding solo, keeping an eye open for license plates on the hot sheet, pulling guys over for violations of the speed limit, which in these parts was sixty-five and not a hair faster.

Oh, some smart-ass types looked down on the highway patrol, smirking know-it-alls who thought there was no danger in handing out tickets and cruising the interstates and the back roads. But they were wrong. There was danger, plenty of it. Any car a trooper pulled over might have some loony-tunes at the wheel with a gun in his hand. Especially in California. In California, people took shots at each other on the freeways; it was like a sport to them. And bodies were always turning up in the Mojave, buried in drifts of sand, feeding scorpions and pomace flies; often they'd been dismembered. There was an undercurrent of craziness in this state that seemed to attract and nurture a certain kind of sociopathic fruitcake. Most of them lived in LA or Frisco, but the desert got its share.

Wendell had been in the highway patrol for only a little over a year, and he had yet to run into any dangerous characters. But he knew they were out there. He heard stories. Like that guy who ...

The voice on the radio faded in again.

"Come in, Lew. Dammit all, answer me!"

Wendell frowned, hearing the note of desperation in Ellyn's voice. Lew Hannah just might be in some sort of trouble. He was still wondering about it when a new voice came over the air, a man's voice, a voice that was strangely cold, even chilling, though Wendell couldn't have said why.

"Hello, Mrs. Hannah," the voice said.

A beat of time passed in silence. Wendell listened, intrigued, while the road hissed under his tires at sixty-five miles an hour.

"Who's that?" Ellyn asked finally. "Who's on the other end?"

"You don't know me."

"How'd you get on this frequency?"

The man answered, but the static had risen again to a buzzing roar, drowning out the words. Wendell turned up the volume, but made out only fragments of conversation.

"What's happened?" Ellyn asked

"... surprise for you ..." That was the man. "Go on. Look."

Then there was no more talk, or at least none Wendell could hear. But at some point during the minute or two that followed, there was a sharp crack, which might have been a beat of static, or ... might not.

Wendell considered picking up the mike and contacting Ellyn Hannah to see what was going on. But he didn't want to do that. If he used the radio, he'd be broadcasting his suspicions to everybody on that frequency. Not smart.

The same held true for calling in a report to his dispatcher. Anyway, he didn't want to call in a report. It was probably nothing. Most likely he'd misunderstood the conversation entirely. Or maybe some joker was playing a prank on a ham-radio outfit; it happened. As for that bang he'd heard—hell, he picked up all sorts of snap-crackle-pop on the radio.

He didn't want to embarrass himself by making a report that didn't amount to doodly-squat. On the other hand ...

Tuskett wasn't far. He could drive into town, take a

look, even check in on the Hannahs and reassure himself that they were okay.

Why not? He had nothing to lose.

Wendell turned the car around, executing a wide U-turn on the empty road, and headed back toward Tuskett, while the memory of his baby daughter's first steps poked at the corner of his mind and made him smile.

Jenny Kirk stood very still, hardly remembering even to breathe, while Jack Evans knelt before Tommy and examined his bare arms and legs.

She knew what the doctor would see there, of course. She'd studied the damage herself, as soon as Rile arrived at her house with Tommy in tow. Her son's skin was peppered with fresh cuts, tinged purple at the edges with dried blood, and huge blue-black bruises standing out sharply like tattoos.

But none of that was the main reason for rousing poor old Jack and his wife, Millie, from bed at a quarter to eleven on a Tuesday night, so Jack could conduct a medical exam in his living room. The reason was that Tommy still wasn't talking, wasn't showing the slightest inclination to talk.

Jack ran his hand over the worst of the contusions, then let out a low whistle.

"My, oh, my. Whatever did happen to you, Tom-Tom?"

Tommy said nothing.

Jenny willed her son to talk. To be himself again. To run and make noise and yell and break things, even.

A memory swam into her mind, the memory of a rainy day two years ago when Tommy, housebound, had been running and shouting and carrying on. Out of carelessness or clumsiness or frustration, he'd body-slammed the cabinet in the hall where she kept her knickknacks, mostly mementos of her aborted trip to LA. A glass ashtray she'd picked up in Little Rock had nosedived to the floor and exploded into a million needle-fine splinters. Damn, had she been mad. She'd actually struck the boy—something she'd sworn she would never do—struck him on the cheek. He'd run to his room, red-faced and sniffling. That had been his punishment for being loud and clumsy and full of life, for being a little boy—and how much money would she give now, how many dime-store ashtrays, to see him like that again?

She lowered her head, fighting back tears, then felt a hand close over hers. Rile Cady's hand. His fingers were callused, leathery; they had the feel of an old glove, careworn and cracked at the tips and joints. She liked that feel.

She smiled at him, a weak halfhearted smile, but better than none at all. He smiled back. A fine smile, a curve of perfect white teeth which served as proof of his often-repeated boast that he'd never suffered a single instance of tooth decay in his life.

That smile suited him. He was getting on in years—he must be somewhere in his seventies—but he was still an impressive-looking man, hale and vigorous, his black face framed with a mane of shock-white hair, his eyes alert and sparkling.

Maybe a tad less alert than usual, tonight. She'd noticed the liquor on his breath as soon as he walked into her house. It didn't matter, and she would never gossip about it; still, it was a small shock. She couldn't remember ever seeing Rile Cady take a drink. It seemed faintly astonishing to think there were some secrets people could manage to keep in a town this size.

Jack Evans finished checking Tommy's injuries, and nodded to himself. He looked the boy square in the eye. "I guess you don't want to talk much about what happened to you, huh?"

The boy looked at him, his face blank.

"It must've been darned scary, that's for sure. But whatever it was, it's over now, and you're among friends, so why don't you tell us what it was?"

Nothing.

Jenny wasn't surprised. If her boy wouldn't talk to her or Rile, he sure wasn't going to open up to Jack Evans, a man known to him chiefly for sticking his arm with needles.

Jack seemed to arrive at the same conclusion. He got up and belted his terry-cloth bathrobe, which had come undone, exposing the faded plaid of his pajamas.

"You know, Tom-Tom," he said in the kindly voice that made him everyone's first choice to play Santa at the annual Christmas party, despite his regrettable absence of paunch, "I do believe my ears detect signs of activity in the kitchen." He pretended to listen. "Indeed they do. I hear ... blueberry pie." He raised his voice. "Millie? Is there a blueberry pie making a racket in there?"

Her voice lilted through the kitchen doorway. "I'm afraid so, Jack. Only way to keep it quiet is to gobble it up. Anybody out there who can help me?"

"I think we can round up a volunteer." He patted Tommy on the behind. "Go on, Tom-Tom."

Tommy went, not running, just walking obediently out of the room. Like a robot, not a boy. Jenny stared after him and tried to keep her eyes dry.

Jack seemed to feel the same way. He shook his head sadly, then crossed the living room to Jenny and Rile. His slippers flapped on the carpet. The left slipper was worn through and his bare toes stuck out.

Dr. Jack Evans, general practitioner, was the only doctor Jenny had seen in the nine years she'd lived in Tuskett, and the only doctor Tommy had seen in his life. It was Jack, in fact, who had delivered her son, and it was

Jack who got Tommy through a night of raging fever when the boy was just four. He was a fine doctor—everybody said so—a healer of the old school, who combined a lifetime's experience with wide-ranging knowledge gleaned from constant perusal of the latest medical journals. Jenny trusted him completely.

He wasn't much to look at, though. Jack was at least ten years Rile Cady's junior, but unlike Rile, he looked his age. Part of the problem was that he wasn't the sort to look after himself; he had a habit of lounging in his pj's till noon, and he rarely remembered to comb his hair or shave his stubble of beard. He was absentminded, always muttering to himself and scratching his chin and forgetting that his fly was unzipped. In all this, he was his wife's opposite. Millie Evans was obsessed with neatness; her kitchen—with its glowing floor, immaculate countertops, and perennial aroma of Lysol—was as orderly and sterile as a chemistry lab.

Jack and Millie retired every night at nine, and rose at daybreak. She puttered around in the garden and the kitchen, and he worked on his collection of Indian arrowheads, painstakingly assembled over the years, and occasionally saw a patient. They had three children, all of whom had left home and gotten married, and who were now strangers save for birthday cards and rare long-distance calls.

"Well," Jack said as he reached Jenny's side, "physically he seems okay, except for the obvious things. A few Band-Aids and some bacitracin will take care of that. He's had his tetanus shots, so we don't need to worry on that score. As for his behavior ... Well, he's had a bad shock."

"What kind of shock?" Jenny asked.

"Beats me."

Rile cleared his throat. "I've been thinking. Suppose he got chased by an animal. Coyote, maybe. That could put a scare into anybody."

"Haven't heard too many stories of folks around here being chased by wild animals," Jack said dubiously. "Coyotes are known to keep their distance, mostly."

"Might've been rabid."

Jenny shivered. "Oh, God."

Jack shot a warning look at Rile that pretty much requested that he keep his damn mouth shut. He patted Jenny's arm.

"Your boy's got no bite marks on him. I told you, physically it's just some scrapes and bruises, the kind of thing every boy gets when he's been roughhousing."

"Didn't say he got bit," Rile persisted, refusing to be put off. "Said he got chased. Why not? It fits what we know."

Jack glowered at him briefly, but did him the courtesy of considering the possibility. "Yes," he said finally, "it does. But there's another thing to take into account."

"What's that?" Jenny asked.

"Well, it's quite a coincidence, don't you think? This happening on the same night when that new fellow shows up in town?"

Jenny blinked, baffled. "What new fellow?"

"That man Kane."

He said it like it was common knowledge. The name meant nothing to her. She glanced at Rile and saw bewilderment on his face as well.

"Kane?" she asked. "Who is he?"

Jack shrugged. "That's a good question. I've heard a lot of speculation on the topic, but I'm not sure anybody knows. Personally I—"

"Jenny!" The voice was Millie's, and it came from the kitchen. "Would you come in here, please?"

There was something in the way she said it that let

Jenny know there was trouble, bad trouble. She broke away from Jack and Rile, crossed the living room at a run, and burst through the kitchen doorway.

Millie Evans was kneeling by Tommy and holding him tight, while Tommy shivered all over like a wet dog. Ribbons of gooseflesh bumped up on his arms and legs. His gaze was fixed on the kitchen table, where the pie was set out on a china serving plate, a large-handled carving knife beside it. The knife was smeared with purplish goo, the blueberry filling, which hung off the blade in dripping, glutinous gobs.

Like blood, Jenny thought. Like dripping blood.

She grabbed the knife and shoved it into a drawer, out of sight.

Instantly Tommy stopped shivering. His legs folded under him. He sank onto the tile floor, lifeless again, showing no expression, no hint of personality, no flicker of the boy he had been.

Jenny knelt beside him and hugged him and ran her fingers through his hair, talking to him, whispering his name, praying for him to speak, to show her some acknowledgement, to be okay, and all the while Tommy said nothing, did nothing, just sat there and stared and stared and stared.

Charlie Grain stepped through the doorway of the Hannah house, looking around warily.

Only a few minutes earlier, he'd been standing in his kitchen thinking good thoughts about Gretchen Lewis and the new life the two of them would build together. He had a can of Coors in his hand, and he'd just popped the tab to pour himself a cold one and celebrate this special night, when he heard a sound—a distant, sharp crack like an echo of the pop-top, or like a gunshot.

He stood listening. The night breeze, warm and sultry, stirred the curtains of the kitchen window. They rustled, ghostlike.

Then he heard another sound, different from the first; it might have been the slam of a car door. A moment later, there was a second sharp crack that sounded for all the world like the report of a pistol.

It had come from close by, somewhere down the street. Only one other house was still occupied on this end of Second Avenue. Lew and Lynnie Hannah's house. And Lew kept plenty of guns around.

Reluctantly Charlie had put the beer can down on the counter and gone outside, into the night, determined to find out what was up.

So far he'd seen no sign of trouble. Lew's car was parked at the curb, as usual. Outwardly, at least, the house was quiet and undisturbed. The front door was unlocked, but that was hardly cause for concern, not in Tuskett. And the living room was neat and orderly. Everything was just the same as always.

Still, he had a feeling. He couldn't put his finger on it, but he knew in some wordless way that something was wrong.

He almost called Lew's name. Then he remembered those sounds he'd heard in the night, sounds that could have been—must have been—gunshots. He kept silent.

Cautiously he made his way through the living room, past the grandfather clock, ticking sedately, and the coffee table scattered with back issues of *National Geographic,* their yellow-bordered covers promising adventure in exotic lands with unpronounceable names, and the cast-iron German shepherd, reproduced in one-quarter scale, which stood guard over a potted candy-barrel cactus.

He looked into the den. It was empty. The TV was on, tuned to the news. A reporter stood on a street corner, his face harshly lit by the glare of an off-camera light. He was talking about a gang shooting in south-central Los Angeles. Tuskett got all the LA broadcasts.

The camera panned down to focus on long smears of blood striping the pavement. The reporter went on speaking, his voice a monotone. Three people were dead, four injured. All were reputed gang members. Minors, he said—which meant they were children. Children who prowled the streets on a Tuesday night, armed with automatic weapons, living the life of jungle animals, ready to kill or to be killed in defense of the graffiti-scarred landscape that was their turf.

It was nothing new. Things like that happened all the time in LA. The city had a sickness, a disease born of drugs and gangs and guns; every night the LA newscasts confirmed it all over again. And whenever he caught a report like this, Charlie would watch with a sense of sorrow—yes, sorrow for young lives so horribly twisted and so thoughtlessly snuffed out—but with a certain smugness too, a sense of superiority that came from knowing that nothing so awful could ever happen here, that in Tuskett he was safely removed from crime and craziness, that here, at least, he was safe.

He didn't feel safe tonight.

He stared at the TV for another moment, no longer seeing the images, just looking at the flickering picture tube and thinking about the fact that the room was empty and the set had been left on.

Charlie knew the Hannahs nearly as well as he knew himself. Lew and Ellyn had spent their earliest childhood years in the midst of the Great Depression, just as he had. The hard times had left their mark. Neither he nor they would ever throw away a perfectly good rubber band or use a hundred-watt lightbulb when sixty watts would do. And under no circumstances would they leave the TV on when nobody was around to watch it.

Not unless something had happened to them.

Charlie turned from the doorway to the den, then stopped, hearing the creak of a floorboard, somewhere on the far side of the house, where the bedroom was.

It was probably nothing. This house was as old as his own, and, as he well knew, the timeworn dry wood could make some darn peculiar noises as it settled in for the night.

On the other hand, it just might have been the sound of a footstep.

He waited. He swallowed once. The click of his Adam's apple was loud in his throat. He heard nothing more.

Part of him wanted to get out. Get the hell out and run for help. Call the state police or the cops in Jacob or the county sheriff. Call anybody.

But another part of him, calmer and more reasonable, told him he had no business leaping to conclusions. What was he going to tell the cops, anyway? That he'd heard some noises that could have been shots fired in the night or a screen door banging in the wind? That he'd gone to investigate and found a TV left on in an empty room?

He had no proof anything was amiss. Just a gut feeling. His gut might be wrong. Lew and Lynnie might have gone for a walk and forgotten to shut off the damn TV; it happened. Or they might be out in the backyard watching the stars. Or in the bedroom making whoopee. Anything was possible.

Before he started making hysterical telephone calls like a paranoid old woman, he needed some solid facts.

He took a breath, then walked quietly down the hall.

The bedroom door was ajar. He peered inside. The room was dark, the lights off. Dimly he made out the silhouette of the bed, its cover rumpled and shapeless. He looked around but saw nothing else.

Carefully he pushed the door open and stepped inside. He groped for the light switch. The lamp on the night table came on. The green-shaded bulb cast a wan, sickly light over the room.

The first thing to catch his eye was the window. The screen had been removed—pried off, it looked like. He hadn't noticed that from outside, what with the bedroom being dark. He didn't like it. It was a sign that somebody might have broken in here. To burglarize the place, maybe.

He glanced from one part of the room to the other, seeking other evidence of trouble. His gaze flicked from the police-band radio on the table by the window, to the framed oil painting of Lynnie's mother on the far wall, to the antique dresser near the closet, to the closet door, sensibly shut, then to the bed with its rumpled spread ...

He hitched in a breath, staring.

The bedspread wasn't merely rumpled. It was stained with a purplish-brown ooze which had run in crisscrossing rivulets through the hills and valleys of the cotton fabric's jumbled folds, and now was dripping off the bedspread's tassels onto the carpet, each drop falling silently, with metronomic precision, like the Chinese water torture, and gathering in thick, viscid puddles, puddles of ...

Blood.

Charlie circled the bed slowly and stared down at the floor where Ellyn Hannah lay on her back, her mouth open, eyes wide and glassy, like marbles. The back of her head had exploded onto the carpet in a spatter of bleeding red meat, which was her brains.

An image flashed in his mind. A hamburger sizzling on the grill in his coffee shop. A patty of ground round, frying in a pool of fat. Crumbs of meat dropping off at the edges. And, he thought numbly, if he were to take that burger and douse it with ketchup till it turned all sticky-red, then stuff it inside somebody's skull—Lynnie Hannah's skull, say—and blow it out her ears, why then, he would have exactly the same pretty sight he was seeing right now.

His stomach rolled. He burped. The sound was gross and tasteless and somehow obscene under the circumstances. He couldn't help it. He would be reverent later, at the funeral. Right now he just felt sick.

Got to close up the shop even sooner than I thought, he told himself as his mind whirled. Can't ever fry up another burger again.

He took a step backward, away from the body on the floor, thinking that now was the time to run and call the cops, because this was all the evidence he needed, and then, very simply, without any fuss at all, the closet door opened and Kane was there.

Charlie looked at him, then at the gun in his hand.

A beat of time passed in the silent room, and in that moment Charlie Grain drew back from the situation confronting him and considered his options with a calm, almost radiant clarity of mind. Kane, he thought, no doubt expected him to do one of two things—either to make a run for it or to stand frozen with fear. In the first case, he would be shot in the back before he even reached the bedroom door. In the second case, he would be shot in the heart. In neither case did he have any chance to survive.

But there was a third option, one that might not have occurred to Kane. He could fight. Yes, he was unarmed, and he wasn't young or agile or strong, not like he used to be. But he was cornered, and a cornered man, no less than a rat, could bare his teeth and make a stand, and maybe, just maybe, take his enemy by surprise.

Kane raised the gun a half-inch, aiming it squarely at Charlie's chest; his finger was poised to pull the trigger.

What the hell, Charlie thought, his calm unbroken, his detachment complete.

He drew back his left leg, as if inching toward the door. He let Kane see it. He watched the slow smile blossom on the man's face like an evil flower, a white rose on a fresh grave. He waited till he was sure Kane believed he was going to cut and run and make a bull's-eye out of his back. Then he struck.

He sprang at Kane, pistoned out his arms, and slammed his bare hands into the man's chest. He felt a hard thud of impact. He caught a glimpse of Kane's face, his eyes wide, smile frozen. Both of them stumbled into the closet door. It banged shut. Charlie's hand closed over Kane's wrist and he squeezed hard, and, miracle of miracles, the gun squirted free and thumped on the floor at their feet.

Charlie experienced a brief thrill of victory, which lasted until he realized Kane was laughing. He kept on grappling with the taller man while his mind raced with fevered questions, trying to figure out what was so goddamned funny, and then he understood.

He had not forced the gun out of Kane's hand. Kane had dropped it deliberately, to even the odds. This was a game to him, a sport, a contest of wills and wits and cunning, nothing more.

"You bastard," Charlie breathed. Kane only laughed harder, his lips stretched wide over chipped teeth and pale, bloodless gums, his breath hot and dry on Charlie's face like the desert wind.

With a sudden sideways move Kane tore free of Charlie's grasp, both of his arms coming loose in an eyeblink, the sleeves of his coat flapping like wings.

Charlie grabbed for him again. Kane whirled, making him miss. His coat twirled like a cape. Charlie tried to catch hold of it, but the fabric slipped through his fingers.

A steel-hard fist caught him in the gut. He wheezed, tasting vomit, and doubled over. Bare knuckles slammed down on his skull and set off a fireworks display. His legs were yanked out from under him. The room tilted. The floor rushed up. He crashed into the carpet. Reality seesawed. He tried to get to his feet. A boot caught him in the side. He heard a crunch, the wishbone snap of a rib. He coughed, and something red and bubbly came up. He crawled on hands and knees, mewling and whimpering like a dog.

Then he blinked, seeing something on the floor, an object he almost recognized.

The gun.

It lay on the carpet, in the shadow of the dresser. If he could grab it, turn it on the son of a bitch, blow his head clean off ...

Just like in the movies, he thought. Happy ending. Everything turns out okay.

A boot toed him in the chest. He grunted. The floor dipped and rolled, swanboating on green swells of nausea. He fought to stay conscious. He still had a chance. One chance.

With his last strength he lunged for the gun. His hand closed over the barrel. Cold steel singed his fingers. It felt good, like the frosty sting of the Coors can he'd taken out of the fridge minutes ago, the can that would still be waiting for him when he got home.

He pulled the gun toward him, and Kane's boot came down hard, stomping on his hand, shattering his knuckles like ice cubes.

Charlie tried to scream, but only a strangled groan came out. He stared at the boot inches from his face as it twisted savagely, grinding his hand into the carpet like a fleshy spider crushed under a sadist's heel. His arm throbbed with pulses of white agony, racing up his neck to sizzle like strokes of lightning before his closed eyelids.

The boot was lifted. Charlie told himself that whatever happened, he had to hold on to the gun, because the gun was his only hope. But it was no use. Every bone in his hand was broken. His fingers drooped like the fingers of an empty glove.

Kane kicked the gun out of his hand and sent it spinning into a corner.

Charlie Grain was a dead man. He knew that now. There was no hope, no chance, no way out. He lay on the floor on his belly, offering no resistance, waiting bleakly for the end.

Kane seized him by the arm and hauled him to his feet and flung him down on the bed like a doll, with a cymbal crash of mattress springs. Charlie landed on his back. He gazed up at Kane, looming over him, and for the first time he noticed how terribly tall the man was, and how cadaverously thin, like a walking skeleton, his leather-tough skin stretched taut over creaking bones.

Then Kane leaned in close, and Charlie was reminded of his daddy bending over to give him a good-night kiss when he was a little boy, half a century ago. His dad had been lucky. He had died in his sleep. That was the way to go. Everybody said so.

Kane reached behind Charlie's head and picked up something and held it in both hands.

A pillow.

Charlie stared, unable to react, as the pillow came down and covered his face. He was swallowed by darkness. He could feel Kane's two hands through the foam stuffing, pressing down hard, driving the pillow into his skin, his bones, cutting off air, smothering him.

His body lashed out. His legs kicked and writhed. He clawed at Kane with his good hand. He felt his fingertips sink into the man's cheek and peel off flesh in long, twisted grooves. Distantly he was aware of the mattress shaking under him like one of those bucking broncos you could ride for a quarter.

It was no use. Kane only pressed harder. And Jesus, the bastard's hands were strong, like slabs of iron, like lead weights, crushing the life out of him.

Charlie heard a dim, hysterical mewling, the sound a puppy would make on its first night away from its mother, and it took him a moment to understand that he was making that sound as he squirmed and flailed, fighting for the life that was deserting him along with the last dribble of air in his lungs.

He opened his mouth wide, sucking air, tasting only stale cotton and foam rubber. His nostrils were pinched shut. His head pounded. His brain buzzed. His ears roared. His awareness was fading out.

His last thought was of Gretchen Lewis and the new life he'd meant to share with her, the life which, like that cold and frosty can of beer, now lay forever beyond his reach.

Meg Sanchez stared moodily at her typewriter and willed it to give her some inspiration. She was sure there was a story here. A lead story for next week's edition of the *Clarion.*

Just think of it, she told herself. A man walks into town—walks, for God's sake, *walks* off the desert on a blistering summer day—and takes a room at Ethel Walston's place. Doesn't explain why he's here or what he's after. Doesn't say a damn thing except that Tuskett is a good place to die, whatever that means, if it means anything at all.

Hell, it was the most interesting development in this town in years. There had to be a lead story coming out of this, dammit.

Only there wasn't.

The problem was, she had nothing solid to report. She didn't know the first thing about the man. Of course, that itself was the story. He was a mystery man. But even the mystery wasn't solid enough, substantial enough, to set down in print. She didn't know how to begin. She couldn't think of a headline or an opening sentence. She couldn't think of a damn thing.

In the coffee shop, as she sat watching Kane and talking with him, she'd been sure there was something strange about him, something not quite right, something that had set off whatever journalistic alarm bell she possessed. But now it was gone. When she thought back on what had happened in Charlie Grain's place, it seemed distant and unreal. Looking at the matter objectively, as a good reporter must, she knew that all that had taken place was that a man had taken a stool at the counter, ordered coffee, been taciturn and peculiar, finished his coffee, and left. Even in Tuskett, that was hardly front-page news. Hell, it wasn't news at all.

She pushed her chair away from her desk; the chair legs scraped irritably on the hardwood floor. She stared into space. She could feel it coming on again, the way it always did. Depression, settling over her like a shroud.

Of course, everybody got depressed sometimes. But with her, it was more than feeling blue. It was as if a black thunderhead had rolled in to blot out every bright light in her life. And it could happen so suddenly, with no more justification than this—a typewriter that wouldn't cooperate by doing her the small favor of writing the story itself, or a story that wouldn't cooperate by agreeing to be bigger than it was. She'd been feeling pretty good an hour ago—hell, she'd been flying, soaring on adrenaline wings, believing she'd finally gotten herself a news item more worthwhile than a bake sale or the pitiful display of terpsichorean incompetence at the July Fourth party. This was the kind of story she'd been waiting for. And now the story had popped like a soap bubble, leaving a vacant space in her mind, which the depression rushed in to fill.

And she was afraid. Because in this inner darkness, this sudden pall cast over her world, she felt she was capable of anything. Suicide, even. One reason she'd never bought a gun was that she didn't feel she could trust herself with it.

She sat very still, her shoulders slumped, her head lolling on her chest, and thought about her life.

Meg Sanchez had been born in Arizona, fifty-seven years ago come September 3. The town she grew up in was dirt poor and dying; she spent her childhood in a fever of anticipation to leave. At seventeen, she did. She set off on her own in a Trailways bus, with no notion of where she was headed; she figured she'd know it when she found it. And when the bus stopped off in Tuskett, she got off for good.

The town had been different then. It was bursting with energy and confidence, a regular boomtown. The interstates had yet to be built, and everybody heading east or west through this part of the country had stopped here. It was hard to remember, but the streets and shops of Tuskett had been crowded back then. You saw all kinds of people here, but especially young ones, single men fresh from the service and couples just starting out—the kind of people who now existed in Tuskett only as flickering shapes on TV picture tubes.

It had been the opposite of her hometown. Tuskett was a place of youth and life and opportunities. She loved it.

So she settled there, and built herself a life. Things happened. She got married and pregnant, not in that order. The baby came early and died. Her husband blamed her for it in a dark, secret, wordless way. That was when the quarrels started, ugly, nightly quarrels that escalated into ten-round fights with no winners. The divorce, when it came, was a blessing. That had been thirty-six years ago; she'd been only twenty-one at the time. She'd never remarried. She'd started the newspaper instead.

She thought of the *Clarion* as the husband and baby she'd lost. It had occupied her days. And it had made money too, enough money to permit her to devote her full time to turning out twelve pages twice weekly, pages stuffed with news and gossip, then eventually more gossip than news. Meg was no psychiatrist, and self-analysis was hardly her strong suit, but even she could figure out that her anxious interest in other folks' lives was a kind of compensation for the emptiness of her own. But she did have the paper. It was enough.

Then a terrible thing happened, more terrible, perhaps, than the death of her child. The interstates were built. And slowly Tuskett began to die.

The town dried up like an old well. The people left. The cars stopped coming. The paper shrank to eight pages, then to four; now it came out only twice a month, and even on that schedule, what news there was had to be stretched out, the way you might stretch a pound of hamburger by mixing in bread crumbs. The paper was no longer a moneymaking proposition and hadn't been for many years. And in her dark moments, like this moment right now, she wondered if anybody in town besides herself even bothered to read its contents anymore.

But she couldn't give it up. To let the paper die was to experience another loss, the most painful one of all. How many of her loved ones did she have to lose? How many children?

Her house was paid for. She had money in the bank.

She'd never been a spendthrift, and when the *Clarion* had been profitable, she'd socked away a fair amount. She could live in modest comfort for the rest of her life. She could afford the small luxury of keeping the paper alive.

Even if there was no news, and no point to it anymore.

She fumbled at the pocket of her blouse and found her cigarette pack. She lit one. They caused cancer, of course. Everybody knew that. She didn't care. Sometimes—most times—she thought cancer would be a blessing, just like the divorce had been. An end to pain.

She exhaled a smoky plume and thought about a seventeen-year-old girl who'd climbed aboard a Trailways bus to escape a dying town. Now, forty years later, here she was in another town, deader than the first.

What goes around, she thought wearily, comes around—and in spades.

She looked at the typewriter. It grinned at her with its shiny black rows of keys. Grinned like a cat.

"Screw you," she told it. She took another drag on the cancer stick.

Of course there had been no story to write. She should have known that. This was Tuskett, California, the ass-end of the universe. Nothing of interest ever happened here.

Shortly after eleven o'clock, Wendell Stoddard guided his patrol car off the Old Road, into the town of Tuskett, and headed up Joshua Street.

His first thought was to check out the police station in the hope of finding Lew Hannah there. But when he glided past the station house at two miles an hour, the place looked dark and empty.

Okay. The next thing to do was check out Lew's home. The problem was, Wendell had been to the house only twice, and he couldn't remember where it was. He wound up cruising the side streets, looking for the Hannah place and hoping he'd recognize it.

At eleven fifteen, he swung onto Second Avenue and struck pay dirt.

Halfway up the street, the Hannahs' house was plainly in view. And pulling away from the curb in front of the house, moving in his direction, was a Ford Tempo, Lew Hannah's car.

"All right, trooper," Wendell said to himself out loud, "let's find out what's going on here."

He rolled down the driver's-side window and leaned out just as the Ford was rolling past.

"Hey, Lew," he shouted. "It's Wendell. Listen, I—"

The man behind the wheel turned his head to look at him.

Not Lew. This was a stranger.

The Ford accelerated with a scream of tires, whipped onto Joshua, and sped off. Wendell gathered his wits and followed.

His thoughts came fast as he raced in pursuit of the shrinking taillights. It had to be the same guy Ellyn Hannah had been talking to. That was how he'd gotten on the police band in the first place. He'd used the radio in Lew's car.

He floored the gas, barreling down the middle of Joshua at seventy miles an hour. The night air knifed through the open window. The motor roared.

The Ford reached the end of town and hung a hard right onto the Old Road, heading west. Wendell followed. He thumbed the switch that set the domelights flashing and the siren wailing like a banshee. The Ford still wouldn't stop.

"Arrogant bastard," Wendell breathed, and grinned at himself as he walked the car up to eighty-five.

He was enjoying himself. Part of him was scared, and part was angry; but most of him, a good ninety percent, was having a ball. Because this was the real thing, folks. This was the first honest-to-God action he'd seen since he put on a trooper's uniform fourteen months ago.

He felt a powerful impulse rise up in him, an impulse to scream his head off, and he gave in to it, raising his voice to the sky like a moon-dreamed dog.

"Yeeeehah!"

He kept his foot on the gas, closing the gap between himself and his prey. The Ford was now only a few yards away. Wendell unhooked the mike from under the dash and jabbed the button that activated the loudspeaker on the roof.

"Pull over," he growled into the mike, and was pleased to hear his amplified voice boom in stentorian tones. "This is the police. You are under arrest."

The Ford kept going.

Wendell swung into the eastbound lane, nursed the patrol car up to ninety, and eased alongside the Ford. For the second time, he looked at the stranger at the wheel. Once again he spoke into the mike.

"Repeat: This is the police. You are under—"

The stranger smiled, a cold smile like icicles, and slowly he raised a pale bony hand, which held a gun.

It went off, blowing out the passenger-side window and planting a chunk of lead in Wendell's right shoulder. He screamed. Instinctively he clutched the wound. The steering wheel spun free. The patrol car went into a skid, twirling crazily. Centrifugal force pinned him in his seat. He was reminded of the Tilt-a-Whirl at the amusement park in Carlyle, and how much fun it had been to ride that iron cage as it swooped and dived and threatened to bring up your lunch. For five seconds or five years the car kept spinning before it bounced off the road onto the desert hardpan, sending up a cloud of alkaline dust, and shuddered to a stop.

Wendell sat in his seat, gripping his shoulder and breathing hard, while dust stung his eyes and drew bitter tears.

"Shit," he mumbled. "Oh, shit."

He turned in his seat and craned his neck to see if the Ford was gone. It wasn't. It had stopped a hundred yards away, and now it was executing a slow U-turn like some dark predatory fish circling for the kill. Its headlights homed in on him, filling his world with lurid ghost-white radiance.

He's coming to get me, Wendell thought in shivering terror. Coming to finish me off.

It was all clear to him then. The stranger had never really wanted to escape. The high-speed chase had been only a ruse to get Wendell out of town, into the wilderness, where he could be dispatched without witnesses.

He knew he ought to call in a report. It was standard procedure in situations like this to get on the horn and squawk. Officer in trouble, request assistance. That kind of thing. But there was no time. He was way the hell out in the middle of nowhere; help wouldn't get here until much too late.

Instead he gunned the engine. The patrol car rolled forward, bouncing roughly over the rubble-strewn terrain, plowing over creosote bushes and mesquite. Wendell lurched in his seat; with every sudden movement, the bullet lodged in his shoulder shifted, sending needles of pain up his neck.

Behind him, the Ford's headlights bobbed up and down, and Wendell knew the car had left the road and was crossing the desert in pursuit.

He fumbled at his holster, clawing at the gun strapped to his hip, but, funny thing, he couldn't seem to get a grip on the handle; his fingers were palsied, spastic.

"Come on," he muttered low under his breath. "Come on, come on, come on."

Finally he got the gun out. He gripped it tight. It was a Smith & Wesson .32, the Regulation Police model. Its three-inch barrel gleamed, catching splinters of red and blue strobe-light from the roof of the car. The only time he'd ever fired the gun was at the shooting range, when his objective had been to put holes in menacing silhouettes. He'd scored pretty well at that game. But the silhouettes never shot back. That was the thing, see. They never shot back.

Up ahead, a Joshua tree, ten feet tall, swam into the glare of his high beams. He jerked the wheel hard to the left and brushed past the thing, its trunk scraping the side of the car.

Behind him, the Ford was closing in. Its headlights splashed white fire over the interior of the patrol car. And then the rear window exploded, spraying glass shards in a glittering rain, and Wendell realized the bastard had taken another shot at him.

He turned in his seat, took aim through the empty window frame, and squeezed off one round. One of the Ford's headlights winked out with a faint tinkle of glass.

"Got you," Wendell said shakily, and he was just taking aim again when more bullets flew in his direction, shattering the windshield, shearing off the sideview mirror, blowing away the headrest of the passenger seat.

Wendell stuck his gun out the window and fired again and again. That was a mistake; he was too badly rattled to take aim. None of his shots connected. Then the gun was empty, and when he pulled the trigger, it made only a hollow click.

He thought about reloading—there was more ammo in his gun belt—and then he glanced through the empty frame where the windshield had been, and saw the black hole of an abyss opening up before him, directly in his path.

An arroyo. The Mojave was littered with the things—riverbeds carved by centuries of erosion, foaming with rainwater in the flash floods that came with the winter storms, dry as bone in midsummer. Some of them were miles long and formed gorges fifty feet deep. Like this one, for instance.

He spun the steering wheel, veered sharply to his right, and sped along the rim of the pit. The Ford hugged his tail, then accelerated, ramming him. Wendell felt the ground squirt out from under his tires. The patrol car skidded closer to the edge. Sand and gravel poured down the sheer slope of the ravine in skittering millstreams. For a second Wendell was sure the lip of the arroyo would give way like quicksand and pull him down to the lightless bottom. Then he got the car back on track.

The stranger shot forward and smacked into him again. Metal groaned. The patrol car wobbled, and there was a bad moment when one of the tires left solid ground and swung out over the abyss. Wendell slammed the gearshift into second and pumped the brake and somehow regained control of the car.

He turned the wheel, trying to put distance between himself and the chasm to his left, but the stranger had other ideas. The Ford plowed into him again and knocked him back into line, then smashed into his passenger side and sent him into a bad skid, a killer skid this time. Wendell tugged uselessly at the steering wheel. His front end tilted down at a terrifying angle and the world was on the diagonal and he was sliding over the edge and there wasn't a damn thing he could do about it.

Wendell screamed.

The patrol car tumbled into the gorge, turning end

over end, sending up flurries of dirt and starting small rockslides as it went. The headlights blew out. The motor died. The domelight exploded. The siren wailed briefly, a ululant death cry, then was stilled. The tire axles cracked in half and flew off in all directions like broken barbells. The radio rattled free of the dash and broke into crazy jigsaw pieces. The lever that adjusted the position of the driver's seat snapped off, and the seat jerked crazily back and forth, slamming Wendell's forehead into the horn on the steering wheel; with each new impact, the horn blatted petulantly.

The car flipped over and over and over. Halfway down the slope, it nosedived into the rock wall, and its hood folded up like a squeezebox, hissing steam from a burst radiator. It pinwheeled for another fifteen feet, then plowed into a scraggly patch of mesquite that had somehow taken root in the sheer rock wall, and ripped it free.

A thousand years later the car crashed on its side at the bottom, teetered drunkenly, then flopped over on its belly and lay there at an angle, exhaling smoke and steam and dust, sizzling like an egg on a frying pan.

Wendell blinked, looked around slowly, and discovered to his considerable astonishment that he was alive. Oh, not for long, maybe. He was in a bad way, no doubt about that. With each breath, he experienced a stab of dizzying pain in his rib cage. His face was bloody, his vision blurred, his ears ringing. His mind seemed to be flickering on the threshold of a blackout. All in all, he'd had better nights.

After a long moment he decided he was not going to pass out. He sat there unmoving, his body alive with every species and genus and phylum of physical pain. He tried to figure out where the hell he was and what was going on. Then it came back to him. The stranger in the

Ford Tempo. The man with the gun.

Cautiously he shifted in his seat. Broken ribs cried out; he gritted his teeth and ignored them. The car was leaning toward the right on a forty-five-degree slant; it took a hell of an effort just to pull himself to the driver's-side window and look out. Somehow he managed it. He gazed up at the rim of the gorge. A huge Cyclopean eye, the Ford's headlight, glared down at him.

So the son of a bitch was still up there. Waiting. But for what?

To see if he was dead, maybe. Yeah. That just might be it.

It occurred to him that the stranger might actually get out of his car, descend the cliff on foot, and inspect the damage firsthand. If so, Wendell was finished. Oh, sure, theoretically he could fight back. His .32 was empty, but he had more ammo. He could load the gun, then crouch low in his seat and wait for the bastard to come near enough to make an easy target.

But he knew he wouldn't—couldn't—do that. He didn't have the strength. He couldn't pop the bullets in their chambers with his hands shaking like they were. He couldn't squeeze off a decent shot with his eyes all watery with tears.

If the man in Lew Hannah's car wanted to come down and finish him off, then Wendell guessed that was exactly what he would do.

He waited.

The Ford backed up, then turned, its headlights swinging in a lazy arc, tracing a trail of white luminescence like a comet tail. The car vanished into the night.

He thinks I'm dead, Wendell told himself, then smiled. Guess that's a good joke on him.

He laughed a little, then was racked with a fit of coughing as blood bubbled out of his mouth.

- — -

Bill Needham was staring out the window, into the black night, when the telephone rang.

He turned slowly in his seat and stared across the living room at the phone as it rang a second time, then a third. He made no move to answer it. He just sat and stared, while a premonition of disaster set his skin itching in a slow spider crawl.

It was eleven thirty. Nobody called at this hour. Not unless there was trouble. But then, he'd known there was going to be trouble, hadn't he? Ever since a man in a battered hat and a long black coat had appeared in the desert like a shadow cast by no object.

He let the phone ring twice more before he got up, crossed the living room, and answered.

"Hello."

"Bill?" It was Jenny. He remembered Tommy, out late, not hearing his mother's cries. He felt cold and scared.

"Yes, Jen?" He forced his voice to stay flat. "What can I do for you?"

"There's a problem. I found Tommya"—Bill shut his eyes in relief—"but ... but he's not himself. Seems scared. Won't talk. Jack Evans just gave him a sedative."

"What happened to him?"

"I don't know. Nobody knows. Like I said, he won't talk." Jenny's voice quavered, threatening tears, then steadied. "Anyway, that's not what I'm calling about. Not exactly ... Thing is, I've just heard the news about this man Kane. And I think ..." She swallowed audibly. "I think he's got something to do with this. I really do."

Bill gripped the phone tight. His voice was a whisper. "So do I."

"That's why I've been calling Lew's place, trying to get hold of him. But there's no answer. I know he was out before, looking for Tommy, because I asked him to. But as soon as Tommy turned up—he was over at Rile's place—I called Lynnie to let her know. That was an hour ago. She should've gotten hold of Lew by now. They should both be home. And nobody's answering."

Bill nodded, his mouth dry. "What can I do?"

"Well, I thought maybe I'd better go over to the Hannah place and take a look." She lowered her voice. "Rile's with me. And I'm sure Jack would go if I asked. But ..." She let the words trail off.

Bill understood. Rile was in his late seventies, though fit for his years. And Jack Evans, at sixty-five, was old before his time. Jenny didn't want to go nosing around Lew and Lynnie's house with those two. She needed a younger man.

Despite the circumstances, he almost smiled. It felt strange, having a woman need his help, his strength. In the nine years he'd known Jenny Kirk, this was the first time she'd ever asked him for anything.

But he didn't want her going anywhere near the Hannah house.

"I'll tell you what, Jenny. I'll go over there myself. You sit tight."

"Oh, no. I can't let you do that."

"Why not? Lew and Ellyn are my friends too. I've known them longer than you have."

"It's too dangerous to go alone."

Which was true, of course. He hadn't been thinking clearly. Funny how fast this macho stuff could go to your head and scramble what little sense you had.

"Okay," he said. "Tell you what. Rile has a gun, doesn't he? A shotgun?"

"I think so."

"Have him get it and meet me here. The two of us will go together. That's two men, one of them armed. Shouldn't be too dangerous that way."

He waited for her answer. "All right. If you're sure."

"I'm sure."

"I'll tell Rile, then." There was a pause; then she added in a whisper, "Thanks, Bill. I ... Thanks so much."

The dial tone hummed in his ear. Slowly he put down the phone. He thought about the way she'd breathed his name, her voice soft like a caress. He hoped he'd get to hear her say it like that again, sometime.

Kane guided the Ford Tempo down the Old Road at thirty miles an hour. The car was streaked with desert dust, its front fender dented and hanging at a lopsided angle; one tire had blown out, and the wheel was riding on its rim. The lone headlight cut a funnel of white light in the darkness.

He reached the edge of town and turned onto Joshua Street, driving slowly. His face was an expressionless mask, lit from below by the glow of instrument gauges on the dash. Beside him, on the passenger seat, lay the Detective Special formerly owned by Lew Hannah, its chambers empty, and the police-band radio from the Hannah house, its wiring ripped free and scooped out like the insides of a melon. On the floor of the car lay half a dozen lead pipes of all diameters and lengths, salvaged from the dump.

The car hit a pothole and bounced on its shocks. In the trunk, something bumped and rolled like a loose suitcase.

Scattered on the backseat was a small-arms arsenal, clinking like dinnerware as the car rattled over the rough road. A Smith & Wesson .32 and a Browning bolt-action rifle, both previously stored in the police station. A Llama .22 automatic pistol, found in the hall closet of the Hannah house. A Colt .45, removed from Todd and Debbie Hanson's home. A Winchester Sporter Magnum, previously owned by George Baker.

Lew Hannah had supplied Kane with the names of all the people in town who owned guns. One by one, the guns had been confiscated, their owners dispatched.

Now there was only one name left.

Kane reached the south end of Joshua Street and pulled into the trailer park. He shifted into neutral and coasted past the dark hulks of the abandoned trailers, overgrown with paintbrush and milkweed. Out of the dozen or so homes scattered here and there, only two gave the impression of being occupied. In both, the lights were out.

He drove to the far end of the field and parked the Tempo behind one of the empty trailers, where it could not be seen from the street.

He got out, then reached into the backseat and took the Colt .45 he'd obtained from Todd Hanson's house. He hefted it, feeling its weight. He checked the magazine. Seven shells glittered in the starlight. He nodded.

He raised his head to study the two trailers that had not been left to the weeds. In one of them, there lived a man with a shotgun, a man named Rile Cady, a man Kane meant to kill.

He moved his eyes from one trailer to the other. A long moment passed in silence.

Then he shrugged his narrow shoulders and started walking toward the nearest one, with Todd Hanson's loaded gun in hand.

PattiSue Baker stirred half-awake, hearing a noise in the darkness.

It came from just outside the door. A low, furtive scrabbling noise, the sound a rat might make running through the walls. She listened, intrigued. Then all of a sudden she knew what it was. She sat up in bed, sleep forgotten.

Eddie Cox was perhaps the only person in Tuskett who locked his door at night. He always had, for as long as PattiSue had known him. She suspected it had something to do with the paranoia always simmering inside him like a pot of bad chili. From her point of view, it had always seemed silly to worry about crime in a town this size; and in the early days of their relationship, before things had turned ugly, she'd even teased him about it. But now she was glad the door was locked.

Because somebody was on the other side of it, working the lock, trying to break in.

An image flashed in her mind, soundless as heat lightning, the freeze-frame image of a man with rattlesnake eyes.

Him. It was him. It had to be.

She rolled over and grabbed Eddie's arm, and for the first time in many months she was grateful for the size of that arm, the rounded hardness of his biceps, the strength that lay dormant there.

"Eddie," she breathed through gritted teeth. "Eddie, wake up."

He murmured. She tugged harder. He groaned.

"Eddie!"

His eyes opened, bleary with sleep.

"Huh? What's the matter, girl?" The words came out slurred, like a drunkard's speech.

She pressed her lips to his ear. "Somebody at the door," she said urgently.

"What?"

"Trying to get in."

He stared stupidly at her. He blinked once. Then comprehension flickered in his eyes.

He cocked his head, listening. PattiSue watched him. She was reminded, irrelevantly, of a dog pricking up its ears with its head tilted at an angle.

The low scrabbling sound went on, filling the stillness.

"Shit," Eddie hissed.

He flung wide the covers and rolled out of bed. He was naked save for yellow-stained Jockey shorts and an undershirt sweated dark at the armpits. His arms and legs were huge and hairy, almost apelike. She all but expected him to pound his chest with his fists and roar, King Kong in dirty underwear.

He padded on the balls of his feet to the bedroom doorway and peered into the living room.

"Fucking son of a bitch," Eddie Cox whispered, and she saw his shoulders bulk up with anger, saw his hands curl into fists, saw him stride through the doorway into the living room; and even though his back was turned, she knew what his face looked like in this moment, because it was the face she'd seen too many times before—the face of a crazy man.

In such a state, he was capable of anything. He might beat that man Kane into a coma. Kill him, even. Kane hadn't looked very strong; he was tall, sure, but all skin and bones. He was no match for Eddie, not when Eddie was wild like he was now.

PattiSue wanted to whisper a warning to Eddie not to hurt the man if he could help it, not to do whatever foolish thing he was about to do. But her voice had deserted her like a cowardly soldier under fire. Only a breathless gasp came out. She sat in bed, stiff with apprehension, gazing spellbound through the doorway at the scene about to be played out in the next room.

Eddie reached the front door and jerked it open to reveal the man on the steps.

PattiSue saw him standing there, the man called Kane, his tall figure outlined in a bluish mist of moonlight. In his right hand there was a steel-blue glitter that was a gun. She drew back on the bed, pulling the covers up around her. Suddenly she wasn't worried that Eddie would beat the living daylights out of Kane.

"Who the fuck do you think you ...?" Eddie began, but the words trailed away as he saw the handgun pointed at his chest.

"Rile Cady?" Kane asked.

Eddie took a slow-motion step backward, away from the door. Kane stepped into the living room, and PattiSue felt chills ripple through her with the awareness that the man was inside.

"Your name Cady?" Kane asked again.

Eddie found the wits to shake his head no.

"He lives ... across the way. You ... you got the wrong place."

Kane smiled. Even at a distance, PattiSue could see how his pale lips stretched up over his white teeth, like a coyote's snout wrinkling to bare its fangs.

"Too bad," Kane said. "For you."

He raised the gun a half-inch, aiming dead at Eddie's heart, and PattiSue knew, just knew, just *knew,* he was going to squeeze the trigger and blast Eddie to hell and then she would be next. She found her voice and screamed.

Kane jerked his head in her direction, and his eyes met hers across a space of fifteen feet. Cold blue eyes. Dangerous eyes. Eyes she'd found fascinating and mysterious not very long ago. And still did. Still did.

For a heartbeat he stared at her and she stared back, and something passed between them, like a current of electricity uniting them both. Her jaws snapped shut, making a single hard click like the snap of a briefcase; she trembled all over, her body rippling with shockwaves. She remembered how she'd stepped out of the shower once, dripping wet, and stupidly flicked a light switch;

she'd gotten a powerful shock. That had been like this.

Then Eddie struck.

Maybe he was taking advantage of the momentary distraction afforded by PattiSue's scream, or maybe he'd somehow sensed what had happened when the woman in his bed had looked into that man's eyes, and had been made reckless by jealousy. Whatever the reason, he threw himself at Kane with a sound halfway between a battle cry and a grunt of pain. He seized Kane's gun hand and wrestled with him for control of the gun.

PattiSue watched from some great distance, her bruised mind slowly turning black and blue.

A thunderclap of sound rolled through the trailer. The gun had gone off. The knowledge seemed remote, unreal.

Those eyes, she thought. Rattler's eyes.

The fight went on. Eddie and Kane were locked together in an insane waltz. They staggered together, banging into walls and furniture, breaking things. The gun went off again. Kane's hat slipped sideways, hanging from its chin strap, exposing a rat's nest of straw-colored hair, pallid in the moonlight.

Then Eddie shoved Kane hard, and the two of them stumbled away out of PattiSue's field of view, and she could only listen, fascinated, to the staccato beat of their footsteps and the intermittent bursts of gunfire and the sound of glass shattering.

The gun went off one last time, then made only a series of witless clicking noises, like the clacking of a single typewriter key, and PattiSue realized its bullets were spent.

That changed things. Eddie had the upper hand now. He could beat Kane's face to hamburger, crack his skull, pound him into the floor. And it would be good if he did that. Wouldn't it? She ought to think so. But the memory of those eyes still held her mesmerized. Eyes that had seemed to glow, catlike, in the dark. Eyes that had spoken to her and made secret promises.

Eddie appeared in the bedroom doorway again, his back to her. She looked past him and saw Kane step into view, watching him warily. He still had the gun in his hand, but he was holding it limply, indifferently; he let it go and it clattered on the floor.

The two men stood facing each other across the narrow living room.

"I'll kill you, man," Eddie said, forcing the words past shallow gasps of breath.

Kane smiled. "I don't think so," he said quietly.

"You get the hell out of here now, and I won't have to hurt you."

Kane just kept smiling. And PattiSue knew with sudden certainty that he was right to smile. Because he was going to win.

In her head, a faraway and dreamlike voice was telling her to save herself, climb out of bed and escape through the window while Kane was preoccupied.

She didn't run. She sat waiting, watching, while those lambent blue eyes danced in her memory, hypnotic as flame, and the small drama before her played itself out.

Eddie Cox didn't know what the hell was going on.

The guy who'd come barging in here was Kane. That much he knew. He matched the description PattiSue had given to a T. But what he was doing here—what it was he wanted with Rile Cady or with Eddie himself or with anybody in this two-by-four town—was impossible to guess.

Well, whatever it was he wanted, he surely wasn't going to get it. With a gun in his hand, he'd been a threat; now, unarmed, he was nothing. Eddie was almost afraid to go for him with his bare hands, out of fear that he'd kill him, really honest-to-God *kill* the son of a bitch. But if Kane didn't haul ass out of here, and soon, he was going to get what he had coming.

"One more time, pal," Eddie said. "You want to skedaddle, or do I have to break you clean in half?"

Kane looked at him and laughed, simply laughed; and it was the laughter that decided things. Nobody laughed at Eddie Cox.

Okay, asshole, he thought with something very much like glee. You asked for it.

He swung out with his fists. Kane ducked and dodged, lightning-quick. Eddie couldn't connect. He kept throwing punches, but it was like shadowboxing; nothing was there, nothing he could touch. Fury welled up. Kane was making a fool out of him. Eddie flailed, pummeling empty space, launching blows at the smiling face that always bobbed clear in the nick of time.

You son of a bitch, he thought in teeth-gritted rage. Come on, stand and fight like a man.

He lashed out again and again, and Kane weaved and parried with the suppleness of smoke, making him miss every time. He seemed to be enjoying himself. And he was smiling, still smiling, always smiling.

Eddie felt a dizzying rush of anger. All he had to do was make contact and he would knock that smile off Kane's face, all right; he'd knock the crazy bastard straight into an early grave. He had no compunction about killing him now. Hell, he was looking forward to it. He would take Kane apart piece by piece. If he could just lay his hands on him.

He couldn't do it. Kane was too quick for him, quick as the very devil. Eddie had to give him that much. But there were other ways to skin a cat.

Eddie picked up a chair, hefted it over his head, and

brought it down in a rush of air, aiming at Kane's skull, intending to smash wood and bone to splinters and put an end to this business once and for all.

But again Kane was too quick. He leapt sideways, his body a blur of motion almost too rapid to be perceived. Eddie had time to think it just wasn't possible for a man to react that fast, and the chair crashed harmlessly on the floor.

"God damn," Eddie Cox breathed.

Then something flashed in Kane's hand—a knife—and it was Eddie's turn to try dodging a blow; but, unlike Kane, he wasn't quick enough, not nearly. He was still tensing his body for a backward leap when Kane's hand shot out like an uncoiling cobra and plunged the blade deep into Eddie's groin.

Eddie stared in stupefied indignation at the knife, buried up to the hilt, while blood dribbled down his thigh.

"Shit." The word came out as an inarticulate wheeze. He clutched at the knife. His fingers closed over the handle. He fought to pry it loose. It was stuck. It wouldn't budge.

Kane was laughing again.

Darkness swam over him. He was going down. Down to the floor, sinking down on hands and knees and curling up in a quivering knot of shock and pain—and then down farther still, down into lightless mineshaft depths where the pain couldn't reach.

I'm blacking out, he thought with a last spark of awareness.

He almost did, and then new pain found him and tugged him up out of that comforting darkness into the ugly glare of reality.

Kane loomed over him, towering like some vast monolithic statue, his head swimming in shadows. One leg of the broken chair was in his hands, a caveman's club. It had smacked Eddie hard in the shoulder, and it was poised to strike again.

The chair leg circled down for a second time, sweeping out of the dark like a descending hawk. It caught him on the side of the head and set off a dazzling light show in his skull.

He blinked, fighting to stay conscious.

"Stop," he whispered. "Just stop, will you?"

Kane didn't stop. He slammed the chair leg into Eddie's knee, cracking bone. Eddie tried to get to his feet, fight back, grab that damn stick out of Kane's hands and use it on him. But his legs wouldn't respond; he kicked weakly at the floor like a baby that hadn't learned to crawl. The chair leg hammered him in the ribs. Immobilized by pain, he rolled onto his belly, cradling his head in his arms and whimpering,

Kane circled him, batting him again and again, while Eddie lay helpless, moaning and snorting up runners of snot and wishing Kane would stop—please, God, make him stop.

"Stop," he said feebly, just before the chunk of wood came down for a final time and split his skull.

PattiSue waited. She knew what was coming. She wasn't afraid.

She'd watched the fight, such as it was, through the bedroom doorway. She'd seen Eddie go down with a knife in his nether regions, and watched Kane beat him to death with a stick of wood from the smashed chair. Part of her—a small, smirking, secret part—had been glad to see it, glad to watch Eddie cower like a dog under the lashing of blows, glad to hear him plead for mercy the way she always had, begging his assailant to stop, and getting no reply but another whack of the chair leg and another jolt of pain. He'd hurt her so many times, and now, at last, he was getting his.

But that was only a small part of her, because the greater part was feeling nothing at all, not satisfaction or horror or fear; it just watched, as emotionless as a TV camera recording an event in which it took no part.

Kane threw aside the bloody stick and rose to his full height, and for a crazy moment PattiSue felt sure he was going to plant a boot on Eddie's corpse and pose like a hunter with his kill. He didn't. He merely stared down at the body, then lifted his head to face her through the doorway. She looked into his eyes once more and was instantly lost in them.

Kane stepped over Eddie's body and into the bedroom. He approached the bed. His breathing was low and husky, like the ragged panting of an animal. His eyes gleamed, feral. His teeth shone like fangs.

He stopped at the foot of the bed, looking at her, and seeing right inside her, into her very soul.

"You're beautiful," he said.

She shook her head. "No," she said, her voice thick and strangely torpid. "I'm not."

"Let me see you. All of you."

A last whisper of her former self reached her ears, pleading with her not to do it, not to let him see. But it was only a whisper, barely audible, and then it was drowned out altogether by the sudden roaring in her head which was a rush of blood.

She pulled down the sheet, an inch at a time, revealing the white snow cones of her breasts, then kicked the sheet aside and lay naked and exposed to him, the purple welts Eddie had given her standing out against her skin. She didn't move. He studied her dispassionately, with an artist's eye.

He nodded once, as if in satisfaction.

"Very nice," he said.

Then, very simply, he bent over the bed and kissed her on the mouth.

His lips were dry and dusty and his skin was cold. It was like ... like being kissed by a corpse. By death.

That thought and the reality of his touch shocked her alert for the first time in minutes.

She twisted free of his embrace. She kicked, fighting to get out from under him, to escape from the cage of his arms. She rose halfway off the bed, flailing, screaming.

"Go away! Don't touch me! Leave me alone!"

He seized her by the shoulders. He forced her down onto the bed. She wheezed in fury and fear. Then he was on top of her, his fingers—cold, like icicles—massaging her breasts and sending ripples of gooseflesh up her back. He was laughing.

"God damn you!" she screamed.

He chuckled. "Too late."

He plunged his mouth into her right breast, biting her, drawing blood. She thrust her fingernails into his face, finding the flesh of his cheek and jaw. She tore at him, seeking his demon eyes, seeking to jam her nails into them and rupture them like egg yolks.

His hands closed over her throat. She felt the power of his fingers, ten steel clamps tight against her flesh.

"No more games," he breathed, a crazed half-smile frozen on his face. "Or I'll choke you. I'll choke you to death and fuck your corpse."

"Bet you'd like it better that way," she snapped, heedless of danger.

"Maybe I would."

She swallowed. Because she had a feeling it was true.

"No more games," he repeated, then let go of her neck.

She stared up at him. His face was slick with blood from where her nails had ruptured his skin. His eyes swam in shadows.

He took her. He didn't even bother to remove his clothes, not even the hat still canted on his head, held in place by the chin strap. That made it more obscene somehow. She was buck naked and he was fully clothed, clad in boots and pants and the heavy black coat that flapped around him like vampire wings.

She put up no resistance. She knew it was useless to try. She lay still, hearing the drumroll of her heart in her ears, as he licked her breasts with his pale, bloodless, sandpapery tongue. It felt like a dog's tongue, only cold. She shivered. She bit down, fighting the impulse to scream.

His trousers were rough against the bare skin of her legs. Through them she could feel the stiffening of his erection. She shut her eyes. She didn't want to see what would happen next, didn't want to be here at all. Dimly she remembered fantasizing about this man as she lay in Eddie's arms. He'd seemed exciting in an erotic way, dangerous but alluring. There was no allure now. There was only terror and humiliation and pain.

He mounted her. He gripped her buttocks and thrust himself deep inside. She ground her cheek against the mattress. He was cold down there too. Cold everywhere. His phallus was stone-hard and stone-cold. It felt flesh-less and dry, like a scrap of bone.

The bed rocked. His breathing became louder, harsh and throaty. She opened her eyes and glimpsed his face, twisted into an animal mask, the eyes bright with fever, lips foaming with spit. She squeezed her eyes shut again.

Finally he climaxed. She knew it from the strangled noise he made, like a grunt of pain, and from his sudden limpness. She'd felt no spurt of semen. It was like he was empty inside. Empty and dry as dust.

He pulled out. He propped himself up on one elbow, still leaning over her, holding her imprisoned by the nearness of his body.

She was numb. She seemed to have no sensation below the waist. She heard low, hysterical sobbing. It took her a moment to realize the sobs were her own.

"Go away," she whispered. "Please."

"Oh, no, little darling." He spoke slowly, languidly, in a lazy cowpoke drawl. "I'm not through with you yet."

She blinked back tears. "What ... what's that supposed to mean?"

"It means I'm going to have you again."

"No." The word was a whimper.

"Oh, yes." He smiled, a slow, sickly smile spreading over his face like leprosy. "But this time ... my way."

He reached out with both hands and his fingers wrapped around her neck, squeezing, and all her world was pain.

The Reverend Chester Ewes sat in his easy chair with the fifth volume of Frazer's *Golden Bough* in his lap, marking a page with his finger, listening to the church bell toll midnight.

The bell was hooked up to a mechanical pulley controlled by a timer. He'd set up the system himself, years ago, and rarely found any cause for complaint about it. True, the timer mechanism was no longer all that accurate, and the chiming of the bell was sometimes off by two minutes or more, but nobody seemed to mind, least of all Chester Ewes himself. He liked to listen to that bell as it sang out in its brassy soprano. He liked to reflect on what its daily song signified.

In his readings on religion he'd encountered the idea that the rituals of any faith, whether Christianity or tribal polytheism, were designed to mark the stages of a human life, to note the pivotal events of birth and death, marriage and parenthood, and so give a sense of order to the meaningless passage of years. It was right that the institutions of faith, arbitrary and irrational though they might be, should do this. And following the same logic, he felt it was profoundly right for the bell in his church steeple to mark the passing of the hours and give the impression of order to the unfolding of each day.

So ordinarily he received a sense of quiet pleasure from hearing the bell. But not tonight. Tonight there was something in the slow, regular tolling that he found ominous, like the distant march of jackboots, the slow tread of death.

He sat rigid in his chair, counting off the last strokes. Ten. Eleven. Twelve.

Then he expelled a sigh of relief, knowing that the bell would fall silent, and perhaps silence his worries as well.

The bell chimed once more.

Thirteen.

He listened, but the bell did not toll again. He heard no sound other than his own breathing, low and ragged in his ears.

Thirteen strokes. But it wasn't possible. He must have miscounted. That was the answer.

Except he knew it wasn't.

All right, then—his mind groped for a logical explanation like sleep-fuddled fingers groping for a light switch—the mechanism must be malfunctioning. It had rung off the wrong number of strokes. That was entirely reasonable, indubitably possible, and a fully satisfactory resolution of the problem. There was no reason to break out in a cold sweat of panic about such a simple thing. No reason at all.

But ... why tonight? Tonight of all nights?

He thought of the Bible quotation his finger had alighted upon, words that Israel's God had thundered to Abel's brother at the beginning of time. He thought of his conversation in the worship hall with a pale-skinned, dark-clad stranger—a man who, it was rumored, had come out of the desert, out of the vast emptiness of the Mojave, where nothing lived but hawks and weeds. Out of nowhere. A man called Kane.

Kane. Or ... Cain?

Chester Ewes shook his head with sudden savage bitterness.

Superstition. Mindless, primitive superstition. As if there could be any significance in a man's name, or in the number of strokes his bell had chimed. Next thing you knew, he'd be picking apart the entrails of chickens to forecast the future.

He lifted the book and began reading again, trying to drive away the nonsense that was clouding his mind. But one thought kept coming back to him.

Thirteen strokes.

He knew it was foolish to be afraid. He was, anyway.

4

Bill Needham had spent the last five minutes loitering on the curb outside his house, uncomfortably aware of the shadows swimming around him and the warm wind whispering like a talkative ghost. A minute ago, the distant church bell had chimed midnight. There had been something wrong with the tolling of that bell, but he couldn't say quite what it was. He shrugged. He was on edge, that's all; everything felt spooky tonight.

He wondered where Rile was. It had been nearly half an hour since Bill had gotten off the phone with Jenny. More than enough time for Rile to get here from the Evans place.

He had just about made up his mind to go back inside to wait, when the ancient Chevy van finally rounded the corner, wheezing and clanking as usual. The van shuddered to a stop, backfiring. Bill climbed in on the passenger side and pulled the door shut, glad to shut out the night.

"Would've been here sooner," Rile said as he put his foot on the gas and eased the van up to cruising speed, "but Jenny passed along your advice, and I must say, it made good sense to me."

He patted the seat cushion at his side, where a Remington Model 1100 12-gauge shotgun rested peacefully.

"Had to go back to my place to get it," Rile added. "And then I had a devil of a time finding any slugs. I guess I'm getting senile or something, because I forgot where I kept 'em. Anyhow, I'm here now."

"See anything out of the ordinary when you were driving?"

"Not a thing. Town's asleep. Quiet everywhere. Well, except in Eddie's place. He must be giving it to PattiSue pretty good, as usual. Heard her moaning and carrying on."

"At least somebody's having fun tonight."

Rile chuckled. "Yeah. Well, maybe we'll have ourselves some fun too. We could use a little excitement in this one-hydrant town, wouldn't you say?"

Bill looked uneasily at Rile, then at the shotgun. "Let's just hope we don't get too much excitement."

Rile didn't answer for a moment. He swung the van onto Joshua Street. His headlights made twin funnels cutting the night.

"I've got a feeling we will, though," he said finally. "Maybe more than we bargained for."

Bill thought about that, and suddenly his fears were not remote anymore. They were very close and very real.

They rode in silence. Bill watched the old man's hands on the steering wheel as he turned west on Second Avenue. Steady hands. They didn't show even a tremble. Tough customer, Rile Cady. Even at his age he was a good man in a pinch. Bill was glad to have him at his side.

Of course, the Remington didn't hurt either.

Framed in the dusty windshield, the Hannah house slid into view, half a block away.

"Stop here," Bill said.

Rile pumped the brake, then killed the engine and headlights. The two men sat in the abrupt stillness.

Suddenly Bill Needham's heart was pounding.

Well, there it was—the house. The house he'd offered to enter alone, and boy, was he grateful Jenny Kirk had talked him out of it. But even with Rile and his Remington for company, he was acutely aware that he didn't want to go in.

He realized Rile was looking at him. Not just looking. Studying him as if trying to determine if Bill Needham had just chickened out. He felt a flush of shame at the thought that he was wondering the same thing himself.

Then he remembered how Jenny had said his name, her voice low—hushed, almost. This was a crisis, and she'd turned to him for help. He couldn't let her down.

His heart quieted down a bit. He turned in his seat and looked at Rile. He forced a smile.

"No use driving right up to the front door." He kept his voice light, casual, the voice of a man used to danger and rather enamored of it. "I mean, it's not as if we were delivering flowers."

"Okay, Bill. I hear you."

The way Rile said it, Bill knew he'd heard too much. He'd heard the words, and the fear that lay behind them.

Heard it—and shared it.

For the first time Bill understood that Rile Cady was as scared as he was. The realization made him feel better.

He put his hand on the door and hesitated, staring out the window at Charlie Grain's house, which sat directly opposite the spot where they were parked.

"Hey, Rile," he said. "Know what I'm thinking? We ought to see if Charlie's up."

"Another member of the posse?"

"Something like that."

"Doubt he'll appreciate it."

"Well, shit. It's not fair for us to have all the fun."

Rile laughed, a sound like dark chocolate, rich and sweet. Bill smiled again—for real, this time.

The two men got out, shutting the van doors softly.

Bill looked around at the dark street under the star-flecked sky. The smile faded from his face. A Joshua tree shivered in a sandy current of wind. He shivered with it.

Together they walked up the front steps of Charlie's house. Bill glanced at Rile and saw that he was holding his rifle in both hands, gripping it tight, poised to aim and shoot, like a man who meant business. That was good.

A light shone in Charlie's living-room window. Unusual for him to be up at this hour; unheard-of for him to leave the lights on after he turned in. Unless he'd poured himself a few cold ones. Then he might be passed out in the armchair, snoring like a power mower. Bill hoped so.

Rile rang the doorbell. It chimed. They waited. Rile tried again. Nobody came.

Wordlessly Bill opened the door—unlocked, of course. He looked in. The living room, at least, appeared to be undisturbed. He was about to go in when Rile took his arm.

"Let me," Rile said. He tapped the 12-gauge. "I've got the firepower."

Bill didn't argue.

Rile entered, looking around warily. Bill shadowed him. They explored the house. In the kitchen they found an open can of Coors, still full, gone flat. That was odd. More than odd. Darn near inexplicable. For Charlie to pass up an open can of beer just wasn't in his nature.

They checked the rest of the house. Nothing else seemed out of sorts. The bed showed no sign of having been slept in. And there was no sign of Charlie Grain at all.

"What do you think?" Rile asked when they were back outside.

"I think we'd better check out the Hannah place." Bill licked his lips. "And we'd better keep our eyes open. Open wide."

Rile nodded, while with one hand he stroked the Remington's ventilated-rib barrel like a nervous soldier on combat patrol.

Bill started forward and Rile followed. Together they headed down the street toward Lew and Lynnie Hannah's house, to see what they would see.

Ethel Walston sat on the living-room sofa and listened to the ticking of an unseen clock. She didn't have to see it to know what time it was. Not less than five minutes ago, the church bell had tolled twelve. In truth she'd thought she counted thirteen strokes; but that was silly. She'd lost track in her counting, that was all. When a woman got to be her age, she found herself making all kinds of little mistakes. It went with the territory.

Twelve strokes were what she'd heard; and twelve strokes meant midnight.

And her boarder, Mr. Kane, still wasn't home.

She peered out the window and contemplated what might be keeping him. In a bigger town, she'd have guessed that he'd found himself a young miss to dally with. But not in Tuskett. There were no young misses here, excepting Jenny Kirk, who'd never go in for that sort of sport, and PattiSue Baker, who was Eddie's girl.

The thought crossed her mind that Mr. Kane might be up to no good. Robbing houses, maybe. She doubted it. No self-respecting thief would look twice at Tuskett. There was nothing here worth stealing. Anyway, thievery would hardly fit in with the romantic image she'd painted of the man. In the past few hours, as she'd thought about him, he seemed to have grown more handsome than she'd noticed at first. Dashing, you might say. Like the men pictured on the covers of the paperback romances she guiltily indulged in. A man like that would never be a crook. Well, maybe a jewel thief on the Riviera, seducing society women as a ploy to make off with their baubles. But certainly not your garden-variety sort of crook.

But what *could* be keeping him?

She couldn't say; and, really, it didn't matter, because there was a more compelling question on her mind, one she'd tried to shake off but which wouldn't budge. She recalled how a tick had once lodged itself in Scooter's neck. Harry had had himself a devil of a time getting it out; the stubborn parasite clung to the dog's flesh, resisting all efforts to pry it loose. This question on her mind was like that—ugly, nasty, and stubbornly refusing to let go.

It was Ellyn Hannah who'd planted the idea in her head, over three hours ago, when she'd asked Ethel what was in Mr. Kane's backpack. Ethel, of course, couldn't say. *Well, how should I know what's in it?* she'd replied a trifle huffily, because anybody would think, from the way Lynnie had asked, that Ethel was some sort of awful snoop like Meg Sanchez. But the question Lynnie had asked just wouldn't go away. What *was* in that pack, and why was Mr. Kane so strangely gentle with it?

Around ten o'clock, her telephoning finished for the night, she'd gone into her bedroom and changed into her nightgown and slippers. Scooter lay dozing on the bed. She roused him gently, figuring it was time for him to go bye-bye in the backyard, as was his nightly custom. And then a strange thing happened. Scooter growled at her. A low growl, barely audible, the kind of noise she felt more than heard, felt in the tips of her fingers as she stroked the spaniel's stiff, wiry fur; but a growl nonetheless. She drew back, startled. She couldn't remember a time when Scooter had acted up on her like that.

She left him there on the bed. He could take care of his own business tonight.

On her way out of the bedroom, she paused, then went down the hall to look in on the guest room. It was empty. The bedside light was on. The backpack lay on the bed.

Well, how should I know what's in it? a voice in her memory, her own voice, had echoed. Only, this time she heard an answer: *Go look.*

She shook her head, disgusted with herself, and hurried down the hall to the kitchen to fix a cup of tea. Tea always served to settle her stomach, and her stomach was a little queasy, what with today's excitement and all. Then she settled down on the sofa in the living room, sipping the hot tea and gazing idly at some back issues of *Sunset* magazine that Marge Baker, PattiSue's mom, had given her.

She hadn't quite had the nerve to confess to herself that she was waiting up for him. Waiting to see him return, and to find out, if possible, where he'd gone off to and what had kept him for so long.

The clock ticked off minutes, then hours. He didn't return. She sat pretending to read, trying not to think about that empty room and that backpack, while curiosity squirmed and twisted inside her like a cat in a sack.

Then, not five minutes ago, the church bells had chimed midnight, and she'd realized just how late it was. And that had only made the curiosity worse.

She shook her head, staring out the window at a featureless rectangle of night.

The man was a mystery, that was for sure. Mr. Kane. She frowned. Here she was, putting a man up for the night, and she didn't even know his first name. She tried to guess what it might be, running through a string of common names in her mind. None fit him.

Maybe the things in his pack held the answer to that question. Identification of some sort. Something to tell who he was and where he hailed from. It was possible. Some clue to unravel the riddle posed by Mr. Kane.

Well, how should I know what's in it?

Go look.

She almost rose from the sofa, then stopped. Suppose he came back and caught her in the act. That would be embarrassing, wouldn't it? Embarrassing—and somehow dangerous. She knew that, although she couldn't say just how she knew or what the danger might be.

Still ...

He'd been gone for hours. Most likely he wouldn't be back in the next five minutes. Anyway, she was sure to hear the heavy tread of his boots on the porch or the living-room floor. She'd have plenty of warning. She could always replace the contents of his pack and escape the guest room before he got anywhere near her.

Besides—and this was the deciding argument—she had to know. Simply had to.

She got up and left the living room quickly, before she could change her mind. She went down the hall, moving stealthily, like a thief—a thief in her own house. She entered Bobby's old room and approached the pack. It bulged in odd places. She touched it, then listened to be sure she caught no sound of footsteps. There was nothing.

Go on, then, she told herself. Open it up.

Her hands shook. She fumbled with the zipper. Finally she got a good grip on it and tugged. The pack opened smoothly.

She reminded herself of how carefully Mr. Kane had treated the pack. It would hardly do for her to spill its fragile contents all over the bed in broken pieces. She took hold of it by the bottom, then slowly tilted it and let whatever was inside slide out an inch at a time. It took her a full minute to empty the pack. Finally its contents lay in a heap on the bed. She put the pack aside and cast her eyes over the scatter of objects, itemizing what she saw.

A spool of electrician's tape. A plastic funnel. A coil of rope. A box of nails. Other things.

The thought crossed her mind that Mr. Kane might be a handyman of some sort. It seemed unlikely. He certainly hadn't acted like one. In her experience, handymen were big and gruff and friendly; they whistled a lot. She couldn't imagine her houseguest whistling a note.

She went back to looking over the things in the pile. She saw a small glass jar with something inside, something she couldn't quite make out; and, next to it, a medium-size box, latched shut. Ethel hesitated, staring at the box, then touched the latch, expecting to find it locked. It sprang up easily. She lifted the lid.

Inside the box was a thick sheet of sponge rubber with a hollowed-out compartment in its center. Nestled in that space, matching its dimensions precisely, was a large metal canister secured by three strips of thick black tape. There was writing on the canister. With her poor eyesight Ethel had trouble making it out. She leaned close, squinting.

$CH_2NO_3CHNO_3CH_2NO_3$.

A chemical formula, she knew, but one that meant nothing to her. But below the formula, there were words.

GLYCERYL TRINITRATE.

Still meaningless. She peered closer. In smaller letters, cupped by parentheses, was one word.

(NITROGLYCERIN)

She stared. Her dentures clicked together once like a clam shell snapping shut.

Nitro. But nitro was an explosive, wasn't it? It was the

stuff they made TNT out of.

Suddenly she was shaking all over. But there had to be some mistake. Mr. Kane couldn't be carrying explosives around with him. It made no sense. Maybe she'd read the word wrong, or maybe it wasn't nitro they used in TNT after all. She was an old woman, easily confused; she'd made a mistake.

Almost against her will, her eyes tracked down to the bottom of the canister, drawn by the bright red letters printed there.

WARNING: HIGHLY FLAMMABLE AND COMBUSTIBLE, SENSITIVE TO HEAT AND IMPACT. HANDLE WITH EXTREME CARE.

Flammable and combustible.

So it was an explosive, after all. She'd made no mistake. No wonder the man had been so gentle with this pack of his. He'd been afraid of blowing himself sky-high.

She almost left the room right then. She knew she ought to. She ought to run down the hall to her bedroom, where she kept a phone on her nightstand, and call Lew Hannah. There must be all kinds of laws against lugging a container of nitroglycerin around in a packsack like it was a jug of Gatorade. And what did that man Kane—suddenly he wasn't *Mr.* Kane to her anymore—what did he want with an explosive, anyway? What was he up to? And why had he stayed out so late?

But she didn't leave the room just yet. Because there was still that small glass jar to look at. Something was inside it; she couldn't tell what. She wanted to know. She was almost afraid to look at it. Oh, but she had to. Simply had to.

She picked it up with trembling hands and held it up to the light. She gasped.

Inside the jar was a tiny, precious hand. A baby's hand, severed at the wrist—not neatly amputated, but sawed off, as with a carving knife. It was floating in a pint of green fluid flecked with specks of gray, like pond scum. Formaldehyde, she guessed. The hand had been cut off the child and pickled like a medical specimen.

She dropped the jar. It bounced on the bed. For a horrible moment she thought the hand inside was moving, the fingers twitching. Then she saw that the thing was merely sliding around as the formaldehyde solution sloshed from side to side, foaming like dishwashing liquid.

"Oh, Lord," she whispered. "Dear Lord."

She took a faltering step backward, then another and another, unable to take her eyes off the pile of things on the bed. She reached the doorway and turned, and Kane was there.

He stood directly before her, a yard from the door, silent and unmoving as a wax figure. He must have been there for some time, watching. His face was pallid in the dim light. His eyes were huge. In his hand, a knife glinted. A knife from her own kitchen.

"So," he whispered, the word a lit-fuse hiss. "Snooping in my things, were you? Did you like what you found?"

She made a sound that wasn't human, a guttural choking sound.

"I take it you've seen my treasure. My little one." Kane smiled. Not a pretty smile. His eyes were oddly red, like droplets of freshly spilled blood. "He's special to me. My first kill, you see."

The smile was wider now, terrifying.

"But hardly my last."

"Their car is gone," Bill Needham said, noticing it for the first time, as he and Rile reached the lawn of Lew and Ellyn Hannah's house.

"Uh-huh." Rile sounded as if he'd made note of the

Tempo's absence right off, and maybe he had. Despite his years, Bill knew, the old man's eyes were as sharp as his wits.

"What do you suppose," Bill asked slowly, "Lew and Lynnie would be doing out at this hour?"

Rile shrugged. "What are *we* doing out at this hour?"

"Looking for trouble, I'd say."

"Well, maybe they are too."

"Yeah. Or maybe they found some."

Rile said nothing, but Bill saw he was gripping the shotgun tighter than before.

They crossed the parched lawn, heading for the front door. Unlike Charlie Grain's place, the Hannah house was dark, all the lights off. Under other circumstances Bill would have assumed Lew and Ellyn were asleep. But not with the car gone. And not with Charlie's house empty ... and that can of beer on the kitchen counter, left to go stale.

They didn't ring the doorbell this time. They seemed to have reached an unspoken agreement not to advertise their arrival. Rile opened the door and crept inside with Bill at his back.

They made their way through the shadowed living room and looked into the den. The TV was off, the lights out, the room empty.

Soundlessly they slipped down the hall, pausing to check out the kitchen and bathroom. At the end of the hall was the bedroom. The door was open. They peered inside.

The bed was empty and unused. The pillows were nicely fluffed, the white cotton sheet neatly tucked in, corners squared with military precision. There was no bedspread, which was funny, since Bill vaguely remembered Ellyn once saying that a bed looked naked without a spread. But, after all, the night was hot, and it was a lady's prerogative to change her mind.

He entered the room and circled the bed. His gaze traveled briefly to the floor. Was that a stain on the carpet? He looked closer. No, he decided, not a stain. Only a shadow. There were shadows everywhere tonight.

Rile crossed the room to the table near the window. He drummed his fingers on the empty tabletop.

"What is it?" Bill asked.

"Didn't Lew used to keep his police-band here?"

"I think so."

"Huh."

"Of course, it's a portable. He might've moved it."

"Must have." Something seemed to catch Rile's eye. He bent over, squinting at the window screen.

"What is it?" Bill asked.

"Holes in the screen. Two or three. See?" He poked his finger through one of them and wiggled it like a worm on a hook. "Awful big hole, this one. Bigger than the others."

Bill moved to his side and looked at the screen. There were a couple of holes in it, true, but he saw nothing peculiar in that fact.

"Worn through," he said with a shrug. "Mine are getting pretty ragged too. Been meaning to replace the ones in the front room."

Rile said nothing, just kept poking at the largest of the holes. Bill couldn't see why.

"Something funny about that window, you think?" Bill asked.

Rile turned away. "No. I suppose not." He sighed. "Everything's wearing out in this town, I suppose."

The two men stood facing each other in the darkness and sudden stillness.

"So," Rile said simply.

"So," Bill agreed. "Looks like nobody's home."

"Looks like."

"What do you think?"

"Don't know."

"Lew, Lynnie, Charlie—gone," Bill checked his wristwatch. "At half past midnight."

"Darn peculiar."

"Sure is."

Silence hung in the room.

"I'm thinking," Bill said slowly, "maybe we ought to give Ethel a call. She's putting that man up, you know. In Bobby's old room."

Rile nodded. "Might not be such a bad idea."

Together they returned to the TV room, where there was a phone. Bill dialed Ethel Walston's number from memory. He listened to the ringing at the other end of the line. Six rings. Seven. He was beginning to worry that something had happened to Ethel, that maybe she'd disappeared too, when the eighth ring was interrupted by a click, and Ethel's voice buzzed in his ear.

"Hello?"

"Ethel? Bill. Sorry to wake you at this hour."

"Oh, it's okay, Bill," Her voice was aflutter with nervous excitement, but Bill figured anybody would be rattled when the phone started jangling at this hour. "I wasn't asleep. I mean ... I was just dozing."

"Well, I'm sorry anyhow. The reason I called ... This might sound strange, but some of us are a little concerned about that man you're putting up at your place. Mr. Kane. We're not quite sure, frankly, what he might be up to. And we were wondering if he was snug in his bed like he ought to be."

"Oh, yes. He is."

Bill blinked. It wasn't the answer he'd expected. "You sure?" he pressed. "Have you looked in on him lately?"

"Not two seconds ago. He was out like a light."

Bill rubbed his forehead. "Look, Ethel, I don't mean to beat a dead horse, but are you positive you saw Kane, and not just some pillows and blankets made up to look like him?"

"Why, Bill Needham, sometimes you treat me just like a child. 'Course I'm sure. Point of fact, the light in Bobby's room was left on—poor man must've nodded off reading, from the look of him—and I could see him plain as day. What's this all about? Why've you got your bristles up about Mr. Kane anyhow?"

"Nothing. Never mind."

"Okay, then. You rest easy, will you?"

"I'll do that, Ethel. Apologize for getting you up and about."

"'Night now."

"'Night." Bill hung up and looked at Rile. "He's there, all right. Sleeping like a baby, she says."

"That's a relief."

"Yeah."

"You don't sound so sure."

Bill frowned. "I'd still like to know where Charlie and Lew and Ellyn went to. Wouldn't you?"

Ethel Walston stared at the phone in her hand as it hummed a dial tone. She wished she were a braver woman. A braver woman would've shouted a warning to Bill Needham, a warning about her boarder, Mr. Kane, who was not fast asleep in his bed with a book open on his chest. He was wide-awake and standing right at her back, gripping her arm with one hand while with the other he held the knife to her throat.

She knew that knife well—she'd used it often enough to carve roasts and slice vegetables. Its blade was very sharp. And Ethel knew that if she had tried to warn Bill, the knife would have sliced through her neck quicker than a straight razor through a stick of butter.

But if she did as she was told, Kane had sworn he wouldn't hurt her, wouldn't so much as touch her. She doubted that his word was worth a damn; still, it was something to hold on to, some small reason for hope.

And she needed hope. She was almost surprised to discover how badly she needed it, how much she still wanted to live. Even now, in her old age, when her days were lonely and her nights restless, when her body creaked with stiffness and pain, when her only joy was a rare phone call or a gift-wrapped package from Bobby in Orlando, Florida—even now, she clung to her life, as stubbornly as that tick had clung to Scooter's hide.

"That was good," Kane whispered. His breath on her neck was hot and stale. "Now hang up."

She replaced the phone in its cradle on the nightstand. She stood waiting for Kane to kill her, as she was pretty sure he would.

Then, astonishingly, Kane let go of her arm and stepped back. She wondered if maybe he would keep his word after all.

Slowly she turned to look at him. With difficulty she found her voice. "Why are you carrying that stuff with you? The explosive, I mean? Just what are you meaning to do?"

"Never you mind, Mrs. Walston."

She shuddered, hearing him speak her name. It sounded filthy and obscene coming out of his mouth, like some foul insect crawling out of a dank hole.

"And I thought you were a nice man," she whispered, speaking almost to herself. "Scooter thought so too. Scooter ..."

She turned to the bed, where Scooter had been dozing when she'd last looked in on him, two hours ago. The bed was empty. The spaniel was gone.

"Where is he?" she breathed. "What ... what did you do to him?" She hated to hear her voice trembling so. But the thought of her dog, so feeble and trusting, getting hurt or ... killed ...

"He's right there," Kane said quietly, nodding at the floor.

Ethel jerked her head down, expecting to find Scooter lying dead in a puddle of his own innards, and saw him poking his small head out from the skirt of the bedspread, gazing up at her quizzically. Unusual for him to be hiding under the bed; he must be scared.

A fine watchdog you are, Ethel told him silently, smiling a little at the intensity of her own relief.

She lifted her head to look at Kane again.

"What are you going to do with me?" she asked, her voice flat.

Kane shrugged. "I told you I wouldn't lay a hand on you as long as you did what I wanted. So I'm not fixing to hurt you. No, I don't mean to hurt you at all."

He moved to the bedroom door. He paused in the doorway. He smiled again, that ugly fright-mask smile.

"But old Scooter now, he might have different ideas."

From under the bed, the spaniel started to growl.

Kane left the room, closing the door behind him. It thumped shut, a sound of quiet finality. Ethel stood in the middle of the bedroom, while Scooter's low growling went on. Slowly she looked down at him again. His eyes were darker than before, darker than she'd ever seen them. His upper lip was curled, exposing a small gleaming fang.

If it had been any other dog, Ethel would have sworn he was getting ready to go for her. But this was the spaniel she and Harry had raised from a pup, the gentlest dog in the world. A dog that could never be a threat to anyone. The very idea that he could ever be a threat to her or to anyone ... Why, it was just ... just plain ...

Scooter wriggled out from under the bed, his eyes crazed, his muzzle wet with spit. He snarled, showing all of his fangs this time. Yellow fangs bared to the gum lines.

Ethel took a step back, staring at her dog, trying to understand how a thing like this could be happening, but of course there could be only one explanation, and she'd known it all along.

Years ago she'd read a spy thriller, one of those paperbacks she liked to thumb through to pass the time. In the book, the villain had broken into the hero's house and injected his dog with something, some chemical formula or other, to make it turn on its master.

Kane must have done that. A man who carried a container full of chemical explosive in his packsack could surely have other evil things on his person. Chemicals or pills or something, anyhow, that had put poor old Scooter clean out of his mind.

Or maybe—maybe he hadn't needed pills or chemicals. Maybe all he'd needed was those damnable eyes of his, eyes so blue with cold they froze your very soul, eyes as hypnotizing as the devil's own. She remembered how Scooter had gazed up at Kane in the hallway this evening, then licked Kane's boot as if in supplication. The dog hadn't been himself since. Had Kane taken him over at that very moment? Stolen his soul—if a dog had a soul?

She didn't know. And it didn't matter. All that mattered was that Scooter was slinking toward her, his fur standing up in wiry bristles, his eyes gleaming like gemstones, and he was snarling and yapping and slavering white spumes of spit.

"Scooter," she whispered. "Stop that now. You just stop that."

It was no use. The dog was past the stage of recognizing her voice. And even though he was only a little dog, barely bigger than a pup, and old and infirm at that, still he had teeth and he knew how to use them.

She kept backing up till she reached the bedroom door. She tugged at the knob. It wouldn't yield. But that wasn't possible. The door was unlocked. It had to open. Then she realized Kane must still be on the other side, holding the door shut.

All right, then. There was another way out. Across the room, on the far side of the bed, was a window, open to let in the night air. All she had to do was punch out the screen, climb through—could she do that at her age, climb out a window?—of course she could, she had no choice. She'd get out somehow and run straight to Lew Hannah's place.

If only she could get past Scooter, barring her path.

She took a cautious step forward, thinking that if she moved very slowly, one step at a time, and didn't get the dog riled up any worse than he already was, she might be able to sneak past him—and then Scooter came at her in a howling rush and sank his teeth into her leg.

Ethel screamed. She beat at the dog with her hands, trying to knock him lose. Scooter clung to her leg, driving his fangs in deeper. His tiny paws scrabbled wildly, catching the thin fabric of her nightgown, shredding it like tissue. She flailed her leg, but the spaniel hung on, swinging crazily from side to side like a furry rag.

She remembered that the telephone was only a few feet away, and if she could get to it, maybe she could call for help before the dog killed her, or maybe she could use it as a blunt instrument to smash his skull. The thought pained her, but not as badly as the fangs and claws savaging her leg.

She tried to walk. She couldn't do it. Her left leg was

useless, nothing but blood and pain. She hopped on her right foot, feeling childish, a little girl playing hopscotch. She had played hopscotch when she was a girl, hadn't she? Yes, and that other game too, the one about cracks in the sidewalk. Step on a crack ... break your mother's back.

She hopped closer to the nightstand, almost close enough to reach the phone. Then she took a bad hop and came down wrong, and there was a snap, which was the sound of her ankle breaking. Pitched sideways, she landed on the carpet with shock waves of pain rippling up both legs.

Broke your mother's back, she thought as girlish giggling rose in her mind. You lose, Ethel.

Finally Scooter let go of her leg, and for a blessed instant Ethel was sure the dog had come to his senses again. But it was only an instant, because next thing she knew, he was scrambling up her midsection, pawing at her gown, yammering and screeching. His eyes rolled wildly in his head like marbles in a tin cup. His fangs swept toward her throat. She threw out her hands in a fragile defense, and he savaged them with his small daggerlike claws, while she heard a hysterical voice, her own voice, screaming in helpless horror, "Scooter, stop it, will you stop it, oh, that's a bad dog, a very bad dog!"

Scooter's fangs tore into her throat, slicing the skin as neatly as a letter opener slitting an envelope. Ethel tried to keep on screaming, but all that came out were helpless gargling sounds. The dog gnawed at her neck, lapping up her jetting blood the way he would slurp at his water dish on the kitchen floor.

Bad dog, she thought incoherently. No supper for you.

Then, just like that. Scooter stopped.

The dog blinked, dazed, and shook his head. His eyes seemed to clear. He drew back from the mess he'd made and whined, a low, piteous, unmistakably apologetic sound.

He stared at Ethel, then slowly lowered his head to her face and licked her cheek, mewling like a spanked puppy, seeking—or so it seemed—to make up for the very bad thing he'd done.

Ethel almost smiled. With her last strength she reached out and stroked the spaniel's fur. She coughed weakly and found her voice.

"It's all right. Scooter. I didn't mean ... what I said. You're a good dog. Always have been. You ... you didn't know what you were doing ... that's all."

Scooter whined again, and went on licking Ethel Walston's face, quietly, desperately, long after she was dead.

Wendell Stoddard gripped the sheer rock wall of the arroyo and prayed he wouldn't fall.

If he lost his purchase now, after more than an hour spent struggling up the slippery slope, searching for footholds and handholds amid the loose boulders and crumbling ledges ... if he tumbled down to the bed of the dry gulch forty feet below—then he would be finished. He might die in the fall, or he might merely break his back and both of his legs, but one way or another, he wouldn't be getting out under his own power, and quite possibly he wouldn't get out at all.

Nearly two hours earlier, he'd been sitting motionless in the wreckage of his patrol car, listening to the hum of the Ford Tempo's engine as it faded into the distance. He hadn't even considered trying to climb out of the gorge, not at first. He was too weak and too badly hurt to move, let alone walk, let alone scale that monster of a wall. Instead he just sat there in the driver's seat, breathing hard and thinking of nothing.

After a long time it occurred to him that he could use the radio to call for help. One glance at the squawkbox dashed that hope. The thing was in a million pieces.

A few minutes later he decided he ought to reload his gun in case the stranger came back. It was no easy job. He had only his left hand to work with; his right hand was useless, its fingers stiffened into claws by the throbbing pain from the bullet in his shoulder. He got out six spare rounds, snapped open the cylinder of the .32, and fumbled the cartridges into the chambers.

Then he holstered the gun. He wasn't sure what made him do that. After all, he wasn't going anywhere.

Except, of course, he was.

He supposed he must have known it all along. Sure, he could stay here and wait for the dispatcher to notice he was missing; eventually a police chopper would spot the car in the bed of the gulch and send down a rescue team. But most likely that wouldn't happen till daylight. And daylight was too far away.

Because *he* was out there. The man in the stolen Ford. A man with a gun and a smile like icicles. A man who must have killed Lew Hannah and Ellyn too. A man who, quite possibly, was on a regular California-style murder spree.

People had to be warned. Every police officer within a hundred miles of Tuskett ought to be out looking for that car and its driver. And with the radio busted, there was only one way for Wendell to get the word out, and that was for him to climb out of the arroyo, then flag down a passing car or walk to a phone or something.

It wouldn't be easy. But he was a cop, and that made it his job. His duty.

With an effort he forced open the door and got out of his seat. He stood up. His ribs sizzled angrily. His head spun. Multicolored lights coruscated across his field of vision. He waited, not knowing if he would pass out.

Gingerly he lifted one foot, put it down. A step. He had taken a step. That was good.

A memory flashed in his mind, the memory of little Melody walking for the first time. And now here he was, repeating the same performance, taking his baby steps.

He kept walking. His boots sank into the powdery soil. He remembered a filmstrip he'd seen, years ago, of Armstrong and Aldren's walk on the surface of the moon. The dirt up there had been a lot like this. Soft and fine, with a lot of give in it.

Maybe I'm on the moon, he thought. He had an irrational urge to lift his head and look for the blue-green ball of Earth in the night sky.

Slowly he advanced, covering only a few inches with each stride. He passed a scatter of driftwood and wondered what it was doing here, in the middle of the desert, so far from the sea. Then he remembered the flash floods that had carved this channel; no doubt more than one prospector's shack had been swept away in those white waters.

His shuffling steps carried him finally to the wall of the ravine. He stared up at it. The wall was made of loose earth and sedimentary rock, dusted here and there with the same grayish talcum he'd been trudging through. Twisted traceries of erosion channels scarred its surface; mesquite bushes, rooted in narrow crevices, tufted the channels like splotches of mold on bread. The lower portions of the wall didn't look too hard to climb; the grade was gentle enough, and there were plenty of rocky outcrops to hang on to. Higher up, the wall became more steeply vertical. He wasn't sure how he would negotiate that section. He figured he'd find out when he got there.

Or die trying, he added silently, and managed a smile.

Wendell stood there for a long moment, gathering strength and courage. Then he began to climb.

Progress was slow. With only one good arm, he had trouble hoisting himself over rocks and loose rubble. He took great care to plant his feet just right with every step. The soil was treacherous, and even the larger spurs of shale and sandstone could crumble unexpectedly under his weight.

About halfway up the wall, he reached the bad section he'd noted from the bottom of the ditch. The gradient was less shallow than before; the larger knobs of rock had thinned out; he saw nothing to grab hold of, only sandy soil flecked with mica and quartz, the kind of stuff that would run right through his fingers if he tried to find purchase there.

He waited, standing on a sandstone spur, catching his breath. Slowly he looked around. To his right, a few yards off, ran a narrow vertical channel studded with rocky outcroppings. That was it. His way up.

He crabbed sideways, hugging the wall, like a man traversing the ledge of a skyscraper; only, this ledge widened and narrowed unpredictably, and he could never be sure when his boots would find solid rock and when they would find only pebbly earth that gave way at the first hint of pressure.

After what seemed like many hours, he had reached the channel and begun wriggling up, using his two feet and one hand to climb from hold to hold. At one point the channel had abruptly funneled down to a gap too narrow for him to penetrate; he'd made a sideways detour into another, parallel waterway and continued the ascent.

And now he was nearly at the top.

He had looked up a moment ago to gauge the distance still remaining, and found he was less than ten feet from the rim of the arroyo. A wide, insanely cheerful grin blossomed on his face. "I'm gonna make it," he said out loud, his voice unexpectedly hoarse and throaty in his ears. "I'm really gonna goddamn make it."

The thought renewed his strength. He started moving

again, swiftly, almost casually snaking up the channel, releasing streams of sand and gravel with every movement of his legs and his left arm.

A yard higher, he found a place where he could actually stand, a thin spur of shale projecting out from the wall like a jutting lower lip. He planted his left foot on the thing to test its stability, decided it was strong enough to hold him, and set down his right foot also.

Not far above his head was a jagged crevice in the shape of a lightning bolt; hanging out of it was a gnarled mesquite bush. If he could grab hold of the bush and pull himself up another couple of feet ...

He was reaching for the nearest branch when the knob of shale under his feet tore free with a terrible rending sound.

He lunged for the branch. His hand fisted over it. He hung there, clinging to the mesquite bush, dangling while his boots searched for a toehold and found only loose gravel sliding away in a hissing millstream.

A moan warbled out of his mouth like the cry of some desert animal in pain.

The mesquite bush shuddered, coming loose, its roots surrendering their hold. In another few seconds it would pop free and he would plunge down, rolling and sliding forty feet over the rocks, to land at the bottom in a tangle of limbs. What would be left of him then, he didn't want to know.

He glanced around frantically, trying to find someplace to stand, and then he saw it. An outcrop of sandstone, probably firm enough to support him. If he could reach it. He swung out his right leg, groping for the rocky spur with the toe of his boot, but the damn thing was too far away.

The mesquite bush jerked down another inch. Its roots were unraveling like strands of a fraying rope. The plant was almost completely out of the wall now.

Wendell licked his lips. He knew what he had to do. He had to let go of the branch and jump. Jump for the sandstone spur and hope he could land on it without having it collapse under him as the shale had done, and without losing his balance and plummeting down.

Yes, that was what he'd have to do, all right. Only, he couldn't. He was afraid. He couldn't make himself let go of the branch. His hand was glued to the thing, his fingers frozen in place.

The branch jerked down another half-inch.

He shut his eyes and pictured Melody, her blue eyes so big, and Jill, holding the baby in her arms.

He had to do it. If he didn't, he would never see either one of them again.

He took a great big swallow of air and fixed his gaze on the sandstone ledge. He tensed his body for the leap.

In the instant when the mesquite bush snapped free, Wendell jumped.

He landed squarely on the ledge. The jolt of impact sent a ripple of sheer agony up his side from his broken ribs. He teetered, pinwheeling his good arm, and somehow got his fingers around an outcrop of quartz. Hugging the wall, he tried to breathe again, waiting for the ledge to give way and drop him into the pit. It didn't.

I made it, he thought in disbelief. Thank you, God. Thank you.

A long time later, he lifted his head and resumed his climb.

It was half past one in the morning. Bill Needham and Rile Cady had been cruising the streets for nearly an hour in Rile's van, looking for something, though neither of them could say what it was. Just looking, that's all. Because things weren't right in Tuskett. Bill figured they both knew that, even if they couldn't put it into words.

If Ethel Walston had told him what he'd expected to hear—that Kane had been gone all evening, Lord only knew where—then Bill could have found the words, all right. He would have figured Kane was out there kidnapping people or killing them. And he would have been on the horn to the state police quicker than you could say "Jack the Ripper."

But Ethel had said Mr. Kane was snug in his bed. And that left Bill not knowing what to think. It wasn't natural, what had gone on tonight—Tommy getting hurt, Charlie gone, and the Hannahs missing too, along with their car. The idea that Kane's arrival in town could be chalked up to coincidence was awfully hard to swallow. But there it was.

"What do we do now?" Rile had asked as he and Bill stood in the Hannahs' parlor, their faces as blank as the TV tube.

Bill had thought it over. "I'd like to take a look around town," he'd answered finally. "See what we can see. Maybe ..." He'd shrugged. "Maybe Lew's car will turn up."

"Okay."

"If you're feeling tired, I can go it alone."

"I'm not tired." Rile had looked at him. "And I don't want you going it alone. Not tonight."

Bill had smiled, hearing those words, relieved to know that he wasn't entirely crazy, because Rile Cady was just as worried sick about this mess as he was.

Before they left, Bill called the Evans place. Jenny answered. Yes, she and Tommy were still there; the boy was asleep, knocked out by the sedative Jack gave him. Bill knew Jenny could have lugged him home, had she really wanted to; but he understood why she hadn't. She didn't want to be alone. He couldn't blame her.

He told her about Charlie's place, and the Hannahs,

and his phone conversation with Ethel. "So it looks like it's not that man Kane," he finished. "There must be some other explanation."

"But what?"

"No idea. Rile and I figured we'd look here and there, see if we can find Lew or the others. They must be around somewhere."

"I guess ... Look, Bill, you take care. You and Rile both."

He smiled. She was worried about him. He liked that.

"We will," he said with more confidence than he felt. "You get some rest now."

But he knew she wouldn't rest. He had a feeling none of them would rest tonight.

He and Rile set out in the van. Their first stop was the police station, halfway down Joshua Street; they figured Lew might be there. He wasn't, but they checked out the place anyhow. The door was unlocked, which was odd, very odd; that was one door in Tuskett that did get locked at night, because inside the station house, in a locked cabinet, Lew kept his guns.

The guns were gone.

"Stolen?" Rile had wondered aloud, his voice echoing off the walls of the empty office.

"Maybe." Bill checked the lock on the cabinet. "But this thing wasn't forced open."

"No sign of a breakin out front, either."

"Whoever was in here had the keys, then. And Lew's the only man in town who's got a set. Carries them with him all the time."

"So you think Lew came over here and cleaned out the place?"

"Looks like." Bill took a breath. "Lew—or somebody who'd gotten hold of his keys."

Rile had said nothing. They left the police station and

continued their search. Bill did his best to recollect how many guns Lew had kept in that cabinet, and what kinds they were. He recalled a Smith & Wesson .32 and a Browning bolt-action rifle. There might have been others.

They drove past Lew's grocery store and found it normal. Then they made a slow circuit of the town, crawling up and down the dark side streets at five miles an hour, seeing nothing untoward. They kept looking, circling the town remorselessly, hoping something would turn up.

Now it was one thirty, and they were still at it.

"You think maybe they left town?" Bill asked as Rile guided the van down Joshua Street for yet another try.

"Doubtful," Rile answered. "Lew would have no reason I can see to go gallivanting about at this hour."

"Unless there was an emergency. Charlie's sister, say." Bill sat up in his seat, warming to the notion. "His sister in San Bernardino. Suppose she got sick, had to go to the hospital. Charlie gets the call. He's got to go see her straightaway. Of course, he's got no car of his own. So he gets Lew to take him, and Lynnie goes along to keep Lew company on the way back."

Rile pursed his lips. "Maybe."

Bill was excited. He was sure he was onto something here. "You remember how Charlie's sister took sick that other time, don't you?"

"Yeah."

"And Lew drove him."

"I recall."

"It might've been something like that." Bill searched Rile's face for confirmation. "It really might."

"Uh-huh," Rile said as he swung the van onto Fourth Avenue. "Makes good sense, Bill."

Bill smiled. A huge weight had been lifted off his shoulders. There was a logical explanation, after all.

"And," Rile added dryly, "I'll bet Lew figured, seeing as how he was headed out San Bernardino way, he'd better take all those guns from the police station with him. Just in case he ran into some of those pesky redskins on the warpath, you know."

Damn.

Feeling like a fool, Bill turned away and looked at the houses creeping by.

"Guess you got me there." He sighed. "I forgot about that. Just about convinced myself I had it all ..."

His words trailed off. He stared at Stan and Judy Perkins' beat-up old Dodge, parked at the curb outside their house. For just a second, he could have sworn he'd seen a furtive human shape kneeling by the door on the driver's side. Then he'd blinked, and the shape was gone. If it had been there at all.

"Rile. Stop this thing."

The van slowed to a halt, creaking like a weary mattress.

"What is it?" Rile asked.

"See that?"

"Punch and Judy's car. So?"

"See anything else?"

"Like what?"

"Like ... like a man, maybe."

"Nope."

Bill stared at the car, then shrugged. "Guess not. Probably nothing."

"Probably," Rile agreed. He picked up his Remington and threw open the van door. "But what do you say we take ourselves a peek anyhow."

He climbed out without waiting for a reply. Bill sat for a moment, wondering why he was sorry he'd said anything, why he was sure something was out there that he didn't want to find.

He flung open the door and caught up with Rile. Together they approached the Dodge. Halfway there, Rile released the safety on the shotgun. It clicked. The sound was loud in the night stillness.

They circled the car. Moonlight glinted on chrome. The dark headlights stared like sightless eyes. Bill watched the shadows.

Nothing was there.

Bill hesitated, then stepped close to the Dodge on the driver's side, where he thought he'd seen the man. He peered through the window, which was rolled partway down. The interior was empty.

He gazed around the street. A scrap of newspaper flapped against a telephone pole. There was no other movement, no hint of life.

He released a long-held breath.

"Sorry. Like I said, it was nothing. My imagination's running away with me, I guess."

"Maybe." Rile's voice was low.

Bill looked at him. The old man's eyes were narrowed in thought, nearly sewn shut.

"But I'll tell you something, Billy boy," Rile said slowly. "I sure feel like we're being watched."

Bill tried to judge if he felt that way too. He couldn't tell. He wasn't sure how it felt to be watched.

After a moment he shook his head. "I don't," he said. "I don't feel anything except foolish. Come on. Rile, let's get back to whatever the hell it is we think we're doing."

Rile hesitated, then nodded. "Okay. Guess maybe you're not the only one with an imagination."

They returned to the van. Bill noticed that Rile kept looking back at the Dodge, keeping an eye on it, and that he was holding tight to his 12-gauge.

I sure feel like we're being watched, the old man had said.

And for a second Bill was sure Rile had been right to feel that way, because now he felt it too.

He dismissed the thought. There was nothing out here. Nothing but a parked car, a dark street, and a restless wind.

Kane lay under the Dodge, spread-eagled on the pavement, gazing out from between the tires at the two men walking back to the van. His backpack, open, lay at his side, next to one of the rusty pipes he'd salvaged from the dump. A gun, the Smith & Wesson from the police station, was in his hand. His index finger quivered slightly, like a plucked bowstring, as if itching to squeeze the trigger.

He didn't do it. His eyes were fixed on Rile Cady's shotgun.

He waited, silent and unmoving as a corpse, till the van had rumbled away down the street, out of sight.

Then he put down his gun, picked up the lead pipe, and went back to work.

PattiSue Baker was not dead.

She'd thought for sure that she was. She couldn't imagine why on earth her eyes were opening, or how she was able to feel the awful pounding in her head and the ache in her neck. Those were things you felt only when you were alive, and she couldn't be alive, not after what had happened.

She remembered every detail of her final moments. There was no mental fog, no amnesia. She remembered how Kane had stretched out his hands to close over her throat and squeeze the breath out of her. Bright lights, like pinwheels of fireworks, had spun before her eyes. She'd heard a high, tuneless singing in her ears; it rose to a screaming pitch as the pressure on her throat tightened and her skin tingled all over and her head whirled. And then—strangest thing—fog had rolled in, a gray fog, blotting out everything, until her only awareness was of a distant pain and that eerie unmelodic singing, impossibly loud now. Turn down the volume on that thing, she'd thought; it's hurting my ears.

Then there had been nothing. Nothing but that darkness and the sudden silence, crashing down like a wave on the shore, leaving her with a blessed sense of peace.

She almost hated coming out of it. Almost hated still being alive. Especially because she hurt. She hurt all over. She was sore everywhere.

She rolled over on the bed, pressing her face to the mattress, moaning. Her stomach churned. Suddenly she knew she was going to be sick. She dragged herself to the edge of the bed, leaned over, and puked a thick, viscid yellow stream. It made a puddle on the floor. She stared at it.

"Oh, jeez," she muttered. "Jeezum crow."

She crawled to the middle of the bed and lay there shivering and hugging herself and groaning.

After a long time she managed to get up. She teetered, then steadied herself. Her legs were so weak. They felt like somebody had driven a tractor over them. She looked down, half-expecting to see jagged treadmarks printed in her skin. She saw only the bruises Eddie had given her.

Eddie.

She'd forgotten him—no, not forgotten—pushed the memory out of her mind like a bad dream. Now it was back.

She gazed through the doorway into the living room. Dimly she made out the huddle of meat on the floor that was Eddie Cox.

A quavering moan escaped her lips. It was the kind of

sound a ghost would make. Is that what I am? she wondered blearily. A ghost?

She took a stumbling step toward the door. She swayed. Her knees trembled, threatening to buckle. She took another step. A yard from the door her legs gave out. She fell forward and grabbed the doorframe, holding on to it until she felt strong enough to walk again.

She went into the living room. Part of her mind, a calm, analytical part, suggested finding the light switch on the wall. She ignored it. The thought was unreal. Everything was unreal. Everything but the pain throbbing in her head and neck, and the body at her feet.

She stared down at Eddie. He was naked except for his underwear. His Jockey shorts and undershirt were bloody and torn. A broken chair leg—the one Kane had used to beat him to death—lay nearby.

She felt sick again. She doubled over, waiting. The feeling passed. She figured she'd just about puked herself out for the time being.

She circled around Eddie, not daring to look at him again. She navigated the darkness, finding her way by feel, seeking the front door. Finally her hand closed over the doorknob.

The door, she noted distantly, was shut. Kane must have shut it behind him when he left.

She paused, while it occurred to her to wonder why he'd left when she was still alive. A mistake, she decided. He'd choked her unconscious and taken her for dead. That had to be it.

Unless ...

Unless he hadn't left. Unless this was a cruel hoax, like promising to set a condemned man free and then leading him to the firing squad instead. She thought Kane might enjoy playing a trick like that. He might be waiting outside the door, waiting to spring at her and finish her off.

A spasm of terror rippled through her. Her hand jerked, twisting the knob. The door swung open with a savage violence that ripped it free of her grasp, and she gasped, staring at the doorway where Kane stood looming over her with death in his eyes.

The door banged against the wall. The firecracker burst of sound snapped her alert. She blinked. Kane wasn't there. The door had blown open on a gust of wind, that's all.

She ran a shaking hand through her hair, fighting to collect herself, then started down the stairs, stepping gratefully into the warm night as if into a warm, healing bath. She was halfway down before she realized, in mild astonishment, that she was stark naked. Her clothes must still be scattered on the bedroom floor, where she'd left them after stripping for Eddie so he could wallop her, hours and lifetimes ago.

She paused on the middle step. That same very reasonable part of her mind advised her, sensibly enough, to go back in and fetch her things. But she couldn't, just absolutely couldn't. Nothing in the world could make her return to that dark place, that fetid cave smelling of blood, or to pass by Eddie's remains again.

So she'd just have to be naked. It didn't matter. All that mattered was to get as far away from this place as possible.

She made it to the bottom of the steps and experienced the wonderful sensation of grass under her bare feet. She began walking aimlessly, randomly, seeking only to put distance between herself and the trailer. Patches of dogbane and beardtongue scraped her legs. She didn't notice. She was doing it. She was getting away.

She reached the edge of the trailer park and started walking up Joshua Street. The intersection with Fourth Avenue was just ahead. Somebody lived on Fourth Avenue, she thought. Somebody she used to know quite well. Oh, yes. Her parents. That was it.

Suddenly a wave of relief—of joy, almost—washed over her and made her feel more truly alive than she'd felt since she regained consciousness. Eddie was dead. He could never hurt her again, never bruise her body, and above all, he could never, ever mess up her face the way she'd feared. She didn't have to be afraid of him anymore.

She was free.

And that meant she could tell her folks the truth now, and they would take her back, and everything would be all right again. Yes. Everything would be fine.

PattiSue smiled for the first time in a long while, thinking of that, and imagining the look her mom and dad would give her when she showed up, buck naked, at their front door.

At two a.m., Bill and Rile pulled up to the gate of the dump.

They hadn't thought to come to the dump before, because there was no reason for Lew Hannah or anybody else to be here. But they'd seen nothing of Lew, Ellyn, and Charlie anywhere in town, and this was the last place left to look.

Rile left the engine running. He got out, toting his shotgun, and Bill joined him. At first they saw nothing. Bill was just about ready to suggest to Rile that they head on back—he didn't much like it here, what with the night wind whispering and the gate squeaking on its rusty hinges like the door of a haunted house—when Rile pointed at the ground.

"Hey. Take a look there."

Bill looked and saw nothing but dirt.

"What am I supposed to be looking at?" he asked.

"Something was dragged along the ground. Something heavy. Left a mark."

Bill squinted. This time he could just barely make out a long, irregular track. He never would have noticed it if Rile hadn't pointed it out. The man's eyes were as sharp as a hawk's.

"Okay," Bill said. "So what do you make of it?"

"Not sure. But it's easy enough to follow. Come on."

Bill trailed Rile while the older man advanced toward the gate with the shotgun gripped in his hands. Rile passed in front of the van's headlights and was briefly thrown into silhouette, a tall, bony figure awash in a white glare. Bill stepped into the light as well, and felt himself illuminated like an actor on a stage.

Then the van was behind them and the glare receded. Darkness began creeping in on all sides once more. Too much darkness. Bill shivered, feeling vaguely claustrophobic at the thought of being surrounded by those black walls of night.

"Too bad we didn't think to bring a flashlight," he said, just to hear his own voice.

"I can see fine," Rile answered without glancing back. He pointed ahead. "Whatever it was, it went through the gate."

"Coyote, maybe. Dragging a rabbit."

"Way too big for a rabbit."

"How big?"

"About the size of a man."

Bill swallowed.

Together they entered the dump. Rile kept his eyes on the ground, following the marks he saw. They walked slowly, haltingly, with only the pale moonlight to guide them. Rile stopped once, scanning the ground, then nodded, muttering under his breath, and moved forward again.

They circled a heap of discarded tires, the old rubber

shapeless and putrefying, half-melted from years of exposure to the desert sun. Then Rile froze, staring at the ground. Bill followed his gaze and hitched in a breath so quick and shallow it sounded like a hiccup.

Lew Hannah was there. Or what was left of him, anyway.

He lay on his back, staring sightlessly at the night sky with unblinking button eyes, doll's eyes. And, like a doll, he was wearing a silly grin on his face, a grin that appeared to be painted in red. It stretched from ear to ear, a demented happy-face drawn by the knife that had slit his throat.

His silver star still glittered on his chest, nearly lost to sight beneath the ragged folds of his shirt, torn open to expose the gaping hole in his chest. Surgery had been performed. Heart surgery. Lew Hannah's heart had been cut clean out of his body.

But even that was not the worst of it. The worst was seeing the bloody remnant of the heart that lay discarded on the ground at Lew Hannah's feet. It had been chewed. Eaten. Eaten raw.

"Oh, God," Bill Needham said, then spun on his heel, bent double, and lost his lunch.

After a time he regained his composure. He looked at Rile, who was standing there, calm as ever, or so it seemed until Bill looked closer and saw that Rile's head was lowered and his shoulders were shaking with soundless sobs.

Bill touched his arm. "Rile. You ... okay?"

Rile looked at him, and Bill was surprised to see that his eyes were dry. He was shaken up, yes, but still in control.

"Lynnie," Rile said in a whisper. "And Charlie too. They're still missing."

"I know."

"You think they're ...?"

Bill didn't answer. He figured there was no need.

"Come on, Rile," he said. "We've got to get out of here. Get help."

Rile nodded. "Okay, Bill."

They made their way back through the dump in the darkness, moving toward the twin beacons of the van's headlights. They walked slowly, and Bill figured he knew why: they were both afraid to run and give free rein to the panic simmering just below their unreal surface calm.

"You think Kane did this?" Rile asked as they reached the gate.

"Yes."

"But ... it isn't ... He couldn't have. No man could do a thing like this."

"He could."

"How do you know?"

"I looked into his eyes."

They closed the gate behind them and walked to the van. Bill got in on the passenger side and sat there trembling like a colt while the image of Lew Hannah's heart, ragged with toothmarks, flashed in his mind like bursts of heat lightning. He still tasted the bitter flavor of puke at the back of his mouth. He hoped to God he wouldn't throw up again.

Rile slammed the driver's-side door and immediately backed up the van.

"There were Indians," he said quietly, almost to himself, the words nearly inaudible over the rumble of the motor. "A few Indians, anyhow. Not all the tribes, not by a long way, but some. Indians who would eat a dead man's heart. Sometimes his brains too. They reckoned you could gain his spirit that way."

Bill shook his head. "Kane's no Indian."

Rile pulled onto the Old Road. "True enough. But he

might have done it for that reason, all the same."

"Might have. I couldn't say. I don't know what moves him. And I don't care. I just want him caught."

"We'll go to my place and use the phone."

"No." Bill took a breath. "We've got to go to Ethel's first."

"Ethel's?" Rile blinked. "Oh, God. You think ...?"

"I think she didn't tell us the truth. And I think she must've had a very good reason not to."

"Maybe he's got her tied up. Or ... or worse."

Bill nodded. "Or worse."

PattiSue had been leaning her fist on the doorbell for what seemed like twenty minutes, and her parents still hadn't answered. Now a terrible suspicion was taking shape amid the confusion of memories and emotions clouding her mind. A suspicion too awful to put into words. A suspicion she wouldn't acknowledge even to herself.

She gave up on the bell and tested the doorknob. The door was unlocked. She pulled it open and stepped inside.

The smell hit her instantly. A putrid rotten-egg stench. The smell of methane gas.

"Mommy," PattiSue whispered. "Daddy ..."

She staggered into the dark living room. It occurred to her that she ought to turn on the lights. Her hand was fumbling blindly for the wall switch when she remembered reading somewhere that you should never throw a switch when there's been a gas leak, because the switch might generate a spark, and a spark in a gas-filled room was the equivalent of a lighted match tossed into a tub of kerosene.

She withdrew her hand hastily from the wall, then stared into the darkness.

"Mommy!" she yelled, her voice coming back at her in echoey waves.

There was no answer.

She half-ran, half-stumbled through the ground floor of the house, heading for the kitchen, finding her way by feel. It wasn't difficult. She'd grown up in this place and she still thought of it as home, even now, when she'd gotten used to spending her nights in Eddie's trailer and hearing him snore like a buzz saw. She knew every inch of the house, the only two-story house still occupied anywhere in Tuskett, the best house in town. Best house in the world, she'd thought when she was growing up.

Only now it was a house flooded with gas. A house of death.

Finally she reached the kitchen. Just as she'd expected, the smell was strongest here. She looked at the oven, gleaming in the chalky moonlight, and saw that its door was open wide, a yawning mouth. The gas burners, pilots out, hissed like snakes.

Got to shut it off, she told herself. Turn off the gas.

She knelt by the oven and groped for the dials, twisting them to the Off position one by one. The serpent hiss grew fainter, till she switched off the last of the burners and the hiss was silenced.

That was something, at least. But not much. There was still plenty of gas everywhere. Enough to be deadly in a hurry.

She got to her feet, then swayed a little with a rush of faintness. The fumes were getting to her. She couldn't keep breathing in this stuff. What did people in the movies do in situations like this? They tore off their shirt sleeves and made face masks out of them. Good idea. Only, she was naked as a jaybird. Her shirt was back at Eddie's place. Eddie, she thought, fetch me my shirt. She giggled. That was funny.

She shook her head, clearing her mind a little, then groped in the dark and found a dishrag near the sink. She pressed it to her nose and mouth, breathing through it. Better.

She ought to run to the back door and get out while she still could. But her mom and dad ... They must be upstairs in bed. Maybe the gas hadn't reached them yet. Maybe there was a chance they were still alive. She couldn't run away and leave them.

She left the kitchen, still clutching the dishrag to her face, and ran back down the hall. Dimly she noticed that the heat in the house was stifling, unbearable; she wondered how it had gotten so hot.

Then she was in the living room again. She found the stairway and started up, taking the steps two at a time. She remembered how she'd bounded down these stairs not long ago with Trevor in her arms. The thought of the stuffed animal, and the childhood memories it evoked, stabbed her like a knife.

She was halfway up the stairs now, and already she was feeling woozy again. Her head was fairly spinning. Waves of drowsiness washed over her.

She reached the second floor. The awful swamp-gas stink wasn't quite as bad here. She allowed herself to feel hope.

"Daddy!" Her voice sounded hollow and faraway. "Mommy!"

Nothing.

She refused to give up. They couldn't be dead. It was unthinkable. Not just because they were her parents, but because ...

Because she'd never said she was sorry. She'd never told them the truth.

The bedroom was at the end of the hall. She staggered to the open door and stepped inside. She stared into the darkness.

"No," she whispered. "Oh, no."

Her father was sprawled half on the bed, half on the floor. He must have been trying to climb out when he was overcome by the fumes. His pajama pants were pasted to his leg with a large urine stain. His eyes were wide and glazed over, glassy with death.

Her mother had made it a little farther. She'd escaped from the bed and crawled halfway to the bedroom door before collapsing. She lay facedown, the tissuey folds of her nightgown tangled around her legs like swirls of ribbon around an abandoned Christmas present. No breath stirred in her body.

They hadn't died in their sleep. There wasn't even that small comfort. Something must have alerted them to the danger—the bad smell, maybe, or the murderous heat—and prompted them to a confused attempt at escape.

PattiSue stared at her parents, unable to move or react; and in the next instant she was on her knees, tugging at her mother's arm, begging her to be alive, please be alive, because there was something very important PattiSue had to say to her, something her mother had to hear.

"I'm sorry, Mommy," she whispered in a voice blurred with tears. "I'm sorry I didn't tell you what was going on with Eddie and me. I'm sorry I made things so bad between us. I'm sorry it all went so wrong. I'm sorry, oh God, I'm sorry ..."

She teetered, nearly overcome by a slow current of faintness. Past the grief, past guilt, she realized the gas was getting to her.

She forced herself to let go of her mother's arm. Unsteadily she got to her feet. Her head swam. Her knees were wobbly. She bit down on her tongue, hard enough to bloody her mouth. It didn't help. The room was spinning. She was going to pass out. She could picture herself dropping to the floor and slumping over, out like a light. She would never come to. The gas would finish her while she slept. Just like her mom and dad. Three bodies in the bedroom. Maybe it would be better that way. No pain, no sorrow. A swift descent into darkness, and then dreamless sleep forever.

No.

She wouldn't let that happen. Kane had tried to kill her and he'd failed. God had given her a second chance at life, and she wasn't going to throw it away.

She slapped herself. Her face burned with stinging pain. It revived her a little. Not much. Not enough.

Groggily she told herself she had to get out of the house. Turn and retrace her steps. Get down the stairs, out the front door.

She almost tried it. A last whisper of clear thinking stopped her. She was nearly unconscious as it was. To dive back into the swirling sea of poison downstairs would be suicide. She would never make it past the kitchen.

She looked around the bedroom. Her gaze came to rest on the bedroom window. It was shut tight.

With the last of her strength, she ran to the window and tugged it open and pressed her face to the screen. She sucked in deep healing lungfuls of clean night air. Each breath was an audible gasp, a great whooping gulp of air, the sound a drowning woman would make as she broke the surface.

Her head cleared. The world came back into focus. She stayed at the window, breathing hard, gathering her thoughts.

She remembered wondering how it had gotten so hot in here. Now she understood. All the windows in the house were shut. The place was sealed up tighter than a coffin. Sealed up to hold in the gas, to prevent it from escaping into the night.

Somebody had come to this house with murder in mind. Somebody had crept, soundless as a shadow, from one room to the next, even into the master bedroom, where her parents lay sleeping, and shut each window in turn. Somebody had slipped into the kitchen, snuffed out the pilot lights on the stove-top burners and in the oven itself, opened the oven door, and turned on the gas jets full blast.

Somebody with rattlesnake eyes.

She took a last breath of air, then left the window and hurried downstairs. She got out quickly. Then she was racing across the parched brown lawn. Racing for help.

There was only one other house still occupied on the east end of Fourth Avenue. Todd and Debbie Hanson's house.

She ran up the walk to the front door. She didn't bother with the bell. She tugged the door open and stumbled inside, half-expecting to inhale that methane stink again—but thank God, in here the air was clean.

She hurried down the hall to the back of the house, where the bedrooms were. There were light switches somewhere, but she didn't take time to look for them. She burst into the master bedroom, where Todd and Debbie lay sleeping, and she was about to yell at them to wake up when she saw that they were not going to wake up, not ever again.

Blood was pooled on the pillows. Viscid trickles flowed from gashes in their necks.

She backed out of the bedroom, moving in a sleepwalker's weightless slow-motion. Next door was Johnny's room. She went inside, knowing what she would see there. And she saw it, all right. Johnny was dead also.

Dead and gazing up at her out of a puddle of gore.

She looked at him. She shook her head slowly.

No. It couldn't be possible. There couldn't be so much killing in the world. Not in one night.

And the night wasn't over yet.

PattiSue stood staring down at Johnny Hanson for a long moment, and then something snapped inside her and she was running down the hall, out the door, into the night, running blindly, heedless of where she was going or why, while a long ululant wail rose in the night—a siren, she thought, a police siren, thank God, help's on the way—and then she realized it wasn't a siren, after all. It was only her.

She was screaming.

Jack Evans stood by the kitchen window, listening to the low, irregular clink of metal on metal, which was coming from outside.

"You hear that?" he asked finally.

Millie was bending over the kitchen table, sponging it off with compulsive cleanliness after having had a piece of buttered toast for a snack and maybe spilling some crumbs, a thing unthinkable to her. She paused in her scrubbing. "Hear what?"

"That."

"I don't hear a thing."

"Listen."

Millie listened, the sponge in her hand forgotten. Jack waited. He could still hear it, more plainly than before. Finally Millie nodded. She heard it too.

"Somebody's out front," she said softly.

"Turn off the light." His voice, too, was hushed.

She got up, found the light switch, and flipped it down. The ceiling lamp winked out. The kitchen became a nest of shadows. Jack leaned closer to the window and drew back the curtains. He peered out.

He saw nothing unusual. Saw nothing at all, in fact, except their car, an '82 Buick, parked at the curb, as usual. But the sound continued, and as he listened, he became certain that it was coming from the car.

He stepped away from the window and let the curtain fall back into place. Millie flicked the overhead light on again. Jack observed that his robe—the robe he'd been wearing ever since Jenny Kirk had gotten him out of bed more than three hours ago—had come undone. He tied the belt.

"Somebody fooling around with the car," he said.

"Fooling around ...?"

"What it sounds like."

"But ... but who?"

"Only one man I can think of."

"Jenny told us Bill reassured her on that score."

"Maybe Bill was wrong."

Millie said nothing.

Jack figured the same things were going through both their minds. They were remembering the talk they'd heard about a mystery man named Kane. A man who'd come into town out of nowhere and given the folks in Charlie's coffee shop a scare. The man who'd hurt little Tommy Kirk.

Of course, that much of the story was pure supposition on Jack's part. He had no proof, and as for Tommy, the boy still wasn't talking. Around midnight Jack had given him a tranquilizer, and the last time he'd looked, Tommy was fast asleep on the living-room couch curled up next to his mom, who was nodding off herself from sheer exhaustion.

"Jack?" Millie pressed. "What'll we do?"

Jack thought it over. "Can't call Lew. He's ... not around."

"How about the state police?"

"It's a thought. I ... Wait a second. Hear that?"

They listened.

Sudden silence filled the night. The noises from out front had stopped.

"Guess he's through with whatever he's doing," Millie said tensely.

Jack licked his lips. Suddenly he was afraid.

"Maybe," he said as calmly as possible. "Or maybe ... maybe he noticed how the kitchen light went off and came on again. Maybe he saw me peeking out the window. Maybe he knows we heard him."

Millie hitched in a breath.

"Jack, call the state police." Her voice was low and urgent. "Call them right now. Tell them we've got a problem here."

Jack nodded. She was right. It was the only answer.

He turned to the phone. It was a fancy one with digital dialing and a wall mount for the handset; he'd bought it two years ago at a Sears store in Phoenix, as a Christmas present for his wife. Other folks were frankly envious. Rotary phones were still the norm in Tuskett; this item had the sleek, streamlined look of a prop in a science-fiction movie.

He reached the phone in two steps. His fingers closed over the handset. The hard plastic shell felt strangely reassuring. He gripped it tight. He lifted the phone and punched one digit—0 for Operator—and behind him there was an explosion.

He whirled.

The window screen had burst out of its frame; the curtains had tangled in it instantly, and the curtain rod had been ripped out of the wall to crash in the kitchen sink.

Jack saw that, but the information barely registered,

because his attention was fixed on the man who'd leapt through the window and landed catlike on the floor.

Kane.

He matched the description given him in the local gossip, right down to the long black coat flapping around him like a vulture's wings. His hat had slipped off his head and dangled from its chin strap. His hair was crazily askew, standing out every which way.

Kane reached into his coat and out of its voluminous folds he withdrew a gun. It was a Smith & Wesson .32 and it was pointed at Jack Evans' chest.

Jack opened his mouth and shut it. There was nothing he could think of to say.

"Operator sixty-four," a small, distant, oddly tinny voice said, and it took Jack a moment to realize it was the voice of the operator coming from the phone he still gripped in one hand. "May I be of service?"

Jack looked at the phone, then at Kane.

"Hang up," Kane said.

Jack hesitated. He knew he had no choice. But he didn't want to hang up. Because then his only contact with the outside world—his last hope, and Millie's too—would be lost.

"Hello?" the flylike voice buzzed. "Hello? May I help you?"

Kane raised the gun a half inch. He pulled back the safety with a sharp snap. His finger drew down on the trigger.

Jack hung up the phone. The handset clicked as it settled into the wall mount. It was a small sound, barely audible, of no consequence to anyone else; but to Jack it sounded like the death of hope.

He met Kane's eyes. Cold eyes. Empty eyes.

"Please," Jack Evans said.

Kane shot him.

The gunshot was loud in the small room. It reverberated off Millie's spotless walls and immaculate Formica countertops like an explosion. Jack had time to think that Jenny, in the living room, would surely hear it; he hoped she had the good sense to grab Tommy and run.

In the next instant it hit him—the pain from the scorched crater in his chest. It felt like gas. Like a really bad bubble of gas after a greasy meal. He doubled over and tried desperately to burp. Only a wheezing gasp came out. His knees buckled and he pitched headfirst onto the floor. He lay in a quivering heap, fighting for breath that would not come. His pajamas and robe were warm and sticky with blood.

Bullet must've punctured a lung, he thought dizzily. Left lung, judging from the point of entry.

He'd seen a case like that once, years ago, when old Devon Tyler had gone out hunting rattlers and wound up shooting only himself. The bullet had ripped through a lobe of one lung and collapsed the damn thing like an air-filled paper bag swatted by a child's fist.

He was aware that he was going into shock. Normal reaction under the circumstances. Oh, yes. It was all very normal. He might be dying, but at least he was doing it by the book.

He gazed up at Kane. The man seemed to have shot up twenty feet. He was gigantic, towering. Jack thought of the Colossus of Rhodes, the bronze statue that had been one of the ancient world's wonders, a human figure a hundred feet tall.

Kane lowered the gun, aiming dead at Jack's face. Jack waited for the blast that would send a bullet ripping through his skull to chew his cerebral cortex to guava jelly.

Behind Kane, a flash of motion—Millie, lunging for the kitchen cabinet, yanking open a drawer, seizing something from inside. A knife. The carving knife that had scared Tommy so badly before, the knife Jenny had snatched up and stashed in the drawer, safely out of sight. Its blade was still smeared with blueberry goo, dark and crusted like congealed blood.

Millie raised the knife. She let out a cry like a Cherokee war whoop and ran at Kane and buried the knife in his left shoulder. Kane hissed like steam.

Jack experienced a brief, heady thrill. Got you, he thought.

Kane clawed at the knife. Blood bubbled out of the wound and ran down his coat to patter on the linoleum tiles. It occurred to Jack that this was the first time his wife had ever deliberately soiled her waxed-and-polished, Mop-&-Glo'd kitchen floor.

Millie backed away, laughing like a schoolgirl. Tears dampened her cheeks.

"So how do you like them apples?" she said in a high, thin voice. "How do you like—"

Kane aimed the gun at her, almost casually, and fired directly at Millie Evans' face.

Her head snapped back. Her legs flew out from under her. For an instant she hung in space like the freeze-frame of a movie comedian doing a pratfall. Then the image unfroze and she thudded on the floor, her face foaming with a red cataract.

Jack stared at her from across ten feet of spotless floor tiles still smelling faintly of ammonia. The pool of blood around his wife's head deepened and spread. Going to be hard to clean that up, Jack thought. Oh, Millie's going to be furious when she sees this mess.

Kane tugged at the knife. With a muffled grunt, he yanked it of his shoulder and threw it aside. He turned to Jack. The gun in his hand swiveled lazily, like the blade of a ceiling fan rotating languidly on a hot summer evening, and came to rest with its muzzle staring at Jack's face. It gazed down at him, a single, unblinking, pupilless eye.

A third shot echoed in the room, but this time Jack didn't hear it.

The crash of shattering glass in the kitchen had shocked Jenny Kirk out of a restless sleep haunted by a shadow figure chasing her son through a maze of night. She sat up on the couch, her body taut.

From the kitchen came low voices. She couldn't identify who was speaking or what was being said, but it must be Jack and Millie because who else would be in there? Something breakable must have hit the floor. A china plate or a drinking glass.

She almost called out to Jack and Millie to ask if they were okay. Something stopped her, some slow spider crawl of fear, sourceless, irrational, but undeniably there.

She waited, as if expecting something to happen, and in the next moment something did.

An explosion.

It rolled through the house like a drumroll of thunder. She thought of firecrackers, cars backfiring, guns.

Guns.

A gunshot.

Beside her, Tommy stirred. The sedative was still in his system, but the noise had been loud enough to reach him in the depths of sleep. He lifted his head and stared into space, bleary-eyed.

"It's okay," Jenny whispered, knowing that it wasn't. "Don't be afraid. We've got to get out of here, that's all."

She scooped him up in her arms. He put up no resistance. He felt so small, like an infant again. She noticed irrelevantly that he had his thumb stuck in his mouth. When was the last time she'd seen him do that?

She rose from the couch. She crossed the living room

slowly, planting each foot with care to avoid making a sound that would give away her presence in the house.

She was halfway to the door when she heard a sharp cry, a screech of fury or pain. Millie's cry. She was sure of it, though she'd never heard Millie Evans make a sound like that, and she doubted anybody else had, either. It was followed by another gunshot and the thud of something falling, something that might have been a body hitting the floor.

Tommy began to tremble. He shook like a puppy in her arms.

She reached the door. She fumbled with the knob.

From the kitchen came a third shot. Jack and Millie were dead now. She was grimly certain of it.

The door swung open under her hand. Warm night air rushed in. She prepared to step onto the porch and run like hell ...

There was another shot, louder than before, and a chunk of plaster was ripped out of the wall a foot away.

Jenny stared in empty astonishment at the rising plume of plaster dust and the perfect round hole in the wall where the bullet had hit.

"Don't move," a voice said from behind her. A hard, unfriendly voice.

Tommy made a strangled sound, his closest approach to speech in hours. Jenny looked down at him and saw his face twisted into an extremity of terror she wouldn't have believed possible, his small fist jammed into his mouth to stifle a scream.

She stood motionless, waiting for instructions.

"Turn around," the voice said. "Slow."

She did so. She stood facing the man across the living room, the man who must be Kane.

It was the gun she focused on first. It was small and black and shiny, like a toy, a plastic pistol from Tommy's toy chest. Her gaze rose to the trickle of blood from his shoulder, pasting the sleeve of his coat to his arm, then to the pale angular face framed by a rat's-nest tangle of straw-colored hair, a face made of the thin bloodless line of his mouth, the hawk nose, and the eyes.

The eyes ...

She stared into those eyes and felt herself float free of her body like a boat cut loose from its moorings. She hovered in space. She felt no fear, no shock. She didn't even exist anymore. There was only this man and his eyes, watching her, probing her soul, and claiming it as his own.

Kane watched her for a moment, then shifted his gaze to Tommy, breaking eye contact with her. Instantly she snapped out of whatever trance she'd been in. Blood roared in her head like a freight train. She swayed with a rush of faintness.

She held her son tight, feeling the pressure of Tommy's fingers on her arm, the trembling of his body against hers. Their two hearts beat as one.

"Hello, Tommy," Kane said softly. "You should have known you couldn't get away."

Tommy stared at Kane, then moaned, a low, childish, bad-dream sound, and buried his face in his mother's blouse.

Jenny lifted her head to Kane, summoned all her courage, and found her voice.

"Leave him alone," she said quietly, the words crackling with tension like power lines on a rainy day. "Don't you dare touch him."

Kane smiled.

"Now, don't you worry, my dear. I won't hurt your little boy. I won't lay a hand on him." The smile faded. "At least ... not until I'm done with you."

- — -

"Holy Christ."

The words were barely out of Bill Needham's mouth when Rile Cady hit the brake and brought the van lumbering to a stop. Ahead, spotlighted in the headlight beams, was a young woman running down the middle of Joshua Street, coming straight at them, naked as a baby. Her long blond hair was in disarray, her face streaked with tears, her body peppered with welts and bruises. It took Bill a moment to recognize her.

"PattiSue," he said. "Hell, Rile, that's PattiSue!"

He hadn't thought anything could surprise him anymore, not after what he and Rile had found at the dump ... and at Ethel's house. They'd gone straight there and let themselves in. The living room was empty. The door to the bedroom was open wide. And there in the middle of the floor lay Ethel Walston, dead. Bill couldn't tell quite how she'd died, but there was a mess of blood, and it surely hadn't been quick or easy.

Lying near her body, curled up in a shaggy ball, was old Scooter. The spaniel, too, was dead. He seemed to have died of shock. Or grief, maybe.

There had been no sign of Kane. They'd checked the guest room and found it empty. The bed hadn't been slept in. All the man's belongings—his coat, hat, backpack—were gone.

Ethel had two phones in her place, one in her bedroom, the other in the living room. Both telephone cords had been slashed. That was no great matter. There were other phones in town. At the Evans place, for one. Where Jenny and Tommy were. If Kane hadn't gotten there too ...

Rile had nearly reached Third Avenue, where Jack and Millie lived, when PattiSue came into view, naked and on the run.

Bill flung open the van door and jumped out. He ran to the girl, still racing toward the headlights. She didn't seem to see him or anything else.

"PattiSue!" he shouted.

She ignored him, kept running. He reached out and grabbed her arm, just to slow her down. She screamed, a torture-chamber sound, and beat at his hands, grunting like an animal, a net of hair plastered across her face.

"Hey, it's me!" Bill held on to her arm with one hand, using the other to fend off the flurry of fists. "PattiSue, it's me, Bill!"

She didn't seem to hear. She was crazed, out of her mind. Ropes of spit swung from her mouth. Her eyes danced like the lights on a pinball machine. She thrust her free hand at Bill's face, the fingers stiff as claws. He grabbed her hand. She struggled and kicked and spun him in circles, fighting to break free.

Then Rile was there. He grabbed her from behind. She howled.

Bill let go of her arm and slapped her hard across the face with the flat of his hand.

She froze up, stock-still, and in the next second her legs folded under her and she sank limply in Rile's arms, boneless as a kitten.

"Let's get her in the van," Bill said, forcing out the words between gasps.

Together they half-carried, half-dragged the girl into the rear of the vehicle and set her down on the carpeted floor. She lay on her back, her pretty face flushed, her breasts heaving. Rile found a denim jacket stashed in a corner and draped her with it for modesty's sake.

Then her eyes, bright and feverish, seemed to come briefly into focus, and she lifted her head to speak one word: "Kane."

"Damn," Rile muttered. "That son of a bitch has been busy tonight."

- — -

Jenny closed her eyes and tried not to scream.

She could feel Tommy's eyes on her, watching. Watching his mother as she stood unmoving in the middle of the living room with Kane's hand on her breast, kneading it, his fingers cold, so cold, like icicles, like death.

She'd known he had something like this in mind. She guessed it even when she was still frozen in the doorway, facing him from across the room. She knew it from the slow sickly smile that crawled across his face as he looked at the boy in her arms, and then at her.

"Put him down," he'd said.

She hesitated, reluctant to part with Tommy, to release her hold on his warm, living body, when she knew she might never hold him again. Then she realized that if she could distract the man, Tommy might be able to escape out the front door. The thought gave her strength. Gently she set the boy down on the floor.

"Now, get over there." He gestured toward the middle of the room.

She went. There was no hesitation this time. Kane was making a mistake. He would have to direct his attention to her and away from Tommy. She would wait for an opportune moment, then yell at Tommy to run, and he would be out the door before Kane could stop him.

She was still running through her plan of action when Kane turned to look at the boy.

"Tommy," he said softly. "You remember me. Don't you?"

Tommy nodded. His eyes were very big.

"Good. I want you to watch what happens now. Do you hear me? I want you to stand there like a good boy and watch. Just watch. No matter what happens."

Tommy nodded again. He made no further movement, showed no sign of life other than the slow rise and fall of his chest with each drawn-out breath.

Jenny stared at him. She knew with irrational certainty that it would do no good to yell at him to run, because Tommy wouldn't hear her now. He would stand rooted to the spot, his face blank and eyes empty, while Kane did what he wished with her.

And she knew what it was he wished. She knew from the look in his eyes as he studied her, from the visible tightness of his throat. She'd known it, she supposed, all along.

"You're lovely, my dear." His voice, low and strangely gentle, wound around her like a ribbon of smoke. "Tell me your name."

"Jenny."

"How sweet. How pretty. I want you to take your shirt off for me, Jenny. I want to see your breasts."

"No."

"Oh, yes." He said it simply, matter-of-factly, as if it were the most obvious, most incontestable fact in the world. "Yes, you will. You have no choice."

"Don't I?"

"No."

"Why not?"

"Because I'll kill your son." The gun swiveled briefly in Tommy's direction. "Blow his head clean off." Then the gun was back on her again. "See?"

She looked at Tommy. He was lost in whatever spell had claimed his mind. His face was vacant. Nobody was home. She supposed it was better that way.

"Do it," Kane said. The illusion of gentleness had vanished from his voice. The words came out hard, cruel, like shards of glass.

Yes, she thought. He's right. You have to do it. Or he'll kill Tommy right now. You know he will.

She raised a trembling hand to her blouse. She fumbled with the buttons. The blouse opened. She shrugged it off, exposing the white cups of her bra, and even though she was no more naked than she would have been on a public beach, she felt a stab of terrible humiliation and shame.

"Come on," Kane said. "That too."

She reached behind her back and found the clasp. The bra fell to the floor.

"Good. Very good."

He crossed the room. He stopped directly before her. For the first time she realized how tall he was. She stared up at him, then looked away, her eyes squeezed shut, not to see the feral glint of his teeth. She tried not to think about anything, least of all what was going to happen next.

He pressed the gun to her ribs, below her heart. The muzzle was cold. She shivered. With his free hand he touched the nipple of her left breast. He rubbed it gently. She felt the breast stiffen and hated her body for its treason.

"Look at me, Jenny."

She wouldn't. She remembered what had happened when she'd met his gaze before—how his eyes had carried her out of herself, into a flickering twilight. She thought of Tommy, mesmerized by the same demonic stare.

Kane was kneading her breast now. His hand rotated slowly, languidly, moving to its own rhythm. A strangely hypnotic rhythm. She felt herself growing torpid, her muscles relaxing, her heartbeat slowing.

No, she thought. Don't.

"Jenny. Look at me."

She moaned. She wouldn't do it. Wouldn't open her eyes. But the slow motion of his hand on her breast went on and on, lulling her to sleep, like a baby calmed by the steady rocking of a cradle. She began to sway back and forth, performing a senseless hula dance. Her head lolled on her shoulders. She was drifting off to sleep.

"So lovely." His voice was strangely soothing. "You have beautiful eyes. Let me see your eyes."

She let her eyelids slide open. She looked down at his hand. His fingers caressed the tender skin of her breast, rubbing hard, leaving long red marks. She thought of a sculptor kneading clay. I'm putty in his hands, she told herself stupidly. The idea struck her as funny. She giggled.

"You like this, don't you? Of course you do. Look at me."

She raised her head a little, then stopped, seeing Tommy. He was watching her. She couldn't tell if he knew what was happening or not. She prayed he didn't.

Don't watch, she wanted to tell him. Don't watch this. Please, Tommy. I don't want you to see what happens next.

She couldn't find the strength to speak. She had no energy left, and no willpower. She was Kane's puppet, his toy. She would do whatever he wished. She would let him take her, love her, kill her. She couldn't fight him.

Too weak, a low reproachful voice whispered. You're too weak, Jenny Kirk.

It's true, she agreed, and lifted her head the rest of the way to look into Kane's eyes.

Colors swirled there in kaleidoscopic patterns. All kinds of colors. Dazzling, like rainbows. She had thought his eyes were blue, sky blue. But now it was as if the sky had come alive with an iridescent aurora, something strange and wonderful. She could watch it all day.

She barely even noticed when he put down the gun, then lifted her onto the couch.

- — -

Tommy stared at the man who'd chased him down in the dump, and who, like a bad dream he couldn't shake off, had come back to terrorize him again. Only, this time it was worse, a million times worse, because this time his mom was going to be his victim, and Tommy could only stand and watch and wait for it to be over.

The man had his mother on the couch now. She lay with her skirt hitched up high, her long suntanned legs splayed awkwardly, her blouse and bra lying discarded on the floor. The man stood leaning over her with a hand on her breast, rubbing hard.

Tommy knew with terrible certainty what was going to happen next. The man was going to have intercourse with her. He was going to force his penis into her vagina, which Johnny Hanson called a pussy. There was a name for that. Rape. He knew all about rape. It was always on the TV news from LA. Ladies were always getting raped by bad men back there. Not in Tuskett, though. Not until now.

On the couch, his mother moaned. The man was kissing her breast now. Biting it. Drawing blood. Pinpricks of red blossomed around her nipple.

Soon, Tommy knew, the man would be inside her, having intercourse with her, and not long after that, he would kill them both.

Rile Cady steered his van to the Evans place in record time. He wanted to find a phone, but more than that, he wanted to check in on Jack and Millie and, above all, on Jenny and the boy.

Some sixth sense prompted him to kill the engine at the corner of Third Avenue, then coast silently the rest of the way.

"Good idea," Bill Needham said from the passenger seat.

Rile forced a smile. "Like the man said, we aren't exactly delivering flowers."

He parked at the curb behind Jack Evans' Buick. He checked his 12-gauge, making sure there were five slugs in the magazine, then got out. Meanwhile Bill fetched PattiSue from the rear of the van. The jacket that had preserved some degree of her feminine modesty slipped loose. Rile noted how hastily Bill snatched it up and helped the girl put it on. A regular gentleman, was Bill.

"You notice the door?" Bill asked, keeping his voice low.

Rile nodded. "I noticed."

The front door of the Evans place was open wide. Maybe to let in some air on this hot night. Maybe Jack and Millie were sitting around the living room, sipping iced tea, talking with Jenny Kirk, while little Tommy slept peaceful as an angel in her arms. Or maybe not.

Wordlessly Rile drew back the hammer on his 12-gauge. He went up the path to the front steps and crept onto the porch, then edged close to the open doorway. Bill followed with PattiSue in tow. Together the three of them peered inside.

The first thing Rile saw was Tommy, standing near the door, his small body oddly still, his head cocked at an angle, shoulders slumped. Then Rile raised his eyes, following the line of the boy's sight, and saw Jenny Kirk, naked from the waist up, sprawled on the couch with Kane all over her, his spider fingers kneading her breasts. The living room was lit by a single lamp on an end table; its yellow glow gave Kane's face a pale sheen, highlighting the man's features, human features twisted into a waxworks mockery of passion, a carnival mask of bared teeth and bulging eyes. He made low grunts, animal sounds, sounds that belonged in the dank recesses of a cave.

As Rile watched, Kane lowered his head to Jenny's

breast and his teeth sank into the skin below her nipple. Rile thought of a vampire drawing blood.

He stood moveless in the doorway, mesmerized by shock, unable to take in what he was seeing, and then PattiSue Baker screamed. The noise shocked all three men alert—Rile, and Bill ... and Kane.

Bill acted first. He reached past Rile, grabbed Tommy by the arm, and yanked him back, out of the doorway, so roughly that the boy fell sprawling on the porch on hands and knees, then lay there stunned.

PattiSue's scream segued into choking sobs. She hung on to the doorframe, her legs sagging. Jenny shook her head groggily, her own hands moving over her breasts, rubbing at them as if to rub away the feel of the alien presence they had known.

Kane was already off the couch, on his feet, his coat swirling around him like gusts of black rain. He reached for the floor, and Rile saw a gun there, a pistol Kane must have dropped in his eagerness to take Jenny—to take her, good God, to take her right in front of her eight-year-old son. Kane's hand nearly closed over the barrel of the gun, and then Rile fired.

The shotgun barked once, a stinging handclap that set his ears ringing. Kane was hit. Blood blossomed on his shirt, red blotches expanding like the petals of a flower.

He was thrown backward by the impact. He slammed into a wall.

Calmly, coldly, feeling no emotion, Rile drew back the hammer and prepared to fire again. This time he would finish the bastard. He'd never killed a man in his life. He would have hesitated even to squash an insect. But this was different. This man had declared war on their town, he was taking no prisoners, and now he was going to perish in that war, as the first and only casualty on his side.

Rile squeezed the trigger in the instant when Kane

leapt away from the wall. The slug plowed harmlessly through plaster, kicking up dust.

Rile swung the gun toward Kane and snapped back the hammer again, swearing to himself that he wouldn't miss this time, and then Kane seized the lamp and hurled it at the doorway. Rile ducked as the lamp burst into a rain of ceramic shards over his head, and the room went black.

For a second time PattiSue screamed. Bill shushed her with a whispered command. Rile paid no notice. His whole being was focused on the shifting play of shadows before his eyes. One of those shadows was Kane. But which? He fired into the darkness, heard the thud of the slug striking wood or plaster, but not flesh and bone, not his target.

Then the living-room window exploded with a cymbal crash of splintered glass. Kane had jumped through.

"He's getting away!" Bill shouted.

Rile knew that. He didn't need to hear it. He didn't need to be reminded that he'd been outwitted and outmatched.

He brushed past Bill and PattiSue, down the porch steps. He saw Kane racing across the front lawn like a black streak. He squeezed off a fourth shot; it didn't connect. Then Kane was in the van—my van, Rile thought in a spasm of rage, the son of a bitch is stealing my van—and as the engine sputtered to life, Rile had time to remember having left the keys in the ignition like a damn fool.

The van thundered away. Rile got off a final shot, emptying the gun. He wanted to hit a tire, but his aim was wild; his hands were shaking in fury and frustration. Then the van screamed around a corner, veering onto Joshua Street, and was lost to sight.

"Damn," Rile said miserably. "God damn."

- — -

The first thing to do was to call the police. The phone, as Bill knew well enough from frequent visits to Jack and Millie's place down through the years, was in the kitchen. He left Rile with the others and went into the kitchen. Just inside the doorway he stopped short, staring down at the two bodies sprawled on the floor in crimson pools.

He wasn't surprised. He'd figured the two of them must be dead. It was the only plausible way to explain their absence from the living room. Still, he hadn't expected to come on them like this. It took his breath away for a moment.

He shook his head, pushing everything out of his mind except the need to summon help. He stepped over the huddle of meat that had been Jack Evans, his doctor and his father's doctor too, and reached for the phone. But it wasn't there. It had been ripped off the wall and flung to the floor. The cord was severed. Like the ones in Ethel's place.

Bill looked at the phone, then reached down and picked it up and put it to his ear, irrationally hoping to hear a dial tone. There was silence.

He let the phone slip out of his hand. It clattered on the floor.

It occurred to him that there might be an extension in the bedroom. He checked. There wasn't. But while he was in there, he did find a dress—one of Millie's, a bright summer dress with flowers printed on a field of blue. He figured PattiSue could use it. He carried it to the living room, where he found the girl seated on the couch, covering her breasts with her hands and shivering. Beside her sat Jenny; she had shown the presence of mind to slip her shirt back on; now she was holding Tommy tight. The boy looked shell-shocked. His face was empty. His mind was far away.

"I don't know what happened to me," Jenny kept saying over and over, to nobody. "It was like ... like being hypnotized. He looked at me and I just ... wasn't myself anymore. I don't know what happened to me. I just don't know."

"It's okay," PattiSue said quietly. "I ... I understand."

The hitch in her voice told Bill she understood only too well.

He gave the dress to PattiSue without a word. She nodded gratefully and retreated into the next room to put it on.

Rile stood by the window, studying the night. Bill moved to his side. He spoke quietly, so Jenny wouldn't overhear. She had enough to deal with right now.

"Jack and Millie are dead. In the kitchen."

Rile nodded. His face registered no surprise.

"Phone's been disconnected," Bill went on. "The bastard isn't taking any chances."

"There are other phones," Rile said evenly.

"Yeah. Closest house is the Lewis place." Dick and Gretchen Lewis lived right down the street. No doubt they'd heard the racket made by Rile's shotgun and were scared silly. Assuming, that is, they were still alive.

"Want me to go over there?" Rile asked.

"Not alone. We're going together."

"We can't leave them." Rile jerked his head in the direction of the couch. "Suppose he comes back."

"We've got to take the chance. He's still out there. He might be after somebody else by now."

"Okay." Rile nodded. "Fetch me that pistol, will you?"

Bill followed his gaze and saw the .32 on the floor. He picked it up and handed it to Rile. Rile checked it and found three rounds in the chambers. The other three, Bill figured, were in Jack and Millie Evans.

"One of Lew's guns," Rile observed. "He kept it in the police station."

Bill looked more closely at it. "Uh-huh. So it is. Tell you the truth, I'd nearly forgotten about that." He took a breath. "All those guns were missing."

"Yeah." Rile looked at him. "Our Mr. Kane has got himself a regular arsenal."

"We'd better get going."

"I'd say so."

"I'll tell Jenny."

"While you're at it"—Rile handed him the .32—"give her this. And make sure she knows where the trigger is."

Bill smiled. "Right."

He crossed the room to the couch and spoke to Jenny in a low voice, which was hardly necessary since PattiSue was still in the other room, changing, and Tommy was showing no sign of awareness. He explained the situation. He avoided giving any details of what he'd found in the kitchen, suggesting merely that she and the others keep out of there for the time being. Jenny nodded. She didn't seem surprised either. Nobody was surprised anymore by what was going on. It was all too much. Whatever defense mechanisms the mind employed in situations like this had gone into action, erecting barriers and stifling emotion. At least for now.

"Okay," Bill said when he finished talking. "Rile and I will be back in a few minutes. Just hang tight. And hold on to this." He gave her the gun. "You know how to use it, right?"

"I guess so."

"There are three bullets."

"Okay."

He started to move away.

"Bill." He looked at her. "Thank you," she said softly. "For ... for rescuing me."

He shrugged. "Rile did it. I just stood there. No need to thank me." It wasn't modesty, just the truth.

"But I'm the one who called you, asked you to look in on Lew and Lynnie. I got you into this."

He thought back to the moment when he'd faced Kane in the dying sunlight at the edge of town. He remembered how Kane had looked at him, his blue eyes cold and mocking. He heard the man's slow voice, telling him how he'd been looking for a place like Tuskett, population twenty-three, where no doors were ever locked at night.

"No," Bill said quietly. "I was in it already. All of us were." He met her eyes. "We still are."

Jenny nodded. She held Tommy tight with one hand and the gun with the other.

Kane was bleeding badly. He had a knife wound in his shoulder and a shotgun slug in his gut. Another man would have been laid up in a hospital, at the very least, after taking punishment like that. Kane was not another man. He showed no outward sign of distress. His face was an expressionless mask.

He drove Rile Cady's van to the south end of town and parked outside the trailer park. He got out, moving swiftly, spilling bright droplets of crimson as he walked, like a trail of bread crumbs. He made his way to the rear of the park, where Lew Hannah's Ford Tempo was safely hidden from sight.

The floor of the car's front seat was empty; the half-dozen lead pipes salvaged from the dump were gone. In the backseat lay three guns—two rifles, the Browning bolt-action from the police station and the Winchester from the Baker house, and one handgun, the Llama .22 stolen from the hall closet of the Hannah place.

Kane stuffed the rifles into the deep side pockets of

his coat. Then he picked up the Llama and inspected the gun. He nodded, his narrowed eyes glinting as deeply blue as the finish on the polished gun barrel.

Still holding the .22, Kane left the trailer park and climbed behind the wheel of the van. He drove the short distance to the end of Joshua Street, where the Old Road began, and where the power and phone cables branched off from the main transmission line. He parked not far from the first utility pole, then got out and stared up at it, the .22 gripped in his hand.

Slowly he lifted the gun, pointing upward, toward the sky, like a referee raising a starter pistol to signal the commencement of the chase.

He was smiling.

It took Bill Needham and Rile Cady less than five minutes to walk from the Evans place to Dick and Gretchen Lewis' house, but it seemed much longer than that. As soon as he stepped out the door, Bill felt the night close over him like the lid of a casket. His heart sped up. His breathing became shallow. He tried to take a deep breath to relax himself, but he couldn't seem to get any air.

Kane was out here. Somewhere.

Bill reminded himself that Kane had gone racing off in Rile's van. But who was to say how far he'd gone? It could be a trick. The man had ripped the phone out of the wall; that meant he knew the folks in the house couldn't get help without going outside. Even now he might be lying in wait with a gun in his hand, ready to open fire and cut them down like targets in a shooting gallery ...

"Maybe we ought to take Jack and Millie's car," Rile said as they reached the curb.

Bill knew what he meant. Ordinarily there would have been no thought of driving to the Lewis house, less than a block away. But tonight ...

He looked into the car. "No keys in the ignition. We'd have to go back and get them." He licked his lips. "Look through Jack's pockets, maybe."

"Forget it," Rile said. "Just a notion."

"It's not far."

"Right."

That was true, of course. It wasn't far. Just a short walk. But the walk to the gallows was short enough too. That didn't make it a Sunday stroll.

By unspoken agreement they walked in the middle of the street, keeping their distance from the houses on either side, any one of which might have concealed a lurking figure. They said nothing. Their shoes crunched on the blistered macadam. The dry air swirled and eddied around them. Somewhere an owl hooted throatily, then was still.

Rile had his shotgun with him, still clutched in both hands, like always. Of course, it was no better than a movie prop now; he'd fired all five slugs. But Kane might not know that. It was something, anyhow. Besides, Bill figured, Rile seemed to like the feel of that gun in his hands. Bill couldn't blame him.

The Lewis place was the last house on the block, near the intersection of Third and Joshua. The gray shape of the water tower on the far side of the main street loomed over it like some immense dark idol. Distant speckles of light, which were shops and homes, were scattered in the darkness around it like so many stars.

Together Bill and Rile mounted the steps to the porch. Rile jabbed at the doorbell. From inside, Dick Lewis yelled, "Who is it?"

Well, he was alive, at least. Alive, and scared. Bill knew as much from his tone of voice, and from the very fact that he'd asked who was there. Folks in Tuskett weren't normally shy about receiving visitors, no matter how late the hour.

"Open up, Dick," Bill told him. "It's Bill Needham. I'm here with Rile. There's trouble."

A moment later the door swung open. Dick was there, dressed in his barber clothes, a fancy shirt and pants that had obviously been tossed on just minutes ago, most likely when the sounds of gunfire roused him and Gretchen from sleep. His thin hair looked greasy and stiff, the way hair got when it had been slept on. His face was ashen with fear. Bill remembered how he and Dick had sat on this very porch only a few hours ago and passed the time. The memory seemed unreal.

"Bill," Dick Lewis said by way of greeting. "Rile. Come on in." His face went through the motions of a smile, but his eyes were fixed on the shotgun in Rile's hands.

They entered. Dick closed the door behind them. Bill experienced a rush of relief at the thought that the night had been shut out.

He looked around the living room. A lamp was lit; the yellow-shaded bulb cast twin cones of light on walls decorated with paintings done in watercolor and acrylic, nature scenes mostly, which Gretchen had picked up at uncounted garage sales in nearby towns. It was a hobby of hers, art.

At the far end of the room stood the lady herself, still in her nightgown, wringing her hands in a pantomime of worry. Without makeup, her face showed its age, and fear had added some new wrinkles of its own. Her eyes were too wide and too alert for this time of night; the lashes fluttered like moth wings.

Bill glanced down at her side, where a half-finished jigsaw puzzle lay in a scatter of multicolored pieces on a coffee table. At the edge of the table, catching the yellow light with its molded-plastic shell, was a telephone. Still hooked up. Still in one piece. Bill's mind eased a little as he saw it.

"We heard some commotion down the street," Dick said. He sounded like a man doing his level best to keep his voice steady and his face calm, to be the same unflappable fellow he'd been on the front porch not so long ago, but failing. "I was just meaning to go on over and take a look."

Which was probably true enough, as far as it went, judging from those tossed-on clothes; but Bill had a feeling the other half of the truth was that Dick had been loitering in the living room, making excuses for not going just yet.

"So," Dick asked, looking from Bill to Rile and back again, "what's up?"

Bill figured there was no way to sugarcoat it and no use trying. "Bad news," he said grimly, and summarized the situation as best he could in a few terse sentences. He couldn't help noticing that Gretchen had gone ghost-pale, like a woman on the verge of dropping in a dead faint, and Dick had put his hand to his chin and kept it there as if it was glued on.

"So we figure there are at least six dead. Four of them—Jack and Millie, and Ethel Walston and Lew Hannah—for sure. Ellyn Hannah and Charlie Grain almost certainly. There may be more; PattiSue was too shaken up to talk about it, and I don't—"

"Oh, Lord," Gretchen said, and just like that, her legs folded and she sank to the floor. She didn't faint, not quite. She simply knelt there, blinking back tears and staring at nothing.

Dick went to her. Unsteadily he knelt at her side and took her hand.

"It'll be all right, honey," he whispered.

She didn't answer; but Bill was watching closely, and

he couldn't help but notice how her lips moved to form one soundless word: *Charlie.*

He glanced at Rile, who nodded to indicate he'd seen it too.

But Dick hadn't. And that was good. Because if he'd seen Gretchen mouth that name, if he'd understood what made her knees buckle like that, at just that moment—well, it would have killed him, simply killed the man; and Bill figured there had been enough killing in Tuskett tonight as it was.

"So that's the story," Bill finished briskly. "Now we need to use your phone. Got to call the cops in Jacob."

Dick gestured feebly toward the coffee table. "Sure," he said. "It's no bother. No bother at all." He said it lightly, as if this sort of thing happened all the time.

Bill crossed the room to the telephone, picked it up, and put the receiver to his ear. He heard the low, comforting hum of the dial tone. Things were finally under control.

He was about to dial 0 for Operator when he heard a sound, like a distant crack of thunder—or a gunshot.

The lamp winked out like a snuffed candle. Blackout.

Gretchen screamed.

"It's okay, now, it's okay," Dick said, but the reassurance rang hollow because his own voice sounded high and shaky, the voice of a man who'd taken a hit of helium and was teetering on the edge of a fit of hysterical giggling.

There was a second crack of sound, a third, a fourth.

Bill remembered the telephone in his hand. He listened for the dial tone but couldn't hear it anymore. The phone was dead.

He heard another gunshot in the night, from somewhere far away, the edge of town, maybe—and he understood.

Kane was bringing down the lines. Shooting them

down, from the sound of things. And Bill most definitely didn't care for the implications of that development.

All the phones would be out now.

But that wasn't the worst of it. The worst was that the lights would be out too. Out everywhere.

Years ago, Tuskett had prided itself on being an oasis in the desert; one of the billboards lining the Old Road still said so, its fading letters spelling out the town slogan for the benefit of the jackrabbits and chuckwallas that were the road's only traffic now. But it was an oasis fed by the juice in those power lines, and without that nourishment, the town was no better than a dry hole. It was power that had kept the refrigerators humming and the fan blades circling, and above all it was power that had kept the lights burning, the lights which, like a ring of campfires, held the darkness and the wild things at bay. The wild, deadly, stalking things.

With the lines down, darkness ruled. No longer was it possible to close a door and shut out the night.

Bill shivered, thinking of that.

In the dark, Dick Lewis went on comforting his wife while she made low whimpering sounds. Bill ignored them both. He stepped up to the front window and stared out at the town, utterly lightless now, blacker than the black void between the stars.

Rile moved to his side.

"Jesus jumped-up Christ," the older man breathed, "in a chariot-driven sidecar."

Bill nodded, seconding the sentiment. "He means business, all right."

Rile turned to him. His eyes glowed in the darkness. "What about a radio, a shortwave? We can use one to call for help."

"The only radio I know of is the one in Lew's car. And the portable police-band set in his house. That one wasn't where it was supposed to be, remember? It was missing."

"God damn."

"You got that right."

From behind them, Dick Lewis spoke up. His voice was taut and crackling with tension, like one of those power lines in the instant before it had snapped; Bill figured Dick Lewis might not be too far from snapping, himself.

"Hell, you two talk like he's got us cornered. Trapped. That's crazy. There's a way out of here. Cars. We've got plenty of cars. We can drive out. Drive all the way to San Francisco if we want to. Drive a good long way from here. And that's what we're doing." He tugged at his wife's hand and pulled her to her feet. "Come on, honey."

"I have to get changed," Gretchen said stupidly. "I'm still in my night things."

"They'll do. We've got to get moving. Before he comes back. Before he—"

"Just hold your horses there, Dick," Bill said softly. He was mildly astonished at the calm authority of his voice. "There's only one way out of town, and Kane must know it. You've got to go down Joshua to the Old Road. Kane'll be there. Be waiting, most likely, for someone to try a stunt like this. He can mow you down with gunfire just as easy as you please."

"For a smart man, Bill Needham," Dick said impatiently, "you can be pretty stupid at times. Who says we leave that way?"

"There's no other way."

"Like hell. Suppose we drive due east on Third."

"That street's a dead end. Nothing but desert."

"Now you're catching on."

Bill almost said something quick and nasty in return, then stifled it as he realized Dick Lewis just might have a point.

"We drive on dirt," Dick went on, the words tumbling out in a headlong rush. "Drive for miles. And when we've put enough distance between ourselves and town, we hook up with the road or the interstate or any damn thing that'll take us to Jacob."

"It might work," Rile allowed.

"Of course it will. But we've got to get going right now, don't you see? Because he could be back at any minute, and then where will we be? He'll know where we're holed up. He's got the dark on his side, and all those guns you said he stole. He can pick us off like fish in a barrel. Don't you see?"

"Yeah, Dick," Bill said, thinking of Jack and Millie Evans, sleeping without dreams in pillows of blood on the kitchen floor. "We see, all right."

"So are you coming or not?"

Rile shook his head. "Can't. Jenny and Tommy and PattiSue ... They're all back at the house. We can't leave them."

"Anyway," Bill added, "we've got to warn the rest of the folks in town." He paused. "Whoever's left, anyway."

"Okay, okay."

Dick plainly wasn't in the mood for further conversation. He put his arm around Gretchen and hustled her to the door. She brushed past Bill, and he saw streaks of tears striping her cheeks, glistening in the moonlight.

Tears for Charlie Grain. Bill was sure of it.

"As soon as we get to Jacob," Dick was saying feverishly, "an army of cops will be on their way over here to say howdy-do to Mr. Kane. Shouldn't take more than an hour, tops, before they get here. Just take care of yourselves till they show up, is all."

He reached the door, then paused with a thought. "And to think I wanted to give that man a discount haircut. It just goes to show."

- — -

Gretchen allowed her husband to help her out the door. As best she could tell from the fragments of conversation she'd managed to pick up, he had some kind of plan, some crazy, half-baked notion of leaving town. She wasn't exactly sure what it was all about; her mind didn't seem very clear, and it was hard to concentrate on what folks were saying; but whatever he was fixing to do, she knew it wouldn't work.

Because Charlie was dead.

And that meant she wasn't going to leave town, not tonight, not next month, not ever. She was going to stay here forever. She was going to die here, and then she'd be buried here, and that would be that.

There would be no new life in Arizona or New Mexico or someplace, anyplace, far away from Tuskett. There would be no golf course where Charlie could practice his swing, and no fishing hole where he could try his luck at casting a line. There would be nothing. Nothing but this town which had been more than half-dead even before that fellow Kane had arrived to hurry along the inevitable. Nothing but corpses, and bloodless half-corpses like Dick, and century plants growing like weeds in vacant lots littered with For Sale signs like grave markers.

Vaguely she was aware that Dick was easing her into the passenger seat of their Oldsmobile. She let him do it. He didn't bother to buckle her seat belt for her, and she didn't do it herself. It didn't matter. They weren't going anywhere. Couldn't Dick see that? Was he so blind?

"Never going to leave this town now," Gretchen Lewis said out loud as Dick climbed into the driver's seat and slammed the door. "Never. Going to die here. Going to die."

Jenny didn't panic when the lights went out. A moan

escaped her lips, that was all, and she held Tommy tighter and stroked his hair with one hand, while with the other she kept a firm grip on the pistol Bill had given her.

PattiSue, sitting beside her on the couch, was a different story. "No," she whispered in the sudden darkness. "Oh, no." Her voice sounded small and plaintive, the voice of a young child on the verge of tears.

"It's okay," Jenny said, though that was nonsense, of course; things were as far from being okay as they were ever likely to get. She wasn't fool enough to think that the power failure was an accident. Kane had done it. She didn't know how, but he had.

"I'm afraid, Jen," PattiSue breathed.

"It's okay," Jenny said again, pointlessly. "Bill and Rile are getting help. We just have to wait it out, is all." The words rang hollow, but they were the best words she could find.

"That man—he's evil." PattiSue's voice was low and wonderstruck, as if she'd never encountered such a thing before, and maybe she hadn't, at least not in so pure a form. "I don't just mean bad. I mean there's something wrong about him, you know? Like a cross hung upside-down. Like the Lord's Prayer backwards. Something sinful." She giggled, a harsh half-hysterical sound. "You hear me talk? Me, going on about sin, after the times I've had with Eddie in his trailer, and ... Oh, God."

Jenny turned to her, straining to make out the girl's pale, waxen features in the dark. "What is it?"

"Eddie." The word was a groan. "I just about forgot. Kane got him too. Beat him to death right in front of my eyes. And that's not the worst of it." PattiSue reached out, and Jenny felt the squeeze of the girl's fingers on her wrist. "The worst is ... I was glad."

"Glad?"

"Yeah. And I still am. I guess I am, anyway. Eddie, see ...

He used to beat me. Used to wallop the living daylights out of me. Giving me a spanking, he called it. Teaching me a lesson." She shuddered. "Those black-and-blues I got all over me—you must've seen them before I put on this dress—they weren't from Kane, except the ones on my throat. Mostly they were from Eddie."

Jenny licked her lips and struggled to find her voice. "How long did this go on?"

"Months."

"Why didn't you tell anyone?"

"I was afraid. But that was before. Before Kane. Now I know what evil really is. Now I know there's worse things than Eddie Cox. Lots worse. Eddie—he was nothing, just a bully. Nothing compared to Kane." The fingers squeezed tighter. Her voice dropped to a breathless whisper again. "Did you see his eyes?"

"Yes," Jenny answered, her own voice hushed with the memory.

"He can make you do anything."

"I know."

"He took me. Like ... like he wanted to take you." She pulled her hand away and hugged herself, rocking on the couch. "He's a demon. Or Satan himself, maybe."

"No, PattiSue, don't talk like that."

"Well, what else could he be? He's no normal man. Not with eyes like that. And did you feel his touch? Clammy like death. I don't think there's any blood in him, not a drop."

"Oh, yes, there is." Jenny remembered seeing the slow trickle of claret from Kane's shoulder when he stood facing her across the living room—and later, the splash of blood from his midsection in time with Rile's shotgun blast. "There's blood in him, all right," she said firmly, holding on to that thought, afraid to let it go, feeling almost as if she were gripping tight to sanity itself. "He bleeds and he's human, and don't go saying otherwise. Don't even think it."

PattiSue seemed about to answer, and then the house began to shake.

The floor vibrated wildly. Floorboards creaked like the limbs of trees in a strong wind. Things began crashing to the floor in the darkness, things that sounded like paintings jostled off their hooks and flowerpots tipped from the tables that had supported them. Tommy began to cry. His small body shook in time with the tremors racing through the house.

Earthquake, Jenny thought in cold terror—and a crazy idea came to her, the idea that Kane was doing this, that he really was a demon, just like PattiSue had said, a demon with the power to make the fault lines shift like grinding jaws and send Tuskett toppling to the ground as neatly as a toy town demolished by a petulant child.

Then the rumbling died away as quickly as it had come, and she realized that it hadn't been a quake after all. It had been the shock wave of an explosion—not gunfire this time, but an honest-to-God explosion from somewhere close. Down the street. Near ... near the Lewis place.

Where Bill and Rile had gone.

"Oh, God," she said in a strangled half-scream.

She pulled Tommy close to her chest and got up off the couch, clutching the .32 in one shaking hand.

"Come on," she said to PattiSue, not waiting for a reply. She reached the door. Then she was running down the porch steps with Tommy in her arms and PattiSue behind her, running toward the wavering glow of a fire lighting up the night.

It took Bill Needham a long moment to understand what had happened. His mind worked slowly, replaying the events of the past few minutes, putting things together bit by bit like the pieces of that jigsaw puzzle he'd seen on Gretchen Lewis' coffee table.

The four of them—he and Rile, Dick and Gretchen—had left the house together. Dick had shut the door after them. Bill remembered thinking that the small thump of the door in its frame was a sound of deadly finality, like the closing of a casket. He didn't like that thought. There was something wrong with Dick's plan—he was sure of it—some possibility he'd overlooked but Kane would not. But Bill couldn't say just what it was.

He went down the porch steps with the others, stepping back into the night. It was darker now without even the glow of distant porch lights to brighten it. The thought of Jenny ran through his mind like a ribbon of smoke; he wondered how she was doing, how she'd taken it when the power cut out. He hoped she was okay.

They reached the Lewis' car, that boat-size Oldsmobile Delta 88, a huge gray whale that was their greatest pride. It was a holdover from the mid-seventies, back when super-premium was cheaper than water and gas-guzzlers were still in vogue, hardly practical today, but then, Dick and Gretchen rarely traveled anywhere, so Bill supposed it made no difference. Anyway, the car had given him some pretty fair business over the years, and he felt a bit partial to it himself.

Dick let Gretchen in on the passenger side, then climbed behind the wheel. The engine coughed to life, and the headlights flashed on, cutting the darkness,

"Good luck to you," Rile said over the engine noise.

"Same to you," Dick answered, and tipped Rile and Bill a wave.

The two men stood watching as the car pulled away from the curb and motored into the intersection with Joshua Street, then began to swing around slowly in a wide U-turn so Dick could drive east on Third, as was his plan. Bill waited tensely, half-expecting Rile's van to rumble into view with Kane at the wheel, firing off shots like a rodeo cowboy.

The night was silent. There was no sign of trouble.

The Oldsmobile was out in the middle of Joshua now, halfway through its turn. The headlights blazed like twin suns. Above the glare Dick and Gretchen were visible as pale ovals of faces behind the breath-fogged windshield.

And then something happened, something Bill didn't understand at all. One moment he was standing there at the curb, watching the car as it executed its turn with the slow majesty of a constellation wheeling in the sky, and in the next moment he was on the ground and the world was rocking dizzily around him while chunks of volcanic ash cascaded on the lawn. He heard a sound, a deafening sound like the clanging of a giant gong, and then he realized it was his ears ringing like anvils from the impact of a noise so huge he couldn't take it in.

He looked up through a haze of shock and saw a fireball of scrap metal where the Oldsmobile had been.

It blew up, his mind told him calmly, almost impersonally—the way he might have observed that it looked like rain today. It blew up. The damn thing blew up.

He knew it was true but he couldn't make the thought real. He'd worked on cars for all of his adult life. They didn't blow up. Just didn't. Oh, sure, there had been that problem with Ford Pintos a few years back, a design error that had left the gas tank vulnerable to a rear-end collision. Sometimes those cars had exploded on impact when the tank ruptured. But that was different. That made sense. That was nothing at all like what had happened here. Because in this case there had been no collision. There had been nothing at all. The Oldsmobile had been cruising along, and then, just like that, for no conceivable reason, it ... had ... blown ... up. Like a cherry bomb, or a stick of dynamite.

Dynamite.

Of course.

Kane had sabotaged the car. Must have hooked it up to an explosive charge rigged to go off once the engine was running. Bill couldn't quite figure how it had been done, what methods had been used, but he supposed it didn't matter now.

What mattered was that the car had blown up—and Dick and Gretchen had been inside.

"Oh, God," he breathed. "Oh, good God."

He struggled dazedly to his feet. Dimly he realized that the force of the blast, even at this distance, had knocked him sprawling on his butt. But he didn't want to think about that. He didn't like its implications. If the explosion had been that powerful, then there was precious little chance that Dick and Gretchen, at ground-zero, had survived. And they had to have survived. Just had to. He wouldn't permit them to be dead.

Because he was a mechanic, goddammit. He worked on cars. He could have peeked under the hood or crawled under the chassis and found evidence of tampering in half a minute. If only he'd thought to look. And he should have. He'd felt in his gut that there was some flaw in Dick's plan, something that had been overlooked. Only, things were happening so fast. But that was no excuse. No excuse at all.

It was his fault. And that meant Dick and Gretchen couldn't be dead.

They were trapped, that's all. Trapped in that steel inferno down the street. He just had to get them out before it was too late.

He staggered across the lawn, heading toward the middle of Joshua Street, where the scorched, melted, flaming ruins of the Oldsmobile Delta 88 lay in a smoldering junk pile. He caught a flash of movement at his feet and saw Rile Cady, sprawled on the grass, coughing and sputtering and shaking his head, but alive. Bill passed him by and kept running, closing in on the car.

He reached it. Spots of fire leapt at his feet like small excited dogs. Smoke blanketed the scene in a choking cloud. Over the alarm bell ringing in his ears he heard the blare of the car horn, long and monotonous.

It must be Dick, he thought with a rush of relief. Dick—alive and honking for help.

The Oldsmobile's doors had been blasted clean off. Bill looked inside and, yes, sure enough, there was Dick Lewis in the driver's seat, leaning his fist on the horn, his face blank, eyes glazed with shock, his clothes burning like kerosene-soaked rags. Gretchen sat beside him, slumped over, unconscious maybe.

But alive. They both were. Thank God.

Bill grabbed Dick's arm and tugged, trying to pull him out of the car, to drag him out of this hell of heat and smoke, and carry him to safety. Dick flopped over in his seat, leaning half inside the car and half out, and Bill realized he must be unconscious too, which was hardly surprising, so he pulled harder, straining to haul the man's limp and unresisting form free of the wreck. He felt the small pops of muscles in his shoulders and arms.

Then gradually he became aware of something—a smell, oddly familiar, rising to his nostrils on waves of oven-hot air—a greasy meat smell, like bacon frying in a pan or pork chops broiling slowly over a barbecue pit. It was coming from Dick, he realized. It was ... It was ...

For the first time he looked at Dick Lewis, really looked at him, and saw how his skin had turned soot-black, and how the flesh of his body was smoldering and sizzling and throwing off fumes of greasy smoke, like one of Charlie's hamburgers on the griddle.

He'd thought the man's clothes were on fire. But it wasn't only his clothes. It was him. It was his whole body. He'd been roasted like a pig on a spit. All he was missing was a baked apple in his mouth and a bed of garden vegetables to lie in.

Bill let go of Dick's arm. It dropped to the ground and lay hissing and twitching like one of those downed electrical wires not far from here.

Slowly Bill raised his head and looked into the car again, where Gretchen Lewis was slumped in the passenger seat. Her nightgown crackled like old newspapers in a fireplace. Blue jets of flame danced in her hair. Her mouth was on fire; her gums were blistering and melting; as Bill watched, teeth began popping loose, spraying her lap like gumballs.

Dead. She was dead. They were both dead. They'd been dead all along. They were still dead. They would always be dead.

That one word, *dead*, drummed in his brain like a mantra, stifling thought, numbing emotion, voiding self. He stood unable to move or react, as his eyes watered from smoke and his skin tingled with the heat of the fire and cinders drifted down onto his shirt and pants, threatening to set him ablaze.

Then there was a hand tugging on his arm and a voice, Rile's voice, yelling in his ear.

"Bill! Get back! *Get back!*"

Bill blinked, coming out of whatever trance he'd been in. He looked at Rile and saw the old man's face damp with sweat, lit crimson by the flickering fireglow. Wordlessly he nodded. Together they retreated to the curb and stood there panting and shaking all over and staring at the night with haggard faces and haunted eyes.

"You all right?" Rile asked finally.

Bill nodded. "You?"

"Guess so. Got the wind knocked out of me when that thing went up." Rile jerked his head in the direction of the car. "What the hell happened, anyhow?"

Bill took a breath. "Kane," he said. The word came out harsh and brittle as an oath.

"Car bomb?"

"Something like."

"Think the other cars in town got the same treatment?"

"Maybe."

Rile looked at him, looked hard. "Then there's no way out. Is there?"

"Only one," Bill said softly.

He inclined his head toward the car still blazing like a bonfire, consuming the last remnants of the bodies in its grip.

"Their way."

5

It was ten minutes to three in the morning when Dick and Gretchen Lewis were incinerated in their car. The explosion, almost dead center in the middle of town, shook Tuskett from one end to the other like a card table rattled by a gust of wind. And the people of Tuskett—those who were still alive—were shocked out of sleep or reverie into the need for action.

Only a few hours earlier, the town's population had been twenty-three. But that was before Lew Hannah gained a smile and lost a heart; before Todd and Debbie and Johnny Hanson were impaled on their pillows like butterflies on mounting boards; before Ellyn Hannah was given a shot, which was not Novocain, by a man who was not her dentist; before Charlie Grain learned he wouldn't be drinking that can of Coors after all; before George and Marge Baker sniffed the gas choking their bedroom and awoke from one sleep only to drift into another; before Eddie Cox found himself on the receiving end of a whupping for the first and last time in his life; before Ethel Walston lost control of her dog; before Jack and Millie Evans made two stains on the spotless linoleum floor of Millie's kitchen; before Dick and Gretchen Lewis drove their Delta 88 straight up the highway to heaven.

In short ... before the arrival of a man named Kane.

There were now nine people left alive in Tuskett.

Five of those nine—Jenny and Tommy Kirk, PattiSue Baker, Rile Cady, and Bill Needham—had already had at least one violent encounter apiece with that man, and were lucky to still be breathing, themselves.

The others—Chester Ewes, Meg Sanchez, and Stan and Judy Perkins—were at home.

Chester Ewes wasn't all that surprised by the rolling thunderclap that trembled through his living quarters at the back of the church and set his bed vibrating in the darkness like a hammock in a breeze.

He'd been lying wide-awake, waiting for the church bell to chime three o'clock. Something had awakened him a few minutes earlier, a series of sharp bangs that hadn't quite reached his conscious mind. Then the explosion hit, roaring like a distant cannonade, and he sat up in bed, shaking his head, knowing in some wordless way that his worst fears had been confirmed.

Because he'd known that something was going to happen. Something terrible, though he couldn't have said what. He'd felt the presence of danger in Tuskett, stalking the streets on padded feet like the black-panther shape of death.

And he was afraid. Afraid to face whatever evil was out there. More afraid still to face the awful implications of that evil—the possibility that there was a devil, after all, not a witch doctor in a totemic mask, not a child's picture-book monster of goat horns and cloven hooves, but a man who'd come out of the desert for no reason anyone could name, a man whose very existence had made the church bell toll thirteen, a fugitive and a vagabond named Kane.

Yes, afraid of that. Because if there were a devil, there

might be a God. And after the books he'd read and the speculations he'd engaged in, God was the very last thing the Reverend Chester Ewes wanted to find.

He shook his head. This was no time for another spiritual crisis. Things were happening out there, things that involved his town and his people—his flock, as the religious imagery had it. Well, they *were* his flock, and he was their shepherd; and there was a wolf in the fold.

He got out of bed. He fumbled for the light on his nightstand and found the switch; nothing happened. He thought the bulb had blown, until he found the wall switch for the ceiling light; that was dead too. Then he understood.

In the dark he tugged on his clothes, then left the bedroom and made his way down a narrow hall. His groping fingers found the door that opened on the pulpit where the altar, draped in red cloth, stood beneath a wooden crucifix. Rows of pews lay before it like the dark, frozen waves of a soundless ocean. Starlight streamed through the high stained-glass windows and made dim pools of violet and blue-green amid the empty seats.

He walked up the nave. He looked back once. Christ gazed down at him with sightless eyes. He'd always felt there was something vaguely disturbing about that statue's stare. He turned away, walking faster, nearly colliding with the door to the narthex. Finally he reached the portal, the large double doors that opened on the night, and he was outside.

He stopped on the front steps, looking around. Power was out everywhere. The whole town was dark. Except ... In the near distance, at the center of town, flickered a faint reddish luminescence. Not an electrical light. No. The glow of a fire lighting up the sky.

He thought about driving there—his car was parked on the street. He dug in his pants pockets, but his keys weren't there; he'd left them inside. The idea of retracing his steps through all that darkness, under the unsettling gaze of the wooden Christ, started him shuddering, just a little. He decided to walk.

Shoulders squared, he headed in the direction of the fire and whatever evil had spawned it.

Meg Sanchez waited for the house to stop shaking, then got up from her chair. Like Chester Ewes, she was hardly surprised. She'd known Kane meant trouble, known it from the moment when she looked into his eyes in the coffee shop. True, she couldn't put her knowledge into words; true, she'd half-convinced herself it was her imagination. But deep down, she knew.

And because she knew, she'd stayed awake, sipping coffee and listening to the night wind walk and talk. A few times after midnight she'd considered making another stab at that proposed lead story of hers. Something stopped her. Maybe it was the wordless certainty that the story couldn't be written yet because there was still much more to come.

Then she'd heard distant gunshots, and the lights had failed. She sat in the dark, listening to the slow, steady beat of her heart and waiting for whatever would happen next. Something would. She would have bet her last dollar on that.

When the explosion hit, she almost smiled. Because something sure as hell was going on out there. And that meant she had a story after all, a genuine headline story, a story that would get on the AP wire, the way her stuff used to do in the old days before Tuskett began to die. Not a bake sale or a July Fourth soiree. Something big and strange and different. A story she could be proud of.

If only she lived long enough to write it.

- — -

Stan and Judy Perkins had been sleeping soundly, lying back to back and grumbling irritably as they fought for possession of the bed sheet, when something slammed into the house like a giant fist and shocked them awake.

"What the hell was that?" Judy Perkins said, listening as the waves of thunder died away.

"Sounded like an A-bomb."

"Oh, come on, Stan." Her voice was thin and agitated. "It wasn't an A-bomb. You always think everything's an A-bomb."

"Well, it sounded like one. Not close. It could have taken out LA. That's a key population center. Or a silo field in Arizona. That would be a prime military target."

Judy sighed. Her husband was always going on about the Russians and this sneak attack they had planned. She had a feeling that, deep down, he was sort of hoping there would be a nuclear war, just so he could be proved right; if the missiles ever did fly, she was pretty sure Stan Perkins would meet his maker with a big cheese-eating grin that said: I told you so.

"Will you hush up about the A-bombs for once," she told him now. "It's the middle of the night and I am in no mood."

"You haven't been in the mood day or night since Hector was a pup," Stan returned testily, then swung his legs out of bed and got up before Judy could determine a suitable reply. He moved to the window and looked out, his short, pudgy silhouette limned by moonlight, his thinning hair sticking out at odd angles. He emitted a low whistle.

She waited for an explanation, then realized none would be forthcoming if she didn't prod him. "What is it?" she asked grudgingly, hating herself for having been trapped into giving him even that much satisfaction.

"Town's dark," Stan said quietly. "I think the power's out." He flipped a wall switch experimentally. Nothing happened. "Yup. No juice."

Judy rolled over in bed and groped for the telephone on the nightstand. She held it to her ear. Silence greeted her.

"Phone's out too," she said, and she couldn't help but notice that her voice sounded a little shaky. All of a sudden she was wondering if it really had been an A-bomb. She supposed it could happen. Stan had certainly gone over the scenario often enough in her presence. A few well-placed missiles to knock out the American silos and bombers. Then an ultimatum delivered to the White House—surrender or else. But there'd be no surrender, Stan always said, so sooner or later more bombs would fall, a rain of bombs dropping all over the country and lighting up the sky with mushroom clouds in a deadly parody of a fireworks show.

She tried to steady herself. This was no time to get panicky.

"Okay, Stanley," she said, "what do you advise we ought to do?"

"How should I know what to do?" he answered irritably. "I don't even know what's going on."

"That's never stopped you before."

"If it was an A-bomb, I guess there's not much we can do except find Chester Ewes and start praying."

"Will you stop talking about A-bombs?" she nearly screamed. "It wasn't an A-bomb. You've got A-bombs on the brain."

"At least I've got a brain. Stop jabbering and toss some clothes on. We're getting out of here."

Less than three minutes later, they stepped outside. From the front of the house they caught sight of the wavering glow of a fire playing over the sky like searchlights at a Hollywood premiere. It was close, Judy figured. Maybe a block away. And that was good. It meant that whatever had made that god-awful noise, it wasn't nuclear. Armageddon, it appeared, had been postponed.

"Gee," Judy said, "it looks like we didn't lose Los Angeles after all."

Stan pursed his lips, and she was certain she detected a hint of disappointment in his face.

"Why don't we go see what it is we did lose," he answered flatly, "and stop yakking for once."

They started walking up the street toward the glow of the fire, drawn like moths to a candle, saying nothing more.

Bill Needham knew what he had to do, and he was on his way to do it when he nearly collided with Jenny Kirk, standing on the sidewalk with Tommy at her side.

"Bill. What happened?" She stared past him at the wreckage; the glow of the fire fluttered on her face like rippling rain shadows. "What's burning?"

Bill looked away. "A car. Dick and Gretchen's. It blew up."

PattiSue, a yard behind Jenny, heard his words and blanched. "Oh, God ..." The word trailed off in a simpering moan.

Jenny showed little reaction. She seemed to have shut off all emotion in favor of a coolly detached perspective on events. She took in the information, nodded once as if to confirm her understanding of it, then asked simply: "How?"

"Kane. He must've planted some kind of bomb in it. He's got it all figured out, I guess."

"What'll we do?" Her voice was steady, inflectionless.

Bill was glad of that. He didn't want anybody to panic on him right now. He had enough to deal with as it was.

"Join up with Rile," he said briskly, because he could think of no better advice. "Stay with him. I'll be back in a minute. There's something I've got to do."

He ran on, escaping further questions. He looked back once and saw Jenny, Tommy, and PattiSue running down the walk to Rile, their figures thrown into silhouette by the flames.

He reached Jack and Millie's Buick, parked outside their house. It was the nearest car he knew of; and he needed to find another car in order to learn if it, too, had been sabotaged. Even if it had been, all wasn't necessarily lost; he was a mechanic, and it was possible he could figure out a way to disarm a bomb. If he didn't blow himself to bits in the process.

He looked over the Buick. There was no obvious sign of tampering. He considered opening the hood, but he felt skittish about it; there was no telling whether his friend Kane had rigged up a booby trap that would detonate the vehicle if he released the safety catch.

Instead he got down on hands and knees and wriggled under the car. Kane's backpack was there, some of its contents scattered on the ground. In the shifting firelight Bill saw a spool of electrician's tape, a box of carpenter's nails, and a much larger box, its lid open, with some kind of metal container inside.

For the moment he ignored those items. He twisted onto his back and peered at the underbelly of the car. He saw Kane's work immediately, lit by the red wavering glow. The man had made no attempt to hide it, and that fact only made Bill madder at himself for not having had the foresight to check out the Lewises' car before letting Dick and Gretchen get in.

The device looked simple enough. A lead pipe—cracked and rusty, the kind of thing you might salvage from a junk yard—had been attached to the Buick's fuel tank with some of that heavy, silvery tape. Both ends of the pipe were taped up too. And inside the pipe, it was safe to bet, there was an explosive of some kind—most likely a blasting powder like TNT. Enough of it to blow the Evanses' Buick, like the Lewises' Oldsmobile, into the great scrap heap in the sky.

He looked more closely at the pipe. The tape securing it to the fuel tank was rough, strangely bumpy. Carefully Bill ran his hand over it. Nails, he realized. There were nails affixed to the pipe, a liberal sprinkling of nails. Well, that made sense. No matter what explosive Kane had used, there couldn't have been enough of it in a pipe that small to demolish a whole car. But if the pipe exploded close to the fuel tank, sending chunks of lead and a spray of nails flying in all directions, it was a sure bet that the tank would be ripped open; the deadly mix of gasoline and air would go up like a torch and do the job quite nicely.

So. That was how he'd done it. A pipe bomb. Very glamorous. The kind of thing you might read about in a spy thriller or hear mentioned in a TV news report from Beirut. Only, Bill was damned if he could see how it worked. Explosive charges didn't just go off on their own; they had to be detonated, usually by heat or by an electric current. He would have guessed the latter in this case. A car bomb, as he understood it, was usually hooked up to the starter solenoid; when the key was turned in the ignition switch, current flowed from the battery, made a detour to the bomb, and set it off.

But this bomb was different. As best he could tell in the dim light, there were no wires coming out of the thing, none at all.

It occurred to Bill that maybe Kane had been interrupted before he'd finished hooking up the bomb. In that case, the explosive by itself was harmless, and the car was perfectly safe. But he was hardly ready to stake his life on that supposition.

Anyway, now that he thought about it, the Lewises' car hadn't blown up at the moment of ignition, had it? No. Dick Lewis had started the engine and pulled away from the curb; he'd been in the process of making a U-turn on Joshua when the Oldsmobile went up in a blaze of fury. As if the heat of the engine, or maybe the rough road surface, had done the trick. But he wasn't sure how that was possible. TNT wouldn't go off that way, and neither would the plastic explosives terrorists used. He couldn't think of anything that would.

He remembered the box on the ground near Kane's backpack. Maybe it contained the answer. He looked at the metal canister inside; there were words printed on its face, but he couldn't make out what they said. He crawled out from under the car, then slowly dragged the box out too, taking care not to shake it. In the mingled light of the fire and the three-quarter moon, he could read the words without difficulty. And now, at last, he understood.

Nitro, he thought dazedly. Good Lord.

Bill Needham knew a little about nitro. Chemistry had been one of the few courses he'd been able to complete in his aborted college career. Nitroglycerin was a piss-colored, oily liquid—highly flammable and combustible, just like the warning on the canister said. And so damned unpredictable it was virtually useless as an explosive in its pure form. Nitro had been discovered in the nineteenth century, but nobody found a way to make use of it till that Nobel fellow, the one who got a peace prize named after him, figured out a way to stabilize it by mixing it with dirt to make sticks of dynamite.

But pure nitro, undiluted nitro—well, it was just liquid death. Heat could set it off, sure; but a shock, even a mild shock, could do the same. Sensitive to heat and impact, the canister said. The kind of impact any car in

Tuskett would be certain to receive before it had traveled a tenth of a mile down any of these streets—much less the rugged, unpaved terrain of the desert, as Dick had been hoping to do. The kind of impact a man toting this canister in his backpack would have chanced with every step he took, every single step ...

Bill shut his eyes. He remembered watching from his service station as Kane strode out of the horizon. In his mind's eye he could see it again—the slow, deliberate, almost gingerly pace of the man's walking—and then with a leap of imagination he pictured Kane tramping through the desert for endless, trackless miles, planting one foot after the other, calmly, carefully, knowing full well that a single false move would shake the contents of his pack and detonate the canister of yellowish liquid he carried there and wipe him out in a blast of white heat, leaving nothing but a black, smoking crater as big as any on the dark side of the moon.

He tried to fathom the hate, the obsession with killing, that had driven a man to make such a pilgrimage, with that awful burden strapped to his shoulders, with his own death hanging over him like a vulture's shadow every step of the way. He couldn't do it. He'd never known a hate that strong or a passion that blind.

He stared at the pipe, taped in place. He knew he didn't dare remove it. It would take steadier hands than his to do the job. A surgeon's hands. Jack Evans' hands, maybe; but Jack was dead.

Carefully Bill got to his feet, took a deep breath, and then suddenly he was shaking all over at the thought of how close he'd been to the pent-up violence contained in that canister. Suppose he'd tugged harder at the box when he was pulling it out, just hard enough to set its contents sloshing.

He backed away. Right now he wanted to be far away

from that box and this car and any other car in Tuskett. Because he knew the odds were good that every other car in town was in the same shape. Kane was a thorough man, a mightily determined man, a man who'd crossed great distances at great risk to get to a town just like this one and do his dirty work; and now that he was here, he could be counted on not to have overlooked a thing.

Bill turned, too abruptly, and hurried down the street toward the fire, where a small crowd was already gathering, huddled close to ward off the encircling night.

Kane stood unmoving and watched the tangled net of power lines as they crackled and hissed and spat up white pinwheels, like sparklers. Ejected shells from the .22 littered the pavement at his feet. He had squeezed off six rounds, nearly emptying the gun. He stashed the .22 under his belt, then turned, the folds of his coat swishing around him in dreamlike slow motion, and got into Rile Cady's van.

He drove, headlights off, to the intersection of Joshua and Fourth. He turned east on Fourth and continued to the end of the street, then pulled onto the unpaved terrain that bordered it. By this backdoor route, bouncing and rattling on the rough ground, he made his way to Third Avenue. Sometime during his drive, there was a great shout of flame from the middle of town, lighting up the sky. Kane showed no reaction.

He killed the van's engine and coasted down Third till he reached the back of the water tower. He left the van, walked to the tower, and stood gazing up at it. The cylindrical tank was huge against the sky. A ladder snaked down the side of the tank. Nearby a sign was posted. DANGER, it warned. NO TRESPASSING.

Kane climbed the ladder. The rifles tucked into his coat pockets swung heavily from side to side as he mounted the risers in his slow, calm, deliberate way.

Not far away, in the middle of Joshua Street, a car was burning and a crowd was gathering around it, like children around a campfire.

When Bill Needham returned to the scene of the car wreckage, he found eight people waiting for him. His eyes swept over the group, taking in each of its members in turn.

There was Rile, of course, watching the others with a haunted look on his face. Next to him was Jenny, looking stoic and unnaturally composed, the gun Bill had given her hanging in one limp hand. Tommy stood at her side; the boy seemed almost catatonic, and Bill wondered if he would ever speak again. PattiSue loitered a few yards back, hugging herself as Millie Evans' blue dress rippled around her.

Those four he'd expected to see. The other four were new arrivals.

Meg Sanchez had gotten there first, he guessed. Judging from the flush of color lighting up her face and the sweaty exhaustion that had set her legs trembling like tuning forks, she must have run the whole distance from her place. Now she was circling the wreck to find the best camera angles, clicking off pictures on her Kodak. Bill thought he ought to hate her, at least a little, for that. He didn't. Her movements were jerky and unfocused, and he was pretty sure she didn't even know what she was doing; her mind must have shut down when she saw Dick's and Gretchen's charbroiled remains, and now she was operating on automatic pilot, going through the motions of being a newspaperwoman because it was expected of her.

Chester Ewes stood off to one side, his thin face and large eyes looking terribly aged, as if he were not a man of fifty but one of those ancient patriarchs in the Old Testament. He was talking to himself in a low monotone. Bill had to strain a bit before he made out the words. It was the Twenty-Third Psalm. "Though I walk through the valley of the shadow of death, I will fear no evil. I will fear no evil. I will fear no evil ..." The reverend seemed to have gotten stuck on that last part, like a phonograph needle caught on a bad groove.

Stan and Judy Perkins were the last of the group. Normally, Bill reflected, that pair wouldn't have been caught dead making physical contact in public; they were hardly the touchy-feely type; they preferred to circle each other warily, like two fighters in a ring, jabbing and parrying. Tonight, Judy had her arm around her husband's waist, and Stan was gripping his wife tight, and neither of them seemed to realize it.

Bill finished his survey, then turned, peering past the crowd into the vast darkness hemming them in. There was nothing to see down Joshua in either direction. Only the dark shapes of empty stores—and, looming over them all, the black bulk of the water tower on the far side of the street, its tank eclipsing the moon and blotting out the stars.

He looked over his shoulder, staring down Third Avenue. It, too, was empty.

Nobody was in sight. Nobody else was coming. Not from any direction Bill could see.

He thought about that. The explosion had been loud enough to wake the deaf. Nobody who heard it would have—could have—ignored it. And it was hard to believe that anyone who'd been roused from sleep at three a.m. by a crash of sound in the center of town would simply shrug, roll over, and go back to sleep. They'd come, all right. They'd toss on some clothes and shuffle on over like these folks here.

But they hadn't. Which meant they hadn't heard the noise, hadn't been awakened. Because the sleep they knew tonight was one from which they would never wake.

He looked at the group before him. Nine in all, he thought grimly, counting himself. Nine people. And only nine.

He'd known Kane had been busy tonight. He hadn't imagined just how busy.

Bill looked at Rile again, and saw that the old man's eyes were wide and frightened and wet with tears. So he'd figured it out too. He knew that everybody still alive was here right now. Less than half of Tuskett's population.

Rile Cady had lived all his life in this town. He liked to boast that he'd been here before there even was a town. Before there was anything other than red-tailed hawks chasing grasshopper mice, and barrel cacti sprouting amid patches of larkspur and thimbleweed. He'd seen the town born, and he'd watched it all but die—and tonight he was seeing its last blood drained away with incomprehensible speed.

Bill reached out, touched his arm, and spoke low in his ear. "You okay, Rile?"

"No," Rile muttered bitterly. A single teardrop, sparkling like a jewel, rolled out of the corner of his eye and wound down his cheek. "No, I'm not okay, dammit. Nothing's okay."

Bill said nothing. He supposed he'd deserved no better answer. He felt like the idiot reporters he saw on TV who asked the dazed, bleeding victims of car crashes and train wrecks: How do you feel?

He turned back to the group. Meg clicked off another picture in time with a burst of light from the flash cube. He touched her arm.

"Put down the camera, Meg," he said, his voice low. "You've got enough pictures now."

She blinked as if coming out of a trance, then let go of the Kodak and let it swing lazily from the strap around her neck.

"Sorry, Bill," Meg said softly. "I guess I wasn't thinking." She gazed up at him with wide, pleading, desperate eyes. "It'll make one hell of a story, though. Won't it?"

Bill managed a smile. "That it will."

He moved away from her and looked around at the others. They watched him with blank faces, waiting for him to speak, to explain things. He wasn't sure why they expected him to be the one. Maybe for the same reason Jenny had called him when she needed somebody to look in on Lew and Ellyn Hannah.

He cleared his throat.

"All right, everybody. This is what's happened. A man showed up out of nowhere earlier today. Calls himself Kane. Now he's killing people. I don't know why, but there it is. Maybe it's a kind of sport to him, like bagging rattlers. Anyhow, he's damn good at it. A lot of people are dead already. An awful lot."

"Who?" Judy Perkins asked, her voice uncharacteristically subdued.

Bill hesitated, letting the question hang unanswered for a moment. "Look around you," he said finally. "I've got a feeling the folks here are pretty much all we've got left."

Chester Ewes spoke up for the first time. "But that can't be," he said very simply, as if he'd just received a phone bill that was unexpectedly high. "Can't be."

"It is."

"But that's ... that's fourteen of them. Fourteen, counting ..." He gestured feebly at the wreckage of the car. "Fourteen," he said again.

"Looks that way."

Chester looked away, his eyes huge, the eyes of a frightened child.

"No ..." Jenny moaned. "Oh, no." She was kneeling by Tommy's side, hugging him, her face shiny with fresh tears. It was as if her stoic reserve had finally shattered like a burst dam, letting naked emotion spill out. "Not ... not everybody. Not the whole town ..."

"No," Bill said harshly. "Not the whole town. There's us. We're left. We're alive. We're all that matters now. There'll be time to cry and mourn the dead later on. Right now it's a luxury we can't afford."

Jenny sniffed back a tear.

"Okay, then." Bill turned back to the rest of the group. "Here it is in a nutshell. We've got no electricity. No phones. No radio. No transportation. As best I can tell, all the cars are booby-trapped like this one."

He let that sink in. He saw a mixture of emotions—relief mingled with fear—on the faces of Chester Ewes, Meg Sanchez, and Stan and Judy Perkins. Relief that they'd chosen to walk rather than drive. Fear because it had been a near thing.

"So Kane's got us right where he wants us. It's a bad deal, no denying that, but we've got to make the best of it or die." He spread his hands. "Well, that's it."

He waited. Nobody said anything for a long moment.

"So what do you say we do?" Meg asked.

Bill looked at her, amazed, because he'd never heard Meg Sanchez ask anybody for advice or instructions.

And then he realized something—something that both pleased and scared him. He was the boss here. He was the leader. He'd supplied the voice of sanity and judgment. And in doing so, he'd taken it all on his own shoulders without even realizing it.

He glanced around him. He saw Stan and Judy, waiting for his orders, and Chester Ewes, meek as a lamb with no Sunday sermons in mind for tonight, and PattiSue, a trembling girl in a borrowed dress, and Rile, looking for the first time like an old and tired man deferring to youth. And finally there was Jenny, still kneeling by Tommy, holding him, her eyes damp with tears for the dead—but gazing up at Bill, her feelings written on her face in a large hand.

The sight of her face strengthened him; he couldn't say why.

"Well, the main thing," he said slowly, "is just to make it through the night. By morning somebody's bound to come along. The mail truck, for one thing. That'll be here in the afternoon. Or ... Jenny, what about the delivery truck for Lew's store?"

"Yes," she said at once. "You're right. It's due tomorrow. Today, I mean. And Mr. Garcia—he's the driver—always comes first thing in the morning. Gets here usually about nine."

Bill checked his watch. It was ten minutes after three.

"Less than six hours from now," he said. "We've got to hold out that long. Once help gets here, we're home free. In the meantime—"

He was about to tell them what they were going to do in the meantime, assuming he could figure it out for himself, when a distant rifle crack rang out in the night stillness and Judy Perkins went down.

It was that quick. One second she was standing at her husband's side, shivering all over, her pale face lit in shades of red by the fire's glow—and an instant later she was sprawled on her back, her body sunfishing crazily as blood geysered out of her chest. And she was screaming.

"*Get down!*" Bill shouted, and dived to the street, skinning his palms on the rough blacktop. A second later everyone was spread-eagled on the ground while Judy's screams went on and on.

A second gunshot boomed in the night, followed by a high, thin, whistle like the whine of a mosquito. A patch of macadam went up in a puff of dirt and smoke, a few yards from PattiSue.

Bill judged that the shot had come from due east. He looked past the fire, at the black bulk of the water tower. Was that where Kane was shooting from? Had he climbed to the top to get a clear view of the nine of them as they stood around the car, lit by the flames, making perfect targets for a man with a sharpshooter's eye?

Judy was still screaming, but the sounds had taken on an oddly muddy quality, as if she were gargling and trying to scream at the same time, and Bill saw that her mouth was filling with blood from some internal hemorrhage. As he listened, the screams segued into moans and labored gasps. Stan lay at her side, propping her head up and whispering incoherent things in her ear.

Bill forced himself to forget about all that. He had to think. As long as they stayed here, they were vulnerable. The next well-placed shot could finish off any one of them. They had to get to cover.

The nearest building was Charlie's coffee shop. It was maybe ten yards away. The door was closed. And that raised an interesting question in Bill's mind. Was it locked? Ordinarily Charlie would never have locked the door to his place, not in Tuskett. But, after all, there was a stranger in town. So tonight when Charlie closed up shop, had he maybe decided to lock the door for once, just to be on the safe side?

Bill didn't know. And that was bad. Because he was going to have to make a run for Charlie's place.

He, and the others too. And if that door was locked, he wouldn't be able to force it open or even smash a window before Kane got off at least one clean shot and took somebody down.

Son of a bitch, Bill thought. We've got to gamble it all on one throw.

There was no other choice.

"All right," he said sharply, raising his voice to be heard over Judy's moans. "Listen up. We're making a break for Charlie's place. All of us at once. And fast. Got it?"

"No," Stan said quietly. "I can't. Can't leave her."

Judy's chest was a mass of blood. Her face was a pale shock mask. She was dying. Anybody could see that. Even Jack Evans and his little black bag couldn't have saved her.

"Stan," Bill said gently, "it's no use."

"I'm not going, dammit." The man's voice sounded wet with tears. "I'm not."

Another bullet struck. Jenny screamed. Bill winced, thinking she'd been hit—she, or Tommy maybe. Then he looked at them and saw that, thankfully, the shot had missed them both. But not by much. A foot at best. The next one wouldn't miss.

"We've got to go for it," Bill said firmly. "Right now."

Meg Sanchez, Chester Ewes, and Rile Cady each nodded. PattiSue looked blank; Bill hoped she understood. Stan kept on holding his wife's hand as her difficult breathing went on and on, a low rasping sound, like snoring.

Jenny tried to gather up Tommy. Rile whispered something to her, some words to the effect that he could carry the boy with no trouble. Bill smiled. The man was a trouper, all right. But running thirty feet under fire with an eight-year-old child in his arms was too much to ask of a man his age.

Wordlessly Bill crawled over to Jenny, reached out for the boy, and draped him over his shoulder. He grunted. The kid was a load. How much did an eight-year-old weigh, anyhow? Sixty pounds, maybe? It was a lot of weight to be handicapped with.

"Okay," Bill said. "Get ready." He tensed his body for a burst of speed. "*Go*!"

He took off and the others followed in a clatter of footsteps.

Time slowed. Funny how it did that. Bill had heard that in moments of crisis, when your life was on the line, the world's clock seemed to wind down, each second stretching to an hour. He'd never experienced the phenomenon firsthand.

He was streaking along like a gold-medal runner coming down the stretch. But he felt like he was moving in slow-motion. Like a man trying to run underwater. Each step was molasses-slow, each thudding footfall a separate drumbeat in a funeral march. His own funeral, maybe.

The coffee shop was impossibly far away. How could he have thought it was only ten yards? It was a mile, at least. And though he was racing straight for it, the door wasn't getting any closer. It was like one of those dreams where you ran and ran and never got anywhere, and all the time death in some incomprehensible form was closing in.

The distant rifle cracked again. He waited through a timeless eternity for the impact. Then he heard the bell-like ring of the bullet as it ricocheted off the street. It was the kind of sound Bill associated with Wild West movies. And this was a scene out of one of those movies, the scene where the hero and his buddies scoot across Main Street in a jerkwater desert town with bullets flying all around them. And even though a thousand bullets might pockmark the street, none of the good guys ever got hit. You could count on it. That was the great thing about movies.

Tommy Kirk, draped over Bill's shoulder, had put on some weight in the last few endless seconds. He now weighed a good six hundred pounds. With each step Bill took, Tommy bounced a little on his shoulder, driving lightning forks of pain down his side.

The rifle fired again, and this time the bullet didn't carom off the street. This time it struck flesh.

Rile Cady staggered with a muffled curse. Bill glanced over his shoulder and saw that the man had been hit in the arm.

"I'm okay!" Rile barked, and the way he was running, it looked like he probably was.

They reached the door.

Bill came up on it fast. He couldn't stop. He swung his body sideways and body-slammed the door. The impact shuddered through him. He held on to Tommy with one hand and scrabbled at the doorknob with the other, trying to find some purchase on the damn thing. His hand was slick with sweat. The knob kept slipping through his fingers. He couldn't get it to turn. Couldn't get in.

That was the worst moment. Standing there at the door, knowing that at any second the rifle would cough again, and he would be the target this time—no question about it: the man in the lead, the man at the door—he was the one who'd be taken down. And not with a bullet in the arm, either. He wasn't running now. He was standing dead-still, a perfect target.

Bill fumbled with the doorknob, and all the while he couldn't shake the feeling that there was a bull's-eye painted on his back, and Kane was taking aim at it, the cold blue eyes narrowing, one bony index finger drawing down ...

Finally his hand closed over the knob and he twisted it savagely and the door swung open.

Unlocked. Thank God.

He rushed inside, thinking he'd been right all along—nobody locked their doors at night in this town.

The others spilled in after him. Meg, Chester Ewes, Rile Cady, Jenny, PattiSue. But not Stan.

Bill put Tommy down, then turned and looked through the doorway.

Stan Perkins was stumbling down the street, his wife a limp rag doll in his arms. He was halfway to the coffee shop. He had no chance.

"God damn," Bill said. "I didn't think those two even liked each other."

He knew what he was going to do next. He didn't want to do it, and some logical part of himself implored him not to try; but he didn't listen. He'd taken it upon himself to act like a leader. And, as a leader, he was responsible, at least in his own mind, for the bullet that had cut Judy down. Now he saw a chance to make partial amends. Or die trying.

He steeled himself for another race with death, then sprinted out the door.

Oddly, things moved faster this time. He reached Stan in a heartbeat. Judy lolled bonelessly in his grip, her legs and arms dangling.

"Get back!" Stan yelled. "I can do it!"

Bill shook his head. He grabbed Judy's arms and let Stan take her by the legs, so that she swung between them, a human hammock. Walking sideways, crablike, the two men hurried for the coffee shop that seemed so awfully far away.

They made easy targets. Kane could pick them off at his leisure. Bill knew it. He wasn't going to make it this time. He'd been lucky once, but now he'd pushed his luck too far.

A gun went off—once—twice—each shot terrifyingly loud and close. But Kane couldn't be that close, just couldn't be.

Then Bill realized Kane hadn't fired these shots.

Jenny Kirk stood in the doorway of the coffee shop, holding the .32 in both hands. It was pointed straight up in the air, aimed at nothing but sky. She wasn't trying to hit Kane, it seemed, only to put a scare in him, enough of a scare to make him take cover.

And it worked, Bill thought in amazement. No more gunfire sounded from the tower.

Jenny squeezed off a third shot just as Bill and Stan brushed past her, carrying Judy Perkins into the coffee shop. Behind them, Jenny slammed the door.

Bill let out a long shuddering breath. For the moment, at least, they were safe.

Gently he and Stan laid Judy down on the Formica countertop and leaned over her. Even in the darkness, Bill could see the lake of blood on her chest, the red bubbles forming at her nostrils, the waxen pallor of her skin. She wasn't long for this world. All they'd accomplished was to give her a better place to die, and to make sure she wasn't alone when she drew her last breath. That was something, anyway.

He turned away from her and looked at Jenny.

"Much obliged," he said.

She ran a shaky hand through her hair. "Anytime."

On the counter, Judy began to speak.

"Stanley? Stanley, are you there?" Her voice sounded as dry and cracked as an old riverbed. Her eyelids fluttered.

"Yeah, Judy." Stan squeezed her hand; she didn't seem to feel it. "I'm here, all right." He cleared his throat. "Didn't think you could get rid of me that easy, did you?"

She turned her head in the direction of his voice. Her face changed, the flaccid muscles tightening in a half-smile.

"No," she said. "I figured you'd keep on hanging around,

just to drive me crazy, like always."

"You know it."

Bill looked around and saw Meg Sanchez with an unlit cigarette dangling forgotten in her mouth, and Chester Ewes mopping his forehead and murmuring a prayer, and PattiSue watching like a child on her first visit to a funeral parlor. Jenny wasn't looking; she'd sat herself and Tommy down at one of the tables and was stroking the boy's head. Rile Cady, standing near the coffee shop's big front window, wasn't watching either; he was busy tearing off the sleeve of his shirt to make a tourniquet for his left arm.

"Hey, Bill," he said, keeping his voice low, "give me a hand with this thing, will you?"

Bill stepped to his side. "We've got to get the round out," he whispered, hating to think of what that would be like.

Rile shook his head and smiled. "Huh-uh. I was lucky. Bullet went right through. In one side of the arm and out the other. Just a lot of sticky stuff, is all."

Bill let his eyes move to the wound, then looked hastily away. Rile had put it accurately, all right. A lot of sticky stuff.

"So are you gonna help me tie on this thing or not?" Rile asked pleasantly enough.

"Hold still." Bill knotted the tourniquet tightly in place. He wasn't sure if it would stop the bleeding. He didn't have any notion of what to do if it didn't.

Judy Perkins started coughing, a hoarse death-rattle sound, and Bill's attention was drawn back to the countertop, where the woman lay on her back in a widening pool of her own blood, and Stan stood beside her, holding her hand and watching her life trickle away.

"You know," she said softly when the coughing fit was over, "it's not so bad. Dying, I mean." She smiled again.

"At least I won't have to listen to you yammer on about World War Three anymore. That's something to be thankful for, believe me."

"You just aren't bright enough to appreciate good old-fashioned common sense when you hear it."

"Probably right. Everybody told me not to marry you. I didn't listen then, either."

"Should have."

She shook her head slowly, with a strange and beautiful dignity. "No."

Wordlessly Stan Perkins lowered his head and kissed his wife's forehead, something Bill was sure, positively sure, he had never done in all the thirty years of their rough-and-tumble marriage. Judy gazed up at him and smiled, and her breathing stopped, just like that, with no fuss or bother, and she lay unmoving as the smile slowly faded from her face.

Stan lifted her hand to his cheek and rubbed her fingers against his skin in a slow, rhythmic motion.

Nobody said anything. There was nothing to say.

After a long moment Bill turned to the front window and looked out at the street framed in the glass.

"He's gone," he said quietly.

Nobody felt the need to ask who.

"He's not on the water tower anymore. He knows where we're hidden. He'll be coming."

"For all he knows, we've still got a loaded gun," Rile reminded him, nodding in the direction of the table where Jenny was seated.

"That might give him pause," Bill said. "But it won't stop him."

"So," Jenny asked, "what do we do?"

Bill looked at her, then swept his gaze over the others.

"We go to the church," he said quietly.

Meg Sanchez snorted. "It's a little late to get religion, Billy boy. For you and me both."

"We're not going there to pray." Bill kept his voice even. "Although it might not be such a bad idea. We're going there because the church is the sturdiest building in town. It's built of stone, not plywood. It's got double doors six inches thick, with a good solid lock on 'em. That lock still work, Reverend?"

"It does," Chester Ewes answered.

"Good. And there's one other thing. The church doesn't have too many windows. Just a few of the stained-glass type, and we can cover those up. We can make the place damn near impregnable, and hole up there, where Kane can't touch us."

"You're saying," Rile asked, "we lock ourselves in?"

Bill nodded. "And lock him out."

"Till when?"

"Morning. When the delivery truck shows up. Then we'll have to figure a way to signal the driver."

"Unless Kane shoots him first." That was Meg, still skeptical.

"That's a risk we'll run in any case."

"I don't know," Rile said slowly. "It might work. But if he gets in, we're sitting ducks."

"We won't let him in."

PattiSue groaned, an anguished, wounded-animal sound, and sank into a chair.

Bill waited through a tense silence. He was pretty sure this was the best plan available. There was no way out of town, no way to get help, no way to fight back. They couldn't stay here; Kane could shoot them through the windows or set the place on fire and smoke them out. The only choice available was to gather together in the safest place they could find or to split up and go it alone. And he didn't think any of them was ready to face the night alone, if it could be helped.

That was how he saw it, anyway. But he needed the others to see it for themselves.

Jenny spoke up in a clear, firm voice. "I think Bill's right. It's our only hope."

Slowly Chester Ewes nodded. "I don't see an alternative."

Rile smiled. "Okay, Bill. I'm with you."

PattiSue swallowed. "As long as he can't get in."

Even Meg Sanchez fell into line. "Oh, what the hell."

Only Stan said nothing. He seemed oblivious of the conversation. He stood at the counter patting his dead wife's hand.

"All right," Bill said, feeling absurdly good about things and more in control at this moment than he'd ever been in his life. "That's it, then. Now we'd better get going. Kane could get here any minute."

"Or maybe sooner," Rile said, and pointed at the window.

Bill heard the noise even before he turned—the distant rumble, a sound like thunder, and at first he was sure it really was thunder, and the white light sweeping over the coffee shop was a lightning streak. Then he spun on his heel and stared out the window. And he saw it.

The van. Rile's old Chevy. Engine roaring, high beams on, brakes squealing as it swung onto Joshua Street from Third and barreled across the intersection, skirting the wreckage of the Oldsmobile, heading straight for the coffee shop at full speed.

Bill couldn't see Kane at the wheel—he couldn't see much of anything past the blaze of those halogen headlights—but he knew the man was there, and probably smiling too, his face lit clown white by the dash, his mouth frozen in a death-mask rictus. He had one of those snakeskin boots of his stamped to the floor, pedal to the metal, and he wasn't going to stop. Bill knew that. Knew it with utter certainty. Kane wasn't going to stop.

"Out," Bill said quietly, so quietly that nobody else could hear him. He raised his voice to a shout. "Get out the back way! Now! Everybody out!"

Jenny was the first to move. Bill heard the scrape of her chair as she rose from the table and tugged Tommy to his feet. She ran with the boy at her side. Meg, Rile, and Chester Ewes followed.

PattiSue sat immobile in her chair, gazing at the light, her eyes and mouth forming three perfect circles. Bill hauled her to her feet. The light was brighter now, a supernova outside the window; the floor and walls were shaking.

"Run!" he screamed at the girl, and she obeyed.

Then there was only Stan. He stood at the counter, still stroking his dead wife's hand. Bill tried to pull him away from the counter. Stan jerked free. "No," he said almost petulantly.

There was no time to argue. The van was closing in.

Bill ran. He reached the hallway at the rear of the coffee shop. The back door was just a few feet away. The engine noise was impossibly loud and close. There was a small, distant thud, and he knew the van had jumped the curb. It would run smack into the storefront at any second.

Halfway down the hall, he stopped. He looked back. He couldn't help himself. Like Lot's wife, he had to see.

Stan Perkins was silhouetted against the glare, holding Judy's hand and looking up for the first time at the expanding headlights in the window. He looked like a man transfixed by a sunset. Or by a mushroom cloud, maybe. Knowing Stan, Bill figured that just might be it.

The van collided with the front wall. Steel met wood. There was a sound like newspaper being crumpled, only amplified a thousand times, as the wall buckled, the vertical struts cracking like toothpicks, the plywood sheets imploding. The windows shattered in a rain of glass. The van kept coming. One headlight had winked out, smashed on impact. Now the van was a Cyclops. A howling, raging Cyclops butting its head against the wall of the coffee shop and crashing through. A table and chairs—the table where Jenny and Tommy had sat—vanished under the Chevy's front end, chewed to pieces by its tires.

Stan didn't move. Bill, watching from the hall, didn't either.

The van swerved, its one headlight homing in on its target, and bore down on the counter where Stan stood waiting. The van struck the counter at an angle, like a car sheering off part of a freeway guardrail. The countertop's chrome edge ripped a long, jagged gash in the Chevy's side door. Sparks flew.

Then the van hit Stan Perkins and he was flung off his feet onto the hood, and lay there like a hunting trophy, and maybe that was exactly what he was.

Bill took a shambling step backward. He knew he had to run, get to the door, get out of here before Kane saw him. Before Kane thought to arrow the van at a new target. He knew all that, but he couldn't quite seem to pass the thought along to his legs.

The van backed up, swinging from side to side like a big shaggy dog shaking its head. Stan, or whatever was left of him, slid off the hood and fell in a heap on the floor. The Chevy rolled backward over the splinters of a table, grinding them down, then sat motionless, its engine rumbling and sputtering, sounding like a tired animal breathing raggedly and tensing itself for a fresh kill.

The van was a wreck. Even more of a wreck than when Rile had been driving it, if such a thing was possible. The windshield had been fractured by the crash, the glass crazed in a dazzling starburst. The front end was banged hopelessly out of shape. Gobs of oil dripped from the hood like spit from a drooling mouth. Bits and pieces of wood were stuck all over it, looking like porcupine needles. The one living headlight seemed to glare at him.

Bill was still standing in the hallway and staring at the van and wondering why he couldn't get himself to run, when with a burst of speed the van surged forward, and this time it was headed straight at him.

The lone headlight pinned him down like a deer on a highway. A picture flashed in his mind, a memory of a coyote he'd seen on Interstate 10; what the damn thing had been doing out there on all that concrete, Bill had no idea, but it had been there, all right, and some big truck—a diesel rig, probably—had ground it down flatter than a fresh-mowed lawn, pounded it right into the road, squashed it pancake-flat, like that cartoon character, Wile E., run over by his own steamroller. He thought of that, and he thought of the table and chairs and how they had crackled to dust as they disappeared under the tires, and how his bones would do the same.

And then he was running.

Behind him, the van slammed into the doorway to the hall. The doorframe was too narrow; the van couldn't get through. Undaunted, the van backed up and shot forward a second time, splintering the doorframe, exploding into the hall. It screamed forward, a berserk, bellowing dinosaur. Its sides scraped the walls, the door handles gouging long horizontal grooves in the plaster. Paint chips pattered down from the ceiling in a light snow.

Bill was nearly to the door when he hit a bad spot in the floor and stumbled and fell.

Damn, he thought wildly. Oh, God damn.

The van was right behind him, closing fast. He could feel the heat of its engine like hot breath on his neck.

He scrambled to his feet. He didn't dare look back. He was afraid the sight of the van, monstrously close, would freeze him in his tracks. The brilliant white light was all around him, blindingly bright. He thought of those tabloid stories about people who said they'd experienced death; it was like going down a hallway toward a bright light, they claimed. In this case it looked like death was getting a little impatient about it and was coming for him.

He ran for the door. It was wide open, thank God. There would have been no time to fumble with the doorknob with sweat-slick hands, not this time.

Like a diver leaping off a board, he threw himself through the doorway. He landed on hands and knees in a patch of dogbane in the vacant lot behind the building.

The van slammed into the doorway, then backed up and butted it again, and again, trying to force its way through, fighting to escape from the building and continue the chase, like a dog clawing at a fence while a rabbit cowered on the far side.

Bill got up. He ran. He had no destination. He stumbled like a drunk, cutting an irregular path through the rutted field. He waited for the van to burst through the back doorway and bear down on him out of the dark. It didn't happen.

At the edge of the lot Bill looked back and saw that the van was dead.

That was how he thought of it anyhow. Dead. It had seemed alive to him for a few moments there, and now it was alive no longer. Its one headlight was still on, but it had lost its malevolent glare; its stare was glassy and cold, the wide-awake stare of a corpse. The van was wedged in the doorway, making no further effort to move; its motor was silent. The multiple impacts had taken their toll; something—the fuel pump, maybe, or the driveshaft—had fatally ruptured.

He supposed there was a chance, a bare chance at best, that Kane, too, had been killed or seriously injured by the punishment he must have taken in the driver's seat. Bill didn't believe it. He wasn't that much of an optimist.

He stumbled out of the lot into the street and started running like a man in a dream, chased by shadows, with death at his heels.

Chester Ewes lingered near the front doors of his church, shifting his weight anxiously and gazing out into the night, waiting for Bill Needham and Stan Perkins to arrive.

The others were already inside. They'd all gotten here at about the same time, and as soon as Bill and Stan showed up, they could lock the doors and get to work. Chester hoped they wouldn't have to wait long. He didn't much care for standing out here on the front steps, exposed to all this shape-shifting darkness. He'd feel a lot better when he was safely barricaded in the worship hall.

He supposed that Bill's plan to hole up in the church—like Joshua in the belly of the whale—was, on the whole, a good one. As good a plan, anyhow, as could be devised under present circumstances. But secretly he suspected that Bill's rationale for it was little more than a surface coating of logic over the deeper impulse that had moved him. The church, as Chester knew well from copious readings on the subject, was traditionally a place of refuge, a sanctuary from persecutors and evildoers, safely beyond the reach of human or inhuman corruption; longstanding folk wisdom held that no evil could enter such hallowed halls.

Bill Needham was not, so far as Chester could tell, a religious man; certainly he never attended Sunday services, a thing which Chester, considering his own ambiguous stance on matters metaphysical, could not hold against him. But Bill had grown up in a country that clung to its myths and rituals, and it was doubtful he'd altogether escaped the influence of the cultural atmosphere he breathed. Chester suspected that at the back of Bill's mind there was a comforting aspect to the idea of the church as a hideaway, a feeling of security that wouldn't have been present if the building selected had been his own gas station or somebody's house. Bill was probably not even cognizant of it himself, but people did many things for reasons of which they were unaware; Chester sometimes suspected that most of human history was the product of unconscious motives given a veneer of rational justification.

The church was the sturdiest structure in town, yes; but it was also the only sacred place Tuskett could lay claim to. Such considerations had been known to play a role in human action from time to time.

The others, he reflected, surely felt likewise. Even Meg Sanchez, that crusty old bird, had dropped her voice to a whisper when she'd stepped into the narthex, though whatever reverence she might have felt hadn't stopped her from lighting up one of her noxious cigarettes. And it could hardly escape notice how the bunch of them had gathered in the pews near the chancel rail, only a few yards from the altar and the figure of Christ. It was as if they'd felt the need to be close to such icons, like primitives huddled around a tribal totem pole or a sacred tree.

Oh, they felt it, all right. All of them. They felt the undertow of irrational belief that tugged at humanity's heels on even the most civilized shores.

Chester Ewes pursed his lips and wondered if he felt it too.

When Bill arrived at the church, he found Chester

Ewes out front and the others waiting inside, scattered among the dark, empty pews near the altar and whispering anxiously.

"Oh, thank God," Jenny said when she saw him. Her voice caught. "We ... we thought he got you."

Bill forced a smile. "Almost."

"What about Stan?" Rile asked.

Bill shook his head.

Chester mumbled something under his breath; another prayer, Bill figured. More words spoken for the dead. He wondered how many more such words would be said before this night was over.

"Okay." He clapped his hands; the noise echoed in the stillness. "Let's get to work."

Chester found a flashlight he kept in the desk near the front doors. Bill gave it to PattiSue and let her feel useful by giving her the job of shining light wherever it was needed; she was too badly shaken up to be good for anything else. Meanwhile Chester got out a box of candles and matchbooks from behind the altar and lit them; they cast a weird wavering glow over the rows of pews and the crucified Christ.

Bill locked the front doors, then set about building a barricade. Luckily the pews weren't bolted down; each long mahogany bench was heavy as hell, but it could be moved. The five of them—Bill, Rile, Meg, Chester, and Jenny—dragged one of the pews to the narthex and braced it against the front doors to form a barricade. Only Tommy and PattiSue looked on.

"What if he breaks through in Rile's van, like before?" PattiSue asked, the flashlight bobbing in her hands.

"He won't," Bill answered. "The van's finished. He smashed it up pretty good."

The other obvious point of entry was the windows. There were four of them, all of the double-lancet variety common in churches—high, narrow slits like the loopholes of a medieval fortress, filled in with stained glass. It was easy enough to seal them off. Easy in theory, anyhow, though in practice it was tough, sweaty work, the kind of hard labor that set off miniature cherry bombs in the muscles of the shoulders and arms—pop-pop-pop—muscles Bill hadn't even known he had and which he was none too pleased to discover.

He and the other four all worked together, upending several pews and leaning them vertically against the walls to cover the windows. Propped up that way, they made respectable barriers; Kane would have the devil's own time finding the leverage to tip one over from outside.

Only after the worship hall was properly barricaded did Chester Ewes remember the window in his bedroom.

"Damn," Bill said when the reverend spoke up. "We should've thought of that right off."

Chester led him to the rear of the church, where his living quarters—two rooms and a bath—were found. There was no back door, a fire hazard under most circumstances, but a blessing tonight.

The window was open wide, with only the wire screen to shut out the night, a respectable defense against bugs, but no defense at all against Kane. Bill shut the window and locked it, a thing that probably had never been done in the church's history. The two of them were casting about for a way to secure it when Chester remembered the plywood sheet he kept under his bed to stiffen the mattress and save him from back pains. The plywood was appropriated for a more urgent purpose. Chester fetched a toolbox, and he and Bill set to work with hammers and nails. When they were done, the window was boarded up good. For good measure, they upended the bed and stood it against the window as an additional barricade.

Chester said he figured that ought to do the trick. Bill agreed. But privately he wasn't sure. There were ways a man like Kane could get in.

If only they had a gun. If only they had some way to defend themselves. If only they could make it until morning, when help was sure to arrive.

Bill returned with Chester to the front of the building, where the others had seated themselves in the two remaining pews, hunched stiffly on the high-backed benches and talking nervously among themselves, their faces lit ghost-pale by the flickering candles in their hands.

The conversation, not surprisingly, was about Kane.

"Who is he, anyhow?" Rile was wondering aloud. "Just who the hell is he?"

PattiSue spoke up tentatively. "*What* is he? That's what I'd like to know."

Meg sucked deep drags off an unfiltered Camel and let out the smoke through her nostrils. "Oh, hell," she said in her gravelly voice. "He's a goddamn nutcase, is all. Some freaking loony-tunes. He got out of the asylum and wound up here. Just our luck."

"I don't think so," PattiSue said softly. "I don't think he's crazy. Not exactly. He's ... he's evil." She looked at Chester Ewes, her eyes luminous in the candlelight. "It's possible, isn't it, Reverend? I mean, for evil, pure evil, to ... to walk like a man?"

Meg snorted.

Chester sat on the edge of the bench. He drummed his fingers on his knee. "I think so," he said finally. "There are stories in the Bible—and in other books too, books of other faiths, some older than our own. Stories about a dark man, humanity's evil brother." He took a breath. "In Genesis, they call him Cain."

Nobody said anything for a heartbeat of time. Then Meg Sanchez laughed.

"Oh, come off it. You're trying to scare the piss out of us. Little late for that. I'm all pissed out as it is."

"It's just something I've been thinking about," Chester said quietly.

A new voice rose in the stillness. Jenny's voice.

"I've been doing some thinking myself," she said. "About something I read somewhere. I don't know if it's true. It might even have been in one of those tabloid magazines Lew stocks—used to stock—at the grocery, and you know how full of baloney they are. Still, maybe there's some truth to it.

"What I read is that sometimes whole towns—little towns, like this one—just empty out overnight. One day the place is full of people, and the next day everyone is gone. Folks come across one of these towns, way out in the woods or the desert or what-have-you, far away from anything, and there's nothing but empty houses. Pots still steaming on the stoves. Laundry flapping on the lines. Maybe a checkerboard with the pieces still in place, the game left off in the middle. As if, one minute, everybody was there, going about their daily business, nice and normal, and then, just like that—gone.

"And I wonder—I know it's crazy, but—I wonder if maybe this man Kane visited those towns too."

Outside the wind kicked up briefly, making high-pitched skirling sounds like a set of bagpipes, then fell silent.

"Nuts," Meg Sanchez said bitterly, and took another drag on her cigarette.

Bill didn't want to contribute to the fear he could feel building in the room, but it seemed he couldn't help him-self. He felt like a kid on a camping trip, huddled with his buddies around a campfire trading ghost stories. It was scary, but it was a pleasant kind of scariness, the kind that seemed almost rational when compared to the unknown terrors that might lie in wait in the darkness beyond the fire's glow.

"I've read about that too," he said, his voice hushed, and they all looked at him. "Only it wasn't in the *National Enquirer.* It was in a history book. Medieval history. There were towns and villages back then, in the Dark and Middle Ages, that just disappeared from the map. All the people, gone. And I remember my professor, who looked old enough to be reporting on the twelfth century from firsthand experience, telling us that stories of that kind aren't unusual. They crop up, it seems, in every day and age, and in every country. Towns that vanish. Depopulated overnight. Everybody gone without a trace. It's been happening for thousands of years, and nobody knows why."

He saw Jenny shiver. Instantly he was sorry he'd spoken.

"Still," he went on, trying to take the chill off what he'd just said, "what's going on here is different. Kane's leaving his mark on this town. It's not like those other cases, when the people just vanished. Here there are ... bodies."

Rile shook his head.

"Maybe not so different," the older man said. "We went to Charlie's place, and Lew and Ellyn's. We didn't spot any trouble there. Kane must've cleaned up whatever dirty work he did. Maybe, if he gets the time, he'll clean up all the rest of it."

Bill thought about that. "I think he left Lew's place in order because he knew Lew was the police chief, and as soon as folks started getting skittish, the Hannah house was the first place they'd go. And he didn't want us to know what was going on. Not right away. He didn't want us calling the state police. He needed to buy himself time, till he could sabotage all the cars and bring down the power and phone lines." He shrugged, trying to keep his voice even. "Nothing mystical about it. It was strategy, is all."

"Maybe." Rile didn't sound sure.

"Yeah," PattiSue whispered. "Or maybe not. Maybe it really was him in all those other towns. Killing people, cleaning up the mess, then moving on and leaving a mystery that couldn't ever be solved."

"For years?" Bill breathed. "For centuries?"

"Could be."

"He's a man, PattiSue."

"I want to believe that," Jenny said. "I ... I used to. But now, with most of the town dead, with only us left, and ... and who knows for how long ..."

"Don't start thinking that way," Bill said sharply.

Jenny lowered her head and didn't answer.

"A fugitive and a vagabond," Chester Ewes whispered suddenly, "shalt thou be in the earth ... A fugitive and a vagabond." His pale face was haunted.

"I say it's all a crock of shit," Meg said, but there was less certainty in her voice than before.

"I hope you're right," Rile said soberly. "I dearly do. Because I don't want to think this man we're up against might be something more than a man—or something less."

Bill was about to say something, he wasn't sure what, and then the church bell began to chime.

"Must be four o'clock," Jenny said.

Meg chuckled without humor. "Time flies when you're having fun."

"It's not ringing four, though." Rile's voice was low, almost hushed. "I've counted five strokes already." He listened as the bell tolled again. "Six."

Meg shrugged. "Maybe the damn thing's busted. Like

everything else in this one-dog town."

"Could be," Chester said. "The timer might've been knocked out of kilter when the power went off."

Bill felt a sudden chill. "But the power's still off," he whispered. "The lines are down."

The bell went on ringing slowly.

"Then how ...?" PattiSue began. The question trailed off with a gasp. "Him. It's him."

Bill nodded.

He knew what had happened. Kane had nosed out their hiding place. It wouldn't have been difficult; whatever tracks they'd left would have led in the same direction. He must have seen how every door and window in the church had been sealed up; but he'd seen something else too. The belfry. It was the one thing they'd overlooked. It had been left open to anyone who could reach it.

Kane had reached it. How he'd managed that feat, Bill couldn't guess. The church steeple was twenty-five feet high, and its smooth stucco face offered no purchase. But somehow Kane had found a way. He'd slipped inside, and now he was up there, at the top of the tower, ringing the bell by hand to announce his presence. Toying with them. The arrogant, cocksure, bloodless son of a bitch.

Bill licked his lips. He was cold all over. He had never felt so close to death.

With effort he focused his mind. No time for panic now, or for telling himself he should have foreseen this. It had been his idea to hide in the church, and now it was up to him to figure out what the hell to do. But that was easy. There was only one thing they could do. Only one option left.

He looked around at the others and saw them watching him, their faces waxen in the feeble candlelight.

"It's him," PattiSue repeated, as if trying to make the

thought real. “He got in. He ... he’s *inside.”*

“Dammit,” Meg breathed. “I just knew this was a lousy idea.”

“We’re locked in.” That was Jenny. She pulled Tommy close to her; the boy moaned, “We barricaded all the exits. We ... we can’t get out.”

“Yes, we can,” Bill answered as calmly as possible. “Through the bedroom window.”

“Then what?” Rile asked.

“We split up. Everyone for himself. We each find a separate place to hide, then wait for daylight and help. Got it?”

They nodded.

“Okay,” Bill said. “Blow out those candles. That way at least he can’t see us any better than we can see him.”

Instantly the candles were extinguished; PattiSue snapped off the flashlight in her hand. Darkness crashed down like a lead weight.

“Good,” Bill whispered. “Now we’ll go to the back of the church, where the bedroom is. Quietly. No need to clue him in as to where we are.”

“Wait,” Chester said. “Listen.”

The bell was silent.

A moment later they heard the slow, regular creak of footsteps on the steeple stairs.

“He’s coming down,” PattiSue breathed.

Bill pulled Jenny to her feet. “Let’s move!”

The seven of them slipped out of the pews and made their way past the altar to the hallway that led to Chester’s living quarters. Behind them, the footsteps grew louder. Kane must be almost to ground level.

Bill stumbled down the hall, feeling his way like a boy in a funhouse maze. He reached Chester’s bedroom, let the others brush past him, then locked the door. PattiSue snapped on the flashlight and swept its beam over the room. Bill saw a large, heavy oak dresser standing against the far wall.

"Chester. Rile. Give me a hand with that thing."

Together the three of them hefted the dresser and eased it in front of the door.

"That ought to hold him. Get to work on the window."

Jenny, Meg, and PattiSue were already doing so. They'd gotten a grip on the bed and were hauling it out of the way.

Chester grabbed his toolbox and found the hammer they'd used earlier to board up the window. Bill set to work using the claw to pry the nails loose, while Rile trained the flashlight on him. The nails were long, a good two inches, sunk deep into the wood of the window frame, stubborn as hell. Bill sweated, struggling to get a grip on the slippery heads.

He froze, hearing the tread of boots in the hall.

"Damn," Meg muttered. "God damn."

Bill got one nail out and dropped it to the floor, then started on another.

The footsteps stopped outside the door.

Bill tugged at the second nail and jerked it free, and an instant later a loud crash of sound rolled through the room and made his heart skip a beat.

"The lock," Chester breathed. "He shot it off."

Tommy whimpered.

Bill pried loose another nail. He'd gotten three of them off, but the plywood still wouldn't budge.

Another rifle crack racketed off the walls, and this time the dresser jumped. Bill allowed himself a backward glance and saw that one of the drawers had been blown out of the thing, spilling Chester's underwear every which way. The rifle poked through a jagged gap in the back of the dresser like the snout of a hungry animal sniffing prey. Kane had blasted a hole clean through the door and the dresser itself.

The others crowded away from the door, into a corner, and huddled there in a shivering mass. Only Bill and Rile stayed put. Bill worked on getting another nail loose. Rile kept the flashlight's beam shining where it was needed. The beam was steady; the man's hand wasn't trembling at all.

Wish I could say the same about me, Bill thought in miserable terror.

A moment later there was another rifle blast, and the dresser shuddered as a second drawer slid halfway out.

Bill pried loose another nail, then another, but the plywood still wouldn't yield. Damn, they'd done a hell of a job on this thing.

The rifle cracked again, tearing off the left side of the dresser. It collapsed like a house of cards. The door shuddered with a violent blow—not a gunshot—the impact of a man throwing his weight against the wood. The rusty hinges squealed. The door began to shudder open an inch at a time. Only the shattered remains of the dresser still held it partially shut, but the thing made a poor barricade now.

Bill looked at the plywood and saw more nails, too many nails, studding its right-hand edge. But the left side was clean. If they could pull it loose ...

"Rile," he snapped. "Help me get this bastard off."

Rile tossed the flashlight to Chester, and he and Bill slipped their fingers under the wood and pulled with all their strength, and the sheet of plywood tore free of the wall and thumped on the floor.

Only the window screen still barred escape. Bill punched it out of the frame and watched it fall away. Finally the window was open to the beckoning night.

Bill resisted the urge to scramble out first. He turned

and scanned the group while a string of words from an earlier age ran through his mind—women and children first. The advice seemed sensible enough. He grabbed PattiSue and hoisted her onto the sill. She scrambled out, nimble as a cat. "Run and hide," Bill told her. She hesitated, just outside the window. "*Go!*" Bill screamed. She went.

By unspoken agreement Tommy was next. Bill and Jenny helped him climb out. Jenny followed.

Kane rammed the door again. It shuddered open a few inches more.

Meg Sanchez was the fourth one to go through. She hit the ground and started running in almost the same instant. Then only Bill, Rile, and Chester were left.

"You go," Rile said to Bill, but Bill ignored him, took his hand firmly, and together he and Chester helped the older man out.

The door banged again. Bill glanced back, and his heart stuttered in his chest as he saw the toe of Kane's boot ease into the room.

"You," Bill said to Chester, but Chester shook his head and pushed Bill toward the window with surprising strength. "It's my church, and I'll be the last to leave it. Hurry, now. Hurry."

Bill didn't argue; there was no time. He hauled himself through the window and flopped down on the dirt, free.

He turned and saw Chester squirming out headfirst. Bill reached out to take his hand, but before he could, a rifle blast rang out and Chester gasped, his face going shock-white.

"Run," the reverend whispered as his eyes rolled up in their sockets.

Bill ran. As he rounded the corner, a shot rang out, ricocheting off the wall, and he knew it had been meant for him.

He kept running, streaking along the side wall of the church, and then something flapped down in his face, and for a second he was sure it was Kane's hand reaching out for him from the night sky. But he caught his breath as he realized it was only a strand of rope. He stared at it stupidly, then raised his head, his eyes tracking up the length of the rope to its other end, looped around the top of the bell tower.

So. That was how Kane had done it. He'd lassoed the belfry and shimmied up the rope, noiseless as a shadow. Such a simple thing, so obvious, so easy to overlook.

Bill broke into a run again. He reached the front of the church and came face-to-face with Jenny, standing there with Tommy at her side. Her hair was a windblown mess wrapping her face like threads of gauze. She stared at him with wide, frightened eyes.

"You were supposed to run and hide," Bill said. "That's the plan."

"I had to know if you were all right. And besides ..." She looked away. "I didn't want to be alone."

Despite everything, Bill almost smiled.

"Nobody does," he said. He took her hand. "Come on."

Then they were off, the three of them together, racing into the darkness. The others—Meg, Rile, and PattiSue—were nowhere to be seen. They must have already scattered in the night. Bill hoped they'd be okay. They only had to hold out till morning; and morning, after all, wasn't so very far off.

Far enough, though. Plenty far enough.

Chester Ewes came to slowly, and found himself on the altar of his church.

He lay flat on his back, staring up at the crucified Christ. He tried to move, couldn't. No part of his body would respond to his silent command. He felt no sensation of any kind. Dimly he remembered having been shot in the back.

Broke my spine, he realized. Bullet cut the spinal cord in half, and now I'm paralyzed and feeling no pain. No doubt it's for the best this way.

He tried turning his head. Nothing happened. But he was able to blink his eyes and shift his gaze. He had that much mobility, at least.

Slowly he rolled his eyes in their sockets. He took in the wavering glow of candles. Candles everywhere. Kane must have gathered them up, lit them, arranged them around the altar. But why?

Silver flashed at the corner of his vision. He forced his eyes to focus on the object catching the light. A knife. One of the steak knives from his kitchen drawer. Embedded nearly up to the hilt in something pink and moist. His hand. Yes. That was it. His hand had been laid on the altar, palm-up, its fingers level with his head, and then the knife had been driven into the soft meat, through muscle and bone, pinning his knuckles to the wood.

He shifted his gaze to the opposite side and saw his other hand likewise impaled on the altar.

There was a rustle of movement above him. He looked up to see Kane leaning down, his blue eyes glinting bright as razor blades. Another knife glittered in his fist, poised to strike.

Chester swallowed. He tried to speak. He didn't know if his vocal cords would still function. They did.

"Mister. I ... I don't know who you are. But I think I know what brought you here." His voice was a croak, the words barely audible. "It's me, isn't it? It's my ... hypocrisy. My lack of faith. I preached one thing, believed another. And now you've come like an avenging angel ... to punish me. Me, and this whole town with me," He studied Kane's face in the flickering light, searching for some hint of a response. "That's it, isn't it?"

Kane said nothing.

"All right, don't answer if you don't choose to. But please ... just tell me one thing. I'll believe you. Because I think you would know, if anybody would." He took a breath. "Is there a God? Have you seen Him? Did you ... did you fall from grace? Is that who you are?"

No answer.

"Or are you maybe someone else? A fugitive ... and a vagabond ... cursed from the earth ...?"

Kane raised the knife.

"You won't tell me?" Chester heard the piteous desperation in his voice. "You won't give me even that much?"

Silence.

Chester sighed, a huge sigh, so big it seemed to deflate his small body like a spent balloon. He waited.

The knife came down in a graceful arc and ripped into the tender skin of his right arm, slicing it from wrist to elbow. Blood foamed out from parted skin flaps, streaming down the altar to patter on the floor in a light rain.

Kane lifted the knife once more. It dripped.

Chester watched, feeling nothing.

The left arm was next. More blood poured forth, spilling everywhere like water from a burst dam. Chester stared at it, mesmerized by the sight of the dark red, copper-smelling fluid gushing out of him in such astonishing abundance.

Kane retreated and stood watching as blood and life drained from the offering on the altar.

Chester knew he was done for, but he was not afraid. He seemed to have stepped back from the situation to some privileged retreat in his mind where he could consider what was happening with impersonal detachment. He thought of Christ nailed to his cross. He thought of druidic prisoners burned to death in wicker baskets. He thought of Odin's faithful hanged from gallows trees. He thought of Phrygian harvesters wrapped in corn sheaves and hacked to death with sharpened scythes. He thought of the King of the Saturnalia, loaded down with his mock crown and wooden scepter, leading the holiday revels, then dying under the knife.

One word rang in his mind, like the tolling of the church bell at midnight, the bell that had chimed thirteen.

Sacrifice. Sacrifice. Sacrifice.

He let his gaze drift upward to the carved Christ. Only—strangest thing—it wasn't Christ anymore. It was changing, its shape mutating, flowing from form to form in a hallucinatory stream. It was a woman with the face of a cat, then a triple-headed goat, then a snake, a bat, a spider. Ancient gods, tribal gods, gods far older than Christianity, that upstart faith. Gods from the beginning of time.

Were they Kane's gods? Was he their servant, their henchman? Was that who he was—not the devil, not the biblical Cain, but a worshiper of dark eldritch forces that predated civilized man? Was that his true purpose, the mission that had brought him here—not to punish an atheist preacher for his sins, but to spill the blood of the innocent and, by doing so, to make his obeisance to gods long dead?

No. It couldn't be. That was insane. These ideas were only superstitious gibberish, a betrayal of everything he'd learned.

He let his eyelids slide shut. He made a last feeble effort to recapture his former rationality. There were no gods, he told himself in the tone of a memorized lesson. There were only myths and metaphors, signs and symbols, and man's poignant need to make sense of the senseless brute phenomena of life and death. What he thought he'd seen a moment ago, when he gazed up at the icon overhead, had been only a fever dream brought on by the emptying of his veins, the slow pitter-patter of his blood on the floor. And Kane was only a man. Nothing more. Of course he was. Of course.

Chester opened his eyes and looked up again, expecting to see the figure of Christ where it belonged, but instead he saw only Kane, towering over him, his lips skinned back in an unholy smile.

The last thing he knew, before black waves washed over him and carried him away, was the sound of Kane chuckling mirthlessly, a dark, dripping-molasses sound, and from somewhere far away—Chester was sure of it, absolutely sure—the answering laughter of something neither human nor divine.

Meg Sanchez had kept one destination in mind from the moment she started running, and now, at last, she'd reached it.

The Tuskett Inn loomed before her, its ragged bulk blacking out the moon.

Nearby lay a scatter of downed power lines, still twitching like electric eels. She gave them a wide berth as she approached the motel.

Kane wouldn't come here. She was sure of it. There was no reason for him even to think of looking in this place of cobwebs and moonbeams and white dust, a place so obviously empty of life.

She climbed in through one of the ground-floor windows—easy enough, seeing as how every window had been busted years ago by kids tossing rocks—and found herself in the lobby. The desk where folks had once waited in line to check in and check out was still there. A potted plant sat near it; the plant was a gray, withered husk. Not far from the desk there was a stairway, metal steps with a metal banister, rising to the second story.

The place was musty with the smell of decay—a dry decay, free of mold and mildew; this was, after all, the desert, where rain was rare and the hot summer sun baked the moisture out of old wood and let it blister and crack. She fancied that the pool hall of an old ghost town might smell like this, which was appropriate, since Tuskett was now a ghost town in everything but name.

She moved forward. Floorboards creaked. A litter of broken glass from the windows crunched under her shoes like new-fallen leaves. She mounted the stairs, stepping carefully in the semidarkness with only splinters of starlight to guide her way.

She wanted to be on the upstairs floor, on the off-chance Kane might come here. It was just possible the man would look in the lobby or one of the other ground-level rooms; but never would he take the trouble to go upstairs and hunt through all that dust and dry rot. And if he did, she'd hear his footsteps on the stairs; that would give her some warning at least.

She made her way down the upstairs hall, past rows of numbered doors. On one doorknob hung a faded PLEASE DO NOT DISTURB sign, printed with a barely legible picture of a man fast asleep in bed and snoring a huge word-balloon Z.

Most of the doors were ajar. She looked into empty rooms, void of furniture, drapes, or even carpets. They made her think of empty coffins waiting to be filled.

She chose Room 209 for no particular reason, and crept inside, wishing she had a flashlight. She stood for a while in the dark, hugging herself. She badly wanted a cigarette but was afraid the glowing tip might be visible through the window. Instead she passed the time by mentally writing and editing the news story she was planning to do about Mr. Kane and his night's work, a firsthand piece of reporting she intended to sell to the highest bidder. She supposed it was ghoulish of her to capitalize on the tragedy, especially one so personal, involving as it did the loss of most of her friends. But what the hell. She'd been editing and publishing the Tuskett *Clarion* for most of her adult life, and she'd never come upon a really big story before. Now that she had one, she was goddamned if she was going to turn her back on it.

We all felt he was a little strange, she thought, running through her lead paragraph. He came walking out of the desert, where nothing lives but collared lizards and red-tailed hawks, into our town of Tuskett, a very small town well off the beaten track, where nobody ever came. He called himself Kane. He had a pack on his back and a cold light in his eyes. He made us afraid, though we couldn't have said why. But now we know. Those of us who survived, anyway.

She nodded. That was nice. It had a certain flavor to it that *Time* magazine might like. Or the *National Enquirer,* maybe. Hell, she wasn't choosy.

She went on putting the words together, like jigsaw pieces, in her mind.

Of course, deep down, she knew what was going on here. She wasn't interested in writing news copy, not with Kane still on the prowl, maybe killing off her remaining friends one at a time. She was trying to keep from going crazy, that's all, trying to keep her head on straight. If she could stay relatively sane by writing an imaginary article, or a dozen articles, or a whole damn book, she'd do it. Because she had to do something.

After a while she decided it would be okay if she had a cigarette after all. She told herself that if she stood with her back to the window, nobody could see her. And besides, she just had to have a smoke. She was, pardon the expression, dying for one.

In the dark she fumbled with her pack of Camels, got

one out, and found her Bic. Shielding the lighter with her body so as not to send up a miniature signal flare that might be spotted from outside, she lit the cancer stick and sucked in a lungful of smoke. She sighed, a contented woman. Somehow the surgeon general's warning, which had flared up briefly in the lighter's glow, didn't seem too important at this particular moment in her life.

She finished the cigarette and had another, then a third. She was thinking seriously about starting a fourth when she heard a distant, faintly metallic echo on the stairs.

She froze.

He's coming, she thought in a sudden fever of fear. He found me. Somehow he hunted me down, the bastard.

She listened tensely. She heard nothing further. She permitted herself to think that the sound she'd heard had been her imagination. She'd gotten herself spooked. Smoked too many damn cigarettes and gotten a touch lightheaded.

From way down the hall, a floorboard groaned, an awful, rasping, haunted-house sound.

This time there was no denying it. She'd heard something, all right. But there was no need to panic. This was an old building, and old buildings, just like old people, were known to make their share of funny noises in the night. What she'd heard might have been only tired wood settling in. She clung to that thought as if to a life raft, and she'd almost persuaded herself it might be true, when she heard the sound again.

It was louder this time, closer. She waited. She heard it again, then again, closer each time, the creaking of floorboards in a deadly, terrible rhythm, and she could no longer pretend to herself that she was hearing anything other than the slow, ominous tread of footsteps.

How could he have known where to find her? How

could he have followed? It just wasn't possible. More than that, it wasn't fair. She'd come up with a good plan, a perfect hiding place; she'd done all that could be expected of her; and now here he was anyway, closing in on her, inexorable as death.

She shook her head. None of that mattered now. She had to find a way to survive.

She crossed the room, taking slow, gingerly steps, careful to make no sound, till she reached the door. It was half-open, hanging at a forty-five-degree angle to the room. She maneuvered behind it, out of sight. Her heart was banging in her chest. She was warm all over, flushed as if with fever; her knees and elbows positively burned; chills shivered up her back. She'd never noticed just how much fear felt like a bad case of the flu.

She could see nothing from where she stood. The door blocked her view of the hall. But she remembered the peephole. Every motel-room door had one. Craning her neck, she gazed through and, yes, she could see something now. She had a fish-eye view of a wedge of hallway washed blue by moonlight. She couldn't see Kane, but she could hear him approaching from the far end of the hall.

Another floorboard protested under his weight. The sound was close now, terrifyingly close. She felt the short hairs at the nape of her neck stiffen like porcupine bristles. She'd always heard that hair acted up that way when you were scared, but she'd never personally experienced the phenomenon, and frankly she would have given a great deal not to be experiencing it now.

She peered through the peephole. She saw a shadow crawl over the floor. In time with another footstep the shadow swam closer. She still couldn't see him, but she could feel his closeness, and she was acutely aware of the thinness of the wall at her side, the wall that was the only thing separating her from him, a quarter inch of cheap plywood. She fancied she could hear the low, steady rasp of his breath, and even the muffled drumbeat of his heart.

He moved forward once more. She heard the whispery rustling of his coat. Into the peephole's field of view floated a pale hand, its shape distorted by the wide-angle lens, the fingers elongated into claws. An arm followed, gliding eel-like through murky darkness, and then ...

Meg Sanchez released a long-held breath and shut her eyes.

It wasn't Kane. It was PattiSue.

"Oh, Jesus," Meg said aloud.

PattiSue shrieked. It was the sound a woman in an old movie would make as she stood on a chair and pointed with a trembling finger at a mouse. She spun toward the door, her eyes wide, clutching her chest with that pale hand, which no longer looked menacing at all.

Meg stepped out from behind the door. "It's okay. Just me."

PattiSue swayed, and for a horrible moment Meg was sure the girl was going to pass out on her, and then she steadied herself.

"Oh, God," she was saying. "Oh, God. Oh, God."

All of a sudden Meg started to laugh. She couldn't help herself. It was funny. All of it. A riot. She stared at PattiSue, running her eyes over the long blue dress she was wearing, the dress that had rustled silkily in a way that sounded like Kane's coat, and she kept on laughing and laughing, until finally PattiSue caught her hysteria and joined in.

They laughed till they were out of breath, bent double and gasping.

"What the hell are you doing here?" Meg asked when she was able to force out speech.

"I thought"—PattiSue giggled helplessly—"I thought it'd make a good place to hide."

"Guess you weren't the only one."

Finally they got themselves under control. PattiSue looked around, shivering. "You know, it's real spooky in here."

"Not half as damn spooky as being out in the dark with Jack the Ripper."

"That's for sure. I still don't like it much."

"Aw, hell. Didn't you ever go to the funhouse when you were a kid?"

"Sure. In Jacob."

"Well, this isn't any different. It's a funhouse, is all. Just think of it that way and you'll be okay."

"I'll try."

PattiSue stepped into the room. Meg noticed she was still barefoot, and now she was limping a little. Her left foot was dark and splotchy with red.

"What happened to you?"

PattiSue glanced at her foot selfconsciously. "Nothing. I cut myself a little."

"That's what you get for not wearing any shoes."

PattiSue looked away. "Wasn't time to fetch any of Millie's. This is her dress, see. My things ... Well, they're back at the trailer ... with Eddie."

Meg understood. "Sorry I said anything." She was still staring at that bleeding foot, while a bad thought began to take shape inside her like an unwanted pregnancy. "You been bleeding like that for long?" she asked as casually as possible.

"Yeah, I guess. I didn't want to take the time to bandage it up. I've been running pretty much the whole time, like a chicken with its head chopped off. Didn't know where to go. I ran from house to house, but nowhere felt safe. Finally it dawned on me to come here. Guess you thought of it right off."

"Um." Meg couldn't take her eyes off that foot, or the

floor behind it, the floor leading out to the hall. "You should've put some shoes on, darling."

"I told you," PattiSue said petulantly, "I couldn't go back to the trailer and there wasn't time. What's the difference anyhow? There's a lot worse things out there to worry about than a sore foot."

"It's not your foot being sore that's got me worried."

"What is it then?"

"You've been leaving a trail of bread crumbs for the big bad wolf to follow, is what."

She pointed, and PattiSue followed her gaze, and both of them stared at the hall floor, where even in the dim light it was possible to make out a trail of blood-red footprints.

PattiSue blinked. "Oh, my God. You think ...?"

"I don't know. Maybe."

"Oh, Meg, ... I'm sorry."

Meg's heart, tough as it was, broke a little to hear the girl whimper like that, pathetic as a puppy, after what she had been through. She brushed the words away.

"Okay, okay. Nothing to be done about it now. We've got to find some other place to hide. The dump, maybe. But first I'm going to get that foot of yours wrapped up, or we'll be in the same fix we're in now."

They sat on the floor. Meg studied PattiSue's foot. She must've stepped on a nail or something; the bottom of the foot had been ripped open in a long ragged line. A nasty wound, the kind that, in a better day, would have prompted Jack Evans to apply stitches. Well, Jack was gone, and Meg Sanchez was no doctor, but she could damn well take care of herself and the Bakers' girl too. She ripped off a length of her sleeve, then wound the cloth around PattiSue's foot and knotted it tight, a makeshift tourniquet.

"That hurt?" Meg asked, getting up.

"A little."

"Can you walk on it?"

PattiSue stood up and limped around the room. "Yeah, I can. Am I still ...?"

Meg studied the floor. No bloodstains were evident. "Nope," she said. "It's working, at least for now. Might come undone. If it does, I'll put on a new one."

"I'm really sorry, Meg. I just wasn't thinking."

"Quit with the apologizing. I told you, it's all right. No harm done." Meg took a step toward the door, then began to laugh again, not hysterically this time, but easily, good-naturedly. "At least you weren't Kane."

She stepped into the hall. She was still laughing when something hard and pointy slammed into the base of her throat, knocking the wind out of her. She stumbled backward and came up hard against the wall and stood there helpless, gazing down the twenty-four-inch barrel of a Winchester Sporter Magnum hunting rifle at the man who was holding it, the man who was, of course, Kane. He was smiling.

She knew, with ugly certainty, exactly what had happened. Kane had picked up PattiSue's trail and followed her here; for all anybody knew, he might have been right behind her the whole time, tracking the girl, soundless as a shadow. He'd climbed the stairs in silence, crept down the hall in a panther tread, no doubt drawn unerringly to their hiding place by PattiSue's footprints and by their stupid schoolgirl laughter.

Then he'd waited. Waited to pounce.

There was a sharp click, the sound of the safety's release.

Meg felt no fear, no anger, nothing but that awful emptiness inside her she knew only too well, the same black cloud that darkened her mind whenever she sat at a typewriter and the words wouldn't come. She remembered how, in times past, she'd been afraid of herself in this mood, afraid she might get hold of a gun and blow her head off to end her misery. She needn't worry about it this time.

Out of the corner of her eye she saw PattiSue standing in the doorway taking in the scene before her, paralyzed by fear. The girl would be next, of course. Neither of them was going to get out of this particular funhouse alive. Meg told herself she ought to feel sorry about that, for PattiSue anyhow, if not for herself; but—funny thing—somehow the emotion just wouldn't come.

Only one regret reached her, even in the depths of the dark place she was in. Regret over the story she could have written.

Hot damn, she thought, I bet I could've sold it to *Time* magazine. Could've made something of my life, and maybe even justified it.

Or maybe it had already been too late for that.

She felt, rather than saw, Kane's finger tighten on the trigger. But when he squeezed it once and the Winchester bucked in his hands, blasting her throat to ropes of bloody meat, she didn't feel anything at all.

The gunshot shocked PattiSue into action.

She'd been standing there like a prize dummy, stuck in the doorway and watching the final seconds of Meg Sanchez' life, dumbstruck by horror; and she might never have moved at all if the rifle hadn't made such a godawful racket when it went off, and if there hadn't been so much blood. It was everywhere, splattering the wall and floor and ceiling, splashing down the front of PattiSue's borrowed dress like so much puke.

I'm next, she thought with sudden vivid clarity. He'll shoot me next.

Meg's head lolled on her shoulders, a flower on a

broken stem. Slowly her body slid down the wall, leaving a long vertical streak of red. She crumpled to the floor and fell over on her side and lay in a twitching heap, the fingers of her left hand working convulsively.

Then, just as PattiSue had expected, Kane swung the rifle around and pointed it at her. But she wasn't going to just stand there and take it like one of Eddie's whuppings. She'd cheated death once tonight. She could do it again.

She opened her mouth and a sound came out, a high, clear, echoing war whoop, a sound you'd expect to hear from an Apache on the war path, but not from a small-town waitress in a blood-smeared dress who'd never lifted a finger in self-defense when her boyfriend beat her black and blue.

She grabbed the rifle by its barrel and shoved it straight up in the air, and it went off harmlessly, blasting a hole in the ceiling, and then she hurled herself at Kane's knees and took him down.

"Son of a bitch!" she screamed. "You son of a bitch!"

They hit the floor in a rolling heap. She clawed at him and bit and snarled. The rifle kept jerking toward her, but each time, she knocked it away with the flat of her hand, easily, almost petulantly, in a brisk shoo-fly gesture. She wasn't scared of the rifle. She wasn't scared of anything. She'd had it with being scared. She'd always been scared, for her whole life, it seemed. She'd been scared of staying with Eddie, and scared of leaving him. She'd been scared of keeping his brutality a secret, and scared of telling a soul. She'd been running like a scared rabbit all her life, and she was sick and tired of it, you bet she was.

"Goddamned ... murdering ... son of a *whore!*" she screamed in a voice that wasn't her own.

The rifle twisted toward her again, and in a spasm of red fury she seized it with both hands and wrenched it halfway out of Kane's grip. She wouldn't let go, and neither would he, and the two of them fought for possession of the gun in a savage tug-of-war, till finally the rifle flew free and boomeranged down the hall, landing somewhere out of reach.

Then PattiSue knew the odds were even, and she went wild, even wilder than before; she was all over Kane, scratching and clawing like a tigress, ripping his ashen face to blood and shrieking a banshee yowl.

She could feel her eyes bulging out of their sockets, her lips skinned back to expose the white of her teeth. An image flashed in her mind, an image of how she must look at this moment, her cover-girl face twisted into a carnival mask, all pop eyes and unholy grin. What the devil had gotten into her? She didn't know, didn't care. All she knew was that she was going to kill this man with her bare hands and nothing in the world would stop her.

She was still going at him full tilt, dragging her fingernails down his face and pounding him with her fists, when she felt a sharp pain in her side, what her mother called a stitch, the kind of stabbing pain you felt when you'd been exercising too hard, except that this pain was worse than that; it was as if a needle had been plunged into her guts and was turning her insides to jelly. She looked down.

A knife, long and sharp, its serrated blade sticky with dried blood, was sinking into her side as neatly as a pin in a pincushion.

She watched, her fury forgotten, as it slid in the rest of the way, vanishing up to the hilt. And then the hand that had pushed it, Kane's hand, released its grip and left it in there like a surgeon's tool abandoned in the body of a patient.

PattiSue made a very small noise, not much different from the sound she might make if she were clearing her throat, as the blue dress began to run red with blood.

Dimly she understood what had happened. It was the coat. He'd been carrying the knife in there. And while she'd been pummeling him and cursing and screaming her fool head off, he must have snaked one arm inside that coat, easy as you please, and drawn out that knife, and struck.

Abruptly it was as though all the wind had been knocked out of her. She couldn't fight him anymore. She couldn't even bring herself to take hold of the handle of the knife and pull it out. It was too much effort. Everything was too much effort.

She lay on top of him, grunting and wheezing, while blood pasted her dress to her skin and waves of pain washed over her like ripples in a pond.

Kane seized her by the arms and pulled her off him. The knife moved inside her. She almost screamed. He dumped her onto the floor on her side, driving the blade in deeper, and the shock wave of pain nearly knocked her unconscious. She rolled onto her back and lay motionless save for the rise and fall of her stomach in time with her labored breathing, while tears dampened the corners of her eyes and ran down her cheeks like droplets of rainwater on a windowpane.

Kane got up slowly. He stood looking down at her. His blue eyes glinted, pinpoints of light in the deep well of shadow that was his face.

"Bitch," he said softly, tonelessly.

He lifted his head, and she caught a glimpse of the damage she'd done, the bloody tracks printed on his face where her fingernails had grooved deep into his flesh. She hoped it hurt. Hoped it hurt like hell.

He turned and walked away, heading back down the hall. He paused once to pick up the rifle, then went on. She felt the heavy thump of his boots on the floor; each new vibration set the knife blade quivering and sent new lightning forks of pain shooting up her side. He reached the stairs and descended, his footsteps ringing out metallically in a slow, regular rhythm like the tolling of a bell.

Then he was gone.

PattiSue was left alone, with only Meg Sanchez' corpse to keep a deathwatch over her. Meg, who'd had no chance even to fight back, who'd been left with no choice but to stare down the rifle's barrel and wait for the bullet to take her head off.

Not me, she thought grimly. I didn't let it end that way. I put up a fight. For once, I didn't take what was coming to me lying down. For once.

The thought strengthened her a little. She experienced a faint swell of pride, pitiful and almost absurd under the circumstances, but there it was.

"I put up a fight," she said aloud, the words coming out painfully hoarse and ragged.

She smiled, and in that moment her lovely face bloomed like a rare flower in the darkness. And another thought occurred to her, a thought that seemed utterly irrelevant, but wasn't.

Kane had left her for dead once before.

6

Rile Cady had gone straight back to his trailer after escaping from the church. He'd had two excellent reasons for doing so. First off, he knew Kane had already visited the trailer park, and it seemed unlikely he'd go back. And second, on the floor of his bedroom closet there was a shoebox full of 2-3/4-inch Magnum shells for his Remington 12-gauge. He figured if he could load the gun and make it useful again, he'd feel a good deal better about his chances of survival, should Kane surprise him and show up.

Entering the trailer, Rile experienced a pang of disappointment so deep it bordered on despair. The place had been ransacked. His bookshelves, piled with musty old books from his childhood, had been toppled, spilling their loads every which way. Paintings had been torn off the walls. The sofa cushion had been slit open; pasty-white stuffing drooled out.

Kane had been here, all right, and he'd been after something. Rile figured he knew what it was. The shotgun. Somehow the man had found out about it; he must have come here to steal it and kill its owner. Rile counted himself lucky on both scores. He'd been out with Bill

Needham, looking for Lew and Lynnie Hannah, and he'd had the gun with him.

Still, he was worried. Because Kane might have found the shoebox and taken the ammo. And that would put quite a crimp in Rile's plans for self-defense.

He made his way through the dark living room, stepping daintily over piles of scattered debris. He entered the bedroom. It was in no better shape. The bed, yanked partly off its frame, listed like a distressed ship. The closet door hung open, exposing the mess inside. Kane had looked in there, and no doubt he'd found Rile's small, precious hoard. Still, there was a chance he'd missed it.

Rile approached the closet, knelt down, and searched the floor, pawing through a scatter of wire coat hangers and rumpled clothes. He knew it was hopeless, he was merely going through the motions, and that was why he was so greatly surprised when his hands closed over the shoebox.

It was still there. And it felt heavy, heavy enough to contain its secret treasure.

He lifted the lid with fumbling hands. The big Magnum shells glittered inside like gems in a jewelry box. Dozens of them.

Rile almost laughed out loud.

He carried the box over to the bed, planting himself awkwardly on the edge of the displaced mattress. Moonbeams filtered in through the window at his back. In the weak light he loaded five shells into the magazine tube. Then the gun was ready for action again, and Rile let out a slow sigh of relief.

Suddenly he felt better than he had in a long while. Yes, indeedy. He half-hoped Kane would show his ugly face again. The way Rile was feeling right now, he wouldn't mind getting another crack at that son of a bitch. But another part of him, a more levelheaded and pragmatic part, told him to be grateful to be hidden away where Kane wasn't likely to look.

Something reminded him of the window at his back, and of the black night beyond. It occurred to him how vulnerable he was, sitting there. If Kane happened to pass this way and saw his outline, he could take him out with an easy shot, as easy as target practice on a rimfire silhouette.

Rile hastily moved away from the window. Better to sit on the floor, where he would be invisible from outside. He hunkered down in a corner of the bedroom and sat with the shotgun in his lap, his fingers drumming the smooth walnut stock.

He let his thoughts drift to remembrances of all the people who'd lost their lives tonight. Lew Hannah, with his easy man's-man smile and his slow, honey-smooth voice. Lynnie, who'd been like a second mother to Jenny Kirk. Charlie Grain, who'd served up the best burgers west of the Mississippi and charged a bargain price for them too. Dick and Gretchen Lewis, who at least had died instantly, with no senseless pain to complicate matters; that was something, anyhow. And all the rest—George and Marge Baker, Jack and Millie Evans, Todd and Debbie and Johnny Hanson, Stan and Judy Perkins, Ethel Walston, Eddie Cox. All of them, lost. Lost forever. Just like Tuskett itself, dead and gone. Rile had known the town was dying, but he surely hadn't expected it to disappear in one night like a candle winking out.

He wondered where he would go. He couldn't stay here, not with nearly everyone dead, and the few survivors—if they did survive—certain to move on, themselves. And yet the notion of leaving this place he'd called home for his whole life was not an easy one to adjust to, not for a man of his years. Starting over at the age of seventy-seven. Damn, that was a hard thing to ask of a person. He wasn't sure he was up to it.

Maybe, he thought bitterly, it would have been better if he had been here when Kane showed up. Then he would be dead already, never to know how many others had died. Never to face this awful emptiness that was all around him, and inside him too.

He sighed. No point in brooding. He was alive, and he ought to be grateful. Though he couldn't help but wonder how the Reverend Chester Ewes would explain the wisdom and mercy of a God who let an old man live while taking the lives of the young. The Lord works in mysterious ways, Rile could hear Chester saying in that solemn, blandly ritualistic way of his. He wondered if that was true. He wondered if the good reverend even believed it himself—or if anybody did.

He let his head droop on his shoulders. He half-shut his eyes. Of course he wasn't going to fall asleep. Nobody could fall asleep on a night like this, no matter how dog-tired he might be. Still, it was good to rest.

He thought about Kane. He knew nothing about the man. If he was a man. Well, of course he was. He had to be. Except, you see, a man wouldn't have chewed Lew Hannah's heart to pieces. A man wouldn't have had the strength to run, fleet as a deer, after he'd been gut-shot at close range. A man wouldn't be able to wipe out a whole town, even a very little town, all by himself in just one night. No, sir. A man, even a crazy man, wouldn't—couldn't—do those things.

But if he was not a man ... then what?

Rile didn't know.

He let his head nod lower. He lingered in that border town between wakefulness and sleep. And in that twilight place, he thought of Kirby Tuskett, the old man with scads of money and an assumed name, the man who'd come to Desolation, California, to hide out from whoever was dogging his heels, who'd given the town its power lines and water tower, and who'd been found dead in a bathtub filled with water from that very tower, water tinted red with his own blood. And it occurred to Rile, as he drifted toward sleep, that nobody had ever known just who Kirby Tuskett's assassin might have been; the killer, nameless, faceless, had come and gone, silent as death, leaving corpses as his calling card.

And then a thought struck Rile Cady, a wild, improbable thought, the kind that could come only on the brink of dreaming.

That killer with no name or form, that shadow of death from so many years past—had he, too, been Kane?

Had Kane visited this town, way back in the summer of '26, to do his dirty work? Had he slipped in and slipped out, soundless as the fall of night? Had he been waiting ever since, alone in the wasteland of the Mojave, like a soul banished to purgatory, waiting for decades, ageless, changeless, clad in his dusty cowpoke clothes? And had he now returned, an agent of some impersonal fate, to finish the job he'd started, to bleed this town built on blood money, to murder this town that had taken its name from a dead man's alias, to punish the town of Tuskett for the sins of its father, and take its life as he had taken the life of Kirby Tuskett in his bath?

Rile moaned.

No. It couldn't be. It was plain crazy.

Sleep took him.

Sometime later—it might have been a minute or an hour—a gunshot sounded from outside, loud and close, shocking him awake.

Rile jerked his head up and listened. A long interval of time passed in silence. Then he heard a second shot, ringing out in the stillness. And yes, it was very close. Right in this neighborhood.

He was wide-awake now. And he knew he had a decision to make. He could stay put, huddled nice and cozy like a rabbit in its den, and wait out whatever was left of the night. Or he could act like a hero, and probably get himself killed. Yeah. Probably. But dammit all, he did have a freshly loaded gun. He was the only person in town, other than Kane himself, who had a weapon worth speaking of. And the way he figured it, that particular fact put a burden of responsibility on his shoulders, a burden he didn't much want but could hardly cast off. He had to do what he could.

Anyway, he'd put a hole in Kane once. Wounded him pretty good, he believed. Just allow him one more clean shot at the man, and he'd blow that bastard's head off.

If Kane was a man, and not a ghost out of Rile's childhood and Tuskett's distant past.

Wendell Stoddard was pretty sure he was dead. Dead and in hell. It was the only explanation that made sense.

Sometime earlier, three hours or three centuries, he had finally made it to the top of the arroyo. The moment when he hauled himself over the rim and collapsed panting on the wondrously flat desert plain was the sweetest of his life. Even the miracle of Melody's first steps paled by comparison.

He'd lain there for a long time, asking himself whether he had the strength to go on. He didn't know. All he knew was that it was so good not to have to climb anymore, so good to rest, to press his face to the dirt and feel rivulets of sweat stream off him like water off a duck. He didn't think he could ever rise again.

But he did rise. He went on. Because a killer was out there somewhere in the hot summer night, a killer who had to be stopped.

He staggered across the desert, retracing the zigzagging course the two cars had taken, following the rare treadmarks still visible in the whorled and drifted sand. Sometime later, he found the Old Road and headed east, shambling zombie-like along the double yellow line, hoping desperately to see headlights wash over him so he could wave down a car.

Unless, of course, the car was Lew Hannah's Ford.

That thought set him shivering all over. He pushed it out of his mind.

He encountered no cars. He wasn't surprised. The Old Road rarely saw much traffic even at noon; now, in the wee hours of the morning, it lay dark and silent.

He trudged along with his head bowed and shoulders slumped, the holstered .32 slapping his hip with each stride. His gaze was fixed on the cracked macadam directly before him; he was conscious only of the slow shuffle of his boots as he covered yard after yard.

At some point he began experiencing symptoms of delirium. Awareness faded in and out like those voices he'd heard on the radio earlier tonight. One moment he knew with absolute lucidity where he was and what he was doing, and a moment later he was staring at the empty road and trying to puzzle out what in God's name had brought him to this desolate place. During one of those feverish, trancelike states, he got the notion that he must be dead, and now he was on a journey through hell, a ceaseless journey down an infinite road bounded by nothingness on either side.

Dead, he told himself. That's it, all right. You're dead meat, Wendell. Maybe you died in the car crash. Or maybe you fell and broke your neck when you were trying to climb out of that pit. Or maybe ...

A sudden sound shocked him alert. A single brief handclap that split the night and left no echo. The sound of a gunshot.

He raised his head. Directly to his left was the outline of a building, one he was sure he'd seen before. The Tuskett Inn. The old motel that had been shut down years ago. But that meant ... that meant he'd reached the edge of town. He'd gotten back to Tuskett.

A second shot rang out. This time he was able to pinpoint its source.

The motel.

Wendell's hand shook only a little as he unholstered his .32.

Rile crept through the trailer park, scanning the darkness. Dry bitterroot and desert candle crunched under his feet. He gripped his shotgun in both hands.

Eddie Cox's trailer passed by, dark and strangely foreboding; no doubt Eddie's dead body lay inside. The thought gave Rile the creeps. He walked faster.

He reached the edge of the field and stepped out onto Joshua Street. The downed power lines weren't far away, snaking and sparking feebly. He made a wide detour around them, then stopped, staring across the street at the black shape of the Tuskett Inn.

A man lurked in the shadows.

From what Rile could tell, the man wasn't aware of being watched. He was wading through thickets of weeds, circling the motel, prowling the darkness. Then he reached the far end of the building and rounded a corner; but before he vanished from sight, Rile saw a glint of metal in his hand.

A gun.

It was Kane, then. He was the only armed man in Tuskett, other than Rile himself.

He found his courage and crossed the street. He crept up to the motel and edged along the side wall. Cautiously he peered around the corner.

Kane was only a few yards away. His back was turned, but the gun was still visible, glittering in his right hand. He appeared to have shed his hat and coat, but not the dark pants and shirt. He moved slowly, limping a little. Well, that was hardly surprising; he'd taken a shotgun blast to the gut.

And now he was going to take another one.

Slowly Rile stepped out from behind the wall, raised the Remington, and got a bead on the target. He drew back the slide handle with a soft click.

Kane whirled, hearing the sound. The pistol in his hand came up fast. But not fast enough.

Rile fired.

Kane staggered back, hit squarely in the chest, gushing blood. The gun dangled uselessly from limp fingers.

Got him, Rile thought with a thrill of triumph.

He fired again, and Kane's head snapped back with a whiplash jerk. The gun flew out of his grasp and disappeared into the weeds. Rile squeezed off one more shot and hit him in the midsection, then watched as Kane fell sprawling on his back. The man twitched and lay still.

Rile started breathing again.

You did it, he told himself. You killed him. You really goddamn *killed* him.

Slowly he approached the body, keeping his eyes open for any hint of movement, still suspecting a trick or a trap. Not that any man could absorb that much punishment and still be alive to brag about it. But then again, with this fellow, you never knew.

He reached the remains and stood over them, staring down, and his tongue clucked once against his teeth in time with an intake of breath.

It was not Kane.

It was someone else entirely, someone Rile had never laid eyes on before. A young man—terribly young, barely old enough to take a legal sip of whiskey, from the looks of him—wearing a state trooper's uniform. His pants and shirt were matted with dirt and dried blood, staining the fabric nearly as dark as Kane's clothes.

Rile stood unmoving by the body of the man he had killed, a man who must have come to Tuskett to save them, a man who'd been hunting Kane just as he himself had thought he was.

"No," Rile whispered. "Goddammit, no." Tears burned at the corners of his eyes.

Then something hard and cold bumped him in the back, and he knew without the need to look that it was the muzzle of a gun, and it was planted directly between his shoulder blades, and the man at the other end of it was Kane. The real Kane this time. Still very much alive, thank you.

The gun went off. Rile felt an explosion shudder through his insides, ripping him to pieces. He staggered but did not fall. With his last strength he tried to pull back the Remington's slide handle and load another shell into the breech. Maybe he could take the bastard with him. Turn and fire at point-blank range. If only he could get the damn handle to slide back ...

He couldn't do it. He seemed to have lost control of his hands. His fingers were numb. His whole body was numb. The shotgun slipped free and dropped to the ground. He stared at it blankly. It seemed very far away. As he watched, the gun turned red. Funny how it should do that. Then he understood that he was bleeding all over it. The bullet in his back had bored a hole right through him, and his guts were spilling out. The thought made him sick. He felt the need to vomit. He lowered his head, but nothing came out of his mouth except a low, piteous moan. He swayed weakly, then fell across the trooper's body and hugged it tight.

Somewhere, Kane was laughing. Had he laughed like that when he filled the old man Tuskett full of holes? But that was crazy, and Rile had no more time to think about it now. He was too busy dying. And after that, he was just too damn busy being dead.

Bill Needham had thought briefly about leaving town on foot, heading into the desert to hide there and let the night pass, and he might have done it if he'd been alone. But not with Jenny and Tommy in tow. They would have had to walk for miles over the rough terrain, and he could see from the look on Jenny's face that she wasn't up to it. And as for Tommy, the boy looked half-dead. Bill could hardly blame either of them.

Instead it occurred to him that Kane might have missed at least one of the cars in town. So he'd taken the time to stop at each parked car they passed. With infinite care, he wriggled underneath to inspect the fuel tank, hoping to find no lead pipe taped there. Each time, he was disappointed, Kane had been thorough. If he'd missed a car, Bill hadn't found it.

So there would be no easy way out. They couldn't leave town, either on foot or by car. They'd have to wait out the night, survive somehow till morning arrived, and with it, at least the possibility of help.

In the meantime, they needed a hiding place. The service station seemed as good a choice as any. Bill led Jenny and Tommy into the dark office where he'd spent so many sleepy hours watching TV and waiting for a car horn to honk. There hadn't been many horns these last few years; from now on, he reflected, there wouldn't be any, ever again.

Tommy was nearly asleep on his feet. The strain of the night's multiple shocks had taken their toll. He lay down on the floor, curled up, and began to doze.

Bill and Jenny set about preparing a defense.

It was no good just to wait and hide. They needed weapons. And Bill had an idea of how to improvise some.

Near the old Coke machine was a garbage pail full of empty bottles. He carried the pail into the office, then found some of the rags he used to wipe his hands when he worked, old, dirty, oil-stained things. From the display rack in the front window he removed some cans of motor oil and pried open the lids. Together he and Jenny poured the contents of three or four cans into the Coke bottles, then stuffed the bottles with the rags, making Molotov cocktails.

"Think it'll work?" Jenny asked, keeping her voice low so as not to wake the boy.

Bill nodded. "All we need is some matches." He opened his desk drawer and found one of the complementary matchbooks he gave away whenever anybody bought a pack of cigarettes. He tossed the matchbook to her. "Hold on to this. You'll have to light the things ... if it comes to that."

"With any luck, it won't."

"Yeah. With any luck."

But he had a feeling luck was one thing they couldn't count on tonight.

They arranged the bottles in neat rows in a corner of the office, soldiers ranked and ready for battle. There was nothing else to do. They settled down to wait. Bill positioned himself against the back wall, with a clear view of the front of the service station through the open doorway and windows.

The building was easy enough to defend. There was no rear exit, no second story. Looking through the doorway, Bill could take in the asphalt fuel area, the full-service island with its three pumps—leaded, regular unleaded, and super-premium—and Joshua Street beyond.

Kane would have to approach that way if he wanted to get in.

Bill and Jenny sat in the dark and said nothing for a long while. On more than one occasion, gunshots sounded from far away. Tommy didn't stir.

"Bill," Jenny said suddenly.

"Uh-huh?"

"I just wanted to say ... thanks." She lowered her head, embarrassed. "Thanks for being here. Tommy and I ... we wouldn't have made it this far without you."

"As I recall, you're the one who fired off those shots at the water tower when I was a sitting duck." He shrugged. "It works both ways."

"Let's call it even, then."

"Even-steven. It's a deal."

She looked away. "You know, I wish I'd gotten to know you better. Everybody told me I should. But I guess ... I guess I was afraid." She laughed. "Doesn't it sound silly, being afraid of something like that? I mean ... after tonight."

He kept his voice low. "I don't think it's silly. I've been afraid of some things myself. Like leaving this town. I stayed because I had the excuse of a father to care for, and then a gas station to run. But they were only excuses, and I knew it." He smiled. "Guess I've run out of excuses now."

"Me too," Jenny said,

There was no sound but Tommy's low breathing.

"So what happens now?" Bill asked.

"You mean, if we make it?"

"We will."

She didn't look at him. "Well ... we move on, I guess. Tommy and I."

"Yeah." He studied her face in the darkness. "I don't

suppose ... I mean ... I don't suppose you'd want the three of us to move on ... together?"

She raised her head to look at him, and he couldn't help but notice that her eyes were wet with tears.

"I think I'd like that," she whispered.

He held her hand, and neither of them said anything more.

Abruptly, Tommy woke up. He tilted his head, as if listening, then shuddered, not like a boy, but like a dog, a dog scared of distant thunder, his small body trembling convulsively from head to toe.

"Tommy." Jenny took his hand. "What is it?"

He kept on shivering, his teeth clenched, while a low whimper escaped his lips.

"Tommy—"

"Shhh," Bill said, touching her arm.

The boy heard something. Bill was sure of it.

The three of them listened. From the distance rose the soft crunch of footsteps on gravel.

Bill licked his lips. Suddenly his mouth was very dry. He stared out the doorway into the night. And, yes, there he was.

Kane.

He was crossing the lot, heading directly for the office where they'd tried to hide.

Bill had no idea how Kane could have tracked them down. Maybe he'd simply gone from house to house and shop to shop, looking everywhere with methodical care, eliminating one possible hiding place after the next, until finally he'd narrowed it down to this one last building. Or maybe some instinct had drawn him here, some wordless wisdom that normal men didn't possess or understand.

Didn't matter, one way or the other. He was coming.

And he had a rifle in his hand.

Bill looked at Jenny. From where she was sitting, she couldn't see the view through the door. He saw the unasked question in her eyes and nodded. She bit her lip, trembling.

He picked up the nearest bottle and snapped his fingers. Jenny tore a match out of the book and tried to light it on the cover, but her hand was shaking badly and the matchstick snapped. She tossed it aside, tried again. Kane was closing in. This time she got the match to light. She touched it to the mouth of the bottle. Instantly the rag caught fire. Bill felt the sudden intense heat through the glass as the oil inside ignited.

He leaned into the doorway and hurled the bottle. It shattered at Kane's feet, missing him by less than a yard, a good toss under the circumstances, but—dammit—not good enough.

Kane fired the rifle. The bullet slammed into the doorframe, sending up a cloud of splinters and dust.

Jenny lit another match, with more assurance this time, and ignited a second bottle. Bill hurled it through the doorway. This time his aim was true. But Kane was too quick for him. He dodged sideways, and the bottle slammed into the asphalt where he'd stood an instant before, sending up a brief shout of flame. Kane squeezed off another round, but he was off-balance from the leap and the shot went wild. Bill heard a low, oddly solid thump, the sound of a bullet striking something hard and unyielding. A gas pump, he realized. It hit one of the gas pumps.

Kane kept coming.

Jenny lit another bottle. Bill leaned into the doorway to throw it, but before he could, there was an echoing rifle crack and a sudden blinding pain in his right arm.

He'd been hit. The impact sent him spinning backward. The bottle flew out of his hand, boomeranged into a corner of the office, and went off like a bomb. Fire erupted, sweeping over the walls, setting maps and calendars and certificates of inspection ablaze. It leapt onto his desk, where old newspapers and Styrofoam coffee cups went up like torches, shooting up showers of sparks.

Bill lay in a heap, blood streaming from his arm. Shot, he thought dazedly. I've been shot. He couldn't make the thought stick. Somehow it didn't seem real.

The flames reached the oil cans stacked in the front window. The cans exploded in rapid-fire sequence, spraying hot oil and scorched scraps of metal everywhere, feeding the fire as it spread out of control.

Bill watched as Jenny scooped up the two remaining Molotovs with one hand, grabbed Tommy with the other, and crawled across the floor, away from the flames, which were climbing higher, reaching for the ceiling with eager, grasping hands. Three walls of the office were curtains of fire, billowing like sheets on a laundry line on a blustery day. The heat was blistering. Thick fumes flooded the room.

Jenny, coughing and watery-eyed, reached Bill's side with Tommy in tow. Bill wanted to tell her to run, get away, but dimly he realized there was nowhere to go. They were trapped. It was over.

As if to underline the thought, Kane stepped through the doorway.

He loomed over them as they lay helpless on the floor. The rifle was still in his hands. He was smiling.

Jenny looked away, not to see that smile. Beside her, Tommy made a little sound that was a boy's manful effort to hold back tears.

The room blazed. Flames had claimed the ceiling. It sagged in blistered patches. Ceiling panels began popping loose. The overhead fluorescents hung down on twisted nets of wires. Fire was everywhere. Smoke choked the air. Kane stood backlit by the red glare, his tall, thin, almost skeletal figure thrown into silhouette, with the folds of his bloodied coat flapping around him, gusting with drafts of superheated air.

His face was a deep well of shadow. Only his eyes were visible, glowing tiger-bright.

"You three are the last," he said in his gravelly gravedigger's voice. "All the others are dead."

He paused, letting the words register. Bill shut his eyes briefly. He thought of PattiSue, of Meg, of Chester Ewes. And Rile.

"Now you'll join them," Kane added. "And my work will be done."

Bill lifted his head to face the man.

"Why?" he asked. "What made you do it? What were you after? What was it all for?"

Kane didn't answer. He only laughed, a soft, dark, oddly viscid sound, like dripping blood.

Very slowly, he lowered the rifle and took aim at Bill from point-blank range.

Bill stared up the length of the gun barrel. He waited. He felt nothing. There was nothing to feel, no grief, no fear, not even physical pain. He was empty inside. Everything had been beaten and bled out of him.

At his side, Jenny moaned, a scared-little-girl sound.

Kane pulled the trigger.

Nothing happened.

There was no blast of thunder, no oblivion crashing down like a curtain on his life. There was only a meaningless click.

The gun was empty.

Kane looked at the rifle, astonished that it would fail him in this moment.

And Bill saw that there was still a chance.

He threw himself to his feet in one headlong motion, disregarding the rush of pain from his wounded arm. He slammed into Kane, shoving him back against the wall. The useless rifle clattered on the floor. Bill drove his knee hard into Kane's gut, then seized him by the arms. Kane sprang forward, fighting to break free. Bill held on. The two men grappled with each other, stumbling dizzily around the office, spinning like riders on some nightmarish merry-go-round, while the flaming backdrop of a hellish carnival wheeled around them in a flickering blur.

As they struggled and the room whirled and flames leapt and roared, Bill gazed into Kane's face, inches away. He smelled the man's breath, like mummy powder, like the stink of an open grave, the smell of decay and dry rot. And a memory came to him—his first sight of Kane, a dark figure rippling in the slow waves of heat like a mirage. He remembered the chill of fear he'd felt as he watched the man's slow, ominous advance. He'd thought of Kane as death. Death all dressed up in funeral black and a vampire cape. Death striding out of the desert to claim the town of Tuskett as its own.

If death ever took human form, then surely he was holding tight to it right now, dancing with it in a lunatic waltz, fighting to cheat it of its prize.

The two men stumbled into a gumball dispenser, which tipped over and thumped on the floor, cracking its clear plastic shell and spilling a rolling riot of gumballs. Bill lost his footing, his shoes slipping on the hard candies that shifted like loose sand, and Kane took advantage of the opportunity to slam him against the wall and hold him there while he leaned in close, filling Bill's field of vision like a close-up on a movie screen, his eyes huge and hypnotizing.

Bill looked into those eyes. He couldn't help himself. They held him riveted, unable to look away, while a dark voice—Kane's voice—rose in his mind, telling him not to fight, not to struggle any longer.

Nobody beats me, Bill Needham—the voice whispered—I always win, you can't cheat me, and you know it too. So just let go, let go, let go ...

Bill felt his grip on Kane's arm relaxing. Yes, he thought, it would be best that way. Best to let death take him, as sooner or later it would anyway, him ... and Tommy ... and Jenny ...

No.

Not them. He wouldn't let Kane have them.

He lifted his head a fraction and gazed deep into those ice-cold eyes and did what Lew Hannah had not been able to do in Charlie's coffee shop. He stared Kane down.

"Fuck you," Bill Needham said.

Kane blinked, surprised by this development, and in that moment Bill felt Kane's grip on him relax just slightly, and just enough.

Bill tore free, then drew back his fist and brought it forward with his full strength, putting everything he had into this one motion of his arm, and hit Kane squarely in the face.

Bone shattered. Teeth sprayed the floor, sounding very much like the gumballs a moment before. Kane made a strangled sound that was not quite a scream. He was sent reeling backward, into the flames.

Instantly he caught fire. His coat blazed. He writhed like a madman, twisting and rolling on the floor, seeking frantically to smother the flames that leapt over him like hungry animals. Abruptly he spun around on his knees, his eyes sizzling with blue fury, and thrust his hand into the burning remnants of his coat to withdraw a gun. A Llama .22. One of Lew Hannah's guns.

Bill knew this gun wouldn't be empty, this time there

would be no reprieve—and then something black and wet splashed in Kane's face, and Kane hissed like a scalded cat as the gun fell from his hand to vanish into the flames.

Bill whirled and saw Jenny standing behind him with a Coke bottle in each hand. One bottle was still stuffed with oil and rags. The other was empty, its contents—he realized—tossed in Kane's face like a cup of black coffee, a pint of motor oil that had ignited on contact with the flames.

He looked back at Kane. His face, dripping with oil, was ablaze; the skin itself was blistering, folding, crinkling as it sent up boiling clouds of greasy black smoke. The dry straw of his hair twisted and writhed. Kane howled, a long echoing wail like the bay of a wolf. It wasn't a human sound. It was the sound of an animal in pain. A dying animal shrieking in agony and rage.

But stubbornly Kane refused to die. He lowered his head, pounding at his face with his hands, beating down the fire, stamping it out, the way another man might stamp out a campfire's embers with the heel of his boot. Bits of skin flaked off his face like dandruff.

Then he raised his head once more, and through drifting clots of smoke Bill saw his face. It was a half-melted horror mask, all scorched flesh and dripping gore. The left eyelid had been glued shut, and the whole left side of his face was skewed crazily, sagging like the face of a stroke victim. Only the right eye still gazed at him, a bright blue marble.

Suddenly, shockingly, Kane pulled the ruins of his face into the parody of a smile. He began to struggle to his feet.

He was down, but not out. Not finished yet.

Bill looked at the office door. The flames had spread to that wall. The doorframe was sagging. At any moment it would give way and they would be trapped inside, and the office would be their funeral pyre.

"Come on!" he shouted.

He snatched up Tommy and ran with Jenny at his side, still clutching the one last bottle in her hand. They plunged through the doorway and got outside, free of the inferno.

They crossed the wide asphalt lot where Bill had squeegeed so many windshields and filled so many tanks. They reached the curb. Bill glanced over his shoulder.

Kane stepped out of the office, a ragged silhouette, just before the weakened doorframe gave way with a rush of sparks and crashed down, barely missing him. He kept on coming, stumbling after them, his arms outstretched, fingers twisted like claws, as if still seeking blindly to tear out their throats with his bare hands.

Bill and Jenny ran across Joshua Street. The church wasn't far away. Bill had some vague notion of taking refuge inside. He veered toward it, holding Tommy tight, Jenny at his side. They reached the verge of the church's lawn, and Bill looked back.

Kane was halfway across the lot, pursuing blindly, heading straight for the service island—the service island, where gasoline was dribbling out of a bullet hole in the skirt of the super-premium pump.

Bill thought of that slow trickle of gas, and of the underground tank beneath the fuel pump, the tank that held thousands of gallons, and he thought of the chain reaction that would be set off if any part of the gas were ignited, a chain reaction that would make their homemade Molotovs look like children's toys.

He put Tommy down on the church lawn. He looked at Jenny.

"The bottle. Give it to me."

She looked down at the bottle in her hand. It seemed

she had forgotten she was holding it. Wordlessly she handed it over, then struck a match. Her face was briefly lit by its glow. She lighted the rags stuffed in the bottle's mouth.

Kane had reached the service island. He was shambling over it, still coming, always coming, not to be stopped.

Bill took aim, knowing that if he didn't get Kane now, he never would; and Kane would get all of them.

He flung the bottle. It smashed at the foot of the super-premium pump. The brief burst of flame from the bottle lit up the island like a floodlight, throwing Kane's blistered features into sharp relief.

And then the gas station was gone. Just gone.

In its place there rose a boiling fireball and a thunderclap that split the night like the howl of a legion of damned souls. It was answered by the multiple cymbal crashes of the church's stained-glass windows, exploding instantly.

The impact hurled Bill and Jenny and Tommy face-forward onto the lawn. They lay stunned as shock waves rippled over them and a fierce wind gusted out of nowhere. Bill raised his head and gazed across the street.

Red fury filled the night. Rising out of the smoke and flame, lifted fifty feet off the ground by the force of the underground storage tank's explosion, was the concrete oval of the service island. It hung in space, hovering over the fiery caldron below like some alien spacecraft, then ponderously sank down. A second explosion, more powerful than the first, rocked the earth with an ear-splitting hammer blow of sound, and Bill grasped that the two adjacent storage tanks, those that had stored leaded gas and regular unleaded, had gone up also.

As he watched, the office and service bay, or whatever was left of them, erupted out of the ground and blew apart into splinters of wood and glass and steel, flying in all directions, marking the night sky with twisted red contrails like the fading afterimage of a fireworks display.

Debris rained down in flaming chunks. Jenny crawled to Tommy and covered his small body with her own, and Bill covered her in turn, and the three of them lay there together as scraps of fire plummeted around them like a shower of meteorites. The lawn began to smoke.

Slowly the deadly rain died out. Bill dared to look again.

There was nothing much to see. A scorched crater was all that remained of the service station that had been his life.

He sat up and stared. Beside him, Jenny and Tommy did the same.

Then Tommy spoke, uttering his first words since Rile found him in the trailer park, lifetimes ago.

"Son of a bitch," the boy said softly, "we *got* him."

Bill and Jenny looked at each other, then at Tommy, and then the two of them were laughing, while Tommy blinked and shook his head, coming fully awake. Bill studied the boy's face and saw that his eyes were clear and alert once more. He looked like himself again. Whatever evil spell had held him in its grip had died along with Kane.

Jenny hugged her son and held him close, and Bill reached out and squeezed her arm, and the three of them sat together on the lawn of the church and watched the last remnants of the gas station smolder and burn.

Hector Garcia had been driving a truck for fifteen years, delivering wholesale supplies to independent grocers throughout the Mojave. Lew Hannah's store in Tuskett was his favorite stop, because Lew and his assistant, Jenny Kirk, were always sweet as cream to him, asking how his wife was getting on and passing the time of day. Lew had even found out when Hector's birthday was and remembered to give him a present every year—most often a Snoopy card with a ten-spot inside. Nobody else on Hector's route had ever done a thing like that for him.

So Tuskett was a special place to Hector, and that was why he whistled a happy tune as he guided the truck off the Old Road into town on this Wednesday morning at nine o'clock. Right on time.

Abruptly the tune died out in time with a squeal of brakes.

Blocking the right-hand side of the street was a tangle of high-voltage wires, some of them still crackling with electric current.

Hector stared out the dirty windshield. He figured the lines must have been blown down during the night. These desert winds could get mighty fierce.

He executed a wide curve around the power lines and drove on. A new sight caught his attention.

"God damn," Hector muttered.

Up the street, two blocks away, lay a heap of scorched, mangled wreckage. It took him a moment to grasp that he was looking at the remains of a car.

His first thought was that there'd been one hell of a car crash. But there was no other vehicle in sight, no evidence of a collision, no crowd of onlookers, no tow trucks or ambulances, not a damn thing. There was just that one car, or what was left of it, abandoned in the middle of the street like so much scrap metal.

Hector braked the truck again, gently this time, and sat there with the engine idling.

Something was wrong here. Something was very wrong.

The town was empty. There was no sign of life anywhere. He turned his head in a wide arc, taking in the familiar shops that lined Joshua Street. None appeared to be occupied.

Of course, Tuskett wasn't exactly the hub of the universe, but under normal circumstances folks would be up and about by this hour, especially with the downed utility lines and a car accident—or something—to talk about.

He saw no one. Not a soul. And that was passing strange.

If it had been any other town, Hector Garcia would have turned his truck around then and there. But this was Tuskett, his favorite stop. He couldn't stand to turn tail until he knew what had happened here.

Shifting into low gear, he crawled cautiously forward at three miles an hour, looking at the shops that passed by on either side.

He reached the intersection of Joshua and Third. Near the wreckage of the car was a coffee shop where he'd been known to have a cup of brew when he was running ahead of schedule and could afford to take the time. The shop was in ruins now. The whole front wall had caved in. He didn't know how a thing like that could have happened.

He turned his attention to the car itself. It looked like it had been blown to bits by a bomb. One of those pipe bombs, maybe, the kind the Arabs liked to use in distant places like Beirut, Lebanon, places he knew about only from the pictures Dan Rather showed him on the nightly news. But that was nuts. This wasn't Beirut, this was Tuskett, and there were no pipe bombs here.

He looked closer, then hitched in a breath.

In the front seats were two charred human figures.

He steadied himself and kept driving. At the northwest corner of town, there used to be a service station where he'd sometimes topped off his tank and bought a Hershey bar. The guy who'd run it was named Bill. Bill something. Nice enough guy.

The service station was gone. What was left was only a huge jagged crater and a scatter of junk, like confetti after a parade. Whatever had done this had been more than a pipe bomb. This was some major damage, the sort of damage you'd expect to see from one of those big shells the size of Volkswagens that were fired from the gun turrets of the battleship *New Jersey.* Only, he didn't figure the *New Jersey* to have been doing much shelling around here. Tuskett was landlocked, after all.

He heard a low, hysterical giggling and realized it was himself. He ground his fist hard into his cheek to cut off the sound.

He didn't know what he might see if he drove down one of the side streets, where the houses were. He didn't want to know. All of a sudden he was certain this was a ghost town. Everyone who'd lived here was dead. How it had happened, he couldn't begin to guess. But they were. Even Lew Hannah, who gave him ten bucks on his birthday, and poor, sweet Jenny Kirk. All dead. All—

"Hector! Over here!"

The voice was Jenny's and it came from behind him. He spun in his seat and saw her and two other people—a man and a boy—stumbling out of Lew Hannah's grocery store. They were waving their arms and shouting to him in hoarse, cracked voices, like castaways on a desert island signaling a passing plane.

He eased the truck around and drove back down the street, where the three of them stood, silent now, in a line. He pulled alongside them and got out.

"We were waiting for you inside," Jenny said without preamble, as if this were all the explanation necessary. "Guess we dozed off." She forced a weary smile. "It's been a long night."

Hector's eyes moved from Jenny Kirk to the boy standing next to her, a boy Hector had talked to once or twice. Her son. Offhand he couldn't remember the kid's name. He shifted his gaze to the man at the boy's side and recognized him as Bill something-or-other, from the service station.

They looked like hell. Hector had seen pictures from World War Two, pictures of air-raid survivors shambling out of the rubble, their clothes reduced to bloody rags, their faces sooty ovals with blank, dazed eyes. These three were like that.

"What the hell happened to this town?" he asked finally.

The man named Bill let out a long, slow, tired breath.

"It died," he said.

By eleven o'clock, two hours after Hector Garcia had driven into Tuskett and an hour and a half after he'd reached the nearest town, Jacob, with Bill Needham and Jenny and Tommy Kirk in tow, Tuskett was crowded, filled with people, people everywhere. For the first time in years and for the last time in its history, it was a boomtown again.

Almost all of the Jacob police force was there, with reinforcements called in from Carlyle and other, more distant towns. The state police had gotten into the act, and there were some boys from the bomb squad who'd flown in by helicopter from Bakersfield to defuse the crude but effective bombs secured by heavy electrician's tape to the undersides of all vehicles within Tuskett's borders, with the exception of Lew Hannah's car, which had been stashed at the rear of the trailer park, hidden from sight.

The phone and power companies had sent linesmen to patch up the lines and restore service. Ambulances had driven into town, sirens caterwauling, to cart away dead bodies. Two-person teams of dog trainers and handlers arrived with rescue dogs in tow, German shepherds mostly, which were set loose to prowl the wreckage of the coffee shop and the service station, sniffing for signs of survivors.

Eventually the dogs gave up, finding nothing, and other people moved in—firefighters in bright yellow jackets and construction crews in orange shirts, who'd kept their distance to avoid contaminating the areas with their scent, and who now set about digging with shovels and with their gloved hands, reluctant to bring in earth-moving equipment until they were sure nobody was alive under the debris.

It seemed everybody and his brother was in Tuskett today, except members of the media, who were being kept out until all the explosives were defused. It wouldn't do to have one of those crazy camera jockeys blow himself and his video rig sky-high.

The police had split up into pairs to check out every building in town. Officially they were searching for survivors; in fact, they were counting the dead. They'd seen things today that none of them would care to remember or would be able to forget. In the church they'd found a man impaled on the altar, his arms slit, his body drained of blood. In one home, a man and his wife and their teenage boy had all been killed in their sleep; their heads were nestled on pillows stained brown by the brackish ooze from their necks. There was that couple who'd roasted in the wrecked car, and another couple who'd suffocated in a gas-choked house. There was even a state trooper, a man known to most of the cops searching the town, discovered lying dead in a thicket of weeds with an elderly local man slumped over him. And others. Many others.

All the cops knew at least the bare outlines of the story Bill Needham and Jenny Kirk had told. And as they went through the town, they kept repeating the same words, over and over, like a mystic mantra intended to ward off any lingering evil that might be here: "One guy. One guy did this. One guy."

It hardly seemed possible. But there it was.

The Tuskett Inn was one of the last buildings to be checked. The old motel had the look of a place that hadn't seen use for years, and somehow it seemed doubtful anyone would be inside. But on the ground floor the two cops exploring the place found a trail of bloody footprints leading up the stairs; and in the hallway on the second story they found two more bodies, both female, sprawled nearly side by side.

One was an older woman, shot in the throat and no doubt killed instantly. The other was a girl, barely out of her teens, lying on her back, her blue flower-print dress blotchy with blood.

She was alive.

They didn't realize it at first, not till one cop saw the barely discernible rise and fall of her stomach in time with a flutter of breath. He knelt at her side and peeled back an eyelid, and one blue eye looked up at him. And the girl smiled.

"Put up a fight," she whispered. "Not gonna lie down and take it. Not gonna get kicked around anymore."

The cop took her hand gently in his.

"That's right, miss. You bet you're not."

In late afternoon Bill Needham and Jenny and Tommy Kirk were escorted back to Tuskett in a police car to pick up some of their things for the night. The bullet had been removed from Bill's arm at a hospital in Jacob; now the arm was in a sling. It ached like a bastard now that the painkiller was wearing off, but otherwise it was okay, and the doctor had assured him he'd regain full use of it in time.

Jenny and Tommy had been cleaned up and looked over, and the medical consensus was that there was nothing wrong with them that rest and relaxation wouldn't cure.

Before leaving Jacob, they'd looked in on PattiSue Baker. The girl was listed in serious condition but expected to make a full recovery. She'd demonstrated, the doctor said, a remarkable will to live; it was the only thing that had kept her going as she lay in her own blood with a steak knife in her gut; but it had been enough. Jenny figured they ought to pick up a few of PattiSue's things as well.

She had some misgivings about taking Tommy back to the scene of last night's events, but she didn't want him left alone, and he seemed to be handling it okay. Better than she herself was, in fact.

The police drove them to Bill's car. Bill checked it over himself before getting in—not that he didn't trust the authorities, mind you, but he wanted to get a firsthand look. The lead pipe that had been taped to the fuel tank was gone. The engine looked untouched. All in all, the car seemed to be in good working order, a fact that had been confirmed by the bomb squad, who'd hotwired it and taken it for a spin before declaring it safe. Even so, Bill was just a tad nervous when he turned the key in the ignition. Then the motor came to life, purring prettily, and everything was fine.

He drove Jenny and Tommy to their house first. They went inside. It was a funny feeling, Jenny said. Bill knew what she meant. The house had been her life, hers and Tommy's, and now it was only a piece of the past, soon to be discarded as if it had never been.

Jenny gathered a suitcase's worth of clothes and sundries, and Tommy found a few favorite toys. Then they left the house, and, as always, nobody locked the door.

Bill's house was next. He didn't like being there, seeing this place where he'd grown up with his father, this place stuffed with old furniture and old memories. He quickly grabbed some clothes and drove on, not looking back.

The Baker house was the last stop they had to make, and the hardest. Tommy stayed in the car this time. Bill wanted Jenny to stay there too, but she insisted on helping him, what with his arm and all. Besides, she told him, a man couldn't be expected to know which items to pick out for PattiSue.

Bill and Jenny made their way through the empty house. The bodies had been removed from the master bedroom, and the house had been aired out; only the faintest whiff of rotten eggs lingered to remind them of the way George and Marjorie Baker had died.

They found PattiSue's room. Bill let Jenny do the picking and choosing, while he waited, humming nervously, and imagined Kane breaking in here last night, stealthy as a cat burglar, shutting the windows, and turning on the gas jets to flood the house with death. He must have enjoyed doing that. Death had been his purpose, his essence, his reason for being. And finally he'd achieved it—for himself. Bill supposed it was possible to take comfort in that.

When Jenny was finished, Bill led her out of the house, into the evening air. The sun hung low in the western sky, red and bloated, painting the desert in stark shades of red and orange, vivid as a backdrop in a play.

He looked toward his car and experienced a moment's painful shock when he saw that it was empty. Tommy was gone. Then he heard young laughter and saw the boy playing in the yard of the abandoned house next door, a yard that had gone to seed in a riot of larkspur and wild buckwheat. He'd found a butterfly, it seemed—a checkerspot, from the look of its red-and-yellow-spotted wings—and he was chasing it happily through the tall, waving grasses and weeds.

Bill glanced at Jenny and smiled. She smiled back. Her eyes, he noted, were a trifle damp. He reached out and squeezed her hand. They watched Tommy playing with unselfconscious abandon, his laughter rising high and easy in the summer air, just as if nothing evil had happened to him in his life. Accepting the day and the sunshine as if the night and its darkness had never been. Well, kids were like that.

At last Bill broke the mood.

"Hey," he said briskly, "we'd better get moving. Sun's going down. And I don't think I want to be here after dark—if you know what I mean."

Jenny smiled. "I'll second that."

She called to Tommy. He gave up his pursuit and climbed into the back of the car, with Jenny in the passenger seat and Bill behind the wheel. Bill pulled onto Joshua. On impulse, he turned up the street and drove to the northern edge of town to take a look at the place where his service station had been.

The lot was a heap of shattered concrete, chunks of asphalt, splinters of steel and glass. A handful of firemen, wearing helmets and dust masks, rummaged through the rubble in the fading light, scooping up litter in their small shovels and sifting it by hand.

Bill stopped the car and got out, leaving Jenny and Tommy inside. He stepped up to the curb.

"Find anything?" he asked.

The nearest man pulled down his dust mask and shook his head. "Not what we're looking for."

"And what might that be?"

"Him."

Bill let a moment pass.

"Well," he said, "it was one heck of a blast."

"There ought to be something, though. There always is."

"So what do you make of it?"

The man shrugged. "I guess if he was right on top of it, he might've been blown nearly to atoms. It's all we can figure."

"That must be it, then."

"Must be."

But the man didn't sound sure.

Bill walked slowly back to the car. He put his hand on the door, then paused. Something drew his gaze to the distant horizon, flaming with the sunset. His eyes narrowed. He stared.

There, at the edge of the earth, a black shape wavered fitfully, a speck of darkness that might have been a shadow ... or a man. A tall man dressed in black, a distant figure shimmering like a mirage behind a tremulous curtain of heat. A man who was out there alone, walking slowly, deliberately, crossing the bleak stretches of gray shale and alkaline sand, shrinking with distance, moving on. Heading over the horizon in search of other towns to visit, maybe, little towns that lay by the side of untraveled roads, towns where all the doors were left unlocked at night.

Bill blinked, and when he looked again, the man—or the shadow—was gone. The horizon was empty.

He got back in the car. Jenny studied his face.

"Bill," she asked softly, "what is it?"

He looked at her. Slowly he smiled.

"Nothing," he answered. "Nothing at all."

Bill turned the car around, and together he and Jenny and Tommy drove out of Tuskett, down the Old Road, into the night.

AUTHOR'S NOTE

As always, I invite readers to visit my website at michaelprescott.net, where you'll find news items, information on my books, and other good stuff.

I wrote *Kane* back in the late 1980s, which is why none of the characters has a cell phone—a gadget that definitely would have come in handy! My agent, Jane Dystel, sold the book for me, and my editor at Onyx Books, Kevin Mulroy, gave me a lot of helpful input.

For this new digital edition, I did a considerable amount of line-editing, excising more than 5,000 words. Originally the book had no chapter breaks, only one-line scene breaks. I still prefer it that way, but ebooks seem to require chapter breaks, so I added some.

My thanks to Diana Cox of www.novelproofreading.com for her careful proofreading of the manuscript. Any remaining errors are mine.

—MP

ABOUT THE AUTHOR

After twenty years in traditional publishing, Michael Prescott found himself unable to sell another book. On a whim, he began releasing his novels in digital form. Sales took off, and by 2011 he was one of the world's best-selling e-book writers.

Made in the USA
Middletown, DE
12 December 2014